QUEST AT
GOLDEN HALL

An Australian Historical Fiction Novel

The Australian Sandstone Series 5

MICHAEL BEASHEL

Title: Quest at Golden Hall
Series: The Australian Sandstone Series Book 5
Author: Michael Beashel

Publishing and Marketing Consultant: Lama Jabr
Website: https://xanapublishingandmarketing.com
Sydney, Australia

ISBN 978-0-6480569-7-3

Cover by Giovanni Banfi
Front cover Details: *I have got it*- Eugene Von Guerard Artist 1854

Author's Note

The great southern land that came to be known as Australia was home to people who created the longest living culture on earth. When Europeans settled there, in the late eighteenth century, they changed the landscape and way of life in profound and distinctive ways, to bring about the unique first-world country that we see today.

The early years of settlement were marked by hardship and conflict. My passion has always been to tell this part of the Australian story using historic events and people as a canvas on which I paint credible characters in dramatic situations that challenge their morals, their ambitions, their loves and their journeys. It is my intention to tell more of this story in future books of The Australian Sandstone Series, so that an international reader can get a reasonably accurate picture of how the Commonwealth of Australia developed in the nineteenth century.

I hope you enjoy the fifth book in The Australian Sandstone Series, which shows John Leary's journey from a troubled recent past to something better. Mystery, attraction and discovery align in two interwoven story arcs.

All novels in The Australian Sandstone Series can be read as stand-alone books.

Michael Beashel
http://www.michaelbeashel.com.au

Contents

Principal Characters

Leary Family
John Leary, widower
Richard Leary, his son
Christine McGuire, John's mother-in-law
Stella Fawcett, housekeeper and nanny to Richard

The Fordes
Liam Forde, John Leary's brother-in-law
Maureen Forde (nee Leary), John Leary's sister
Michael Forde, their son
Irene Forde, their daughter

The Gleesons
Gerry Gleeson, John's uncle
Moira Gleeson, Gerry's wife

The Ryans
William Ryan, wool broker
Constance Ryan, his wife
Donald Ryan, their son,
Catherine Ryan, their daughter

The Harrigans
Mary Harrigan, widow
Reginald Harrigan, her son

The Connaires
Sean Connaire, John Leary's business partner and director of Leary
Contracting
Veronica, his wife

Contractor
Harry Shelby

Prospector
Thomas Barnes

Chapter One

1859

The May breeze lifted the dark-blonde hair from the boy's forehead and his hands were active, touching metal. His blue eyes were inquisitive as he looked up at his father. 'Read it to me?'

John Leary looked down at the brass sign set into the garden where his son had been playing. The brass plaque standing about four inches above the soil spelled 'BEDE HALL'.

The Learys' Labrador dog, which had been wandering the garden, came up and sniffed the sign. Three-year-old Richard grinned. 'Parnell found it!'

John patted Parnell's head. 'He did indeed.'

There were two signs identifying John Leary's house, the other one being near the front door. This plaque at their feet held the first name of the house, and until the dog found it, it had lain under weeds and soil. If John had known of its existence he would have changed the lettering to Golden Hall, the name on the other sign.

The boy patted the soil beneath. 'Someone under there?'

John shook his head. 'It's not a gravestone. It says the first name of the house.'

The boy stood up and looked around, his gaze taking in the vista to the west and north. The house was on the high point of the headland of Point Piper, with sweeping views over Sydney Harbour. Then he turned to the house and pointed at the sign near the front door. 'There!' he cried. 'Not the same name!'

'Not quite. That's clever of you,' John said, impressed with his little son's powers of observation. 'That says "Golden Hall".'

The boy was already looking back at the sign on the ground. 'Nobody under there?'

3

'No.'

'But Mother's in the dirt.'

The words sounded brutal, but John knew his son's thoughts were not. On their last visit to Waverley Cemetery, he'd explained some things to Richard about his departed mother. He clearly needed to say more. 'But part of her is in Heaven.'

The boy picked up a toy soldier and straightened its bayonet. 'Which part?'

'The best part, Richard.'

The boy frowned. 'Mummy is in a good place?'

'I think she might be,' John said. His feelings saddened. 'And she might be looking down on us.'

The eyes looked up and searched the blue sky. 'Can't see her.'

'You mightn't be able to see her, but she can see you.'

John looked at Parnell, who was now lying inside a model fort that John had constructed in timber. The walls were high enough to conceal the dog when he had his head on his paws, but he raised it when the two moved forward to look down at him.

John picked up a rasp from his toolbox by the open gate of the fort. 'Now, let's try and get these battlements sorted out.'

'What's a batterment?' Richard wiped his cheek, smearing more dirt onto it.

John pointed his rasp to the crenellations he'd cut into the top of each wall. 'These cut-outs, that's what,' he said and tapped one. 'From these, the soldiers shoot their rifles, and they can hide behind them when the bad men fire at them.'

Richard touched one battlement, then jerked his hand back. His face became red and he looked at his finger, which had a splinter in it. Tears came and his lips trembled, but he didn't want to cry.

Parnell the dog sprang up and stuck his nose under Richard's armpit. John took hold of his son's finger. 'Our Captain's got a wound, Parnell. Give it a lick, there's a boy.'

Richard stuck his finger out and the dog did the honours.

'That's why we have to smooth the timber down,' John said, 'so you don't get splinters like this.'

Richard examined his finger. 'It hurts!'

'If you can wait until I finish this filing, we'll get Stella to take it out and you can have a biscuit.' Stella Fawcett was the boy's nanny, who had also been John's housekeeper since the death of his wife Clarissa, twenty months before.

'Will it hurt?'

'What? Having a biscuit?' John smiled.

He was met with a puzzled look. 'The splinter!'

'A little bit, perhaps, but not as much as when it got in. Now, while I'm doing my work, pick up the soldiers and put them back into the box. Can you do that with your sore finger?'

'I can, Father.'

John applied himself to the timber, glancing at times through the wrought-iron front fence at the harbour shimmering in the autumn haze. 'You know why you have to have the fort right here?'

Richard frowned, trying to remember. 'To fight the baddies.'

'And why near the front gate?'

'Baddies could come in there.'

John ruffled his son's hair. 'That's right, my boy.'

'Hit them when they come,' Richard said with pride. 'You're Jason, father. Got a head of Molden Fleece!'

John smiled again at son's comment. 'It's golden.'

'You're big!' his son continued. 'Got a cut too, from an axe.' John didn't want to spoil his son's opinion of him by telling him that the scar over his left eye, was the result from a miss-struck nail. 'You're a giant,' Richard went on, 'ten feet tall!'

John laughed. 'Not ten, but over six feet. Remember your numbers?'

Richard got his soldiers, lined them up and started counting them. He got to five and frowned.

John added another soldier and said. 'That's six and there's another four till there's ten.'

Richard pointed back at the house. 'Seven and nine. Our house.'

'Good. It's number seventy-nine and it's in Wolseley Road.'

Footsteps sounded down his front path and John turned as Stella Fawcett joined them. A slim woman in her mid-twenties, she had the same hair colour and eyes as Richard. Not for the first time, and with the same pang as always, John reflected that to outsiders she might appear to be Richard's mother. But Richard's mother was lost for ever.

Stella smiled gently. 'It's time for his bath, Mr Leary.'

'So soon?' John said. He was disappointed not to be able to play with Richard for longer. Only his boy could lift his mood. He tried to smile back. 'Thank you, Stella. We're nearly finished and we have a wounded officer to look after.'

Richard proudly held up his finger.

'My goodness,' Stella said, 'but it's a dangerous wound, Master Richard. Perhaps we should seek a hospital?' She grinned.

Richard's eyes expanded in wonder. 'A hostipal?'

Stella got him on his feet, brushed down the dirt from his pants and took his hand. 'Ho*spit*al. No, I don't think so, but we have to get that splinter out. Do you think you'll be brave and not cry?'

Richard glanced at his father and shook his head. 'Won't cry. Promise.'

'Good,' she said. 'And you can show your wound to your cousins tonight.'

Richard smiled.

Yes, of course, John thought. Tonight was their family dinner, always held on the last Sunday of the month. It used to mean so much to Clarissa. The invisible shroud returned, and he felt its weight again. Richard brought brightness to his life for the time he spent with him, the darkness taking a holiday. It would be good if he could carry his son around with him all day and all through the night.

He watched the pair disappear into the house and then resumed his filing, at times pushing away the inquisitive Parnell. Finally he returned the rasp to his toolbox. Packing up his tools and putting a canvas cover over the fort, he returned to the house. On the way he looked up and nodded to the sky. Clarissa was there, he knew. And he missed her.

John's uncle, Gerry Gleeson, turned from the parlour window as John entered the entrance hall. 'The boy was enjoying himself out there,' he said with a smile.

His nephew's bright face dissolved into a plain mask. 'He was,' John said. He seemed about to add something, but just nodded. 'I've got to clean up.' He continued on his way.

Gerry shook his head. Since Clarissa's death, every time his nephew spent time with Richard, the man changed into something human. But without his son by his side, John seemed lacklustre and depressed. Gerry looked at his wife, Moira, seated on the lounge. 'Worrying, that,' he said.

'What's that, my dear?'

'The way he changes. One minute he seems happy and next he's dead pan.' Gerry went to the drinks trolley and poured himself a Bushmills. 'Would you like a sherry, dear?'

'No, thank you,' his wife replied.

Returning to the chair, Gerry sat down and pondered. 'It's been like this since her death.'

'He misses her. You'd expect that. But I agree with you. It's twenty months since Clarissa died and he hasn't found a way to cope.'

'September 1857, that's right,' Gerry said. 'Cancer is cruel. She was just twenty-five.'

'And so sudden, Gerry. It was awful for John, only married four years. We've seen him angry and denying it happened and now this.' She paused. 'I really hope he finds love again. He's handsome and loving. I pray so.'

Gerry sipped his whiskey and said, 'Thank God for the boy.' Moira was very fond of him, he knew.

'Yes, he's a dear one,' she said.

And whenever Richard was with his father, John was different, more like his old energetic self. For the life of him, Gerry couldn't think what else he might do to bring his nephew back to the man he could be.

At dinner that evening, John was at the head of the table, his son on his right. His mother-in-law was seated at the other end. Next to Richard sat John's sister Maureen and her husband Liam. On John's left was Gerry, with his wife Moira beside him.

'Shall we say Grace, John?' Christine McGuire said.

'Liam,' John said, 'will you give thanks?' John liked his brother-in-law; a slight man in height but a big man in courage. Liam loved John's sister and had married her in Ireland, knowing that she'd been raped months before by her landlord. A situation not many men would have taken on with such acceptance and understanding.

Liam completed the Grace and looked at John as the cook served the soup. 'How is the bank job going?'

'All right,' John said. 'Sean's got good control of it and the building's ahead of schedule.' Sean Connaire was his business partner, not invited this evening, which was for family.

'And what of your other projects?' Maureen asked. 'Are you happy with those?'

'My son-in-law,' Christine said, 'has the business well in hand.'

John looked at her for a second. She was shutting down the topic at the family table, even though she was part owner of Leary Contracting. Why?

'Now, Maureen, tell us about your moving house. It must be happening soon?'

'In ten days,' Maureen said, accepting the abrupt change of subject. 'Liam and I are very excited about going to Glebe.'

'I'm not surprised you're leaving Surry Hills,' Gerry said. 'The neighbourhood's changing. There's more crime there, I'm sorry to say.'

'Just last week,' Liam said, 'there was another murder just two houses down from where we live.'

'Horrible,' Moira said. 'Maybe Redfern's next.'

'Now, now' Gerry said. 'Let's not get ahead of ourselves.'

'So, we can't wait to be in Glebe,' Maureen said. 'We'll have extra bedrooms and that big back yard. John's men have done such a grand job, building the house. There's a few things to do, but ...'

John glanced through the window. As Maureen's excited words faded, he was back in a different place. On a ship to New South Wales in 1850, when he'd first met Clarissa McGuire and her mother. He was a twenty-year old immigrant carpenter from Kildare and she from Dublin, all on their way to New South Wales to make a new life. She was upper-middle-class, he was from a farming family that had income despite the famine. He had somehow felt inferior to her and had sensed that difference throughout the voyage and for the years thereafter.

'John?' Christine said, exchanging a glance with Gerry. 'What do you say about all this?'

John shook his head. 'I'm sorry, I missed what Maureen said.'

'We were discussing the new house,' Gerry said with a worried look. 'She just asked me about the slate. Well, my answer is that it's imported and should give you many years of service, Maureen.'

Maureen, too, was looking at John. 'Thank you, uncle.'

'We still have to do the garden,' Liam put in, 'but we'll wait for spring before we plan anything.'

The cook cleared away the soup dishes and returned with the main course: roast lamb, vegetables and gravy.

The others busied themselves with the food and John sat silent. He knew he wasn't contributing to the evening but he couldn't summon up anything to say. He sat looking at Richard, who was starting to fidget. Fortunately Stella came in, right on cue.

'Come, Master Richard,' she said. 'You can join your cousins in the kitchen and finish your dinner there.'

Richard looked at John, who simply nodded, and the two left.

It was his mother-in-law who broke the rather awkward silence, by speaking about the Leary country property, which was inland, near Bathurst. 'It would be nice to go to Clontarf before the weather gets too cold. We'd all benefit from some time away from Sydney, in peace and quiet.'

'I'd like that,' Gerry said, 'but we're busy on site at the moment. It's all hands to the pump.'

John didn't think the company was that busy. 'All hands to the pump' included him—wasn't he doing enough? He realised he didn't really know. Maybe Gerry was right. Sean Connaire, John's partner and a Leary Contracting minor shareholder and director, had said in their last conversations that John had to have more involvement in the business. Even Christine, who was a major shareholder and a silent partner, had privately urged him to do his part more. But wasn't John already doing his best?

'Perhaps we could travel out there just to spend a long weekend,' Christine said. 'We could do that, surely? Richard and your children, Maureen, would love the fresh air.'

'Let's just get over our new move,' Maureen said. 'Then we could think about a little trip.'

'We don't need to go as far as Bathurst,' Liam said. 'There's places south of Sydney, not far out of town …'

Soon they were deep in talk about other destinations and John wandered off again in his mind. These days, whenever he tried to remember the best moments of his happiness with Clarissa, he felt overwhelmed instead by guilt. The guilt of an adulterous relationship during their marriage that had occurred between himself and a former love. It had led to confrontation, shame, and daily knowing he'd done the wrong thing by his wife. Everything reminded him of his guilt, even Clontarf. It was there that Clarissa had found out about his infidelity.

The woman he'd had an affair with was Beth Blackett, a former friend, who as silent partner had held fifty-one per cent of Leary Contracting shares. His mother-in-law, on discovering his infidelity, had taken revenge for her daughter's sake, by purchasing the shares from Beth Blackett. So Christine McGuire, the wily and intelligent woman sitting opposite him, controlled the company he loved. For weeks after Clarissa's death, John had felt anger in the midst of his grief and was determined to get back his controlling interest. But then his anger had been replaced by the terrible reality of Clarissa's passing, and since that time he'd lost any will to achieve anything through his building business. The only thing that kept him from slipping into a pit of despair was his son, because Richard was the one in whom Clarissa lived and he was the link to her.

Again, he came back to the present and to silence around the dinner table. He looked at each of his relatives in turn, wiped his face with a napkin, stood up and left the room.

Maureen stood to follow him and Liam placed a hand on her arm. 'Leave him be, dear.'

'But Liam, I can't see him go on like this. He's—'

'He's done the same to me in the past three months. Just not even said goodbye. Just left.'

'It's a habit he's got,' Gerry said. 'He's deteriorated and I'm concerned for him.'

'Oh dear,' Moira said.

'John's a strong man.' Christine said, as if to dismiss the subject. 'He'll get back. He showed drive and ambition when he came to New South Wales.' She paused and forced a smile. 'He'll be that man again.'

Maureen's eyes became wet. 'I fear not. I feel I have to look after him now that he's alone. But I'm not sure how.'

'What's Sean's view of all this, Gerry?' Liam asked.

Gerry stood up and closed the sliding doors of the dining room, their height just about matching his own. He came and sat down. 'Sean's as worried as the rest of us. The company is only marking time. Without my nephew's passion to run it, it will shrink.'

'It's John I'm worried about,' Maureen said, 'not the company.'

'We all are, dear,' Christine said. 'Is there something we can do? There must be. There has to be a way.' She sat back and looked around the table. All solemn faces and none of them meeting her eyes.

* * *

At six-thirty the next morning, Gerry Gleeson entered the site for the new Bank of Australasia building, on the corner of Jamieson and George Streets. Part of his job was supervising the stonework for the façade of the Renaissance revival building. No matter how many stones he'd laid over his thirty years—and he'd laid a few since coming to the colony as convicted felon, Gerry Riordan—he never tired of it. Of course, at fifty-one years of age his days of lugging and cutting were over: and so, with gladness, he was planning work and supervising others to do the heavy lifting.

'Good day, Gerry.'

He looked around as Sean Connaire came up to him. 'Good morning, yourself.' Sean was general foreman running the site and Gerry liked him. The five-foot-five Irish carpenter with the nuggety frame was all muscle and experience. He might be a director with nine per cent share of Learys but he was also a down-to-earth tradesman with no-nonsense views. 'Have you got some time before work starts?'

Sean nodded. 'I've got water boiling and we can chat.'

They entered the site shed. Sean poured tea into a billy, swished it round and let it settle. 'What's on your mind?'

'It's John.'

'I figured that,' Sean said.

'At dinner last night we lost him again,' Gerry said. 'He can't seem to talk to us for more than a couple of minutes and he's off in his head somewhere. These episodes are coming up more and more.'

Sean filled two mugs and handed one to Gerry. 'It's got me stuffed. The men see it, they do. He turns up but he seems to be going through the motions. He doesn't keep tabs on the competition. He's letting other builders like Harry Shelby get the better of us.'

'Shelby's won another job?'

'Surry Hills. One that we bid on and all—but John doesn't seem to care. Yeah, the company's doing fair but it's not gonna stay that way. You know John, Gerry. He's always been restless, always wanted to grow, always wanted to be the best and the biggest—and sometimes that busted him. But he's lost the edge.'

Gerry sipped his tea. He'd had the same thoughts. When he'd been made a Ticket-of-Leave in 1830, he'd changed his surname from

Riordan to Gleeson—new life, new freedom, and new name. Over the years, he'd grown closer to his nephew. He'd sensed character there and courage. John had taken risks and made mistakes, sure, the worst one being the affair with Beth Blackett. But he'd always bounced back, and Gerry believed he genuinely loved Clarissa. But since her death, John had changed.

Gerry could see what John was going through—it was despair. He'd seen it on the convict road gangs, in men who talked little and, bitter with resentment, just removed themselves in mind and spirit from the fellows around them. He'd been in that space himself a few times. 'I'm open to all ideas,' he said. 'Maureen is worried, Christine is worried, everyone's bloody worried!'

'If I could just get into his head,' Sean said, 'I could clear out some garbage in there and give him some blue sky.'

Gerry took another gulp of his tea and put the mug down. 'I'll try and think of a way. The one thing that strikes me is, being with his son seems to enliven the boy.' Gerry made for the door. 'Thanks for the brew. Let's talk again, maybe with Christine, and see if we can think of something.' He waved and walked away.

* * *

On that same Monday afternoon, John's first appointment was with Ian McCreadie, a wool broker. For fifteen minutes, they talked in John's office about a new job.

'I'd like you to do it, Mr Leary,' Ian McCreadie said. 'We know you. You supervised the last job for me and the workmanship was sound.'

'Thank you.' Some seven years before, John had been the supervisor for another contractor, who'd built a wool store for the McCreadie firm in Market Street. Now that he had his own show, he should be grabbing this opportunity, but it didn't excite him. 'It's a simple alteration that any contractor could do. Why come to us?'

McCreadie looked irritated. 'As I said, business is best when you work with people you know. But if you don't want to do it, I'll get somebody else.'

John tried to think about the job strategically. His best clients were his past or existing customers, so why was he hesitating? Yes, the job was small, but the profit could be handsome. He sighed. 'All right. We'll have a crack at it for you. Let's see those plans again.'

McCreadie looked pleased and pushed the architectural drawings closer to him. 'I want to use part of the existing wool store as an office, put up some walls. Maybe a—'

'Yes, I see a mezzanine floor on the plan. Is this where you want your office?' John pointed.

'It is,' McCreadie said, 'and one for my assistant. Do the walls have to be in brick?'

'Your architect says so, but I think we can do them in timber.'

'The only fancy room I want,' McCreadie said, 'is where we meet clients. The architects have specified timber panelling for that.'

'When would you like the quote for the build?'

'As soon as you can, but latest Monday the sixth of June.'

John raised his voice. 'Frank!'

Footsteps sounded from next door and a big strapping man stopped at John's office door.

'Come in,' John said. 'Ian McCreadie, this is my chief estimator, Frank Cartwright. Frank, Mr McCreadie is a client of ours.'

'Hello, Mr McCreadie,' Frank said.

John pushed the drawing towards Cartwright. 'Mr McCreadie would like some alterations to his wool store. Have a look at it for us and give us your view, please.'

'Surely. Got a few things to do today but I can get onto it first thing in the morning. Is that all right?'

John nodded. 'Have the quote by Friday, Frank, thanks. That will be all.' The estimator collected the drawings and left. John sat back and looked at the wool broker, remembering what he knew of McCreadie from the past.

Instantly, he was thinking of Clarissa. At one time, McCreadie had proposed to her. Had John himself been the right husband for Clarissa? Maybe if she'd accepted McCreadie, she would still be here. But, no. Clarissa's illness would have taken her no matter where she was or whom she was with. John had let her down by having the affair, but he had not caused her death. He sensed the man looking at him. He forced a smile. 'Is there anything more we can do for you?'

McCreadie stood up and extended his hand. 'No thank you, Mr Leary. I'll await your quotation.'

John stood up with him. 'Agreed. I'll see you to the door.' He led his client outside into a small hall, past Frank's office and that of his accountant Dan Reynolds, and then downstairs.

Ian McCreadie paused to look round at the meeting room, work desks and kitchen that all faced out onto George Street and had a view of nearby King Street. 'You've been in these premises a while now. Do they still suit you?'

John tried to bring himself back into the present. He felt a bit dazed. It was as though he had just arrived at work for the day. The surroundings suited him, yes. A bit worn, maybe. Under the lease, he was entitled to have them maintained; he made a mental note to contact the landlord and get them painted. 'They're all right for us now.' He escorted his client to the front door, where McCreadie put on his hat.

'Good day, Mr Leary. My father sends his regards and asked me to inquire into your well-being.'

John's well-being? He wasn't ill. Well, he thought he wasn't. But the way McCreadie was looking at him he got a sense that he might appear under the weather. Odd.

John opened the door for him. 'Goodbye, Mr McCreadie. Please tell your father that I'm quite well.'

McCreadie hesitated just a fraction, then left the building. John turned around and went back up the stairs to his office.

* * *

15

Christine McGuire's eyes hovered over her mantelpiece, and she made her decision. It needed a change to its surrounds. Her Point Piper house wasn't old; John had built it seven years before, three doors down from his own handsome abode in Wolseley Road. But her fireplace stonework was dated. It wasn't polished like the one she'd seen in Lady Dalkeith's house. Christine had to alter it.

The mantelpiece was uncluttered, displaying only a daguerreotype of Clarissa. Sadly, Christine stroked the frame, which was as smooth as her daughter's skin. Clarissa had not only been beautiful: she had inherited her father's wilfulness and held society-challenging attitudes about women and their role in the world. While feeling quite unlike her daughter, Christine had admired her determination and brought herself to support some of Clarissa's decisions—she had even come to accept John as the husband Clarissa had chosen. Yet it was fair to say that the mother-daughter relationship was not deep in affection. Why should she feel such a pang now? It wasn't Clarissa's birthday, or any other event associated with her, but the moment caused her pain.

Christine's maid entered the parlour. 'Would madam like her tea now?'

'Yes, thank you, Elizabeth. I'll have it on the back veranda.'

'It's chilly out there, madam. Shall I bring out your wrap?'

'I'll get it.' Christine left the parlour and went upstairs to her bedroom. The emptiness of the house after her husband's death had scared her at first, and she had considered going to live with her daughter. But since Clarissa's death later that same year she didn't mind the vacant rooms, because Richard often filled them with his laughter. Being three doors from her son-in-law initially had been very difficult for Christine, because she was always debating with herself whether John was worthy of Clarissa. But now, being near her grandson was a benefit and a blessing. In some ways, her life here was good.

She collected her wrap from her wardrobe and returned downstairs and onto the back veranda, which had a view of Blackburn Cove. She settled into a chair out of the southerly breeze, as her maid brought out the tea with a sweet cake. 'Thank you. That will be all for now.'

'Yes, madam.'

As Christine sipped her tea, welcoming its strong brew, she thought about John and his abrupt exit from dinner two days before. He was getting strange. So different from the young man who had come to the colony in 1850. Neither well born nor successful in his career at first, John Leary had been a man possessed when it came to Clarissa! Clarissa had fallen in love with him on the voyage out to New South Wales and, despite Christine's consistent attacks on that relationship, she had failed to move him on from her daughter's mind. Despite John's honesty, hard-work, intelligence and ambition, in the early days she had continued to be angry at her daughter for countenancing such a poor suitor. Later, even after John had proved that he could keep Clarissa well provided for, Christine had harboured doubts about the marriage. She had not been mistaken there: John's affair had vindicated Christine's view of him as a poor choice. To protect her daughter's future, she had managed to purchase the 51% share in Learys from John's mistress. She had a non-executive role and was satisfied with that; but had the time come when she perhaps needed to step in?

What she hadn't allowed for, and what every parent feared, was the death of a child, and Clarissa had been so young. A tear slipped out and Christine dabbed it with her handkerchief. No revenge, sweet as it was, could equal in emotional depth the shock and sorrow of Clarissa's passing. But she had told herself to be strong. She'd grown to accept her daughter's loss and there was a proportional relationship between her fading grief and the growing love of her grandson, Richard. That was something to cling to.

John had tried to fight her for the shares after Clarissa's death but his defence had fallen apart as guilt corroded him. She'd acknowledged that his grief was genuine: it was the least a man could feel for the loss of such a superlative woman. These days, he'd become more or less acceptable to Christine. They did not have a close relationship, not yet, but she treated him in a polite and sometimes friendly way. However, over the past four months he'd changed, and that worried her for two reasons, both of equal merit. One concerned the man himself: if he continued in this way, he would not only harm himself but the relationship with his son. But then she checked herself. Ironically, John was always happiest when he was with Richard. She finished her tea and poured another one. The second reason was commercial. It did not concern her other family holdings, which she had inherited from her husband, David McGuire. McGuire Wire and Superior Sheeting firms were in well-managed hands, and they were trading well. No, Leary Contracting was the prize—and to her dismay she'd heard Gerry and Mr Connaire talk on three occasions about trouble ahead if John lost his firm hand on their dealings.

The company needed John Leary to be in control and manage his company well on a day-to-day basis. If he did not, the company's income would decline, its profits would shrink and so would its value to her.

If only there were some way to get John to lead the charge once more.

* * *

On the second Saturday of June, winter hit with chilling rain and driving wind. Maureen Forde, seated beside her parlour fire, could hear nothing of the wildness outside. She smiled.

Liam, sitting opposite her, said, 'What's so amusing?'

'There's no moaning sound, dear. I was outside five minutes ago to see off Michael with his friend and was nearly blown away. But in here it's quiet as an empty church.'

'You expected banshees to follow us from Surry Hills?' Liam smiled. 'Surely not.'

'Not ghosts, dear, but the sound wind makes coming through the gaps.'

'Aye, we get none of that here. I guess that's because your brother's a good builder. No draughts, no whistles and no moans. This Glebe place of ours is well-built.'

'It is.' *If only its builder were as good in mind as this house is in quality.*

'You're frowning,' he said. 'What's wrong?'

'The usual,' she said. 'John.'

Liam sighed and put down his newspaper. 'Is he turning into a recluse, do you think?'

'Not really. He's not unsocial. He does go to balls, outings and so on. Now and then.'

'Friends?'

Maureen shook her head. 'No one close. They're only work colleagues.' She paused. 'Perhaps female company might assist. A friendship.'

'But we know he's not the gallant type. Don't get me wrong. I've seen him enjoy himself in female company, but not I'll admit for a while. Then … there's Richard.'

'There is,' she said. 'A sweet boy. But John shouldn't depend on him too much. I don't mean he can't love him as a son, but he mustn't use Richard as a crutch.'

'That's a bit harsh.'

'I don't mean that he doesn't put Richard's happiness first. He does, but …' As a mother with children, Maureen understood and cherished John's relationship with his son. But as long as he could find someone who could love Richard too, was there any reason why he shouldn't remarry? He was tall, handsome, with the family's deep blue eyes, and he had a great future. Something needed to happen so another woman could enter his life. There was nothing wrong with doing a little social scheming for her brother, and she couldn't think of any other way to coax him out of his depression.

'You've been quiet for too long,' Liam said. 'Still thinking?'

'Yes, dear, still thinking. And I've got a few ideas.'

* * *

John drove his gig into the stables at his Point Piper mansion and alighted. It was early Sunday afternoon and he'd just returned from

Waverley Cemetery and a visit to Clarissa's grave. His face lit up as Richard ran towards him down the path and he scooped him up and lifted him into the air. 'How's that wound?' he said.

'Good,' Richard said and examined his finger.

John put him down. 'That's grand. Now, what would you like to do this afternoon?'

'Play soldiers,' Richard said and pointed to the fort.

John nodded as Parnell the dog joined them. 'We can. You take the cover off and be careful of spiders.'

Richard's eyes expanded. 'Spiders?'

'It's been two weeks and sometimes they want to get in out of the rain and weave their webs. Here I'll check for you.' He lifted the cover from the fort and an orb-weaver scurried out. Parnell inched closer and sniffed it.

Richard stood back behind his father. 'There *is* a spider!'

John smiled. 'It's only a small one and it isn't harmful. Now, let's get your soldiers and your old shoes and clothes. Stella can help you. I'll get changed as well.' He held his son's hand and they walked back into the house.

Mary Harrigan was feeling anxious as she and her companions headed east in an open carriage along South Head Road, outside of Sydney town. But she hid her tension from Constance and William Ryan as they all drew closer to something she'd once held very dear. It was a house, Bede Hall, that she had had to let go when misfortune struck four years before in 1855. Was returning to Sydney the right thing to do? She had the feeling that the wealth she had lost could only be regained here, but was that just a pitiful dream? Her forehead perspired and she hoped her nervousness wasn't obvious to young Catherine Ryan, seated next to her, or to her parents opposite.

Mary wouldn't be here in Sydney again if she hadn't sold her first husband's telescope. Its value had enabled her to pay for the cost of the voyage and return to the country that had offered her and her first husband, Peter Smith, such riches. Without that optical wonder, she would still be in Norwich, England. Yes, she would, and she'd still be wondering if her former house held treasure.

At the height of his fortune, Peter had had their house built on the headland at Point Piper. The origin of Peter's wealth was a lucrative gold strike that he had used to start a haberdashery business and build Bede Hall. He had often told Mary, 'There is a fortune in this house.' She had always assumed that the land itself was worth a great deal, and that was why Peter said those words with such a proud, significant look at her every time.

Peter and Mary Smith had no high-class connections in Sydney, but colonial society was tolerant of its well-off citizens provided they appeared respectable. Peter's wealth was welcomed, and Mary was well-educated, attractive and an addition to good company wherever she went. Her life with a husband whom she loved seemed charmed.

But Peter's good fortune did not last. His business failed, he suffered ill health and eventually died. With Peter's failure and death, everything changed for Mary, because he left immense debts. She did not have the income or the courage to keep up her position in Sydney society, and she had to sell their grand mansion. An agent managed to get her a very good price, from a buyer, a merchant named McGuire, and as soon as she had paid Peter's debts, she left the colony in November 1855 with her young son Reginald, to return to relatives in England.

During the first six months there, she had had to be dependent on her family. Then the flamboyant James Harrigan, a property developer and speculator, had courted her, and they married in June of 1856. When her second husband had fallen to his death from an icy scaffold, in January 1858, Mary had begun dreaming about Bede Hall and the 'fortune' that Peter used to boast about.

So, Mary had taken a gamble. She had used her second husband's modest estate to re-establish herself in Sydney for a few months and try to discover some hidden remnants of Peter's fortune. She took ship in February 1859 and her mission began well. On board, she met a woman called Constance Ryan and her daughter Catherine. The three enjoyed one another's company. In particular, Constance Ryan admired Mary's education and saw her as a good influence on her daughter. Mary would live modestly in Sydney, but she already felt part of its social circle once more.

Their carriage turned into Wolseley Road and when she got a glimpse of the house, her heart beat faster. It took her breath away. Two high pinnacles that book-ended a central domed skylight, paid homage to the one that she remembered on the nearby Henrietta Villa, demolished some time ago. Solid sandstone walls covered every elevation, punctuated with full-height windows. A slate roof and a radical inclusion for the colony, a veranda, ran the length of the front, protecting it from the fierce Sydney sun.

At that moment, John and Richard were preparing for combat near the front gate of their house, John holding the Red platoon of soldiers and Richard the Blue.

'Where did you get those?' John said touching two solid brass cylinders about eight inches long.

'In the garden,' Richard said pointing near the fort. 'There.'

John picked them up, curious. They were cylindrical ferrules, pitted and marked from their time in the dirt. They weren't his, he knew. 'For now, we can use them as a bridge to cross the moat.'

'Good.'

Wheels sounded nearby and Parnell barked. John, squatting behind the front fence, glanced through the wrought-iron railings as an open carriage stopped near them.

'Quiet, boy,' he said.

Sightseers weren't unusual up here, as the view from the point was spectacular. He was able to examine them because they were unaware of the man, boy and dog concealed by the shrubbery behind the fence. Richard stayed quiet, as though he and his father were playing at ambush, and John peered at the newcomers through the foliage.

It struck him that the four people weren't looking at the view but *at his house*. Did he know them? The older couple he did not recognise.

One of the other ladies looked slightly familiar. She was well-dressed and in her late twenties, with a pleasant face that had a mole high on her left cheek. The younger woman seated next to her was attractive, and John concentrated on her. Her light blonde hair struck him first, gathered under a smart bonnet. Her eyes and facial features were pleasing to the eye. Taller than her companion, she looked to be in her late teens.

'Got you!' Richard cried, diving down on an enemy soldier while John was preoccupied.

John looked down and grinned. Their cover was blown. 'That's two prisoners you have. I have none.' He concentrated on his campaign and willed the spectators to move on.

'That's it,' Mary Harrigan said. 'That was my home.'

William Ryan brought the carriage to a halt. 'It's a handsome residence. I'd heard of it but never seen it. Do you miss it?'

'I do.'

Catherine Ryan was looking at the house with admiration. 'The view must be magnificent from every room that fronts the harbour.'

'My husband loved the place, Catherine,' Mary said. 'He loved Henrietta Villa, too, which was just down on the water in front of us. Unfortunately, it was demolished the year our house was built.'

'It must have been hard to say goodbye to this,' William Ryan said.

'Indeed,' Mary continued. 'But circumstances forced my hand.'

There was silence for some time. Mary sensed the Ryans' embarrassment for her. The mansion that she'd once owned was no longer hers.

'Oh,' Constance Ryan said. 'There's people near the front fence. They'll think us rude just staring. Come dear,' she said touching her husband's jacket, 'we must get going.'

'Indeed,' Ryan said and geed the horses. 'If it's not too impertinent of me to inquire, or upsetting for you, Mrs Harrigan, can you tell us a little more about your life here? I regret that we never met while you were in Sydney before. Would you like to tell us?'

Mary could see no harm in sharing her past with William Ryan. The family seemed genuine people. Mrs Constance Ryan, her daughter Catherine and son Donald had been visiting Bournemouth the previous year to look after Mrs Ryan's ailing mother. After she had passed, they'd come to London before returning to Sydney to be with William, who was a wool broker. During the voyage from England to New South Wales, Mary had got to know Mrs Ryan and her daughter well. This had continued and through them she would make a smooth entry back into Sydney life. Yes, she'd explain some things about the house and its fascination for her. 'Well, if it's not too boring for you?'

'I'd love to know!' Catherine said. 'Please tell us.'

'Excuse my daughter's enthusiasm, Mrs Harrigan,' Constance said. 'She loves exciting stories.'

'I wouldn't know about exciting,' Mary replied looking back from the harbour to her companions, 'but it's certainly not dull.'

Their carriage progressed to the end of Wolseley Road and William eased it around for the return journey. 'Let's stop at Double Bay for some refreshments,' he said. 'Now, Mrs Harrigan?'

'Very well. Peter, my husband, was no businessman but he was a hard worker. He'd worked for a haberdasher in England, and he knew his fabrics. We arrived here in 1851 and he went to Bendigo to try his hand at mining.' She smiled. 'He got lucky and found a golden hole. He returned to Sydney a rich man and used the proceeds from the gold to build Bede Hall. The house was finished in the middle of 1853, and he loved it. We were happy there.'

'How fascinating!' Catherine said. 'Was it you who chose that name?'

'No. Peter named it after a great scholar, the Honourable Bede, who was an astronomer. Peter loved astronomy. He had a telescope mounted and used it frequently for ship spotting and especially watching the stars.' She was silent for a moment.

'If this is hard for you ...'

'No, Mrs Ryan. I'm all right, thank you.' Their carriage turned into the toll road and headed west. 'Peter used the rest of the gold to set

up a clothing business in Sydney. He built a warehouse in Surry Hills.'
Mary was self-conscious about the next bit of her past and decided
not to tell all. 'He worked hard for two years, suffered ill-health as a
result and passed away.' Tears filled her eyes. 'I sold the house and
returned to England with Reginald.'

'That's very sad, losing your husband like that.' Catherine said.
'But why did you have to sell the house? Why not stay on, if you loved
the place?'

A question Mary feared. She hesitated.

'I think Mrs Harrigan has been very open with us, Catherine,'
Constance Ryan said, looking at her husband. 'It's too distressing for
her to continue.'

'Thank you, Mrs Ryan,' Mary replied. She decided to lead the
conversation in another direction. 'I had to return to England. I was
lucky enough to find my second husband there, but I'd only been
married eighteen months when he died in a site accident.'

'Yes,' Catherine said, 'you shared that with us on board. Very sad.'

'I did keep some items that were specifically mentioned in Peter's
will. I didn't want to sell them, so when I left Sydney I put them in
storage with the bank.'

'How touching. Could I see them?' Catherine asked.

William Ryan pulled the carriage to a stop in Double Bay. 'Let's
talk more of this over some refreshments.'

Chapter Two

John left his house for work the next morning. He pulled his gig up outside ten terrace houses that were under construction in Kent Street. It was halfway through the project and all seemed to be going satisfactorily. He entered the site for a quick look-see and spotted the foreman, a bricklayer by trade and a six-year Leary employee. 'How's it going?'

'We've had a bout of good weather, Mr Leary, and that's helped us.'

'That it has.' The brickwork and scaffolding were up to the roof level, with the timber roof framing started on the first three terraces.

'And I've got a new roofing contractor, boss. Fitzgerald. Heard of him?'

Maureen's house! There was something important about Maureen's roof when her house was under construction. But what could it be?

'Mr Leary?'

The slate yes, that was it, and where it was stacked. 'Have you got the slate ordered?'

The foreman seemed confused.

'The slate, man,' John said in anger. 'Have you got it or not?'

'We have, boss. First lot's coming tomorrow.'

'Make sure it's dry and keep it under cover.' John said and mounted his gig. 'I'm going to the office. If you need anything, get your boy to call in.'

The foreman hesitated, then touched his hat. 'That I'll do, Mr Leary.'

John spent the next two hours in his office checking the progress reports on four projects, including the Bank and the Kent Street terraces. At ten o'clock, he entered the meeting room where his fellow partners, Christine McGuire and Sean Connaire, were in conversation.

'Here's the board papers, Mr Leary,' his secretary said, coming from behind him.

John turned and took them. 'Thank you, Mrs Dawes.' He glanced at them and thought: had he read them? He must have.

'Can we start, son-in-law? I'd like this to be short.'

'It will be, Christine,' John said and looked at the agenda. Ah yes. May's cash on balance, McCreadie's renovation and other business. 'Let's start. Previous minutes?'

'Accepted,' Christine said.

'Seconded,' Sean said. 'I've seen the cash flow. I'm no bookkeeper but it's been heading south for two months.'

'I noticed the same,' Christine said looking at her papers. 'Any reason, John?'

He looked at the amounts, in five columns with the project names against them. For some reason there was no pattern to the figures, but he sensed that in the past he must have been able to understand them. Then he picked out a trend: last month's figures showed a decline from the month before. But was it a trend or a temporary glitch?

'John?' Christine asked again, then glanced at Sean.

'It's just a cycle we're going through,' John said. 'We expect this mid-year.'

'Expect?' Sean asked.

'Last year,' John said. 'You remember? We had the same.'

'No,' Sean said and pushed a single page of figures towards him. 'Cash flow was higher last year and the year before, with the same number of jobs. The contract sums for each year are also alike. See for yourself.'

John looked at the figures and compared them. Sean was right. So why hadn't John noticed himself? He was usually abreast of all this, wasn't he?

'The cash flow is out of kilter because our clients are paying us too slowly, John,' Christine said. 'Mr Reynolds says they're becoming bad debtors, especially the Australasia Bank.'

'They'll pay, don't worry Christine.'

'Perhaps,' she replied. 'But only if you make them. Learys is a business first. We have to be paid for our work, on time.'

'They're good clients.'

'A good client, John is one who pays his way,' Christine said with emphasis. 'I'm not an expert on cash flow but I do know that you have to have more money coming into the business than going out from it.'

John tried to keep sarcasm out of his voice. 'Indeed. I'll talk to Dan and get onto it.'

Sean nodded. 'Let's see how you go and we'll have a look again in two weeks.'

'We've got more time than that: the next board meeting's a month away.'

'In two weeks,' they both said at once.

Talking down to him and changing his schedules! John became irritable. He held 40% of Leary stock but the way he was being treated didn't indicate that. 'That's enough,' he said. 'Now, McCreadies. We should get started on their renovation job. He's agreed our price.'

'The profit's handsome,' Christine said. 'Sean?'

'If we put a team on that right away,' Sean said, 'it'll suck up what men we have left. We need a bigger project with a bigger profit. Another wool store would be ideal. There's a huge wool store job coming up—'

'No, let's do McCreadies,' John said.

Christine looked at Sean. 'When does this huge job come up for tender?'

'It starts next week,' Sean said.

'I don't think we should have a go at another wool store,' John said.

'I talked to Rupert Jenkins,' Sean said. 'He knows Ian McCreadie and he's happy to have a crack at the renovation under Learys name. He'd have his team on it and that would free up our men if we win the other tender.'

'But Jenkins is old,' John said. Jenkins had been his first boss when he'd first come to the colony.

'Still can organise a good job, John.'

'That's a good idea, Sean,' Christine said. 'Agreed. Any other business?'

John looked down at his papers, irritated again about being voted down. He could think of nothing else to talk about. 'No,' he said.

* * *

Mary Harrigan and Catherine Ryan were following a bank employee along a musty corridor. Mary was pleased that Catherine had agreed to go with her to the bank's store in Redfern. Ever since Mary had seen her old Point Piper mansion three days previously, her excitement had increased.

The trio descended a flight of stairs. The man stopped, repositioned a large envelope under his arm and unlocked a door. 'This is the store room,' he said.

Greeting them inside was a series of forty-foot-long shelves rising to the ceiling. Each shelf was partitioned off into six-foot sections. Between each shelf was a walkway. Their guide passed the third shelf and went halfway down it. He stopped and referred to the notes in his hand. 'This should be them,' he said, looking at the bundles on the shelves beside him. 'Left with the bank for safe-keeping by Mrs Mary Smith.' He nodded at Mary. 'Mrs Harrigan, would you care to help me identify these, please?'

Mary looked up at a large object on the shelf above her, wrapped in fabric. Recognising the shape, she said, 'This must be the chandelier.'

The man consulted his notes. 'Yes, there's a chandelier, a set of fireside irons, a miner's lamp, some silk curtains and a grandfather clock.' He moved a ladder from nearby, climbed it and read off the labels attached to each item. 'They're all here except the clock.'

'I think this is it.' Catherine's tall form was crouched down so she could examine the lowest shelf. 'It's in a really long box and the label says, "Smith".'

The clerk nodded. 'The bank will arrange for these to be delivered to you. When would you want them, Mrs Harrigan?'

The previous Sunday afternoon, when Mary had told the Ryans that she was reclaiming some of her belongings from the bank, Constance Ryan had kindly offered a part of her stables at Potts Point to store the five items, for a while at least, until Mary could sell them. It was a kind offer, but Mary wanted them to hand, even if they took up space in the terrace she was renting. 'Tomorrow morning, please,' she said. 'At number twenty-two, Bourke Street, Woolloomooloo.'

'Very well, Mrs Harrigan. Now, if you're finished here, I'll escort you out.' He stepped away and stopped. 'Of course. How remiss of me. Here's an envelope we found with the five items. It should've been given to you at the time you left for England, but it must have been misplaced at the time.' He handed it to Mary.

'Thank you,' she said and her excitement returned. She looked at the envelope, thinking she might see Peter's handwriting, but the outside was blank. Did it contain letters to her? Might they give some explanation of why Peter thought these five items were important? She might learn about the *treasure*!

On their way back on the tram, Mary was anxious—too anxious to open the envelope while she was with Catherine. She couldn't wait for tonight, to read the contents of the envelope and examine the goods she had retrieved. 'It's very nice of your mother to loan me a part of the stables,' she said.' But I think I can fit all those bits and pieces in my little house.'

'I hope you'll let me help you unwrap them?'

'Of course,' Mary smiled at Catherine's keenness. 'It's still a mystery to me why my husband set such value by them. I need to examine them carefully to find out.'

'What if they are *very* valuable?'

'One or two of them could be, I suppose. In which case I'd have the option of selling them off.'

'Or keeping the best items,' Catherine grinned. 'What about your chandelier? What if some of the drops or pendants are really diamonds?'

'Who knows?' Mary smiled. Catherine's excitement was infectious. Despite the thirteen-year age difference, Mary had grown closer to the younger woman this last month, furthering the friendship that had formed on the voyage out. Nineteen-year-old Catherine had an outgoing personality and a sense of adventure, but her spontaneity did not stop her from being mature.

'Your first husband told you there was something valuable in your house?' Catherine asked.

'He did. But I've never worked out what.'

'Maybe the fireside tongs are solid gold!'

Mary smiled. 'Let's just try and keep calm. My five items may have nothing extraordinary about them at all.'

Catherine shook her head. Some blonde hairs masked her blue eyes and she pushed them back into place. 'But what if they lead you to something grand that's hidden away?'

Mary shook her head. 'I must try not to be greedy, Catherine. My husband Peter was lucky in his life, but he was also very unlucky. Riches do not necessarily lead to happiness.'

Catherine nodded, and her expression changed. 'Yes, I know what you mean. This is worldly treasure we're talking about, not eternal.' Catherine, who was pious but not preachy, had taken Mary's comment seriously.

'I'm trying not to get your hopes up too much, Catherine. Or mine.'

Both the women fell silent and Mary thought once again about Peter's insistence that their Point Piper house was valuable. At first, Mary had decided that its value lay in its location and in the money Peter had poured into its construction. She had believed that nearly all of his gold strike at Bendigo had been invested in building his house and setting up his business, and there was no gold left over to be stashed away.

However, leaving New South Wales nearly four years ago, she'd met a member of the original prospecting team, Mr Thomas Barnes, who had discovered the gold with her husband. Barnes had told her of the fortune they'd made and what her husband's share was. Mary was flabbergasted at the amount that Barnes named, which was much higher than Peter had ever mentioned to her.

Mary instantly felt she needed to know more, but was guarded with Barnes; she didn't know whether to believe him and certainly didn't trust him. He had been dressed in patched workman's clothes at the time and appeared down and out. She felt he might be exaggerating the size of the gold strike as a prelude to claiming that he hadn't received a fair share of it. She had no trouble getting rid of him, once she had outlined how badly off she was after Peter's death.

But later that day, with pad and pencil, she'd sat down and worked out how much it had cost her husband to create his new life as landowner and businessman. Even allowing for the construction of their new house, the costs of the haberdashery business and building the warehouse, their living expenses in Sydney during the time of their business and their debt, they were still well short of the fortune that her husband had made, according to Mr Barnes. So where was the rest of the money?

Mary sat looking out at the Sydney streets, tapping the thick envelope on her knee. Had Peter told her the truth about the value of his Bendigo strike? If he had, then he might have been lying about their Point Piper house holding 'treasure'. On the other hand, maybe it had been Barnes who lied about Peter's vast wealth—out of bitterness and spite.

'Catherine,' Mary said, 'I want to be sensible about this and I know you'll help me. I'll be grateful if you'll come to Woolloomooloo on Saturday and examine those pieces with me.'

* * *

John was cooling his heels waiting for his appointment with the bank manager. He was no stranger to a bank, its people and its promises. Since coming to the colony and having his own business, he'd had more fights with the bank than months in the year. At one time, a director of one bank had been compromised in a fraudulent scheme to try and bring him down as a contractor. Even though he had no proof about the man—Harold Shelby—John always suspected his building competitor had been the culprit.

'Please come in,' the clerk said. 'Mr Jones will see you now.'

John followed the man into an office and Mr Edwin Jones stood up and held out his hand. 'Good morning, Mr Leary. Please take a seat.'

John sat down and eyeballed the manager. 'Good morning. The project is progressing satisfactorily, Mr Jones.'

'Indeed, Mr Leary. I was at the site the other day and your Mr Connaire showed myself and another representative around. We're impressed.'

'I'm glad,' John said. 'However, unfortunately, we have an issue with your last two progress payments. Both of which are late. One by fifteen days and the other by twenty days. It's now the seventeenth of June and our next claim to you is on the twenty-fifth. If that payment is late, we shall be charging interest on it, as we're entitled to do under the contract. Our business depends on payments at due date.'

Mr Jones sat back, steepled his fingers and frowned. 'You understand that the Australasia Bank is a conservative organisation. It needs to be sure that the money it pays for its assets is accurate and only for the building work completed.'

'I know that,' John replied, 'but the certificates for both payments were signed by your quantity surveyor as being accurate in work completed and to the pound. So, there's no excuse for payments not to be made in accordance with the contract.'

Jones's frown deepened. 'You're adopting an aggressive attitude, Mr Leary.'

In the past, John would have upped the ante and demanded that the bank toe the line immediately. Banks had to be jolted, sometimes, to keep them honest. But for some reason he felt uneasy about confronting this man over the bank's bad debt. Why? What he'd just requested seemed logical and businesslike, not aggressive. However, he felt himself wavering, as though he'd offended the man and had to set things to rights. 'I'm sorry, Mr Jones, for my directness. But can't you see that the bank perhaps may be at fault here?'

Jones seemed to relax somewhat, as though he'd won the first round. 'That's better, Mr Leary. We want to continue our relationship with you but it has to be on the basis of mutual trust. I'll see what I can do to ensure that our payments are made in accordance with the contract.' He smiled condescendingly. 'I can't promise anything. You know the accounts in this place, they're often slow and sometimes payments are delayed for some reason beyond our control. But I can at least look into it.'

It didn't seem like a commitment, and John felt as though he'd conceded something he shouldn't have. 'Thank you, Mr Jones. I shan't keep you any longer.'

On the way out, John felt confused. Had he made his point? Would Learys get their money any time soon? This kind of thing had never happened to him before.

In the week that followed, John had no luck with the developers of the Kent Street terraces, who cancelled two appointments with him. He decided to write them a letter. He would get his meeting, for sure.

* * *

In the covered back area of her terrace home in Woolloomooloo, Mary Harrigan looked at Catherine and giggled. 'You look like you've just cleaned a chimney!'

Catherine wiped her cheek, which smeared more dirt on her nose. 'It's dirty work, all right.' She removed the last nail from the top of the long box by her feet. 'Give me a hand to lift this lid, Mary. Don't just stand there.'

They took off the lid and Mary looked down at the packing material concealing what she hoped was the grandfather clock. Catherine bent down to rip away the covering.

'Be careful,' Mary said, tickled by Catherine's enthusiasm and energy. 'If there's nothing inside the clock, we'll have to repack it in this box.'

'Yes, captain.'

It would need them both to get under one end of the clock and lift it from its packing. Mary had an idea. 'Give me a moment.'

Reggie was in his room reading a book. 'Would you like to help us, dear?' Mary said.

The boy's eyes lit up. 'You bet.'

She loved his smile. It was like his father's. He also had Peter's blue-grey eyes and thick, dark curly hair. 'Then, come on.'

The pair came into the parlour. 'Hello, Miss Catherine,' Reggie said.

'Hello, Reggie.'

'Reggie, we're going to pick up a clock from this box. Will you make sure there are no things under our feet to trip us when we stand it up?' Mary smiled. 'All right?'

'Yes, Mummy.'

'Good boy.'

The women unpacked the clock and manoeuvred it upright. 'It looks very expensive,' Catherine said admiring it, 'and what elegant numbers on the face.' She ran her fingers around the sides and touched a keyhole. 'Is there a way of ... how do you open this thing?'

'There should be a key taped to the underside of the clock. Have a look, Reggie.'

'I see it, Mummy! I'll get it.'

'Thank you, dear.' She brought it to the keyhole in the back door of the clock. The key turned, it opened and they stood looking at the inner works.

'What are we looking for?' Catherine said.

'I don't know.' Mary peered closer at the pendulum, weights and chains. 'If there were diamonds here or perhaps gold dust ...?'

'Or the pendulum is gold,' Catherine said, her blue eyes excited.

Mary went round to look through the glass front at the pendulum. 'No, it's tarnished, and gold doesn't tarnish.' She came around to the back again. 'If there are any precious stones or metals here, they're probably behind the clock face.' She felt around. 'Ouch!' She brought her hand out and showed Catherine a dot of blood on her fingertip. 'There's something pointy back there! I'm not feeling any further. I'll need to find a clockmaker to disassemble this enough to see what's really inside.'

She went back to the other two items they'd examined over the last hour. One was a fireside tong, which they'd tested by scraping the surface with a file. The tong wasn't gold, simply iron. She guessed the other two tongs in the set would be the same.

The chandelier, which had been packed in newspaper, consisted of hundreds of drops and pendants, each measuring over half an inch in length. A diamond of that size would be of colossal value, and neither woman thought they were likely to find one on the chandelier. But nor could they be certain.

'So, what do we do?' Catherine said. 'You're right, it would take a clockmaker to take this thing apart, and that would be expensive for you. And if there's nothing there, we've just wasted our time and your money.'

'I know,' Mary said. 'It's frustrating. What's the time?'

'Half past three.'

'Right. We have a good hour of daylight left. What's your choice? Examine the other two tongs or start on the pendants?'

'But there's hundreds!' Reggie said. 'Thousands.'

Mary smiled at him. 'We didn't think it would be easy.'

Catherine's shoulders slumped. 'How are we supposed to tell diamonds from glass?'

Mary brought out a small book and stroked its cover. 'Peter gave this to me. He once bought me a diamond bracelet and he got this little book from the jeweller as well.'

Catherine's eyes lit up. 'Do you still have the bracelet?'

'Unfortunately, no.' *It went to pay our debts.* 'When he bought the bracelet, he wanted to be sure that it was genuine.' She smiled. 'The jeweller was taken aback when Peter demanded he test it. In the end, it was all good.' She opened the front cover of the book. 'It gives the ways you can check the difference between a diamond and glass: by breathing on it, using a loupe to examine it, which I have, or reading a newspaper through it. So, what do we do? Start?'

Catherine sighed. 'I'm game.'

Mary opened her book. It had been in the envelope the man at the bank had given her, along with a sheaf of other documents. Opening the envelope had been a disappointment. There had been no letters for her, and certainly no map to buried treasure. There had been no communication from Peter at all—just letters from other people to him. These documents had told her nothing, just raised her doubts and posed more questions.

'What's the first test?' Catherine asked.

Mary referred to the right page. 'You're supposed to place a newspaper behind the object and try to read it. That's to test whether the object refracts light. Too hard—how could you read anything through these pendants, the way they're cut? I don't have a loupe, so I can't examine any of the pieces up close. Let me see. Ah … no … breathing on the glass to get it wet. Perhaps.' She was quiet for a moment and then she smiled. 'Reggie, please, bring me a jar full of water.'

'Mary?' Catherine said as Reggie ran out.

'If any of these stones are diamonds, Catherine, they'll be denser than glass, so they'll sink more quickly to the bottom of the jar. Let's check a few that way.'

Catherine smiled. 'All right, let's try.'

* * *

John entered his Leary Contracting meeting room on the third Monday of June. Seated there were Frank Cartwright, his estimator;

Graham Edwards, the purchasing manager; and Sean Connaire. On the table were a set of plans, specifications and bills of quantities. A sketch on the first drawing showed a massive wool store. They were about to talk about the new bid.

'I've had a quick look,' Frank said as he tapped the drawings, 'and the building's pretty straightforward. It's a brute. Eighty thousand square feet.'

Sean rubbed his hands together. 'Right up our alley! What do you think, John?'

John looked at the pile of documents. It was as if he'd never seen anything like them. He made no attempt to flick through because he felt he wouldn't understand a line.

'John?' Sean said again.

He had to make some sort of response. 'How big is it, then?'

Frank cast an awkward glance at Sean and repeated, 'Eighty thousand.'

John shook his head, trying to get his mind straight. 'Can we do a job this big?'

Sean cleared his throat. 'Sure, we can. Do you remember McCreadie's wool store? That wasn't half this size, but we had it up in no time.'

Yes, of course John remembered the store they'd put up at the end of Market Street. In the time when Clarissa was around. Another world.

'Perhaps, Mr Connaire,' Frank said, 'how about I take a hard look at these and write a summary of my points. I can then give it to you two men to think about?'

'All right, Frank,' Sean said. 'Do that. Graham? Would you like to give him a hand?'

'Happy to add my three pennies,' the purchasing manager said.

Frank grinned. 'I'll take them and more. Come on.'

Sean watched them leave, then he closed the door and sat beside John. 'John, what's the matter?'

'Nothing ... nothing at all.'

'There is and it's time to talk. Now.'

John turned to him and forced a smile. 'Come on, we have a job to win, don't we?'

'The job can wait an hour,' Sean said. 'It's you that's got me beat. You're not yourself and it's getting worse. The family sees it and the lads here see it.'

'What do you mean?'

Sean sat back. 'I'll give you the picture. There's no fire in you and hasn't been since Clarissa's death. I can only guess as to what you must've been going through after she passed.' John said nothing and Sean continued. 'You picked up for a while and we thought you might be getting back to your old self. But these last three or four months you're … changed.'

'How?'

Sean's eyes rounded. 'You haven't noticed?'

John did feel different at times, more alone within himself, as if he was detached from everyone, like a spirit in the room. This was silly! A spirit, what was he on about! And yet, and yet. 'Sometimes… sometimes,' he said, 'I do feel I'm alone, even though there's people around me. And I'm tired. All the time.'

Sean's shoulders sagged and he half-smiled. 'At least you're talking about it.'

'The tiredness I can understand. The hard work, the stress—'

'John. You may think you've been working hard but you're not doing things at the pace you used to.'

'I am.'

Sean shook his head. 'No, you're not. So, something is distracting you from work.'

John felt his temper rise. 'According to you! But you're on site, you don't see me in here grinding away. You—'

'We're all concerned about you losing your grasp on things. Frank, Graham, the staff here, and your family.'

John was shocked. 'All of them?'

Sean nodded. 'Yes. You're not how you used to be. Look, I'm no doctor but I've seen men in dire straits like yours get worse, not better. Gerry is as worried as I am. He's seen the poor souls on the road gangs go downhill. They lose contact with the people around them. They can't talk to anybody, just stare and mumble.'

'You're comparing me with *them*?' This was too much. 'Sean, you're being ridiculous. Look, I feel a bit out of sorts, that's all. It'll pass.'

'So, you're not going downhill? I want you to prove that to me,' Sean said, his look intense.

'What?'

'I want you to take an interest in this wool store. You should be onto it—it's a huge opportunity. In the past, by now you would have had a gang in here, working through all the ins and outs. Getting the best prices and getting a run on your competitors. Your enthusiasm was like a drug to everybody. They loved it and they respected you for it. But this tender seems to mean nothing to you. I sent Frank and Graham away just now. Do you know why?'

'They had to study the drawings.'

'That's what they're going to do, yes, but I couldn't let them see one minute more of your lack of interest. John, we need this work. There's builders out there watching you. The word's out that you're not strong any more. The hounds are yapping.'

John laughed, but Sean's face was still grim. 'That bad?'

'That bad.'

So, Sean, his staff and his family had cottoned onto his inner confusion. He must really be sick. Jesus! When he was with Richard, he felt good, but the rest of the time he not only felt under a dark cloud—everyone else could see the cloud too. It seemed incredible. But Sean was his conscience, and they were close, their friendship spanning nearly nine years.

'Bloody hell. But what can I do about it?'

'Simple stuff at first,' Sean said. 'Listen to people and answer when they have a question. Don't walk away in the middle of a conversation. Don't walk away at all without a reason.'

John winced. He knew he'd done that more than once. 'All right.'

'This is only me speaking, mind. But I think it will help if you stick to one thing for a while. Choose something that'll take your time, that'll interest you, like this wool store.'

'That won't do it.' Sean looked disappointed and John realised he needed to be honest with his friend, who was taking such trouble to discuss his problem. 'Work doesn't excite me, Sean. It used to, but now it's just not enough.'

Sean opened his arms as though John were making progress. 'Champion. You're searching for an answer. Well, if it's not work, let's find you something else. A lady, perhaps?'

That surprised John. He still didn't feel he had a right to look beyond his memories of Clarissa. 'I don't know, Sean.'

'You could start simple. There's a do on this Saturday. The Wool Growers or something. Maureen wants you to go with Liam and her. She got an invite from Ian McCreadie.'

John didn't need to meet more people. 'I don't think so.'

'John. Do this for your sister. She worries about you.'

John mused. 'Very well.'

After a few moments, Sean said, 'Let's keep talking, mate. The more you talk about your problem—and believe me, it is a problem— the more likely we'll find a way of helping you, get you stuck into something that matters to you. Gerry and Christine want to help, too.'

'I'm not addled, Sean.'

'Didn't say you were. But you're troubled, not in the body but in ya head.' He clasped John's shoulder. 'We'll beat this. We will. Now, let's you and me nut out how we're going to beat Harry Shelby to this job.'

* * *

On the last Saturday of June, the Grand Hall of the Australian Museum in College Street was ablaze with lights and packed to the walls with guests, all there to celebrate another bumper year for the Wool Growers' Association. Maureen cast her brother an anxious look as they entered together. John would put her mind at rest tonight. He must. She was one of a select few who wanted him to be here. And she wanted him to be well again. He had to give her that much.

'I'll be on my best behaviour,' John said. 'I promise.'

She gave him a relieved smile and threaded her arm through his. Her other hand gripped Liam's elbow. 'There's Mr and Mrs McCreadie. Let's join them.'

John McCreadie, Ian's father, was with his wife. John's late father-in-law, David McGuire, had known and competed with the McCreadies. They were in conversation with another man and two women; one middle-aged and one younger, who had blonde hair and was strikingly tall for a woman.

McCreadie spotted them and said, 'Good evening, Mr Leary, Mr and Mrs Forde.'

'Evening, Mr McCreadie,' John replied, 'and Mrs McCreadie.'

Liam and Maureen nodded and smiled at the patrician wool broker.

'Mr Leary,' McCreadie said, 'let me introduce Mr and Mrs Ryan and their daughter, Catherine. My dears, Mr John Leary and the Fordes.'

John sensed that he'd seen the Ryans before, but he couldn't place them. 'How do you do?' He made way for a waiter who came up with a tray of drinks, wine and champagne. The Ryan women each took a glass, as did the Fordes.

'Whisky, Leary?' McCreadie asked.

'Thank you.'

'I'll get them, sir,' the waiter said, turning away.

'Mr Ryan's in my game, Leary,' McCreadie said and smiled. 'He competes with me and sometimes wins.'

William Ryan acknowledged the compliment. 'Thank you.' He turned to John. 'Mr Leary, I was an admirer of David McGuire. He dabbled in wool broking, I know.' Ryan grinned. 'I always hoped that he'd keep dabbling and not take on broking full time. He had a knack of winning work.'

John had been looking at Catherine Ryan all this time and had to think about the last bit of what he'd heard. Yes, David, his late father-in-law. 'A great man,' John said. 'He's still sadly missed.'

'Game of whist, Mr Leary?' McCreadie asked as the waiter came back and he took two whiskies off the tray. 'Ian's got a table. The dancing's not due to start for a bit.'

'Yes,' John replied.

'Mr Forde?' McCreadie asked.

'I'll decline, thank you.'

'Very good. Ladies and Mr Forde, we'll take our leave.'

John left with them but realised he would rather have stayed and talked to Catherine Ryan. She was the first woman who'd pleased his eye that way for many months. How old was she? Her smile was captivating. She had bright eyes and a fine nose that was perhaps a little long, but that was not a fault—it made her distinctive.

Maureen watched John walk away with the other men and was a little disappointed. She would've liked him to stay so he could get to know Catherine Ryan. However, Maureen had seen him look in a way that showed he found her attractive.

Maureen compared herself to Catherine, bemoaning her own curly brunette hair: Liam loved it but curls were not fashionable. Still, her figure was in proportion and appealing, and her necklace of semi-precious stones showed off her fine skin.

'You are a schoolteacher, Mrs Forde?' Catherine asked.

Maureen looked into Catherine's eyes, which were a pretty aquamarine. 'I am, and what do you do?'

'Catherine,' Mrs Ryan said, as though to get an unpleasant truth out as soon as possible, 'is a part-time milliner at Madame La Roche in Pitt Street.'

Maureen raised her eyebrows at Catherine. 'Do you like the work?'

Catherine looked at her mother as she spoke. 'It's interesting, but I'd like to be doing more. One day, perhaps, I'd like to manage a business of my own. At the moment I'm getting experience.'

'Never mind,' her mother said, 'it won't be too long before you're married and have a family.'

Catherine opened her mouth to speak, then closed it. Maureen was intrigued by Catherine's controversial activities, her candour and her tact. Young middle-class women were not expected to work for a living—they lived with their parents until marriage and did not engage in commerce. Catherine seemed proud of what she did but at the same time considerate of her mother.

'Excuse me, ladies,' Liam said. 'The music's starting earlier than we thought.' He turned to Maureen. 'Would you care to dance, dear?'

Maureen nodded and went with him. She enjoyed the Chusan Waltz. After it ended, she touched Liam's arm. 'Dear, could you ask Mrs Ryan to dance?'

'But we just started! Can't she wait a bit?'

'I'd like to get to know Miss Ryan a little better.'

Liam smiled and touched his nose. 'Not playing Cupid, are you?'

She tried to appear innocent. 'I don't know what you mean.'

'John's a widower,' Liam said and smiled again. 'Miss Ryan is a spinster?'

'Really?'

'Maureen!'

She smiled with him. 'Go. The music's about to start.'

'All right.'

Maureen returned to Miss Ryan and found her alone. 'May I join you?'

'Please,' she said with a smile.

'Now, tell me all about the millinery trade.'

Catherine hesitated. 'Well … it's more of a means to an end, for me.'

'So, you're working to expand your horizons in a man's world?'

'Is it that obvious, Mrs Forde?'

'Tell me, are you in favour of women taking more responsibility for their own future?'

The young woman's eyes widened, and she nodded. 'As a matter of fact, I do.'

'So,' Maureen said. 'Tell me your thoughts.'

* * *

On the Monday morning, John was waiting in his George Street meeting room, thinking about the ball the previous Saturday night—a great success, with its immaculate decorations, amazing food, wine and lively music. And he was thinking about Miss Ryan.

Sean and Christine came into the meeting room and sat down. There were no papers tabled and only one item to talk about. Cash flow.

'Good morning, John,' Christine said.

'And to you.'

'I'll come to the point,' Sean said. 'How have you fared with the debtors?'

'All right. The bank said that they'd look into their payments. I've had no reply from the Kent Street clients, so I'm not sure when they're paying up. But it's only been a week.'

Sean glanced at Christine. 'Are you sure they've got the message? If they pay late next time, they'll get hit with our ... what you call it?'

'Letter of demand,' John said. 'I think that's the term.'

'You *think*?' Christine said.

John was about to protest when Sean said crisply, 'I'd give the responsibility to Dan. He can handle the bad debtors from now on.'

John bridled. 'I've got it in hand, Sean.'

'Sean's right, John,' Christine said with conviction. 'Delegate this. We need you to concentrate on winning our next job.'

John was about to argue with them but their expressions forbade any more talk. He was outvoted.

* * *

Mary Harrigan needed a plausible explanation for being outside her former house but she couldn't think of one. It was not a day for a pleasant walk around Point Piper. Even at one o'clock, on this second-to-last day of June, the southwest wind was chilly, picking up moisture from Blackburn Cove that coated the trees around her. She looked at her old house from behind a tall gum tree, convinced it was her last resort in the treasure hunt.

Catherine and she had spent two Saturday afternoons examining each pendant of her chandelier. The hours of work had discovered no diamonds. She had not yet had the grandfather clock examined, because of the expense. And there was nothing hidden amongst the silk curtains or in the miner's lamp. The silk curtains were of Chinese design, as though they had formed part of a screen. Pretty, but surely not valuable.

Catherine removed a twig that had stuck to her dress and decided that the horse and gig that she'd left on the road told their own story—in an idle moment, while her son was at school, she was taking herself on a drive out of town.

'Good afternoon,' a voice said.

Mary, surprised, turned to its source. A woman in her mid-twenties was looking at her from inside the house's front fence. At her side she held the hand of a young boy. She was not unattractive, and Mary recalled her from the past. She had been a servant in another Sydney household. Mary regained her composure. 'Fawcett?'

The woman moved closer. 'Why yes. I know you?' She smiled. 'It's Mrs Smith.'

Mary smiled also. 'It was. I'm now Mrs Harrigan. How do you do? And who's this young man?'

'This is Master Richard Leary. Say hello to Mrs Harrigan, Richard.'

The boy smiled, nodded, then part-hid behind Fawcett's dress.

'I am well, thank you, Mrs Harrigan,' Fawcett said, 'and yourself?'

Mary looked back at the harbour. 'I've missed this.' She sighed and looked back at her old house. 'And you're now in service, here?'

'I am, to Mr Leary.' Fawcett looked sad for a moment. 'Mr McGuire passed on. He was Mr Leary's father-in-law.'

'Oh. It was Mr McGuire who bought the house in November 1855. Did he sell it to Mr Leary?'

'No. He gave it to him. I keep house for Mr Leary. I look after Richard here, and I live in. All Mr Leary's other servants are hired help, so it's quiet for us here most of the day. Mrs McGuire still lives at number seventy-three. Do you remember her?'

'Of course, I do. I see, the owner is *that* Mr Leary?''

'Yes. He's a widower. Mrs Leary, Clarissa, passed away in fifty-seven.' Fawcett held up Richard's hand. 'This is their son.'

Mary remembered Clarissa—a lovely young woman—and the tall, good-looking John Leary. 'I'm very sorry to hear that. The family has my condolences.'

Fawcett's eyes started to glisten, and she nodded. 'It's very sad. But what a surprise to see you. It's been what? Three years since you've left here?'

'Nearly four.'

'You'll see some changes to the house, I imagine.' She pointed towards the house sign near the front steps. 'Mr Leary changed the name to Golden Hall in January fifty-eight. But he likes to keep it handsome, as it was when you were here.' Miss Fawcett looked at Mary's gloveless hands, simple dress and bonnet. 'You're back in Sydney to stay?'

'I would certainly like to stay.' Mary decided to be up front. 'But I live quite modestly now in Woolloomooloo with my son Reginald.'

'And your husband?'

'Mr Harrigan died in England in January last year.'

'You have my condolences.'

'Thank you, Fawcett.'

Fawcett said. 'How old is your son?'

'He'll be ten in October.' Mary paused. 'I'd like to bring him here one day, not to disturb Mr Leary, just to show Reggie where he used to live.'

'You must come and visit, then! I'll ask Mr Leary's permission for Richard to play with Reginald.' Fawcett smiled. 'He's only three, but he'd enjoy it.'

Excellent, Mary thought. 'Thank you, Fawcett. Please write me a note to number twenty-two Bourke Street, Woolloomooloo, if I can bring Reggie. Goodbye. Goodbye, Master Richard.'

Mary went back to the gig, untethered the horses and set off along the toll road to her home. She had made a good start. Fawcett had come up a little in the world by being housekeeper at Bede Hall, no ... Golden Hall, but she still look flattered by Mary's attention. She seemed an open, friendly person that Mary would not mind getting to know. It must be lonely for Fawcett being shut up in Point Piper all day with a small boy for company. What she needed to do was to make a casual friend of Fawcett, which shouldn't be too hard. Such a friendship that would enable her to be at, and in, her old home without suspicion.

If there was treasure in number seventy-nine, she was one step nearer to it.

Chapter Three

Harry Shelby looked at his staff in his Kent Street office. 'Mr John Leary's not cutting it,' he said and smiled. 'The man's down and out and we'll strike!' His construction manager and estimator looked at him. 'Strike, I say,' he continued. 'Win this job and keep winning until Leary is out of our hair.' His men smiled at him. 'When does the other tender close?'

'Tuesday, the nineteenth of July,' his estimator said.

'That gives us two weeks. Get the best prices you can and find out what suppliers are quoting to Learys and to Hoxtons.' Shelby pounded his desk with his fist. 'I want this job and I'll win it. You men are the key. There'll be a bonus in it for you, so prove to me you've got what it takes. Now, go.'

He watched them leave and swung his chair around and looked out onto Darling Harbour. Leary! Always a bloody thorn in his side. For two years now the up-and-coming builder had won, no, *taken* jobs from him, good jobs including the Sussex Street store, the Bank and the prestigious Council memorial hall project in Park Street. Despite Shelby orchestrating an accident to harm the man, he'd come out with just a scratch! Well, not this time. Carpenters and bricklayers on Learys' Australasia Bank building had talked. They'd said that Mr Leary, since the start of the year, had seemed disinterested in the work, paying scant attention, whereas in the past he'd been a keen and disciplined builder. All sweet news to Harry Shelby. Yes, Leary had lost his young wife. Tough that, but all was fair in love and building.

John Leary was a tall man and had a foot in height over him. Shelby fretted over his own stature, and he compensated that with fine clothes, a sparkler here and there and a ready wit. But Leary's height, looks and reputation wouldn't count a jot now. Harry Shelby had an ace. Leary had not grabbed the opportunity—another example of his competitor's laxity— but he, Harry James Shelby, had. Newly developed mechanical saws, driven by steam engines, could rip through hardwood in a twentieth of the time it took for a pit-saw process. Shelby had bought two. Just the ticket to win and make money on this big new job.

* * *

John reviewed the status report on the wool-store bid. It all looked right. He placed it down and lamented his mood. He couldn't get excited about winning a new job, and that disappointed him. Sean's words reverberated. John had to find something that stirred him, something that would get him back to his best! Whatever the hell that was.

It was nearly midday on a Wednesday and he grabbed his files, filled his satchel and summoned his secretary. 'Mrs Dawes, I'm going to work from home. I'll see you tomorrow.'

'Very good, Mr Leary,' she said.

He mounted his horse and set off for Point Piper. One thing would raise his spirits: playing with Richard. When the boy was asleep tonight, John would take care of the paperwork in his satchel. On the way he thought about Miss Ryan. Since the ball over a week ago, he'd had thoughts, not wild ones, but thoughts. And if he met the young lady again, he'd be pleased.

Approaching his home, he spotted a woman and a boy seated on a rock shelf on a bare spot of land in front of his house. They were looking out over the view. At times, the woman would glance at his house. As he got nearer, the woman, in about her early thirties, seemed familiar. Yes. He wasn't certain, but she looked like one of the women in the carriage who had stopped outside his home on a Sunday afternoon just over three weeks previous. She had the same curly brunette hair that topped an attractive face. It was too coincidental that the woman was here again. What was her purpose? He aimed to find out and rode up to the pair.

He touched his hat and glanced at the wedding ring on her finger and on a mole high on her cheek. It was the same woman. 'Good afternoon, madam,' he said. Then he remembered: he knew her from Point Piper years before. 'It's ... Mrs Smith, is it not?'

The woman seemed pleased as she stood up, along with the boy. 'Good afternoon, Mr Leary. I'm Mrs Harrigan now.'

Mary Smith, as she was then known, and her husband Peter had moved into number seventy-nine in September 1853, when the house was completed. Over the next two years, they had been John's neighbours. Peter Smith had then lost both his house and his business because of poor decisions. 'Fawcett told me you'd come back,' he said. 'How do you do.'

'I'm very well, Mr Leary. Reginald, say hello to Mr Leary.'

The boy removed his cap. 'How do you do, sir.'

'You have grown,' John said and smiled. 'I'm not surprised that you've come up to see this again.' He glanced over the harbour. 'It's magnificent, isn't it?'

'It is,' Mrs Harrigan replied.

'Do you come up here often?' Before she could answer, John continued, 'Forgive me, weren't you here some weeks ago on a Sunday?'

The woman hesitated. 'I was. You see, I love this spot and my son does, too. Yes, I spoke to your housekeeper last week. I'm sorry to hear about your dear wife and father-in-law.'

His good mood took a hit. 'Thank you.' He looked at her for some time and finally said, 'Feel free to bring Reginald up to play with Richard during the week. Just send a note up to Fawcett.'

'I shall and thank you, Mr Leary.'

'Then I'll leave you to your solitude and vista and bid you both good afternoon.'

'And to you, Mr Leary.'

John led his horse through his front gate. He had itched to ask more questions of Mrs Harrigan, but he had no desire to invite her to Golden Hall on a social visit. Arranging such things was still beyond him—he wanted Golden Hall to be for himself and close family. But he wondered what had brought her back to Sydney. Rumours had circulated about her having to sell the house in a hurry and he was unsure of what had actually happened to Peter Smith's affairs. The lady had changed. There were lines on each side of her mouth and around her eyes. What was going on with her? This was the third time she had come here to linger around. Was Mrs Harrigan nostalgic about her past? Probably, but John sensed another reason and was curious.

Was she a lover of architecture? Was she an artist? There was no sign of that, nor had there ever been. So, why was she here and what was her relationship with the Ryans, who he suspected had been her companions in the carriage? Perhaps he should call on the Ryans and find out.

* * *

As Mary Harrigan waited to be served in the busy George Street bank, she thought about the previous day. It was all coming together well. She'd drafted a letter addressed to Fawcett to request acceptance to come to Golden Hall; she would now address it to Mr Leary himself. She suspected he would welcome a companion for Richard, even though there was six years' difference between the boys. That idea was good; a way to get access to Golden Hall.

A man seated at the corner of the public area took her eye. Although it had been over five years since she last saw him, Mr Thomas Barnes was a man she couldn't forget. He was looking at her.

'Here are your deposit slips, Mrs Harrigan,' a bank teller said.

'Thank you.'

She turned and left the bank. It was rude of her not to wait to speak with Mr Barnes, but she hadn't wanted to. She walked up George Street towards the tram stop.

Thomas Barnes couldn't believe his eyes: it was Mary Smith, who'd gone back to England when Peter's business failed and he died.

Or was the woman he'd just seen a look-alike? No, the mole on her cheek was distinctive.

He had to make sure. He had to act. The loan he'd requested from the bank hadn't been approved and he'd been here this morning to confront the loans officer and demand an explanation. His funds were exhausted, and he needed cash. But maybe that could wait. He might have another way to get him out of his troubles.

Armed with an idea, he went to the teller who'd served the woman and said, 'Excuse me, you just dealt with a Mrs Mary Harrigan?'

The teller seemed displeased with Thomas's well-worn garb. 'We can't disclose customers' names, sir.'

'That's all right. I heard you call her that.' Barnes smiled. 'You see I'm a relative of hers, just back from England. It's been years since I've seen her and I didn't want to come on to her here and startle her. I'd best go and try and catch up with her. Thank you.'

The teller gave him a look. 'Good luck with that.'

Barnes left and stood in George Street. He guessed she'd head south, and he set off. After fifty yards he spotted her waiting at the tram stop. He'd follow her and find out where she lived and why she was back in New South Wales. He suspected she'd not come back just for the sunshine.

Two days later, Thomas Barnes stood and admired the Point Piper mansion. He'd done some searching and a tally clerk at the waterfront, who owed him a favour, had found out from the passenger lists that Mrs Harrigan's former name was indeed Mrs Smith, and she was now a widow again. Barnes also knew that his old prospecting mate, Peter Smith, had built this house, number seventy-nine. Smith had gone bust before he died, but mightn't there be a little left over, hidden somewhere? If so, Barnes was going to find it.

Mary Harrigan lived in Bourke Street Woolloomooloo, and she was Peter's widow, all right. Four years came back to him in a flash. Before she'd left here to go back to England, he'd confronted her about Peter. She'd been shocked when he'd told her what both men had taken out of Bendigo—3,300 troy ounces each, thirteen thousand pounds! A twentieth of what had come out of the ground in that year. Looking at the house now and guessing what a business might have cost, Barnes had told Mary there had to be money—a lot of it—left over.

So, she was back here in Sydney, and he guessed why. She was also looking for Smith's lost fortune. The mansion he looked at was impressive. Was gold buried within it or on its land? Was there cash secreted in a hidden compartment? Barnes would find out. He pulled out his watch. Time to go. His nightwatchman duties for a Saturday night shift beckoned and he grimaced. It wouldn't be long before he had back his gold cufflinks and posh carriage. If he couldn't find Peter's treasure, he'd follow Mary Harrigan. She knew where it was buried. He was sure of it.

John moved the parlour curtain and saw him. A man was shielded in part by a tree and was looking at his house. John was startled, then fascinated. Was it a coincidence or was it a plan? Hardly. Mary Harrigan's visits here were just nostalgic. And yet, another curious onlooker here and in such a short time? The man wore coarse clothes, not quite a tramp, but likely a labourer. He was of average height and had a big head with fair hair. The stranger was giving his home a thorough going over. John was about to race outside and confront him when the man vanished.

Had he been a curious bystander? Possible, but unlikely. John suspected that he could be working with Mary Harrigan. Why did he think that? Well, Mary Harrigan might resent John living in the house that she considered was rightfully hers. The two might be casing his house for a robbery or worse. A kidnapping? John's blood ran cold. He wasn't rich, but his Point Piper home shouted wealth from its pinnacles. Richard had to be protected, at any cost. For the first time in months, John felt charged with a challenge. He had a job: to find out why his house was so intriguing to certain people.

* * *

Each Sunday morning, early, John reviewed his household staff. On the Friday, Stella would enter short details in a book about their grievances, requests and so forth and John would read them and act. Besides Stella, who lived in, his groom/driver, handyman/gardener, cook and daily maid all lived elsewhere. After half an hour he had approved leave for the gardener, reprimanded the groom for poor behaviour and complimented the cook on her new dish of smoked snapper.

For the rest of the day, John thought about his house's inquisitive onlookers. He'd been extra protective of Richard and wondered if he should bring his domestic staff into his confidence about his suspicions. But they might think him odd, as everyone else seemed to do these days, and not take his fears seriously. He'd find out more about Mrs Mary Harrigan first.

On Monday morning, following the team meeting, he decided to pay William Ryan a visit. It might well have been the Ryans in the carriage that June Sunday afternoon. He needed a pretext for the meeting. Perhaps the Ryans needed a new store built as well, like McCreadies? 'Mrs Dawes,' he said. 'Please find out where the Ryan Wool Brokerage is and make an appointment there with Mr William Ryan.'

'Yes, Mr Leary.'

It was midday and cold as John set off for his next appointment, a meal in Day Street.

Cochranes Hotel was the first job John had worked on when he'd come to the colony in 1850. The two-storey building was now eight years old and as he came near it, it was still in fair shape. The barge and fascia boards had faded and could do with paint, but otherwise, all good. He went inside and spotted a short, red-haired but now greying middle-aged man. There was a half beer in front of him and he was reading the newspaper.

'Mr Jenkins,' John said.

Rupert Jenkins smiled, took off his glasses and held out his hand. 'John, it's grand to see you.' He paused as he scanned John's face. 'Grand.'

'Another beer?' John said.

'Why not? And order two of those stews. They're the shot.'

'Right,' John ordered the beers and food. Jenkins had been his first boss and a fair one. When John wanted to set up his own building company, he'd approached Jenkins to buy a share but the little Irishman had refused, with grace. John then got his capital investment from David McGuire, Clarissa's father.

John put the beers down while a girl placed two steaming plates in front of them.

'Grand,' Jenkins said and rubbed his hands together. 'Let's dig in.'

They ate and said little for a while.

John sipped his beer and put it down. 'How's the store renovation going?'

'We've just started,' Jenkins said. 'Pulled down a few walls and put up some protection. Straightforward job and Mr McCreadie is a good client. Knows when and when not to stick his nose in.' He paused. 'And, how are you?'

It took a smart man to outfox Rupert Jenkins and John wasn't about to hide anything. 'It's been tough.'

'I heard.'

'From Gerry?'

'The same,' Jenkins said, 'and Sean.'

Right, John mused. 'It's been hard for me to get up and running. Her death hit me more than I'd thought.'

'You've paid for that, John and whatever your sins, you didn't kill her. It was the bedevilled cancer.'

'I know, Mr Jenkins, but I changed, or so everyone tells me.'

'I saw it. It was like a banshee had sucked the stuffing out of you.'

A good interpretation, John thought. 'I felt like that. Sean's had a go at helping me.'

His friend eyed him keenly. 'He's been worried. Like we all have.'

'Yeah, well, I'm alive and doing my job and I think I might have something to get stuck into.'

Jenkins used some bread to mop up his remaining stew. 'Good,' he said. 'Want to tell me about it?' John hesitated and Jenkins smiled. 'It's not madcap or illegal?'

'No.' John smiled with him.

'Then whatever it is, grab it with both hands. I've said this to you twice. You're made from the right stuff and you're a fighter.'

John was chuffed. 'Thank you.'

Jenkins finished his beer. 'My shout.'

As John watched his former mentor, he considered his plan. Protect his house? It was safe already, but he'd make sure. Keep guard? There was Parnell. Golden Hall? David McGuire had bought the house for Clarissa and himself. So, if robbery or kidnapping wasn't the aim, then what was? What was Golden Hall's attraction? For the nearly four years he'd been there, the house hadn't whispered to him of its secrets, nothing unusual to demand inquiry. So, what the hell was bothering him? Whatever it was, he couldn't ignore it.

Jenkins placed the beers down. 'I haven't seen fire in your eyes like that for a while. Planning something big?'

John sipped his beer and got his thoughts straight. 'I might be,' he said.

* * *

John strode into the Learys meeting room on Tuesday morning. He was rubbing his hands together. 'Right, what have we got?'

Sean looked up in surprise at John's exuberance. 'Well ... most of the suppliers' quotes on the wool store are back and we've got a rough price.'

Frank Cartwright chimed in. 'It's a good price we're asking, Sean. But is it a winning price?'

'What's the margin you're recommending?' John asked.

'Three per cent,' Sean said.

John whistled and grinned. 'Skinny!' Sean was looking at him in an odd way and John sensed his fellow director was wondering about his changed mood. 'We're going to win this,' he said, 'and we're going to win it sharp!'

'Mr Leary?' Graham Edwards said.

'Harry Shelby,' John said, 'has bought two steam-driven saws.'

'Where'd you hear that?' Sean said, surprised.

'From the supplier. I was thinking of doing the same but Shelby's beaten us to the punch. Macphersons won't be receiving any more saws for at least six months. Those machines are going to cut Shelby's labour time in half. Most of the wool store's internal columns are 12 inches by 12 inches Ironbark. Once set up, those saws will be worth their weight in bullion, ripping through timber in no time. Here's my figures to prove it.' John brought up his file and lifted two sheets of paper with numbers scribbled on it.

Sean's eyes rounded in shock, and he opened his mouth then closed it. 'He's won the job already, then.'

John's team had become solemn, and he let them suffer for a time. He'd worked late into the night and gone over the client connections on the wool store. In the documents, on which they had to tender, there was the investor client list. By a stroke of luck for John, Mr William Ryan was on the board of the wool grower who'd commissioned the store. So now John had a reason to visit him. In practice, contractors seldom dealt with clients who wanted buildings built and who paid their bills. The architects were the gatekeepers of the tender/bid and supervised the construction. But John knew the secret: save the client money and you most certainly would have an edge.

'So,' Sean said. 'What do we do?'

'What do we do?' John said. 'We change the design. That's what we do.' Sean and Frank looked at him as if he'd gone mad. John smiled at them. 'Halve the number of columns, increase the size of the ones remaining and use bigger beams for the spans in between. Iron beams.'

'But ...' Frank said.

Sean nodded. 'Could work. With fewer columns taking up pricy floor space, means there's more room and so more bales can be stored. That's what the customer is all about. Wool, not how the bloody thing is built. But we have a week left to lodge, John.'

'Then you'd best get cracking. Go over and see Brunel's. I dropped in there before work and got them to give my idea the once over. Frank, if you're happy with your prices, leave that bid in. We'll put a non-conforming bid in on the lighter structure. It'll win it, I'm sure. Go there now, get Brunel's design, measure and cost it. Go.'

Frank grinned at him. 'Yes, boss.'

'Graham,' John said, 'get onto Sydney Steel. I want the best price supplied to Darling Harbour.'

'Right.'

When they'd left, John looked at Sean and he grinned.

'What's up?' John said.

'What's up? You, that's what's up! What magic potion have you swilled?'

'No potion, Sean. I just feel different.'

'Is it this bid?'

There was no reason to share with Sean his weird idea that someone might be trying to rob his house or kidnap his son, and so he told a half-truth. 'Some. My mind's clear again. I don't know if I'll stay this way, but I feel better.'

'Well, let's work on what we've got now. I'll get the boys humming. We might have our next job.'

'We will have, mate. Will have.'

* * *

William Ryan's office was in Pitt Street, not far from Learys. On Wednesday morning, John waited in the reception. He was ten minutes early and keen to get two things—a favourable view of his leaner wool-store structure and more background on Mary Harrigan.

His review of their bid the day before was on his mind. He hadn't forced himself to be upbeat with his team. He just had been that way. This morning he'd felt the same and went to work in a good frame of mind, the first for many months. And Christine's expression was different during the board meeting this morning. Maybe Sean had forewarned her on his changed demeanour.

Mary Harrigan was the key. Her being near his home was deliberate and had a purpose other than general inquisitiveness. He was sure of it. Then there was the strange man outside his house.

'Mr Leary,' a woman said to him. 'Mr Ryan will see you now.'

John followed her into a large office and Ryan stood up and held out his hand.

'Mr Leary, hello again. Please sit down. Some tea?'

'Black, please,' John said. 'Thank you.'

'Mrs Brooks, could you?

'Certainly, Mr Ryan.'

William Ryan sat down. 'Now, what can my company do for you?'

John smiled. 'Award us the wool-store job.'

Ryan's eyes opened in surprise then he smiled as well. 'Bring us your best price and we'll see.'

'Of course, of course.' John paused. 'I do have something that would be worth your while. Something that could save you money.'

'We're always ready to hear about that,' Ryan said.

'Right. Do you know much about wool-store design?'

'Not really. Mr Bardell is the expert there.' The door opened and Brookes brought in the teas and a plate of biscuits.

John took his cup and accepted a chocolate biscuit from his host. It tasted good and he was reminded that it was the first time in many months that he'd enjoyed one. 'Architects want the store to look good and be built properly.'

'Indeed.'

'But if you could get more wool stored, Mr Ryan, wouldn't that be better for you?'

Ryan paused. 'Of course. But the store's all been designed.'

John enjoyed more of his biscuit and sipped his tea. 'Learys is looking at a new design. One that'll reduce the number of columns and that'll mean more room to store wool under the same roof.'

'Wait.' Ryan got up and lifted a set of drawings from his side table and returned to John, who looked at them. They were coloured, non-technical, client-type drawings. On the plan, black dots aligned in three rows marked the column positions. 'Show me how you'd design it differently,' Ryan said.

John removed a pencil from his jacket and leaned over. 'May I?'

'Please.'

John put a mark through each alternate column in the three rows. 'There. We don't need these. We've now halved the number of columns.'

Ryan looked at him. 'Are you sure? You're a builder. You build to a design by others—how do you know this would be sound?'

'Brunel's, Mr Ryan. They're the engineers who have designed the new structure. It'll work.'

'Then Bardells must be told.'

John smiled. 'We'd like this to be kept quiet. After all, we're in a competition.'

Ryan paused then nodded. 'You'll still have to price the architect's original design. That's what the tender's based on.'

'We have,' John said, 'and we'll submit that. We'll also submit an alternative. There'll be a cost reduction.'

'How much?' Ryan asked.

'That, sir,' John smiled again, 'you'll find out in six days.'

Ryan glanced at his desk calendar. 'The close of tender is the nineteenth of July.'

'We'd like favoured treatment.'

Ryan packed up his plans and returned them. 'It all sounds good, Mr Leary, but I'm just one vote on a panel of four.'

'Money saved on your store will be money to your shareholders.'

Ryan paused, thinking. 'Very good. I'll consider your offer, if it proves valid and cost effective and saves us money.'

'That's all we want. Now, I've another question.'

'What's that?' Ryan said.

'My house.' John took a chance now. 'Have you seen it?'

Ryan smiled. 'As a matter of fact, yes. It's a handsome residence. We were out your way some time ago, on a Sunday.'

'I think I saw you outside that time.'

'My apologies for appearing to gawp but we weren't. It was our new friend, Mrs Harrigan, who pointed your house out to us.'

'Your friend?'

'We were sightseeing, and she asked if we could come by your way.'

It sounded innocent. 'I see,' John said.

'She says that she and her husband once owned the house.'

'That's right.'

'Why do you ask, Mr Leary?'

'No particular reason. You didn't know Mrs Smith back then?'

'No. My wife and daughter met the now Mrs Harrigan on the ship coming back here. Constance and Catherine had to go to England to care for my mother-in-law in Bournemouth, who was dying. After she passed, they got her estate in order and returned here. On the voyage they befriended Mrs Harrigan and her son, who were coming back here.'

'I wonder what made her return,' John said, almost to himself.

'I don't know precisely. Now, anything else?'

John was going to ask after Catherine, the man's beautiful daughter, but decided against it. 'Thank you, Mr Ryan.' John stood up. 'I appreciate the chance to convince you about our better bid.'

Ryan gripped John's outstretched hand. 'We'll be in touch through Mr Bardell, no doubt.'

'Goodbye, Mr Ryan.'

John thought about Mary Harrigan as he returned to George Street. Why would she rejoin the society where her husband had failed so spectacularly? Wouldn't she have been better off staying in England?

* * *

Maureen pushed open the front door of her new Glebe home and confronted the chilly wind that accompanied her visitor. 'Miss Ryan,' she said and smiled. 'Please come in, quick. Can I take your coat?'

'Thank you.' Catherine Ryan's clear skin was blushed from the air and her blonde hair captured by an attractive blue bonnet.

Maureen accepted her visitor's jacket and muff and placed them on the hall stand. 'It's bleak out there. There's a cosy fire inside and afternoon tea.'

'Lovely.'

Maureen preceded her guest into the parlour. She'd invited Miss Ryan here this Saturday afternoon for one reason: to get to know her better on John's behalf, though of course she hadn't shared this with John. 'Please sit down. Tea?'

'Black with lemon, please.'

Like John, she thought. Maureen sat and poured.

'How is Mr Forde?' Catherine asked.

'He's well, thank you, and tutoring this afternoon.'

'Now, Mrs Forde, we last spoke about women's rights.'

Right to the point: Maureen smiled. 'We did. Women's rights—an interesting phrase. By law we have very few. A cake?'

'Thank you,' Catherine said as she took the cake, then sipped her tea. 'I just want you to know that I'm no revolutionary. I'd like to make it clear that I believe women should seek independence, but I have no difficulties with getting married and raising children. That's what our religion teaches us. In fact, I'm looking forward to it.'

'I had no doubt of that.' She'd passed the first test for Maureen, whose main passion was for women's education, whatever their marital status.

'It's just that women should have more say in a marriage,' Catherine said. 'Take more responsibility for how they live their own lives.'

'That's a refreshing view.'

'Yes, thank you, Mrs Forde. Women can think and use their brains and should have careers.'

'That's bold,' Maureen said.

'You are a teacher.'

'I am. But up till six years ago I couldn't teach if I was unmarried.'

'You see,' Catherine said. 'Discrimination.' She ate more of her cake. 'This is delicious. Can I have the recipe?'

'It's a simple rock cake.'

Catherine grinned. 'It's doesn't taste simple. I like cooking, especially making difficult recipes.' *Another tick.* 'So, some women are achieving. Miss Nightingale is trying to set up a nursing school in St Thomas's Hospital, London. Miss Blackwell in the United States became a doctor and even in the architecture profession. Why, Mrs Forde, one day we could have our first woman architect in Sydney!'

Maureen laughed. 'My brother would find that a challenging idea.'

Catherine nodded and smiled. 'I bet he would.'

'You're well read.'

'I'm excited about what women can do, could do,' Catherine said. 'What does Mr Forde think about you teaching? I hope you don't mind me asking.'

'More tea?'

'Please.'

'Liam is progressive himself. I think that's necessary in a marriage. To have respect for each other's views.'

'And your brother?' Catherine said. 'What are his views?'

'Would they matter to you?'

For the first time, Catherine seemed discommoded. 'I ... well. Not really, however he's in a man's world of building. Having any woman in such an industry would be ... revolutionary!'

'Radical at best,' Maureen said and smiled again. Did Miss Ryan like her brother? 'So, let me hear you talk about your activities outside work. I'd hazard a guess that your tasks as a milliner fill your day.'

'They do. But they don't fill my mind. Let me explain ...'

As Miss Ryan spoke, Maureen witnessed the passion in her voice and the excitement in her eyes. Yes, she was formidable in her views and that might challenge her brother. Then again, that's what John

might need, a challenge. Over the next hour, Maureen warmed more
to the young milliner.

* * *

On the twentieth of July, Mary Harrigan was sitting in her gig, in
Wolseley Road and beside an acacia tree which gave her some
protection from the biting southerly wind. Her request to visit her
former home had been accepted. But Mr Leary wanted Fawcett to
meet with her, not him. Mary felt put out and she pondered if Mr
Leary was snubbing her. Perhaps. But perhaps he was cautious about
whether she and her son were suitable for Richard to play with. He
might have asked Fawcett to vet her in that way.

She thought about the papers Peter had left for her. Some
troubled her and others made her think that there was no fortune left
at all. Peter had known a gambler, a Mr Ian Dunstan, and there were
letters that indicated their friendship had been strong. Had Peter
loaned the man money? Or worse, gambled it himself? Then there
was a Mrs Marie Carter, last living in Balmain, whose first letter to
Peter disturbed Mary greatly. She opened her purse and took it out.

30th April 1852
Bendigo Diggings.

Dear Mr Smith,

*I want to give my appreciation to you for how you've supported me and the children
over these last weeks in my bereavement. Additionally, my deep-felt thanks to you
for trying to save my husband's life last month. With no thought to your safety, you
unselfishly placed yourself in harm's way in a dangerous place, to try and save my
trapped husband, with likely more shaft collapses following the fatal one that killed
him.*

*Peter, and I think I'm entitled to call you that, since you have been very dear
in my thoughts because of your heroic act, as you know my late husband's diggings*

were near your own. I cannot let you pursue your life without reward. My husband had said that after he'd exhausted the claim that he'd worked on, he was going to make a start on a claim for a quartz bearing section not far away. It looked favourable, and it has proved to be so. It gives me a pleasure that counteracts the pain of my loss to give this claim to you. I will transfer the title claim to your name.

I sincerely hope that you benefit from my gift. It is the least I can do for such a wonderful man as yourself. You will always be in my thoughts.

Sincerely
Marie Carter

Was this woman calling Peter a wonderful man out of gratitude— or were they closer? Could she have been Peter's mistress? Mary hated to think so, because her marriage to Peter had been warm and intimate, and she had never suspected him of having affairs. But Mary was jealous of Carter, and it was an emotion that would not go away.

The other letters were also about money. There was a note that indicated he'd paid money for acreage in Western Victoria, only to find that it had been a dud. All overwhelming and worrying.

Mary folded the letter back into her purse and alighted from the gig.

The house number seventy-three sign caught her eye. A middle-aged woman dressed in high fashion was sitting on its front veranda. Mary continued walking, not wanting just yet to meet a former neighbour. The lady was likely to be Mrs McGuire. Even in the winter sunshine, the house looked well designed, with wide verandas to shade the colony's summer heat. When her own home was being built, she would have liked a similar design, but it wasn't to be. Their architect had adopted the gothic revival style. A pity. Still there was some benefit. The architect, at Peter's insistence, had designed a front veranda facing west.

After opening and closing the front gate of number seventy-nine, she paused. She felt a sadness, because right on this spot nearly four years earlier she'd discovered Peter's unconscious body. He had been working alone in the garden and collapsed next to an empty harnessed wagon and a trolley. They'd taken him to Sydney hospital, where he'd been pronounced dead from a heart attack. Shaking herself from the memory she glanced down and saw the old brass sign for the house, partly concealed by weeds in the garden. It was just under two feet long by a foot and a half wide, and stood about four inches above the soil. Mary was puzzled. It still spelled out 'Bede Hall', though Mr Leary had said that he'd changed the name of the house.

She ascended the steps to the front veranda and rang the familiar bell. Adjacent to the entrance door was a brass plate with engraved letters which spelt out 'Golden Hall'. Why hadn't Mr Leary changed both the garden sign and this one at the same time?

Fawcett greeted her and invited her in. Despite the different decoration in the entry vestibule, she felt right at home and that both excited and saddened her. There was a hall stand with a set of keys. By habit, she turned left into the drawing room at the front of the house, where a coal-fed fire clipped the chill from the air.

'Sit down, please Mrs Harrigan,' Fawcett said.

The boy Richard was playing with blocks on the carpet in front of the fire. 'Good afternoon, Master Richard,' Mary said.

Richard smiled at her.

'Where is Reginald today?' Miss Fawcett asked.

'He's in school at St Vincent's at Darlinghurst. I tried to get him a free day today but there was a test he had to sit. I'm sorry I couldn't bring him. I will next time.'

Fawcett frowned. 'St Vincent's, run by the Sisters of Charity.'

'Yes, Catholic, I know. But we are Church of England and I'm hoping to get him into Sydney's first Ragged School. They have them in Melbourne and Hobart. Reginald attended one in England.'

'Ah,' Fawcett said and stood up. 'I see. Could you watch Richard while I bring the teas?'

'Surely.'

Mary sat closer to the boy, who eyed her shyly, then concentrated on his task. 'What are you playing?' Mary said.

Richard showed her two blocks. One was numbered and one had the letter "A" on it. The other blocks, over a score, were similar, with letters and numbers one to ten. He placed four letters together. 'Fort,' he said and pointed outside. 'In the garden.'

Mary was impressed with Richard's intelligence. 'Then you must show it to me.'

He nodded and Fawcett returned with the tray of tea and a large cake, its aroma pleasant.

'They're his cousin's blocks,' Fawcett said. 'Michael, Mr Leary's sister's son, gave them to him. How would you like your tea?'

'White with two sugars, please. And is that a date cake?'

'I just made it,' Fawcett said.

'I'll have a piece, thank you.'

Fawcett prepared the tea and Mary glanced around. It now felt strange being here. She would love to poke around. But only if she could do so alone. How to manage that?

'There you are,' Fawcett said handing her the tea and a slice of cake. 'I hope you like it?'

Mary took a bite. 'It's delicious.' She sipped her tea. 'Sydney's changed. It's busier and there are more people.'

'There are. What else have you noticed?'

'The carriages,' Mary said, 'and the carts coming out this way on better roads. But I know the weather hasn't changed. I missed the sunshine when I went back to England. It's cold now but I can't wait for summer and light clothing.'

'And now you're not in easy circumstances,' Fawcett said. Mary was shocked and yet Fawcett's face showed no gloating. 'Fate was not kind to your husbands or you.'

Mary forced a smile. 'True.'

'I'm sorry, Mrs Harrigan, if this is a tender subject. It's just that I remember you as a nice lady and it's good to see you back. Whatever the … you know what I mean?'

Mary settled down somewhat. 'Thank you for the compliment.'

'And I have news, too. I'm engaged to Mr Samuel Fruin, Mrs McGuire's coachman.'

'Good for you, and he's close by!'

'He is.'

'And tell me, Fawcett, this house's new name, Golden Hall. Why did Mr Leary choose it?'

Fawcett smiled. 'The gold strikes happened when Mr Leary was courting Clarissa.' She took a deep breath. 'Mr Leary always felt that he'd had a golden age with Clarissa here, and in January last year he changed the name.'

'Very sweet. Yet the garden sign is unchanged.'

'It wasn't found until recently. He'll get round to changing it, I expect.'

'I see.'

The front doorbell rang. 'Excuse me,' Fawcett said and left. Mary's pride still stung at Fawcett's words about her circumstances. Yes, she had come down in the world. All the more reason to find Peter's money.

'Come in, Mrs McGuire,' she heard Fawcett say. 'There's someone in the drawing room you might know.'

Oh dear, Mary thought. Having tea with a housekeeper was one thing. Reminiscing with a former wealthy neighbour was quite another.

Both women walked into the room. 'Mrs McGuire,' Fawcett said, 'this is Mrs Harrigan, who used to live here.'

Richard jumped up, ran and wrapped his arms around his grandmother. She patted his head. 'Dear boy. How do you do, Mrs Harrigan.' She smiled. 'It's been a while. Are you well?'

'Thank you, Mrs McGuire, I am. And you?'

Mrs McGuire sat down opposite her. 'I am, thank you. Fawcett, if there's tea left, I'll have some, and some of that luscious cake. Now, Mrs Harrigan, you've been back to England?'

'I have and I was married again there, but for a short time. I'm widowed once more. But the colony has beckoned me to return.'

'My condolences,' Mrs McGuire said.

Mary remembered her manners. 'I was very sorry to hear about the deaths of your husband and daughter. All in one year.'

Mrs McGuire took a deep breath. 'Thank you. Sadness strikes still, at any time.' She looked at Richard and smiled as her eyes glistened. 'But I have my dear one here and that consoles me.' Mrs McGuire sipped her tea. 'Each winter I seem to get more aches and pains. Summer's best here.'

'It is.'

'Look, grandmother,' Richard said. The three women looked at his blocks, all in a line, spelling out 'I love yu'.

Mrs McGuire smiled. 'Thank you, dear. But there's an "O" in "you".'

Richard frowned. 'That's silly.'

'It might be, but that's the English we know,' McGuire said and ate some of her cake as her grandson inserted the missing block. 'You have a son, Mrs Harrigan, I recollect?'

'I do, Reginald. He's nine and he'd love to play with Richard.'

'That's nice but he's a bit old for him, surely?'

Mary had to have a reason to come back here, and Reginald was her key. She said, 'He likes playing with young ones and he's not rough.'

'Mr Leary would like that,' Fawcett said.

'I'll talk to John about that, thank you, Fawcett.'

'Yes, Mrs McGuire.'

Fawcett cast her eyes down. Ever since Mrs McGuire had come in, Fawcett had changed her demeanour.

'And tell me, Fawcett,' McGuire said. 'Have you got things organised for Clontarf?'

'Just about, Mrs McGuire.'

'We go up country in a week,' McGuire said and turned to Mary. 'Here we are talking about sunshine and we're off to Bathurst at the end of this month. The whole family.'

'The papers said it snowed yesterday up there,' Fawcett said.

'Indeed,' McGuire said. 'But it'll be lovely to have everyone there. Richard, perhaps you can build a snowman.'

Richard started jumping up and down.

There would be no one in the house, Mary thought! She'd have time to snoop. But how to get access? Now was the time to reconnoitre. 'This place hasn't changed much,' she said. 'Has Mr Leary done anything to the back yard?'

'I'll show you,' Fawcett said, but turned to Christine McGuire 'Mrs McGuire? Do you think that would be all right with Mr Leary?'

'Of course. You go. I'll play with Richard here.'

Fawcett led Mary from the drawing room into the north-facing, sun-filled dining room. The walls still had the same panelling but there were different paintings and more bottles of drink on a sideboard. She followed Fawcett into the kitchen beyond, which hadn't changed.

Mary laid the rest of the house out in her mind. On the left side of the entrance hall was an office with storeroom and scullery behind that. Upstairs there were five bedrooms and bathrooms accessed from a central staircase.

Fawcett reached for the back door and Mary noted that the key in its lock had a faded pink mark on it. Mary got excited. Could it be the same key that she used to use? Fawcett opened the back door and stepped outside onto the back veranda, where a big dog greeted her. Mary stopped and pretended to adjust her clothing, glancing closer at the key. Yes, it had been hers.

'See,' Fawcett said gesturing at the rear.

The stables against the back fence were of the size Mary remembered, and now housed an expensive carriage and three horses. The acacia tree had grown, and the lawns were more lush. A dog was nudging into her hand.

Mary patted the dog, a Labrador, and the dog's tail wagged more briskly. 'What a boy.'

'He's the master's dog all right and Richard dotes on him, too. He smells the cake,' Fawcett said. 'Parnell! Away.'

The dog wagged his tail and seemed friendly but Mary knew he would be a problem if she came back here alone. However, she had an idea to deal with that. 'It was always nice to be out here,' she said.

'But the front of the house has the view,' Fawcett said.

'It has,' Mary agreed and walked out and down the back steps. She looked back at the rear of the house and up at the first floor. No change there but her heart thumped with the thought that she had found a way to get inside the house. She still had a copy of the original back-door key and it looked as though the locks had not been changed since she and Peter lived in the house. 'Thank you, Fawcett.' She shivered. 'Can we go back to that fire?'

'Of course.'

'So, when do you go with the family to Bathurst?'

'On the twenty-eighth. We come home on the third of August.'

As she followed Fawcett in, Mary started to plan. They hadn't changed the locks! Well, the back-door lock anyway. When she had lived in her old home, she had dabbed pink paint on the back-door keys to make them easy to identify on her big household key ring. When she handed them over to the new owner, she'd kept one of the back-door keys as a memento and taken it to England with her—the last sentimental remnant of her life with Peter. She still had it—and she would try to get in with it when the Learys were away.

Walking back into the drawing room her face became flushed, not from the fire's heat, but of being a step closer to finding Peter's gold.

* * *

John had returned to Clontarf four months after Clarissa's death. In that 1858 summer heat he'd swum in the Macquarie River, which marked the southern boundary of his three-hundred-acre property. While under water at one time he'd contemplated not surfacing, just ending his misery in the clear and silent world. But Richard had saved him—not by rescue, but by his very existence.

Now on a late July evening, after a light dinner, he looked at his son sleeping on a lamb's wool rug by the fire in the overseer's cottage. The logs blazed and the heat was welcome as snow fell. It had been a long trip by coach to Bathurst and a further six miles to the property. The Fordes, their children, his uncle and aunt and mother-in-law were settling in at the main house, which was detached from the overseer's cottage. Footsteps padded behind him and Stella Fawcett stood by his armchair.

'Time for the little man to be in bed,' she said.

John brought a finger to his lips, bent down and picked up the sleeping child. Richard grunted, but was out to it, and John carried him into one of the two bedrooms and tucked him in. Stella's bed was alongside it.

The mountain air had made her eyes sparkle and her skin glowed. She must have felt self-conscious for a moment, because she ran a hand through her hair. 'Good night, sir,' she said. 'Don't stay up too late.'

'Good night, Stella.'

He returned to the fire and poured himself another Jamesons. There were just the three of them here in this cottage, because the overseer was staying in town. John thought for a moment about Stella's situation. It had been so long since he'd felt the comfort, scent and closeness of a woman. But he would never take advantage of Stella, whatever her attractions: she had looked after Richard since he was a baby and he needed her as a housekeeper. She was engaged to Christine McGuire's coachman, Samuel Fruin, and Christine made it clear to any gossips that Fawcett's presence under John Leary's roof was entirely respectable.

So why had her nearness disturbed him suddenly? Was he becoming susceptible to women once more? He found himself thinking about Catherine Ryan, wondering how he might meet her again. But she was so young and pretty—why would she be interested in him? He forced himself to think about work instead. He'd heard nothing of the bids he'd submitted on the wool store. It was now nearly ten days since the lodgement and no news in this business was bad news. He'd get to William Ryan when he returned to Sydney.

He was about to fill up his glass but stopped. Time for bed. Placing another log on the fire and adjusting the screen, he took his lantern and entered his bedroom. Tomorrow, if the weather cleared, he'd play with his son, nephew and niece. When they got back to Sydney Richard would enjoy having a new playmate: Stella had told him of the meeting with Mary Harrigan and he had approved of the mother and child coming around once in a while. He didn't think Mary Harrigan was snooping at her old home; she only wanted a companion for Reginald, who after all was new in town and had no friends.

Stripping down in the cool air, he slipped on his nightshirt and got into bed.

* * *

Mary was on edge, conscious of every sound and movement, but she chastised herself for being nervous; there was no one here at Golden Hall. John Leary's family was in Bathurst and the back door was hidden from all eyes but hers. It was Monday morning, horses' birthday, the first of August.

She inserted her spare key into the lock and turned it. It met resistance. No, no! She removed it and with a pencil in her perspiring fingers she rubbed the lead along the key and tried again. This time it went all the way. She applied pressure to turn it, worrying that the key might snap. But it didn't and she relaxed, put her gloves back on and looked behind her. Parnell was munching on a bone she'd brought for him. Pushing the door open, she stepped inside.

Glimpses of their life here came back to her. Peter was a loving husband, and he entertained all sorts of people here. He had a wicked sense of humour, a sympathetic ear for a sad story, secret or confession and was the perfect host. Often, guests entered their house as strangers to each other and left feeling lifelong friends. No glass was ever left empty, no appetite unsatisfied when Peter held a party. And Mary went along with the fun of it all. Mary admired Peter's drive and ambition. It was his heart, not his will for life, that failed him in the end.

The kitchen smelt of fried sausages. There was a stove, stone benchtop and cupboards full of utensils and equipment. No hiding places here, unless one of the cupboards had a false back. She glanced in, but the walls looked solid. She went into the dining room, where the biggest piece of furniture was the well-stocked sideboard. She considered the timber panelling above it, wondering if there might be a secret panel, but everything about the room had the firm, clean lines of the rest of the interior.

The drawing room, where Richard had been playing blocks just twelve days ago, was timber-panelled around its north-facing fireplace, but again the panelling was smooth.

The door to the housekeeper's office was accessed from the entrance hall. Turning its knob, Mary found it locked. Fawcett would have the key, so that space would have to wait.

There was a cupboard under the staircase to the upper floor. Mary opened it to a very dark space that seemed to be full of the usual things one would find in a hall cupboard. Its shape matched the contours of the stairs: there were no secret compartments here. She continued her snooping to an adjoining pantry and scullery that led through to the kitchen. Functional rooms with no secret spaces for concealment.

On the first floor there was a hall at the top of the central stairway, capped by an impressive dome, that gave access to five bedrooms and two bathrooms. One of the bedrooms was furnished as John Leary's study. She felt guilty going through these rooms, which were well-furnished, ordered and immaculate. Even the boy's room and Fawcett's room next to it were tidy and pleasant. She didn't look into the wardrobes and drawers: she was looking for discrepancies in the architecture that hinted at compartments behind the walls. But there were none.

In the hallway ceiling outside the second bedroom there was an access manhole to the area beneath the roof. But to place treasure up there, of solid gold bullion, would need special reinforcing of the ceiling beams—a big job and one she would have remembered. She retraced her steps, looking for anything that appeared out of the ordinary, like false panelling. A clock struck eleven, making her jump.

The floor underneath her squeaked. She hadn't seen any places where floorboards in the upper storey could be lifted to place anything underneath, but what about the area under the house? She would have to crouch while looking around, as there was under five feet between the dirt and the underside of the timber flooring. But she knew where the access was: there was an entrance to the underfloor area that led in under the dining room, and from there through to all the other spaces beneath the ground floor. She would have to come back another day, in clothes that could stand the awkwardness and dirt.

Mary went quickly downstairs, let herself out the back door and crept around to the small door that gave access under the dining room, taking care that foliage screened her movements from neighbours' eyes. The low door had a new padlock. How to open that? The only way was to take Fawcett's keys and get a copy of the padlock key.

She walked despondently across the grass at the side of the house, ready to creep out of the garden. What if the treasure wasn't under the house, but buried in the garden? Her heart sank: she could hardly dig it up! If it was buried in the ground, then it was there for ever. This was going to be more difficult than she imagined.

Suddenly Parnell licked her hand and the shock made her pull it away. She smiled, despite her worried state, and whispered, 'Money doesn't worry you, boy, does it? You're only interested in filling your belly and sleeping in the sun. Wish we were all like that.'

Safely outside the house and in the street, she looked back at number seventy-nine. She had found no fortune—and perhaps in the end there was none. Peter might have gambled the last of his money away or given it to the addict Ian Dunstan or— and this was the most horrible thought— he'd led a second life and plied his mistress Mrs Marie Carter with all manner of luxuries.

She looked up at the handsome façade of the house, with its dome and pinnacles, and hope revived again. Of course! The architect. He'd have the plans, which might show up a hidden cupboard or storage area that only the owner and the builders were aware of. Yes, yes, that was the man to see.

* * *

John had decided to beard the lion and he'd picked late Friday afternoon to do it. Most firms were closing down from the week's work and he might get a meeting on short notice. He hoped so. Architects first, then Ryan. It was two days since he'd come back from Clontarf and he had to know about his bid. His company needed the project and it was a prominent one in Wattle Street, Ultimo. John knocked on the door and entered the architect's office. He made his introduction and request.

'Mr Bardell doesn't see persons without an appointment,' the plain-faced secretary said as she looked at John.

'It is important.' John smiled and tried charm. 'Please. I won't take long.'

The woman sighed. 'Then wait here. I'll ask Mr Bardell if he can see you.'

She disappeared into an adjoining office and closed the door.

A minute later, the door opened and the woman re-appeared. 'Mr Bardell can see you for ten minutes, Mr Leary.'

'Thank you,' John said as he passed by her. She closed the door behind him.

Bardell, a small, thin man in a well-tailored suit, stood up. He looked at John through thick spectacles. 'Good afternoon, Mr Leary. Please sit down. I assume you're here about the wool store?'

'I am,' John said as he sat down. A model of the big store was on a corner table.

'We're still assessing tenders,' Bardell said, 'and we'll decide next Monday. All bidders will be advised then on the outcome.'

'Is Learys preferred?'

'I cannot say. Your bid ... bids were compelling but there's much to consider.'

'Such as?'

Bardell sat back. 'I'm not obliged to give you a running commentary on who's favoured. In the documents there's—'

John was offended by the man's tone but decided to keep calm. 'Yes, I know, Mr Bardell, there's other criteria like turnover, safety and capacity. But what about the money saved on our other design? That must have been appealing to your owners?'

Bardell sidestepped John's question. 'We may pause on announcing the successful tenderer. We are thinking of issuing a new design to all original tenderers and ask them to quote on that.'

John became suspicious. 'What sort of new design? One that will cost more to build—or less?'

Bardell stood up. 'I'm sorry I can't give you more time, Mr Leary, as unfortunately you came here without an appointment.'

'If I'd have had one, would you have told me more?'

Worry lines intensified on the architect's brow. 'You'll be notified by mail next week of our intentions.' He moved from his desk and opened his office door. 'Now, I bid you good afternoon.'

John remained seated. 'You're going to use our better design, aren't you? You're going to base the tender on that?'

Bardell gave him a condescending look. 'Leave the design to the experts, My Leary. Just you concentrate on building.'

Coming here was a waste of time. John would now have to get to the owners.

Bardell opened his door wider. 'You'll hear all about it next week. Now, good day, sir.'

John was stuck for any ideas to attack the architect. He stood up and held his temper. 'Good afternoon, Mr Bardell. We'll await your letter.'

John left the office in a foul mood. He'd bet Sydney to a sandstone block that Bardell had pinched his better structure design and wanted the other tenderers to quote on that.

He entered his George Street offices and spotted Sean and Frank Cartwright, who were having an end-of-week beer with the foremen in the ground-floor kitchen. 'Come with me,' John said, 'and bring more beers.'

He led them into the meeting room and closed the door. 'I've just been to see Jim Bardell and its bad news. He's going back out to tender, with our design.'

'He said that?' Sean asked.

'No,' John said, 'but he will. He said he had a new design and I'll bet it's ours. Bugger.'

'That's the risk we ran,' Cartwright said, 'putting in another bid.'

John opened his bottle of beer and took a long swig. 'I know. Our price on the leaner structure must have been so low as to knock out the lowest price on the conforming bid. In other words, our leaner structure was a winner. We should have been accepted.'

'So now,' Sean said, 'bidding starts again and we're back in the same boat as the other bidders. Hoxtons will beat us.'

Hoxtons was a fierce competitor. 'How?' John asked.

'They have their own steel supply,' Frank said. 'They'll beat Sydney Steel any day.'

John sat down, drank and brooded. Sean had a worried face to match, though John suspected it wasn't about losing the job but how John would take the hit. Would John slip back into his funk? Not bloody likely! 'Right, we're still in this,' he said. 'We won't hear from the architects till next Wednesday at the earliest. That's the tenth ... or maybe we won't hear until the eleventh. We've got a lead. Frank, crack open three more beers, Sean get a set of our alternative plans and some tracing paper.' He smiled. 'We'll be here for a while. Is that a problem for anyone?'

Frank shook his head. 'The missus won't expect me home before eight.'

'Sean?' John asked.

'You're supposed to be coming for tea at our place. Remember?'

'Of course.'

'What's on your mind?' Sean asked. 'More smart ideas?'

'Pricing the Bardells design won't win us this job now. I've got a few other ideas that might, though.'

'I'll get the plans,' Sean said.

Chapter Four

A week and a day after she'd snooped around Golden Hall, Mary Harrigan heard a knock on her back door in Bourke Street. She opened it.

A tall man in a grey dust coat faced her. He took off his cap. 'Good morning,' he said. 'I'm Brian Harrison, the clock servicer.'

'Please come this way, Mr Harrison.'

'Thank you.' He carried his box of tools and followed her into her modest parlour.

'Here it is,' she said pointing to the clock.

He smiled. 'Now, here is a clock!' he said. 'James Crawford of Liverpool and a longcase special. Is it yours?'

'It was my husband's. I'd like the mechanism serviced.'

'My pleasure.'

'Do you mind if I stay and watch you?' she said. 'I'm wondering if there are items inside that might have fallen into the works.'

'Not at all.'

Mary sat on an armchair. Now to find out.

Harrison opened the mechanism door with the key that was in the lock, then he opened the bonnet casing above. 'Most likely all we'll find is dust on the workings.' He looked at the packing. 'How long has it been idle?'

'Nearly four years.'

He nodded. 'Then it'll be dust, I'm sure, on the governors and gears.'

Harrison placed a dust sheet on the floor and pulled out the clock from the casing. Behind the face were wheels and ratchets, one of which had hurt her finger when she and Catherine examined the clock. Mary could see there were no valuables amongst the complicated machinery.

Harrison used a screwdriver to disassemble the parts and she looked at the centre of the seven-foot-long oak cabinet with its rods, weights and cable pulleys. There was plenty of space there to place valuables but nothing had come to light. So, there was nothing hidden behind the clock face or amongst the central mechanism. She was disappointed.

As a last resort, she glanced at the weights. There were two, about eight inches long and two inches in diameter.

'What do the weights do?' she said.

'One controls the hour and the other the chime. These ones are polished brass.'

'Thank you.'

But they could be gold! Yes, they could. She rubbed her hands in nervousness.

Harrison had removed four sections from the clock and with fine brushes and rags commenced the cleaning. 'There's little corrosion as the parts are brass,' he said, 'and I'll oil most of them.'

Each weight was connected to its cable by a threaded brass ferrule that could be removed. Excellent. She could hardly wait until Harrison had gone, so she could see for herself the gold Peter had left her.

'I'll leave you to your work.' Mary went into the kitchen and resumed her silver cleaning. As she applied the cream, she tried to contain her excitement. The frustration of her risky visit to Point Piper came back to her. She felt she had wasted her time there, when her fortune might have been sitting at home, waiting to be collected!

Then again, it might not.

* * *

John Leary glanced at the rain beating down on the George Street pavement. It was a bitterly cold and dreary day. The letter in his hand, dated 9 August, two days previous, just made it drearier. He placed it down on the meeting-room table. 'It's from Bardells, and it says what we suspected. They want us to price their new design.'

'And it was ours to start with,' Ron Alexander, the Brunel's engineer, said with exasperation.

'It is, but that's not important now. The architect thinks he's now got us all back to square one.'

'We should sue,' Alexander said.

'We could, Ron, and we would be entitled to, but not just yet. If we don't win this job, we'll have a crack at them by law.'

Alexander nodded.

'So, what do we do, John?' Sean asked. 'Lower our price again just to ward off Hoxtons and our mate Harry Shelby?'

'No.'

'Then what?' Frank Cartwright asked.

John smiled and brought up a plan. 'Ron, you tell them.'

Alexander unrolled and smoothed out the engineering plan of the wool store. 'With this,' he said.

Sean looked at it, shocked. 'Good Lord! Now you've taken out two rows of columns.' Graham Edwards and Frank pored over the drawing. 'How's the roof going to stay up without collapsing?' Sean said.

Alexander pointed with his pencil. 'The original tender design from Bardells had three rows of columns running the full length of the building. That's acceptable, given the weight of the beams they support.'

'However,' John said, 'in our first shot at this, we took out every second column in each row and increased the beam sizes connecting the remaining columns just a bit. Still safe from the weight-bearing point of view and it gave the owners more space to store their wool.'

'Then how do you justify this?' Frank Cartwright said, placing his scale rule on the plan, 'this shows *only one* row of columns running along the centre of the building. The wool store is one hundred and fifty feet wide! That's two seventy-five-foot spans.' He shook his head. 'I'm no engineer, but one row of central columns can't support that roof!'

'Look at the cross-section, Frank.' Sean said. 'There's two massive trusses, each pair joined at the centre column. Christ on His cross! They must be ten feet deep at the ridge.'

Alexander smiled. 'Eleven, actually. All made from timber with steel rods in tension to reduce weight.'

'Never seen monsters like that before,' Sean said rubbing his forehead.

'They'll be the first in Sydney,' John said and smiled again. 'It gives our client over twenty per cent more capacity to store his wool.'

'But the cost, John,' Sean said, 'the cost.'

'I've done a quick estimate,' John said, 'and it should be no more than our latest design. Frank can check it for me.'

'Oh, I will Mr Leary,' Frank said. 'I will.'

'There's less material,' John continued. 'Yes, the trusses are big but we'll make them in a factory and bring them to site.' Frank and Graham looked at him in astonishment. Sean just looked worried. 'In a factory out of the weather,' John said with confidence, 'and we'll use special wagons to transport them to Wattle Street.'

'And we'll need a crane to lift them,' Sean said. 'But I haven't seen one big enough to do that.'

'It will be my job to design the crane,' Alexander said.

'I don't know,' Sean said, more to himself than the others. 'Won't this piss off the owners and Bardells? Are we being too smart for our own good?'

'Financially, they have to be impressed,' John said. 'We gave them a bid that saved them money the first time. Now, with this even better structure, we can *make* them money.'

'The design will work,' Alexander said. 'It's radical, yes, but it'll work.'

'I'm willing to have a go,' John said. 'Sean?'

Sean tapped the table and looked around at the others. They all seemed keen. He turned to John. 'All right.'

'Good,' John said. 'Let's get on with it. We lodge Friday week.'

The rain had stopped and a weak sunlight filled the room. A sign perhaps? John hoped so.

* * *

Sean was sitting down at the Learys meeting-room table. He wondered why John's mother-in-law had invited him here half an hour before their monthly board meeting. 'Good morning, Mrs McGuire.'

'Thank you for coming on short notice, Sean.'

'No problem at all. What's on your mind?'

Christine took a breath and exhaled. 'John. I want to know how he's coping here. At home and in Bathurst I've seen a change in him. A little one, I'll admit, but for the better.'

Sean glanced at the closed meeting-room door. 'He's better at work too,' he said.

Christine smiled. 'Good. Good.'

'I've received a letter from the Australasia Bank,' Sean said. 'John went to see them last week, reminding them to pay what they owed. It was a follow-up meeting from June. They said in their letter that they didn't like his bullying.' Sean smiled. 'But with their letter was a payment to us that was two days earlier than when it was due.'

'So, he's showing gumption again.'

'He is, Christine, and you should've been here yesterday. At first, he didn't want us going for Wattle Street, had no interest in doing another wool store. Well, I don't know if he saw Jesus on a cloud but he's thrashing along now, keen as mustard.'

'We're having another go at it?' She seemed surprised.

'We are indeed. With a very smart design that John has championed.'

Christine poured herself a glass of water from a pitcher. 'What made him change, do you think?'

'I don't know.'

'Maureen doesn't know either, and nor does Gerry.'

Sean smiled. 'So, it's a mystery. But what of it? Whatever's got him out of that funk has done him and us a big favour.'

'Will it last?'

'I'm hoping it will.'

'So do I, Mr Connaire. So do I.' Christine opened her board papers. 'Now, there's something in today's papers I wanted explained to me. What was it?' She put on her spectacles and started to read. 'Ha, here it is. Scaffolding costs. John gets short with me when he explains it. It's simple for him. He lives with it.' She smiled. 'Before he comes, perhaps you could enlighten this woman on the details.'

Sean smiled. Christine was a partner he could deal with any day of the week. 'Surely.'

* * *

Six-year-old Irene Forde was standing on a stool beside her mother. She leaned on the kitchen countertop and touched the bream fillet that Maureen had on a plate.

'Right,' Maureen said, 'pick up the fish and dip it in the flour.'

'It's slippery.'

'It is, but it won't bite you,' Maureen said. 'Now, pick it up. Come on.' Irene did and dipped it in the flour. 'Now, the egg yolk.' That she did also, getting the sticky mixture on her fingers.

'The bed cumbs next?' Irene said.

'Bed *crumbs*,' Michael said, coming into the kitchen and standing beside his sister. 'Here, I'll do it.'

'Let your sister do it, thank you,' Maureen said. 'She has to learn. Both sides, dear. Michael, you can peel the potatoes. '

Irene smiled at her brother, who made a face. She placed the first completed fillet on a plate. 'Why do we have fish every Friday?'

Maureen struggled for a simple answer. 'It's because we're Catholic. We don't eat meat on Fridays.'

'That's the day Jesus died,' Michael said.

'That's what we believe,' Maureen said, 'yes.'

Irene wiped a hand across her face, which left flour on her cheek. 'So, Jesus dies every Friday?'

Maureen smiled. 'No. He died once, but we remember that each Friday and that's why we have fish instead of meat.' She glanced at the wall clock. 'Now, less talking, or we're not going to be able to get dinner for father. It's four-thirty already. So, my boy, more potatoes and Irene, more fillets.'

'All of them?' she asked.

'The lot. I'll watch you and I've got a treat after dinner.'

'What?' Irene's eyes expanded.

Maureen removed a tea towel beside her and uncovered their sweet.

'Apple crumble!' Michael said looking at the bowl. 'My favourite.'

'You'll have none if your homework's not done,' Maureen said. 'Is it?'

Michael looked down. 'Not all of it.' He looked sheepish. 'It's Friday and I've got all weekend.' He eyed the bowl with its thick crust and tasty smell. 'I'll finish it tomorrow, Mother. I will.'

She gave in. 'I'll see what you've done so far, then I'll decide. But for now, young man, the potatoes are calling. And you, miss, can help him. When you've done the fillets, you can wash the potatoes.'

Michael picked up his peeler while Irene continued her ducking and coating.

Maureen enjoyed time with her children, especially preparing meals. She liked trying new recipes and had taken up a correspondence with Catherine Ryan to exchange recipes. It was now nearly a month since Catherine had been here, and she needed another excuse to see her. Perhaps a visit to town? She could drop in at the milliner's where Catherine worked and suggest luncheon. Another chat and another opportunity to get to know the young woman better.

'Will we see Uncle John this weekend?' Michael asked, grimacing as he peeled a tough part of a potato.

'Not for a couple of weeks yet.'

Michael nodded. At last month's July family lunch, Maureen had seen little change in John. Perhaps, next time, he would be on the mend. If that were the case, Maureen thought, how might she get her brother and Catherine together?

* * *

Mary Harrigan entered her son Reginald's room and smiled at the book he was reading in bed, William Howitt's *A Boy's Adventures in the Wilds of Australia*. 'Still liking it?' she said.

Reginald nodded. 'I wish I could go where he goes.'

'William Howitt is a fine writer. Now, time for sleep.'

'There's gold in this story,' he said.

Mary took his book as he slipped under the covers. 'There is.'

'And Bendigo too, where Father was.'

His look was sad and Mary patted his hand. 'He was and he struck it rich.' She ruffled his hair. 'He loved you, my son. He did. And you look just like him.'

'I don't remember much. Some bits.' His eyes brightened. 'How much did he dig up again?'

'A lot.'

'Hundreds of ounces.'

'Thousands, my darling. Now to sleep.'

'Golly. And how—'

'Reggie.'

He smiled. 'Goodnight, Mother.'

She kissed his forehead and blew out the candle on his bedside table. She took three steps down the hall, went into the small front room and sat on a chair. The kettle was on the hob in the adjoining kitchen and she waited until it whistled. She contemplated her home, so small in comparison to Golden Hall. A two-bedroom rented cottage was what fate had left her.

The kettle boiled and she made a pot of tea. She missed Golden Hall but she didn't want it back. There was a feeling of loneliness in her rather than resentment against Mr Leary. No, what Mary wanted was some joy in her life. Friendship with Catherine was something, yet she wanted more. She was not aged. She was thirty-two and widowed, twice, and she would like the company of a man. She poured a cup and added milk and sugar. Despite coming from a humble background, Mary felt that New South Wales still held promise for her. In the three years she'd lived here with Peter, she'd proved that it was a place where class differences were blurred. Yes, there were the big landowners and wool growers, but here one could make a future and build wealth, despite who they'd been in England. That's what Peter had done. He'd dug up a fortune, built a life as a cashed-up businessman and had been accepted as such. She sighed: Peter was no longer here.

But his gold could be.

One place it wasn't was the grandfather clock. Her hope about the weights in the clock had been dashed—they were plain brass. So, three of the five items she'd kept hadn't yielded wealth. That just left the silk curtains and the miner's lamp. Both seemed worthless.

As she sipped her tea, she picked up and read the fair-handed letter she'd received from Peter's female phantom, Mrs Carter, on the fifteenth of the month. It gave an answer to Mary's initial letter to her and confirmed what had transpired between Peter and Carter. She had indeed received a modest sum from Peter during Peter's lifetime. It had been a consideration to her because her own husband, who'd done well in Bendigo, had died at the diggings in a cave-in. Peter had been supportive of her and her children in their bereavement and to show her thanks, she'd indicated to him a good place to dig and try his luck. Peter and his companion Barnes had been successful in their find. Mrs Carter had praised Peter's generosity in the letter that Mary had found among the documents left to her by her husband. In this latest letter, Carter mentioned that Barnes had given her nothing.

Mary put the letter down and refreshed her tea. Was Carter lying—had she been more than an acquaintance of Peter's? Mary had written to her but had not had the courage so far to confront her in person. However, nine days previously, Mary had gone to Carter's house in Balmain. Standing in Short Street looking at it, she found it ordinary, just like its working-class neighbours, timber clad and needing paint. If Peter had bestowed his fortune on this woman, she hadn't spent it on her abode.

As Mary washed her cup in the sink, she decided that Carter was likely telling the truth. Mary had to believe that Peter had been faithful to her and only given Carter what she had said.

Turning off the gas and going to her bedroom, she thought about Ian Dunstan. She'd written to him at the same time as she had to Carter, but so far, no reply. Maybe she should visit the gambler and force herself to meet him, face to face.

* * *

Gerry Gleeson leaned forward in his armchair, catching the smell of the roast that was cooking in the Leary kitchen. 'It smells good, nephew. Nothing like it in winter.'

John smiled as he watched Richard playing with his cousins. 'Then it'll be the last. Spring is just four days away.'

'With its warm weather,' Maureen said.

'And its light clothes,' Liam added, sitting beside her.

'I don't know about that,' Christine said. 'September can be bleak.' She looked out the window to where a southerly was foaming the wave tops in Blackburn Cove. 'And it's not the weather I'm alluding to. It's not a month I like.'

John reached over and patted her shoulder. 'I know.' He nodded. 'I'll be going to the cemetery on the first and I'll take Richard. Would you like to join me?'

Christine covered his hand with her own. 'Thank you, John.'

Nice touch, that, Gerry thought, and Moira nodded as well, recognising John's compassion. The man seemed to be more aware of his loved ones now, something that a month or two ago was lacking. Gerry sipped his whiskey and hoped his nephew's demeanour was here to stay. 'How's it in Glebe, Maureen?'

'In a word, uncle: good.'

'And the back garden?'

'A work in progress,' Liam said, 'which I'll have to address if we want to keep it from overgrowing.'

'Sean's got two labourers who are idle,' John said. 'I'll get them over to your place with a wagon and they can get rid of all the heavy stuff for you.'

'That's decent of you, John, but I couldn't afford their wages. It's just, right now we've—'

'No need,' John said standing up and looking towards the kitchen. 'Stella's given us the signal. Let's eat.'

'But, John,' Liam continued, 'Learys still has to pay them.'

John placed his hand on his brother-in-law's shoulder. 'Liam, no more. It's my pleasure and it'll keep them from sleeping in and going to the pub.'

Gerry followed his wife into the dining room where the soup was already poured for the six of them. He sat in his usual place and watched as his nephew hosted, laughed and talked with interest to all of them. Please God, this would last. Golden Hall was a better place for it.

On the first of September, John opted for the closed carriage to go to Waverley Cemetery, and he was glad of it. On the South Head Road the weather was foul. He remembered the day had been like this when his father-in-law was buried. Christine, sitting opposite him with Richard, seemed to feel the same.

'I'd like to see David's grave as well, John.'

'Of course.' David McGuire had died in same year as Clarissa. The man had been fair, firm and friendly and had, like Christine, tried to discourage Clarissa in her feelings for him. But, after the marriage David had accepted John without reservation, including bequeathing John ten per cent shareholdings in his McGuire Wire and Superior Sheeting companies. Nevertheless, John had taken advantage of David's trust and had tricked him out of his Leary majority. It wasn't something John was proud of.

Richard was fidgeting beside his grandmother. They had forty minutes to go and John had to distract him.

'Your grandfather was a great man, son. He was a pioneer to the colony.'

'What's a pie and ear, father?'

John smiled. 'It's someone who comes to a place before anyone else does.'

'Why?'

'To see what it's like, stay there and work.'

'A long time ago, my dear,' Christine said. 'Men from England came to this land when there was no one here.'

'Natives,' Richard said. 'They were here.'

Christine's eyes expanded. 'Who told you that?'

'Reggie.'

'Who?' she said.

'Reginald, Christine,' John said. 'Mary Harrigan's boy.'

The carriage jolted over a pothole and Richard fell forward. John caught him and sat him on his lap. An arrangement of flowers shifted beside him.

Richard brought out his picture book and opened it. 'Reggie said natives are like red Indians.' He pointed to a coloured picture of an early American settlement. 'Is grandfather in here?'

'No, dear,' Christine said and smiled. She looked at John. 'My David's in Heaven.'

'Like mother,' Richard said pointing upwards.

'Yes, my darling, like your mother. Now, sit beside me again and show me more of that book. It looks exciting.'

John positioned his son alongside her and soon they were absorbed in the pages. He looked out the window at the wind blowing the trees. His feelings now didn't seem as raw as they had been. For some reason he felt a quietude now that he hadn't felt for a long time. It wasn't a quietude of contentment; it wasn't as grand as that, but it was like a respite. A pause in his climb out of his depression. And for the first time in months, he felt that he was clambering out of a hole; as if he'd been captured for a long time without being able to move. Now he was gaining ground. What had changed him? For some reason, he felt something for others and felt something for Learys.

Their carriage was passing Bondi Bay and that reminded him of his visits there with Clarissa. Tears came to his eyes but they weren't the tears of pain, rather tears of … nostalgia. So, what had changed him? What had happened in the past months that was new?

'See, father,' Richard said pointing to two red Indians in a canoe. 'Boat. We should go sailing.'

'When you're a bit older, I'll take you. I've got a boat at Double Bay.'

'Like this?'

'A little,' John said.

Richard grinned and turned the page.

John suddenly realised what was new in his life. It was his curiosity about Mary Harrigan and that man who'd hung around Golden Hall. Those two people had made him *think*. Made him try to work out a reason for their interest in where he lived. He had this vague sense of threat, as though a criminal act was waiting to happen. Robbery? He looked at Richard, talking enthusiastically with his grandmother. Kidnapping? Then he chided himself—maybe there was a simpler explanation for them hanging around. What if there was something in Golden Hall that he didn't know about? Was that the reason why Mary Harrigan had returned all the way from England to New South Wales? After all, one didn't just pull up stumps and travel that long distance on a whim. He felt excited. What was so intriguing about his home? He'd find out.

Their carriage stopped at the gates to the cemetery. The trees bent in the wind but the rain had stopped. John's driver opened the door and he helped Christine out. John handed his son down and alighted with the flowers. A shaft of sunlight lit the area of Clarissa's grave, her headstone shining. Was that a sign? As he picked up Richard and followed Christine, he felt as though he wanted to talk to Clarissa about the mystery of his house. Like old times when they used to chat. Getting closer, he wasn't overcome by the despair he'd felt on his many visits here. As he placed the flowers on her grave, there was a fleeting sense that he could still share things with her.

* * *

It was late Monday morning, four days after John had been to the cemetery, and Mrs Dawes came into John's office. She was carrying his mail in a folder, as was her usual practice. And she was smiling.

'The first letter will be of interest, Mr Leary,' she said. 'When I date-stamped it, I couldn't help but read the first few sentences.'

His secretary had been with him for four years. She was young, fair-haired, efficient and trustworthy; plain faced but not unattractive. He took the folder, opened it and read the opening paragraph of the three-page letter. He made a fist and punched the air. 'We've got it! We've got it. Mrs Dawes, it's a wonder you didn't read the lot.'

'Congratulations, sir,' she said sharing his excitement.

'Thank you, but we all won this wool store, not just me.'

'I've checked your schedule and taken the liberty of getting Mr Cartwright and Mr Evans to the meeting room.'

'Well done. And Mr Connaire?'

'I've sent a boy to Jamieson Street. He should be here in ten minutes.'

'That'll give me time to read the rest of this.'

'Shall we celebrate?' she said.

'You bet we will.' She opened her notebook and stood poised with her pencil. 'Clear the desks and chairs downstairs,' he said. 'Get two half-hogsheads and plenty of pies. Four-thirty start.'

'Yes, Mr Leary.'

'And make sure Mr Gleeson is there too.'

'Right.'

As the door shut, John started to read. He had to check it was all doable. Maybe there was a sting in their award letter; maybe some onerous conditions that would test Learys. He grabbed a pencil and made notes in the margin as he read. His excitement mounted as he ticked the paragraphs. Bardells had approved the radical truss concept design and wanted to see the final design—no problem. They had accepted the Learys demand for full payment of each completed truss before it left the factory. That was essential. He didn't want the cost outlaid for making the trusses and then having to wait until they were

93

all installed, months later, before getting paid. In exchange, Bardells wanted a banker's guarantee from Learys for the amount his clients would have to pay for each completed truss. John had already allowed the cost for this guarantee in the job's costing.

Cash flow was king. That's what David McGuire had pounded into him every day of their business relationship. Profits were welcomed and assets essential—but without cash, businesses failed. He picked up the letter and went to the meeting room.

At four-thirty sharp, there was a buzz of talk in the ground-floor office area when John went in. Sean and Bob Jones were there, as were the foremen Ed Larkin and Barry Watson. The hogsheads of beer were ready, and the smell of the pies permeated the place. Before Clarissa died, John had mixed with clients and their champagne and cigars, thinking that he was one of the elite. Since her death, he realised he didn't care about the social round of Sydney. How false that had been. Tonight, and for as long as he was boss, he'd prefer to share the company of the men who'd made Learys. He raised his hands and the conversation died down.

'Tonight,' he said, 'we celebrate winning a grand job. New South Wales has profited on its gold but there was gold here before 1851, and that was wool. Learys are proud to be part of that wonderful industry and to provide storage for its valuable fleece.' All the men started clapping. 'Right,' he smiled, 'let's get stuck in.'

Ed Larkin headed his way. The Learys Annandale warehouse project would be finished in November and Larkin would be looking for his next job as foreman. But he wouldn't be the 'gun' on the wool store. This morning John had agreed that choice with Sean.

'Afternoon, Mr Leary,' the big Irishman said. 'A fine win.'

'You bet, Ed, and you'll be on it.'

The man looked keenly at him. 'Will I run it?'

'You'll run its most crucial part.'

The man paused and John sensed he was disappointed. What he'd say next would influence John's judgment of the man. 'And what part's that?' Larkin said.

It was stated with no sarcasm or bitterness and John was relieved. 'The trusses, Ed. There are sixteen of the brutes and they'll be the biggest ever built in this colony. I want a good man in the factory. If the trusses aren't made to spec, or they're late, then the job's stuffed.'

'How big?'

'Eleven feet high at the ridge, tapering to one foot high at the eaves. They are seventy-five feet long, each.' Larkin's oath could be heard in George Street. John smiled and led the man aside. 'Exactly, so, are you up for it?'

Larkin shook his head then smiled. 'Timber?'

'Hardwood, and they'll need a strong hand and a keen mind. So, use both and there'll be a bonus in it for you.'

Larkin shook his hand. 'I won't let you down.'

Sean and Barry Watson approached them. Sean, as a former alcoholic, held his customary lemonade. Watson held three beers. Four years earlier, Watson had been foreman on the Park Street Memorial hall project under Sean and had done a great job on the monumental Council building. He'd just come off a stores building in Redfern. Watson handed beers to himself and Larkin.

'Here's to a smooth job,' Watson said raising his glass looking at all three men.

'Barry will head the job, Ed,' Sean said.

John waited for the truss foreman's reply and was gladdened when Ed Larkin touched his glass against Barry's. 'And I'll give him a hand,' Ed said.

'Thanks,' Barry replied, 'and I'll need it,'

'I've got a few ideas.' Larkin said.

'Then don't mind us,' Sean said and smiled. 'Find a quiet corner and have a chat, but don't make it too serious. We're here to celebrate. There'll be enough time for worrying later.' Sean watched them go. 'There's room for another foreman on the job, John.'

'I know.'

'Bob Jones comes off Kent Street terraces in December. We can put him on the brickwork.'

John drank and finished his beer. 'That we can.'

Sean looked at John's empty glass. 'Another?'

'You bet. I'll come with you.'

As they made their way to the hogsheads and through the talking and laughing men, John caught Gerry's eye. His uncle raised his glass and nodded. Yes, it was going to be a good night. He felt relaxed and that surprised him.

* * *

Mary had been at Golden Hall for one hour, so Reggie could play with Richard, and she had no idea where all the house keys were kept. Perhaps in Fawcett's office downstairs, but she didn't have an excuse to go in there. She didn't like to ask Fawcett directly, but she had to find those keys. Without them she couldn't get access to the two places she needed to explore.

Outside, Reggie was laughing at something Richard had done and Mary peered through the drawing-room window. The boys were playing with the fort in the front garden in the first week of cool spring sunshine.

'Richard enjoys the company,' Fawcett said, entering the room behind her.

'Reggie's not too heavy handed with him?'

Fawcett smiled. 'Not at all. Your boy's unusual. He seems to sense Richard's age and is gentle with him.'

That's my son. Mary felt proud. On the wall beside the fireplace was a painting of the battle of Waterloo, highlighting a triumphant Duke of Wellington in the foreground.

Fawcett followed her gaze. 'Mr Leary said there were over eight thousand Irish soldiers in that battle.'

Mary had an idea. Of course. She tried to temper her excitement. 'I'd like to ask a favour of you.'

Fawcett sat down. 'What's that?'

'Peter laid down two vintage bottles of 1815 Waterloo Port under this house. I'd like to get them, if I may? For Reggie, later, you know.'

'Well ...'

'I know that they must be Mr Leary's property,' Mary said trying to reassure her friend, 'but without me he'd likely never find them. I know where they're stashed away. Please, may I fetch them at least?'

'Well, they would be his by law. But I don't suppose Mr Leary would mind your looking for them. However, it's dirty under here,' Fawcett said tapping her shoe on the floor.

'I've brought a dust coat,' Mary said.

Fawcett looked puzzled. 'You carry one around with you?'

Mary realised she'd gone a bit too far. 'It was needed at school,' she lied. 'I just picked it up from the teacher who borrowed it. But about the port ... When I find the bottles, you can present them to Mr Leary, and he can decide to keep them or let me have them. All right?'

Fawcett seemed relieved. Of course Mary didn't care about the port. She wanted to know where Fawcett kept all the keys.

'We'll do it now,' Fawcett said and glanced at the front yard. 'Will the boys be all right?'

Mary said eagerly, 'You don't need to come with me. I can go.'

'No, you'll need a key. There's a padlock on the door that leads under the floor.'

'I see. Where's the key?'

'I'll get it.'

Good, Mary thought. She followed her into the kitchen, where Fawcett opened a cupboard above the bench. As she reached in, she glanced at Mary and noticed her watching. Mary turned away. 'I can search around for the bottles by myself. It'll be too messy and dirty down there for you.'

Fawcett hesitated, then nodded. 'Thank you. I still have work to do.' She held out a ring with a big bunch of keys on it. She picked out a small one and passed the ring to Mary. 'Here's the key to the padlock. Good luck. I'll pop out into the garden and check on the boys.'

'Grand.' Mary went to the bag she'd brought, which was sitting on the kitchen table, and drew out a dust coat that she'd bought at a ragpickers. It was too large for her, but it would do. She took her time in putting it on and waited until Fawcett had exited the front door. Looking down at the bunch of keys, she set to work. The housekeeper's office was her first job.

Fawcett came up to the boys. Reggie was on the ground kneeling. Richard was sitting playing with his soldiers and Parnell was lying down watching them.

'We're coming out!' Reggie said. He opened the front doors of the fort and brought through them a miniature knight on horseback, fully armoured. He mimicked a canter across a metal bridge over a dry ditch.

'I'm ready,' Richard said. He brought two archers along the ground and positioned them to confront the mounted horseman. 'Stop, sir knight.'

'I shan't.'

'Shoot,' Richard said.

The knight stopped and the horse fell over. 'I'm doomed,' Reggie said.

Fawcett smiled. The bridge across the ditch was dull metal that she hadn't seen before. 'Where did you find your bridge?'

Richard looked at her and smiled. 'I got a knight! I got a knight!'

Reggie grinned as well. 'It was a lucky shot, but fatal.'

'Lovely.' Fawcett bent down and pointed to the two pieces of metal. 'Where did you find these?'

'Parnell found them,' Richard said. 'In the garden. There.' He pointed about a yard away from the fort.'

Reggie said, 'They're brass or something.'

Fawcett glanced at the two solid tubes again. Odd items to be found in a front garden. But she could see the boys were eager to get on with the game.

'Well,' she said. 'Can I play? I have a few minutes to spare.'

Richard's eyes rounded. 'Play? Soldiers?'

'Why not? I can lead your cavalry, Richard.'

'All right,' he said. 'Here.' He handed her six mounted soldiers.

'Right,' she said. 'Sir Reginald! Prepare for a charge on your front.'

Inside the house, Mary stood at the door of Fawcett's office. She tried the keys until she found the one for the office, memorised it and unlocked the door. She stepped inside and looked around. It had more furniture than the butler had in her and Peter's day—two more cupboards and two chairs. Glancing outside to the front garden, she could see Fawcett was still involved with the boys. Good.

Reinforced into the outside walls were two plastered columns, one in each corner facing the garden. She went and pressed her fingers on them, with no result. She even grabbed a chair, standing on it and then the desk to feel around the upper sections. Once again, no sign of any false panels. All solid. Stepping down, she examined the floor. The floorboards showed no sign of a storage space beneath. The desk covered a large section. Yes, there could be a hidden cache under it, but couldn't move it. She was wasting time.

Exiting through the kitchen, she made her way to the low door that led into the underfloor area. Unlocking the door, she stooped and went in. A cobweb strand startled her, and she brushed it away. The place was musty but dry, with a loamy soil surface under her feet. Heavy footsteps made her jump, but it was just Fawcett returning to her work in the dining room above. Mary turned from the sunlit side opening and closed her eyes. After a minute she opened them, allowed her eyes to adjust to the darkness, and went at a crouch to where the bottles used to be stored, in the central stair foundation adjoining the dining room. Putting on some gloves because she was apprehensive of spiders, she felt her way into the dark recess, discovered the two bottles and pulled them out.

With the bottles in her hands, she considered her surrounds, for a later date. The staircase where she crouched was in the centre of the house and she was facing towards the front. The office, entrance hall and drawing rooms were in front of her and behind her were the kitchen, storeroom and scullery. Where would a treasure trove be? Today wouldn't do to search—she'd have to return with a lantern and perhaps a trowel, even a spade. At least she knew where the keys were.

Fawcett and the dog greeted Mary when she came out into the sunlight.

'You took some damage,' Fawcett said, pointing to Mary's hair.

'I did,' Mary said. 'Here they are.' Parnell sniffed the bottles, then lost interest.

'Grand. I'll clean them up before I show them to Mr Leary.'

Mary removed her dust coat and brushed herself down. 'We must go. Thanks for letting me under there.'

'No gold found?' Mary's expression startled Fawcett and she laughed. 'Just joking.'

Mary recovered herself. 'That *would* be a joke. I'll get Reggie and go.'

'Richard needs to come inside, too.'

As Mary went towards the boys, she felt like giggling. Fawcett had been so close to the truth.

* * *

Harry Shelby nodded to the doorman and entered the Australian Club in Macquarie Street. He was in a bad mood and wanted to get drunk. Upstairs on the first floor he spotted a friend at the bar and approached him. 'Afternoon, Mr Thomas.'

The tall, broad-shouldered man turned to him and nodded. 'Harry.'

'Can I buy you a drink?' Shelby said.

'I'll never say no to that.' Thomas's red face and manner were testimony to an afternoon on the bottle. Bill Thomas, big drinker, had been on a par with Shelby as a building contractor but the grog now besotted him. If it were not for his inheritance he'd be on skid row. Two years previously, Thomas had worked with Shelby in order to knock Leary down a peg or two, but they hadn't succeeded. Now, Leary was on the rise and had won again.

'Double scotch for me and give me the bottle,' Shelby said to the barman. 'The same for my friend.'

'Yes, Mr Shelby,' the barman replied.

'Let's grab a table, Bill,' Shelby said. 'I'm in for a long night.'

Harry led his friend to a quiet area in the plush surroundings of walnut and leather. He sat down and took a big swig. 'Leary again. The bastard haunts me, Bill. He bloody does.'

Thomas exhaled. 'I heard from Hoxtons that Leary has scored another big job, Wattle Street wool store.'

'The bastard!'

Thomas refreshed his whisky from the bottle. 'Hoxtons says that he didn't win on price.'

'No. Some fancy new design. Untested.'

'Pity,' Thomas said.

Shelby slapped his thigh. 'More than that, Bill. A bloody blow for us. We've tried to build wool stores for years and got knocked off. I had the best price for this one and with only two per cent margin. Two per cent!'

'Low.'

'But not low enough,' Shelby said his voice raised in anger. 'The man has outfoxed me again.'

Two men sat down at an adjoining table and Bill Thomas lowered his voice. 'You told me last time we met that the man was stuffed. Broken-hearted and busted from his wife's death.'

'That's what I thought. No, that's what I knew.'

'His bid didn't show that, mate,' Thomas said. 'It sounded smart.'

'Bill! I don't want compliments about him. Please.'

Thomas sat back and his chair squeaked. 'What are you going to do about it?'

Shelby was silent for a time. Last time Leary had stolen a big Kent Street job from him, he'd set up an accident for the young builder, but the man had escaped with cuts and bruises only. Now, could he go further? 'Those trusses,' Shelby said. 'Bardell told me about them. Monsters. Never been built before.'

'Are they being made on site?'

'No,' Shelby said. 'In a factory.'

Thomas smiled. 'Any new thing built always has problems, faults and setbacks.'

Harry looked at him. Setbacks? Yes. Nothing that would hurt or maim but slow the job and bankrupt the upstart. 'Come on, Bill,' Shelby said, 'empty your glass. The night's young and we've got thirsts to quench and anger to unleash.'

* * *

Maureen waited in Mrs Wicks's tea shop in King Street. She was ten minutes early and had an appetite and a guilty conscience. The first she would satisfy within half an hour, the second was an issue. Was she pushing this too hard? Catherine Ryan seemed a fine young woman: moral, intelligent, attractive and single. John needed a companion. But was she unwise in trying to force the two to meet? She couldn't force them to fall in love, and love was required for a happy marriage. She'd learned that with her Liam. There was attraction when she'd first met him in Dublin, and over the past nine years, that attraction had grown to deep feelings.

Catherine was walking up King Street and Maureen noticed that the tall milliner in her cream dress and red jacket had an elegant carriage. A smart morning cap with a navy bow was attracting admiring glances. Maureen remembered John's look at Catherine at the Wool Growers' Ball. It was a look she knew—curiosity, yes, and more. Her brother was interested. She now had to nurture that interest into something stronger and assist him in doing something about it.

'Mrs Forde,' Catherine said, sitting down opposite her and smiling. 'How are you?'

'I'm very well, thank you. And you?'

Catherine laughed. 'Frenetic at work.' She raised her eyebrows. 'I'll have to be back in twenty minutes.'

'Then we'd better order,' Maureen said.

'It seems that this spring, everyone wants the new fashion.'

'What you're wearing *is* smart,' Maureen admitted.

'Thank you. The cap is the same as last season's but the ribbon's bolder.'

'I like it.'

After they had confirmed their needs with the waiter, Maureen returned to the fashions. 'So, what's popular?' she said.

'Wide straw hats with primary-coloured ribbons. We can't make them quickly enough. It's just the first fortnight in September. If the orders keep up, the shop will do very well.'

Maureen wanted verification that Catherine's head was not just for fashion. 'Do you have an interest in the business? Not a shareholding, of course, but the business side of the fashion?'

'I'd love to get into management, Mrs Forde. You see, the proprietor has a passion for her work, is artistic and welcomes the custom of fashionable ladies.'

Their teas arrived and Maureen poured. 'All that's good, isn't it?'

'Yes … but.'

'Go on.'

'She could make more money if she made her customers pay on time. You see, ladies don't like to pay with cash, and they set up accounts. Many of those are late being paid.' She paused. 'Don't get me wrong, money isn't everything. It's worldly and won't last, that's what the gospels tell us.'

'Your scruples are strong,' Maureen said.

'I just hate waste and poor management of … anything.'

'How do you know so much about the accounts?' Maureen said as she placed two ribbon sandwiches on her plate.

Catherine blushed the colour of her jacket. 'I overheard Madam trying to be severe with her bad debtors. But she doesn't take the right approach.' She sipped some of her tea.

'Sandwich?' Maureen said.

'Please.'

Maureen gave her two. 'Can't you raise this with Madame?'

'I'd like to. But there's four on staff and I'm the youngest and least experienced and only part-time. I'll bide my time until I sense I can say something.'

Now to steer this to John. 'You're in a business that is strictly female.'

'We do sell some men's hats. A few Bollingers. But I know what you mean.'

'My brother's wife, Clarissa, worked in one of her father's businesses. Their most lucrative product was fencing wire.'

Catherine paused with her cup. 'Surely as a hostess.'

'No,' Maureen said, 'right in the thick of it. In fact, she once negotiated a wool brokerage fee between two of the leading firms in town.'

'Really?' Catherine said impressed.

'She did, and managed books of account, general management. All that.'

Catherine seemed surprised. 'Didn't your brother's father-in-law have sons?'

Maureen swallowed some of her cucumber and chicken sandwich. It was delicious. 'No, and that's the point,' she said. 'Clarissa started working with her father as soon as she came back to Sydney from Ireland in October 1850.'

'Was Mr Leary all right with that? I know that's an intrusive question but I'm curious.'

'They weren't married then. I suspect he assumed once she was married her working life would be over.'

Catherine nodded. 'Of course.'

'But it wasn't. Oh, she didn't work over the time she had Richard, but not long after Richard's birth she was back, just for three days a week, I think. It was hard for John but he loved her so.'

'Mr McCreadie talked to me about her recently,' Catherine said. 'I gather he knew her well.'

'Yes, he did,' Maureen said.

'He told me of her death. How do you think your brother is? You know, after her passing and everything?'

Maureen refreshed both their teas. Good, Catherine seemed to care about John's feelings. 'He had a hard time for months, but these past eight weeks he's improved. I've noticed the change.'

'That's grand.' Catherine caught Maureen's eyes. 'He's a handsome man.'

Better! 'He is. And a good one. But then I've got a sister's bias and he dotes on Richard. A dear boy.' Maureen smiled. 'And what about yourself? Have you a beau? Or someone who likes you?'

'Mr Ian McCreadie has taken me to three functions. It's just a friendship.'

So, here was a risk and a possible threat to John. 'Ian McCreadie's what? Early thirties?'

Catherine nodded. 'Thirty-two.'

'What about men your own age?'

Catherine glanced out the window and back to Maureen. 'They are immature, Mrs Forde. I prefer the company of older men. But now, I have to go. I'll pay my share.'

Maureen took a liberty and placed her hand on the young woman's wrist. 'You'll do no such thing. This is my treat.'

Catherine stood up and smiled. 'Thank you. That gives me the chance to repay you another time. Can we do this again?'

Maureen stood up. 'I'd like to. Goodbye, Miss Ryan.'

'Please call me, Catherine, Mrs Forde.'

'Very good. Goodbye, Catherine.' As she watched her go, Maureen was now more convinced of her suitability for her brother.

* * *

'Weaver and Kemp Architects, 181 Pitt Street.' Mary looked at the sign and reminisced. She and Peter had come here on three occasions to look at the plans of their new house. That was an exciting period. Flushed with gold and wealth, she had pinched herself many times at their luck. Now, on a mid-September Wednesday afternoon nearly six years later, things were different.

Opening the street door, she stepped in and went straight upstairs, where she knew the office was. She wouldn't tell Mr Kemp that she'd left Sydney and had returned to New South Wales and in different circumstances. She wouldn't tell him anything about herself at all. The architect had made her feel uncomfortable and had a bad habit of looking at her figure all too often. She had remarked on this to Peter, who'd laughed it off. But precisely because of Mr Kemp's failings, to get what she wanted today she'd worn a daring, tight-bodiced blouse with a hint of décolleté.

The woman at the counter in the hallway upstairs greeted her and asked her to wait, and two minutes later Mr Kemp appeared.

'Good afternoon, Mrs Harrigan,' His look settled on her bosom. She tried to keep her face calm, but her skin crawled. 'Please come this way,' he said.

She followed him into the drawing office. In an atmosphere filled with tobacco smoke and body odour, ink-spotted and dust-coated men bent over their drafting tables. Some were using pens and pencils and others guided set- and T-squares over their tracings. Kemp entered his office, which had its own drafting table. He closed his door and gestured her to a chair.

'It's been quite a time,' he said. 'If my memory's right, your house was finished in July fifty-three.'

'June actually, Mr Kemp.'

'Mr Briggs did a fair job building it for you.'

Mr Briggs of Point Piper Road had done an excellent job; she and Peter had been pleased. 'He did.'

'How can I help you?' He smiled. 'Or should I ask Mr Smith? Is he coming?'

She'd expected this and was prepared. 'My husband passed away in September of 1855.'

Kemp's sombre look was phony, Mary thought. 'My condolences. You have been a widow all these years.'

She felt his glance again at her breasts and was disgusted. 'Yes.'

'Do you need another house designed?'

'I have some thoughts of that, Mr Kemp. What I'd like to do is to look at the plans of my former home and perhaps get an appreciation of spaces and dimensions.'

'Quite the design student, aren't you?' he said, leaning towards her over the desk. 'We can do all that here.' He would like that. She suspected that when they were in conference he'd sit near her and pursue other informalities. But today he simply pulled a notepad out. 'Now, where is the land you want to build on?'

'It's not necessary to go into detail right now, Mr Kemp. But if I could see a copy of our original plans, that would be wonderful.'

He smiled again. 'As you wish. Dimensioned plans?'

'Yes, please.'

'Can you read them?' Her look must have given him an answer. 'Of course, you can,' he said. 'I have the original drawings and you can have them on loan for a modest fee. I can drop them off on my way home. We could go over them together,' he leaned closer and looked at her mouth, 'in privacy.'

He thinks I'm a woman who needs a man's attention. She did, actually, and she acknowledged the thought because it was true. But Kemp's reaction to her flustered state was wrong. He thought she was interested in him! Time to defuse this. 'That's not necessary,' she said, standing up and opening his office door. 'I'll wait in the reception and take them with me. If you could kindly locate the plans for me now. Both floors, elevations and two sections.'

Kemp's attempted seduction seemed on hold, and he retreated. 'Very well, Mrs Harrigan. I shan't be long.'

Later that afternoon, before Reggie returned from school, Mary laid out the plans on her sunlit kitchen table. She put the kettle on. Those plans were her key. They held the answer to what she was looking for. Rummaging in her drawer she brought out a notebook and pencil, sat down and listed the points where secret voids might be made; the underfloor area, corners of rooms, columns in the walls, timber panelling, fireplaces.

The kettle whistled and she made her tea. Returning to her notes, she commenced her scrutiny. She lifted the plan and went to a separate drawing which showed the section. It was as if a giant saw had cut the house in two and she was could see into the rooms on both levels. It gave dimensions: the underfloor area, for instance, had a height of 4'6" and the roof space was of varying heights because of the dome and pinnacles. The fireplaces were highlighted, and the voids they contained. She poured her tea.

Gold was heavy, therefore it wasn't likely to be stored above the ground floor, since no extra supports had been built in. For the moment she discounted the top floor and the roof area. She concentrated on the lower floor. On the drawing, parts of the rooms had circles drawn beside them, with numbers written in. She knew that these numbers referred to other drawings, which showed that particular area in greater detail and to a bigger scale. Sipping her tea, she chastised herself for not asking for those drawings as well. They would run to many extra sheets, but it would have been good to have them.

The Golden Hall drawing room, dining room and hallway had timber panelling on most walls. It was six inches in depth, plain timber that was framed and fixed to the masonry walls. Sheets of polished walnut or oak, in parts decorated with grids of stars, were then fixed to the timber framework. By using larger timbers for the structure underneath the costly panelling, and leaving a gap between these, one could form a void in which to store gold bullion. But where to place this void?

It would have to be low down, say four feet above the floor for easy access. She started listing areas where she thought the treasure could be. Maybe, and this was a dampener, Mr Leary had already found the fortune in the house and had invested it. He was a man who wouldn't advertise his discovery. But now wasn't the time to dwell on that.

The back door opened. She rolled up the plans.

Reggie came into the room and smiled at her. 'What's for afternoon tea?'

'Come and give your mother a hug.'

He placed his satchel down and did so. 'I'm starving.'

'Then we'll see what we've got,' she said and went to the cupboard. At least it wasn't bare—she wasn't that poor. And this afternoon's work had drawn her a few yards closer to her missing fortune. She hoped.

* * *

It had been two weeks since he'd won the wool-store tender and now on a bright, clear Monday, in the middle of the vacant Wattle Street site, John wanted to start the big job now. If he had a shovel in his hand he'd be digging. There was an urgency in him that had been absent for many months. He grinned.

'What's the joke?' Sean said standing with him.

'None! It's nearly three weeks into spring and we've got a new job.' The weather was good and great for building.

Sean smiled with him and glanced along the site.

'It's got a ten-foot fall on its longer side,' John said.

Sean nodded. 'You wouldn't think it.'

'Temporary drainage pit in the northwest corner,' John said. 'Sheds alongside the street.'

'Aye. But built over the footpath.'

John looked puzzled. 'Why not on site?'

Sean tapped him on the chest. 'Because the wool-store walls are built on the boundary where the sheds will be. I don't want to move the site compound again. Over the footpath it goes. We'll build a structure and a staircase up to it from the street.'

'Good idea,' John said and started walking, with Sean following. John kicked the ground. 'Loam to three feet, then sandstone. Drainage?'

'Have to cut the rock, John. No way round it.' Sean grinned again. 'You're right into the nitty gritty, aren't you?'

'The devil's in the details, Sean.'

'It is and you're a terrier with it. Barry Watson's due in ten minutes. We'll jaw about what we have to start first. Now, gas and water. They're over there.' He pointed at the far corner of the site. 'Let's go.'

They set off and Sean brought out a notebook. 'What's changed you?'

John looked at him. 'What do you mean?'

'Mate, two months ago you were two bricks short of being a recluse. You ignored the boys and wouldn't talk to the people who matter.'

John had some idea what his partner was on about. 'I did feel strange.'

'Strange! I'd call it something different. So now, I'm dumbstruck.'

Could he tell Sean about his preoccupations? Would his partner be curious as well about the mysterious man at his house and about Mrs Harrigan's sudden return to the colony? He might.

John trusted his instinct. 'Golden Hall. That's what. But you might think me daft.'

'Go on.'

John laughed. 'It's dumb, but I'm puzzled. The woman who used to own it has come back to Sydney and for no stated reason. I think she has a huge interest in the house.'

'What?' Sean said. 'She travelled back eleven thousand miles just to look at her house?'

'It does seem daft.'

'It has to be more than that.'

'Maybe,' John said. 'It might be silly of me but I can't help thinking she has a secret reason.'

'Well,' Sean said, 'I can't blame her. It's a nice house.'

'True, but as it happens there's a man who's been hanging around too. Weird coincidence, don't you think?'

Sean picked up a broken length of copper pipe. 'And he's got you suspicious. Why? It's a nice house in a nice spot.'

'I know, but what if there's a crime being hatched? Like a robbery? Or a kidnapping?'

Sean kept walking. 'Are you that nervous? You've got a posh house, and people have heard of you. All fame and power get people's

110

jealousy and resentment up. It's part of your success. Surely it's no more than that.'

John said, 'But … and this sounds downright silly, but I think there's something in the house itself that's of interest to people.'

Sean stopped and placed a hand on his arm. 'What?'

'I'm serious, mate.'

Sean continued walking. 'Is there anything else that makes you think that?'

Now he was on thin ground. 'Sean, it's a hunch, a strong feeling. So, I'm going to find out what it is about my house that attracts attention. It'll do no harm to investigate. It's got my juices going and my brain active for the first time in months.'

Sean bent down and flipped the lid of the water meter. Beside this was a three-inch gas main that terminated two feet above the ground. 'We'll need to move both of these,' he said. 'And I want a thirty-foot gate installed here in two leaves. We have to have turning room to get the trusses onto site.' He sketched the services, took two measurements and looked at John. 'Look, what you've said sounds odd, but it doesn't mean what you think it means.'

John spread his arms in resignation. 'Forget I've mentioned it, then, but I'm still going to take a good look around my house. I'm going to get the original plans and examine them.'

Sean stood up. 'It's up to you. And you say that you're better because of this feeling of yours? This suspicion?'

'Aye.'

Sean pointed a finger at him. 'Well, whatever it is, keep it up. Our world's a better place for it.' He looked behind John. 'Here's Watson now. You need me any more?'

'No. Sean this is between us, all right? I might be completely off beam, but it's got to me.'

'I'll say nothing.' He smiled again. 'Just let me know if you find anything valuable. We're partners, yeah?'

'Thanks, Sean.'

Chapter Five

It was the twenty-first day of September and Mary was walking to William Street, where she hoped to meet and confront a person from Peter's past. She had left her Bourke Street home with apprehension and excitement and had not far to go.

She headed south, anything to avoid the stench of sewage. Three houses below hers in Woolloomooloo and down towards the bay, backed-up pipes and stinking overflows were a feature. There was talk of a Commission of Inquiry into it as filth, sickness and rats prevailed. To counter it all, her own terrace home was always kept spotless, with good seals on windows and doors.

Ian Dunstan, the man she intended to meet, was a gambler. From Dunstan's letters in the envelope Peter had left for her, she could see that Peter had given Dunstan sums of money. For gambling? Or could she get some of that money back?

She deduced that a gambler's day probably started in mid-afternoon, then extended into the night and early morning. That morning she'd checked what horse-race meetings were scheduled for that day in case one had lured Dunstan out of town. But there were none. So, he might be home, unless there were gambling haunts near where he lived. It was just after one-thirty and Mary knew it was a long shot trying to pin him down.

The air cleared as she walked westwards down William Street. The temperature was warm and she perspired not so much from the sunshine but from what she was feeling about questioning the gambler, if she found him. He was unknown to her and would be guarded in his response, especially if Peter had subsidised his addiction. Still, he was another probable clue to wealth.

She turned right into Riley Street, where the terrace houses were a little better built. There were subtle textual differences in the details of façades and the choice of wrought iron. On finding Dunstan's house, she opened the front gate and knocked on the door. Half a minute later she knocked again. No answer. Mr Dunstan was not there or possibly sleeping. She crossed the road and waited. After fifteen minutes, she tried again on the door, but to no avail. Going back to her position, she felt she was too exposed and sat on an adjoining bench. In one hour, Reggie would be home from school. Over the next forty-five minutes, no one went into or came out from the terrace and she became very familiar with the exterior of where Mr Dunstan slept and ate. Disappointed, she got up and walked home. She would come another day, maybe a little later in the afternoon.

On the Saturday following her unsuccessful attempt to collar Mr Dunstan, Mary was sitting at her kitchen table looking at the fourth item that had been in storage: her miner's lamp. She decided it was time to take Catherine Ryan more into her confidence. Two heads were better than one and Mary wanted another's view on her sometimes wild imaginings. Catherine seemed just the young woman needed.

Although Catherine went to dances and other social functions on Saturday nights, the weekends were their opportunity to meet, and soon Catherine was hanging her bonnet in Mary's three-foot-wide entrance hall. Her brother Donald was at Sydney University and her parents were out for the afternoon.

Peter's memento was a simple miner's lamp. It was nondescript and Mary wondered about its significance to Peter—why keep it? It was made of metal and had a glass lens on its front, a place for the candle inside, with a reflector behind it, plus a handle and insignia on the back.

Catherine entered the kitchen and sat down. 'Ah, the miner's lamp.'

Mary smiled. 'To all intents and purposes it's not special!'

Catherine picked it up and examined it. She looked at its back. 'There's a raised star insignia. And there's a match-head sized hole in the middle of the star.'

'Perhaps that star is the symbol of the firm that made it.'

It was puzzling, Mary agreed. 'We had this lamp on display at Golden Hall. It held pride of place on the dining-room sideboard. Peter insisted it should never be moved. It had to stand under a painting of the Bendigo goldfields that hung two feet above it … Wait a minute.' Mary picked up the lamp again and looked at the back. 'Yes. This star is about the same size and design as the ones on the timber panelling. Peter said that if you had an eye for detail, and you looked carefully at the painting, you could see the location of his golden hole.'

'What?' Catherine said.

'A golden hole is a very rich vein of gold. It was the Bendigo find that made Peter wealthy.'

'I see. And could you see the exact spot in the painting?'

'Peter swore that he could,' Mary said. 'But I never paid it much attention.'

Catherine looked again at the lamp. 'Where is the painting now?'

'I don't know. Probably lost or sold when we moved.' Mary became excited. It had been mounted on the star-studded wall panelling! Why were the stars on the panelling exactly like the one on the lamp? A clue to something hidden behind them?'

'Mary?' Catherine said looking at her.

'Catherine, we've looked at the chandelier, tongs and clock.'

'And there was nothing in any of them.'

'Right. So, we have this … *lamp.*' Mary gestured to it. 'There's no gold or diamonds in that.' She squeezed her friend's forearm. 'But there might be, in Mr Leary's house.'

'Where?' Catherine seemed astounded.

'There might be something hidden where the painting used to hang. It's our best shot.'

'If so,' Catherine said frowning, 'you have no means of getting it without speaking about this to Mr Leary.'

Mary paused and wondered if she should speak her mind. 'No, but we could try without him.'

'Mary!'

'I know. I know but if it's there, we—'

'Whatever is there now is Mr Leary's. He was left the house by his father-in-law, David McGuire. Sorry, Mary but it is. Legally, doesn't Mr Leary own the land, the house and everything in it?'

Mary's shoulders slumped. 'I know. I'll have to look into this somehow. But if there's gold, and it isn't listed in the title deeds, couldn't it revert to the original owner—Peter—and therefore me?' She looked at the miner's lamp.

'You're really thinking about it, aren't you?' Catherine said. 'Going there and looking for a secret panel?'

'No ... no of course I'm not.'

* * *

John spent the Tuesday and Wednesday of the first week of October 1859 inspecting each of his four building jobs. It was the first time he'd done the rounds in months, and he was eager to see what his men had built and to what standard. His enthusiasm intrigued him, and it was still within him, not evaporating into indifference as he'd suspected it would. Smiling, he put it down to Golden Hall. He'd explained some of his obsession to Sean, but if he told others of his belief in his house's horde, he'd be laughed off his horse. And this could still be his problem. Was he inventing something puzzling just to stimulate his mind? Or was he having some form of mental collapse and going into a world of unreality? Possibly, but the light-heartedness he felt and determination to be again good at his calling didn't seem to point to that.

Starting early on Tuesday before sun-up, he made his way to town. The air was humid and before long he raised a sweat. A lightning visit to the Kent Street terraces surprised his foreman Bob Jones, who had his hands around a mug of tea.

'Good morning, Mr Leary,' Jones said. 'It's a good day. Care to look around?'

'That's what I'm here for.'

'Then let's go.'

John followed his foreman up the staircase of the corner-facing terrace. With two months to complete, the project was well advanced and into its finishing stages. John cast his eye about, dreading to pick up minor imperfections or slovenly work, although with a foreman of Jones's experience this was unlikely. Plaster finish was even and all cornices scribed to a workmanlike quality. The bite of turpentine met him when he entered the main front bedroom. Drop cloths crowded the floor and John scrambled through ladders to inspect the plumbness of the box-framed front windows. All good.

'We've tried a new joiner,' Jones said. 'Mr Jenkins recommended him. 'He's coming up trumps.'

'Where's he live?'

'Surry Hills.'

'Previous work?'

Jones hesitated. 'I don't know.'

'So,' John said, 'you accepted him without checking him out?'

Jones looked away then back to him. 'Mr Jenkins said he was all right.'

'Listen, Bob,' John said. 'Mr Jenkins is fair, and his judgment is sound but don't rely on it. We're all only as good as our last job, including Mr Jenkins's. That joiner might've made a mess of his last job. You should have checked and please still do. Now, let me see the drainage and the water lines.'

Jones nodded and led John back downstairs. At the end of an hour Jones's notebook was fattened by John's pointers.

The man kept silent until John was ready to leave. 'You've given me plenty to do,' he said. His look was not bitter and John sensed that he'd given him a grilling, but a worthwhile one.

'Our name will be on this job when it's finished, Bob. I want us all to be proud of it.'

Jones smiled. 'Right.'

'I'm off. See you next week.'

As John exited the site gate, he glanced back. Jones was scratching his head and looking at his notes. John smiled. Another pair of eyes than Sean's had found issues here, not big ones but ones that needed attention. John was glad that he'd been interested enough to find them. Now, for the Australasia Bank job.

* * *

Mary was at Riley Street again to track down Mr Dunstan. Reggie would stay back at his school, so there was no rush for her to be at home. It was a fortnight since she'd been here and the early October sun had a bite in it, even at three in the afternoon. She was anxious. A quarter of an hour passed and her worry heightened. What if Mr Dunstan wasn't at home? She'd have to come here again. What did he look like? If two men came out of the terrace at the same time, how would she know which one he was? She breathed out and got control.

The terrace front door opened. A large-framed man emerged, dressed in dark trousers and a jacket covering a faded white shirt. It wasn't a gentleman's garb but it would be accepted around a card table, she assumed. The man stopped, squinted at the sun and gave out a hacking cough. Mary went up to the front gate just as the man wiped his face with his handkerchief. His blood-shot brown eyes were small, his skin pock-marked and his teeth stained.

'Are you, Mr Dunstan?'

The man looked her up and down. 'That's me.' He looked around Mary and behind her. He smiled. 'All alone?'

'Mr Dunstan, my name is Mary Harrigan. I was formerly Mary Smith and I'd like to talk to you about my husband.'

Dunstan became guarded. 'Your husband? What about him?'

'You knew him,' she said. 'His name was Peter.'

Dunstan sniffed. 'I may have. I'm off to a ga— to a business meeting in William Street. I can't talk now.' He coughed again.

'Can I walk with you?'

'Please yourself,' he said and set off up the hill. She joined him.

'I possess letters from you to my husband,' Mary said. 'In them you admit he helped you with money. What did he mean?'

'Why don't you ask him yourself? How is he, by the way?'

'He's passed away.'

Dunstan stopped and looked at her. 'I'm sorry to hear that. He seemed like a good man.'

'Why did he pay you sums of money?'

Dunstan set off again, now near the William Street intersection. 'We had a … business connection.'

'In what way?' she said.

He smirked. 'Can't you tell from those alleged letters? I'm afraid I can't say.'

'Mr Dunstan. Be frank. Why did my husband give you money?'

The man was silent for a moment. 'He asked that our arrangement be kept confidential.'

'What for?' Mary had to push. 'That obligation now ends, sir. My husband is dead. Your letters suggest that you are a gambler.' Then Mary had an uneasy thought. 'Did my husband gamble himself?'

Dunstan laughed, bringing on another coughing fit. 'All life's a gamble, Mrs Harrigan.'

She knew that. 'But did he?'

Dunstan stopped. 'I don't know if he gambled himself. He did give me money for my … investments.'

'How much?'

'Not a lot.'

'Are you sure?' she said.

The man stopped outside an open doorway. 'I'm sorry that your husband's dead. I am. Be assured that he gave me little, just enough to cover me when I came up short.' He smiled again. 'You have some idea what I'm talking about.' He touched his hat. 'Goodbye, Mrs Harrigan.'

'How many times did he give you money?'

'My colleagues await,' he said. 'I'm sorry.'

She was going to reply in anger about his obsession, but she hesitated. 'Thank you, Mr Dunstan, for your time. Good day.'

Mary walked back to her Bourke Street home. Was Peter a gambler too? Was that where all the money had gone? But if that were so, why didn't Mr Dunstan mention it? No. Peter had kept Dunstan's letters simply to prove that Dunstan owed him money. Well, Peter had never got that money back, and nor would she.

Golden Hall. It kept calling her back. It wouldn't be too long before she was there again, and this time she might get lucky.

* * *

John left his office at eleven. Crossing George Street and weaving between trams and two hackneys, he went up King Street. Now he felt he was on the trail. Now he was confident that something hidden within his house was valuable. Unsure as to what it was, he was still determined to pursue his instincts to the end. The challenge had become a quest. He smiled and a young woman thought the smile was directed at her and blushed. He wasn't being cheeky, although the young woman was attractive, it was just that 'it' might turn out to be a chimera. Not to worry. Just being on this quest had enlivened him. It was the sixth of October; for two months he'd felt a change in him, and that change was good.

Now to get a look at what secrets his house could reveal: he spotted the King Street number and went upstairs.

Mr Kemp was expecting him and John followed the man into his office.

'Please sit down, Mr Leary,' Kemp said. 'How can we assist you?' The man smiled. 'Perhaps you'd care to be added to our tender list of preferred contractors? With your reputation, it would be a simple matter.'

John knew the architect was aware that he himself had built the Point Piper home for his in-laws at number seventy-three Wolseley Road, but that wasn't the house John was interested in. 'Our projects now are of a more commercial nature, Mr Kemp. But thank you for asking. No, I'm planning to add to my own home, a downstairs bedroom at number seventy-nine.'

Kemp brought a writing pad in front of him and started to make notes. 'What size do you estimate?'

John didn't actually need an extra bedroom. Or not for many years yet, when he himself might not want to live higher than the ground floor. But what of the future? Would he remarry? Would his family grow? He was just twenty-nine and if he met a young woman ... Catherine Ryan came into his mind.

'Perhaps sixteen feet square plus an additional adjoining bathroom.'

'Very good.'

'Do you have a copy of the house plans?' John said. 'I'd like to review them.'

Kemp smiled. 'Your house is very popular of late. I've had another client who wanted these same plans, and they currently hold them on loan from this office.'

John was startled and tried to control his expression 'Who?'

'I'm not obliged to say, I'm sorry.' Kemp smiled. 'We could make a copy of them, of course, but that would be expensive. Is your need immediate or could it wait till I have the plans back here in the office?'

John was puzzled and excited. This was another pointer to interest in his house.

'So, Mr Leary?'

'I'm prepared to wait till those plans are returned, Mr Kemp. Please write to me when that happens.'

'Certainly, Mr Leary. Is there anything else I can help you with?'

'No thank you.'

'Very well, Mr Leary.'

As John walked back down the stairs, he pondered. Another person looking at the plans of his house? It could be anyone, as Kemps were known to design fine residences. Generally, clients liked to put their own stamp on their new house. Their own identity. Why copy someone else's? Someone who was interested in the plans of John's house must have another motive. For instance, they might be planning a burglary. Perhaps it was the strange man seen near his house who had borrowed the plans. So it might be robbery. John considered walking back in to get the name of the other inquirer out of Kemp. But no, better to do his own digging in private. John had to find out what the bloody hell was going on.

* * *

John reached for his October board papers. The meeting would start in twenty minutes, and he leafed through and scanned the back page, which was standard for each meeting. In the middle of the page the share proportion between the three stockholders was shown: Christine's fifty-one per cent share, Sean's nine and his own forty per cent.

The arrangement was hardly new but for some reason today it rankled with him—again. Learys was his company, with his name prominent, yet he didn't own the controlling share. That circumstance was his fault. His sin. His ego and the risks he had run. Yes, all of that, but now he wanted to change it, for the better. How to do that? Capital. He had to have money to buy out Christine, or at least get his majority back. She'd have to agree to part with at least eleven per cent of her share for him to have control. And because of the short time that had passed since he'd violated her daughter's trust, he assumed she was in no hurry to sell him what he most needed. He couldn't blame her.

Until he'd suspected that others were interested in his house, he'd lived with the guilt of adultery like a wound that wouldn't heal. So, how to win or buy his share back without alienating Christine? Did he, deep down, believe that he could start to build a relationship with his mother-in-law? One existed now, a bond of sorts. Was that bond just business? No, it was more. It was a charged emotional one for many years, one that he'd partly loathed because Christine knew all about him. She had spotted his ambition from the outset and it was her opinion that he'd use anyone or anything to get what he wanted. Clarissa's death had been a horrible way to make him recognise his failings, and Christine's loss of her daughter had brought her no closer to him. Could he make amends? The simple life he'd led since was unrewarding and for the last few months he'd been underachieving in his job. Starting a conversation with Christine about the future loomed like a gigantic hurdle.

'Good morning, John,' Christine said as she poked her head into his office. 'What's wrong?' She smiled. 'You look startled.'

'I'm sorry, it was just a … site issue,' he lied. 'Good morning to you. I'll be with you in ten minutes.'

Christine nodded and left him. *There. She's polite to you and has never broached your past. So, what does that say? Well, that she's very much in control of her emotions, which a lady of her class would be, and that she might be trying to improve the bond that you both have together.* Richard was their link and they both loved the boy. John sat back.

Learys was profitable. He was its managing director and to most the boss of the company. By seeding his relationship with Christine with honesty, hard work and humility, he might get into a situation where his mother-in-law would be more amenable to giving him control.

Collecting his papers, he got up from his desk. Smiling, he knew that hard work was needed to build a trust with his mother-in-law. And it was worthwhile to have a go at it.

* * *

Mary Harrigan remembered how she'd loved to sit on the back veranda of her former house and welcome the morning sunshine. Now, she stood under cover and watched as Mr Leary, his son Richard, Fawcett and Christine McGuire rode away in Mrs McGuire's carriage. It was nine-fifteen on a Sunday morning. Just before ten o'clock the carriage would deliver them to St Mary's for Mass. Reggie was spending time with a school friend for the morning and Mary could set to work.

After greeting Parnell and leaving him a treat, Mary entered the back door and headed for the dining room, with a linen bag in her hand. Excitement raised her pulse at the thought of maybe finding gold.

Standing to face the sideboard, she scanned the timber-panelled wall above it. Each three-foot square panel was marked at its corners by stars, which were inset into the panelling and all looked alike. Or were they? She placed a chair against the sideboard, took off her shoes, stood up on the chair and gave the stars a closer look. They seemed identical, but Mary suddenly noticed two stars, one at each end of the wall panelling, that had small round protrusions positioned in the centre of each, about half an inch long. What was the purpose of these protrusions?

She got back down, removed the lamp from her bag and got back on the chair. On the back of the miner's lamp was a star that stood proud of the surrounding metal. In the centre of the star was a small hole. Was this star fashioned to fit over one of the stars on the panelling? She'd find out. Mary swung out the hinged back of the lamp and moved it up the wall to the star that was closest within reach. She lifted it slightly to lay it over the wooden star beneath and felt a thrill when it fitted exactly. The metal was flush with the wall and the small protrusion on the wooden star stuck out through the hole in the metal star.

Excited now, she wondered what she should do next. Keeping the weight of the lamp firm against the wall, she tried to turn it, first right and then left. But it met resistance.

Mary got down, repositioned her chair and prepared to step up on the sideboard, so that she could reach the second star, further above. There was an ashtray where she needed to stand, so she moved it aside. She climbed awkwardly onto on the sideboard with the lamp, positioned it in the same way and repeated the process with the second star.

At first, the clockwise turn was stiff, but she persevered and was able to turn it ninety degrees. As she did so, there was a creaking sound and a panel popped open, six inches below the lamp, which Mary nearly dropped in surprise. Placing the lamp hurriedly on the sideboard, she looked at what the panel revealed. A small space that you could fit a butter dish into. There was no gold. Instead it held a leather wallet.

Disappointment flooded her. She took the wallet, stepped down and sat on the chair, her eyes welling up. Another bitter experience. Mary removed the wallet, musty from its hiding place, and from it brought out a single piece of paper. It was not even written in English! Even more upset, she wiped her eyes and concentrated. It was an Asian inscription, perhaps Chinese. She was after gold and all she had was a bit of paper. All this risk for nothing.

A sudden noise alerted her. It came from outside, near the dining-room window, and she froze in fear. Parnell the dog? Then she heard him barking, further away. Somebody really was outside. Pocketing the piece of paper, she returned the empty leather wallet to its space and clicked the wall panelling back. Replacing the chair, putting on her shoes and thrusting the lamp in her bag, she moved to a corner of the window. Careful not to be seen, she scanned the side area of the house and found no one. Closing the back door and trying to control the affectionate Parnell, she whispered, 'What was that, boy? Hmm? Let's see.'

She went around the side of the house with caution. There seemed nothing. But there, a broken branch, near the dining room window. It was wet with sap from a recent break. Parnell's doing? Perhaps. Still, she'd better be going. Skirting the house, she exited onto the street.

Thomas Barnes watched Mary's departure from the Point Piper house. He'd followed her here and seen her go inside. It was the confidence she'd shown on entering that had surprised him. And then he had it. Of course! Harrigan had a key, which was canny, and she'd also waited until all the Learys had gone to church. Keeping an eye on the munching Labrador, Barnes had gone around the front of the house rather than attempt to go via the back door and alert the dog. Peering into the windows from the front veranda, he'd not seen the woman. A window stood high on the side of the house that could be accessed by a nearby tree. Barnes had climbed it and peered through a gap in the curtains. Below him was a dining room. Harrigan was on a chair and had her hands on the wall above a sideboard.

All at once the thin branch on which he was standing gave way and he had to jump. A bark from the dog hastened his movement and he fled over the front fence and got out of sight across the road.

For the past three months he'd tried to keep track of Mrs Mary Harrigan, especially on her forays to Point Piper. Each Sunday since July he'd come to Point Piper, while the Learys were at church, and today he'd got lucky. Making his way to his horse, he was certain Mary Harrigan had found something in that house. Maybe gold or if not that, then the means to get it. He would return at the same time next week and make sure.

* * *

John was at home and feeling constricted in evening wear on this steamy Saturday night. He was in two minds about going out, suspecting that his sister might be on her match-making hobby horse. His invitation to attend a Celebration Ball tonight three weeks into October was just one more way that Maureen was going to raise his interest in women again. There was one woman who had attracted him and that was Miss Catherine Ryan, and he'd not seen her or taken steps to see her for months. Perhaps he'd change that. Yes, he would.

There was still time before his carriage was ready. He wanted a drink and got up from the sofa and reached for a glass from the trolley. There wasn't one and he remembered that the house maid had washed them all and would return them tomorrow before Mass. Going from the drawing room into the kitchen, he passed the sideboard and glanced down. There was something about the arrangement of objects on it that irritated him. That's right—last Sunday after he'd come back from Mass, he'd noticed that a marble ashtray was not in its usual spot. It was a memento that his Uncle Gerry had made for him about two years ago. It was always in the same position, yet while they were all at Mass it had been moved—and not by the house maid, because he'd asked her about it. No one's carelessness could be blamed for the ashtray not being in its usual place, and you couldn't knock it going by—it was too heavy. So, there was only one explanation: someone had got into the house and gone through the dining room, at least.

His drink would have to wait. He left by the front door, as his groom finished hitching the horses to the carriage. Was he going mad, worrying about this trifle? Nothing was missing—it was just that an item had been shifted without reason. Was his house being searched for something? On the way to town, John ruminated on this problem. He remembered the bottles of port that Mrs Harrigan had unearthed. He'd asked Stella to thank her for finding them. Might she have been back to look for more? But the idea was outrageous—and how could she get into the house?

When his carriage stopped at Government House, John alighted. He walked in, presented his card, and at once found his sister and Liam in conversation with another couple. Maureen smiled and walked up to John. His whiskey foregone, he was looking to quench his thirst. But etiquette first.

'Ah!' she said. 'A man in an evening dress suit is always handsome.' She linked her arm with his and he kissed her cheek. 'And because the man's my brother, he's doubly handsome.'

'Go on with you,' John said but he was pleased with the compliment. 'Good evening, Liam,' he said as his brother-in-law came up.

'John,' Liam replied. 'I'll get you a drink.' He hailed a waiter, who brought a tray, and John took a beer. It was cold and refreshing. 'A hot night,' he said, 'but one that'll be enjoyable.'

Maureen smiled. 'We'll make it that way! Take his drink, will you dear. I want to dance with my brother.'

He was about to protest but Maureen led him onto the dance floor, where they joined a quadrille. As they were the lead couple he was concentrating on the steps and not on the other dancers, but still he received a shock: one dancer was a young woman he knew.

Dressed in a short sleeved, low-necked pale blue top and pale blue crinoline skirt, she moved with rhythm and grace.

'Miss Ryan looks lovely tonight,' Maureen said, noting his look.

John said nothing but kept Catherine in sight. She glanced at him more than once.

'We've met a few times,' Maureen said.

'Met?'

'She has an interesting mind and is a great conversationalist. I find her very open, too.'

Interesting but possibly irritating at the same time, John thought. This confirmed his suspicions that Maureen was on a campaign to see him married again. And yet he was glad that his sister was pushing that barrow. Miss Ryan sounded confident about her own ideas. Clarissa had been a woman who had views in advance of her time and had proved worthy in managing her father's business. John was one of few men who understood and supported women in roles that heretofore hadn't been open to them.

The music was captivating and for the first time in months he was enjoying himself. The orchestra, the movement to the beat, smiling faces, all held him in thrall. And, among the hundred or so guests, there was Miss Ryan, feminine from her blonde ringlets to the white satin bows on her shoes. And, according to his sister, a working woman. 'She's employed as a milliner, I hear.'

'She is, but she has more interest in managing finances than fashions.'

Looking at Catherine Ryan now, John was not thinking of business but of beauty. He was attracted to Catherine, and felt a surge of happy emotion.

'We have become kind of friends,' Maureen said.

He smiled. 'And your basis of friendship was to talk women's issues?'

She didn't look at him and smiled. 'Of course.'

'Not to find a partner for me?'

Maureen didn't answer. The dance was ending, and they joined in the applause, then with the other couples they left the floor. Maureen eased John towards Miss Ryan and her partner, a uniformed officer.

'Good evening, Mrs Forde,' Miss Ryan said, 'and you, Mr Leary.'

'And you, Catherine,' his sister replied. John was startled at the familiarity.

'Captain Phillips,' Catherine said, 'this is Mr John Leary and his sister, Mrs Forde.'

Phillips came to attention. 'My pleasure, Mrs Forde. Good evening to you, Mr Leary.'

'Good evening, Captain Phillips,' Maureen said. 'That dance was wonderful. I could have gone on all night.'

Miss Ryan was looking at John. 'I love to dance as well. Is your table near?'

Maureen gestured towards a corner. 'There. And yours?'

'We're not far from you. Perhaps we'll see each other later.'

'Let's do that,' Maureen said. 'Good evening.' Maureen and John returned to their table and John kept his eyes on the young milliner.

'She's attractive, isn't she?' Maureen said.

'She is that.' He then felt a sadness. Should he let himself be attracted to another woman? He had loved Clarissa. But she wasn't here, but just by looking at another woman, it was as if he was being unfaithful to her, betraying her once again. He pulled a chair out for his sister.

'What are you thinking about?' Maureen asked.

Liam was dancing and John sat beside his sister. 'Nothing, really.' He poured them both a glass of wine.

'Come on. I know you,' she said. 'Out with it.'

John shook his head. 'Daft it is. I'm thinking of Clarissa.' He glanced at Miss Ryan's table and she was laughing at something her officer partner had said. 'I've still got feelings for her.'

Maureen touched his forearm. 'Of course, you have, and you always will.

But life does go on, dear. You cannot stand still, or worse, withdraw into yourself.' She squeezed his forearm. 'Despite what happened in the past, Clarissa would want you to be happy and to love again.'

Liam joined them, wiping perspiration from his forehead. 'What? You two still talking! There's fun to be had and feet to be moved.' He took Maureen's hand. 'I'll pinch her for a bit, John, and give your jaw a rest.'

John smiled as Maureen stood up. He watched as they went off together. The waiter refreshed his glass and John pondered. Confidence. That's what it was, or the lack of it. He did not lack confidence to approach Miss Ryan. No, the confidence he needed was to be able to be clear in his mind and make way for a new relationship. He knew he needed a woman in his life, who could replace Clarissa as his wife and be a mother to Richard. Clarissa was still front and centre, despite that. Was he using her as an excuse not to be in love again? Glancing through the noisy and laughing crowd at the elegant young milliner, he didn't think so.

His sister's words reverberated. He shouldn't build a shrine around Clarissa. Love wasn't like that. It constantly changed into its various forms, improving on the way. He shouldn't stagnate, because that would prevent him from growing into a person who could give love to another, again. But then, was a new love too much to hope for? Why not just have a peripheral relationship, one that was not deep and serious. John grinned. His ego again. This was all presupposing that Miss Ryan even entertained the idea of keeping company with *him*. Approaching her might be all for naught.

He sipped more of his drink, looked around and spotted Mary Harrigan, then Ian McCreadie standing by himself. John stood up and made his way to the wool broker. As John did so, McCreadie walked towards Miss Ryan's table, bowed and took her hand. She stood up and they went to the dance floor. John was a little shocked but then admitted to himself that Catherine Ryan was single, available and well-featured. As his sister had said, time did not stand still. John might have to make his move sooner rather than later if he was to have even a friendship with Miss Ryan.

* * *

While John Leary, Richard, Fawcett, Mrs McGuire and her coachman were at Mass, Mary Harrigan had a big job to do and two hours in which to do it. Even at nine-thirty the sun was warm on this last Sunday in October: it would feel stuffy under the house. Hiking up the patched and worn dress she used for cleaning around her cottage, she opened the gate to the underfloor area of Golden Hall. She lit her lamp, picked it up with basket and short-handled spade and made her way among the cool and musty confines.

She had not yet found a translator for the note in Asian script that she had found hidden in the dining room just above her. If it was a clue to gold buried under the house, she had yet to decipher it. Meanwhile another precious Sunday had come around and she needed to take advantage of it. This time she was physically digging for gold, not just clues. Mustering courage to fight off insect and rodent, she edged towards the front of the house and on a rough pattern she started her dig. After half an hour, with perspiration masking her, she discarded her jacket and worked in dress alone. It was hard, smelly and grinding work.

At the end of one and a half hours she was in the rear part of the house under the scullery. She downed tools, sat back, wiped grains of dirt from her face and sipped her drink. Today's efforts had been a waste of time. There was no gold at this level. Either there was none at all, or it was buried deep and bigger tools would be needed to uncover it.

Parnell started barking. It had a higher pitch to it, and it could mean danger. She put out her lamp, collected her things, placed her lamp behind a brick pillar and crawled out towards the blinding sunshine, checking the surrounds before she exited by the low door.

Once she had padlocked the door, she dusted herself down, placed her basket down and went to check on the dog, which had now gone quiet. On her first visit she'd locked Parnell up in an enclosed wired space in front of his kennel, and then on leaving she'd set the Labrador loose again. It was now time to do the same. There was no one around when she reached Parnell, and he looked pleased to see her. She released the bolt on his gate.

Suddenly a calloused hand gripped hers and another pressed her throat, and she was dragged back behind an acacia tree. Good Lord, had Mr Leary come home to catch her out? What would he do to her? But as she struggled, she could see that the cuff of the man's shirt was frayed. And his breath was sour as he hissed in her ear, 'Ah! The delightful Mrs Harrigan. We meet again.' Mary clawed at his arms to free herself, but he held her tight, with surprising strength. 'I've been following you each time you've been here, and now you're going to tell me everything.'

It was Barnes! Fear almost choked her.

At Mass, John was concerned. It was after the Consecration and Richard, who had drooped all through Mass, was looking ill. He could see creases on Stella's brow, confirming that his son was in distress.

'I'm sorry, Mr Leary,' Stella whispered, 'but I'll have to take him home. He's burning up.'

He whispered to Christine that they were about to leave, and why. Discreetly, he led Richard, Stella and Mrs McGuire's coachman, Samuel Fruin, out of the pew to the aisle. They genuflected and, avoiding the glances of the other parishioners, exited from St Mary's. 'Let's get him home and into bed,' he said. 'We'll call in the doctor on the way.'

Parnell was barking and this time the sound was deep and accompanied by growls. The dog knew that his friend was in distress, and he wanted to attack her assailant.

Mary was in pain as Barnes dragged her into the stables and tied her to a post. She screamed, 'No!' and 'Help!' as he wrenched her hands behind her and the rope that he'd picked up bit into her wrists, but there was no one to hear her. Mr Leary's coach horses looked at her in a startled way from their stalls but when her screams ceased they went back to eating hay from the nets hung on the walls. The carriage stood in the middle of the big space, empty, with one door slightly open.

'Now, little lady,' Barnes said, coming around to stand in front of her with a leer, 'you're going to tell me everything.'

Mary stuck her chin out. She was terrified, and he looked very determined, but if she could keep him talking, someone might turn up. 'This is outrageous! Let me go right now, Mr Barnes. How dare you do this?'

Barnes smiled. 'You're not the lady of the house any more, my dear.' From under his jacket he pulled out a knife.

Mary glanced at its glinting blade and her terror increased. But she must feign strength and composure that she didn't have.

'So,' he said, 'where did my former partner hide his hoard?'

'I don't know what you mean.' She was trying to ease her wrists out of the rope, but it was pulled tight.

'Don't go simple on me. You've done the numbers and I've done the numbers. Peter had more than what he gave away, invested or put into this house.' He smiled again. 'It's such a pretty house. And so is its former pretty mistress.' He leaned towards her and ran a hand across her thigh.

Dear God! He wouldn't do *that*, would he? His eyes kept moving over her. Yes, he had designs on her. She had to keep him talking about the gold. 'If Peter had money left over then—'

'He did.'

'Well, I've found none of it. And if it is found, it will be mine. You've got no claim on it. What makes you think you have?'

'Well, I helped him dig it up, didn't I? You remember that, don't you?'

'Yes, I do. And I remember you got your fair share, and you spent it. If Peter didn't spend all his, then what's left over is mine.'

'I'm glad to hear you talk about fair shares.' Barnes was talking in a lower voice now, with less threat in it. He moved closer and gave her a gloating look. 'Come on, what would a widow woman do with all that money? She'd need a man with her, a man who would look after her, advise her on what investments to make,' He stroked her hip and she flinched. 'And you could trust me. Trust me to see that you want for nothing.'

The man was mad but the man held a knife. Parnell had stopped barking, which was a further worry. If only Mr Leary were coming home soon; Mrs McGuire's carriage would pause at the stable doors to let him, Richard and Stella alight. So she had to stall Barnes until then. Gathering herself she said, 'If Peter left me gold, I've no idea where it might be. But there were five things he left that might give us a clue.'

'There! That wasn't so hard, was it? What were you fiddling with the last time? In the dining room, whatever.'

So, the noise outside that day, and the broken branch of the tree, had been caused by Barnes, snooping around. She'd been stupid, thinking that she was getting away with her comings and goings. 'It was a lamp, a miner's lamp that Peter left me,' she said. 'I used it to open a panel in the wall.'

He moved the knife towards her. 'And?'

'There was nothing there.'

'So, the cupboard was bare, my dear.' His blade was now inches from her face, then he lowered it to her bosom. Her blood seemed to freeze within her. 'Not telling Mr Barnes porky pies, are you?'

'Peter left me four other things,' she said, trying not to show her panic. 'Two fireside tongs, curtains, grandfather clock and—'

His ugly face was animated at once. 'Did you say curtains?'

'Yes. Silk ones.'

'The silks! So, he never let those out of his hands? He had more sense than I ever thought. I'd have thought he'd need to sell them; they were so valuable. And you've got them?'

Mary tensed. Those things she thought were just curtains, were they Peter's real treasure? She said hastily, 'They're in the bank.'

Barnes grinned and shook his head. 'So, you tell me. But when I go to your terrace cottage, I'll find them. Won't I?'

In terror for Reggie and herself, Mary managed to free one of her hands without allowing him to see. 'You haven't heard about the other things. Don't you want to? They might be important. There's a grandfather clock and a chandelier.' She decided to lie. 'I'll let you have them. Please Mr Barnes, let me go! If you let me go, I'll work with you and—'

'Good,' Barnes said and sneered. 'Nice to know you're seeing sense. All right, enough talk for now. Leary will be home soon. You and I will have to continue our little chat somewhere else. Somewhere cosy.' He smiled again.

All at once a horse's whinny sounded outside. Alarmed, Barnes glared at her. She lowered her eyes and stood very still, as though he had subdued her completely. She wasn't going to cry out when he held the knife so close to her.

After a second's indecision he turned away, slipped the knife into its sheath, crept to the door of the stables and peered through the crack between them.

She had to get further away from him. Freeing her other hand, she looked around. Barnes was not looking at her. There was no back door to the stables, and she couldn't hide in the horse stalls, but if she could slip away out of sight and wait, there was a slim chance of escape.

Barnes continued to peer through the gap in the doors to the outside, his face still turned away from her. 'Four of them,' he muttered. 'Damn.'

There were four people outside! Mr Leary must be home early from Mass. Indeed, Parnell was now barking up a storm, welcoming his master.

She must slip into hiding while Barnes was preoccupied. The carriage! Mr Leary's carriage. Mary ran to it, put one foot on the step and slipped inside. There was a folded blanket on the seat and she got down between the seats and covered herself with it.

There was a scraping sound as though one of the stable doors was opening, and sure enough the sounds from outside could be heard more clearly. There was the thumping sound of boots on cobbles and a shout that reverberated around the yard outside and into the stables.

'What the hell? Stop!' Mary recognised the voice without difficulty—it was John Leary's. There was a cry from a woman—perhaps Stella Fawcett—and then other footfalls, from someone wearing hobnail boots.

Barnes must have made a bid for freedom. And he was being pursued by someone in boots, maybe Mrs McGuire's coachman who was yelling as he tore across the cobbles, his nails scrabbling on the stones.

'Go, boy!' John Leary yelled. Seconds passed, and the sound of the pursuit faded. Neither the man nor the dog had caught Barnes. He'd taken them by surprise and his desperation must have lent him speed. A minute or two went by and Mary could hear the man and dog return.

'Damn it,' Leary said. 'What the hell was that man doing in the stables?'

There was not a sound from Stella Fawcett or Richard. They must have gone into the house.

'Do you want to get the police, Mr Leary?' a man's voice said.

There was a pause. 'No. Fruin, you'll take Mrs McGuire's carriage back to church and collect her. I'm going in to look after my son—he's my first priority. Just check the stables for me, though, if you would. See the horses are all right and nothing's been damaged. That bloke had nothing in his hands, so he didn't manage to steal anything, thank God. Bloody glad we got back when we did.'

Mary recognised the name 'Fruin'. He was Mrs McGuire's coachman, who'd driven them all to Mass. When he came into the stables, he would see that the horses were untouched, and if he glanced into the carriage he'd never spot her if she didn't move. He might see the rope lying on the floor but that wouldn't mean anything to him.

Mary stayed motionless, as she heard the sound of footsteps at the stable doors. When they came up and stopped by the carriage, Mary pressed her eyes together and held her breath. After a while she heard the coachman mutter to himself, or perhaps to the curious horses, then all sounds faded away and the stable door closed.

Mary wanted to sneeze but controlled herself. She waited what seemed like fifteen minutes. Then, easing the carriage door open, she looked out into the yard. There was no one around: everyone including the boy Richard must be in the house. Ducking under cover where she could, in order not to be seen from the windows, she made her escape. Thank goodness it was Sunday, so Mr Leary's groom or gardener would not be turning up to surprise her. She was still trembling with nervousness. This had to be her last time exploring her old home.

As she made her way back to Bourke Street, she wondered what else she could do to follow up Peter's possible treasure. But the silk curtains were all she had left. She must get that note from behind the panelling translated—they were in an Asian script, so they might relate to the curtains.

Meanwhile the thought of Barnes haunted her. He had managed to escape, so he remained a dangerous threat to her and Reggie.

The basket! She'd left it outside the underfloor access door. Hopefully, Barnes would be blamed for that, but it was still sloppy of her.

It might be the time to be open with Mr Leary. Deceit and stealth had got her attacked—and exposed her to risks that were even worse.

* * *

The Leary monthly family dinner was held as usual that evening. Richard had recovered from his brief fever and he enjoyed having his cousins at the table. The children were not told of the attempted break in, but after dessert they were excused from the table and the intrusion became the topic of conversation.

'It's so extraordinary,' Liam said. 'And during the day.'

'Not if you add things up,' John said. 'He looked like the man I saw outside the house back in July, I think. He could have been lurking over the street like before, and come creeping around the house once we'd all driven off to church.'

'But he wasn't after your horses,' Maureen said thoughtfully. 'He had ample time to steal one of them before you came back.'

'You're right,' John said. 'I've felt all along it's the house he's interested in.'

'Well, thank God he didn't get in,' Christine said. 'It's outrageous.' She shook her head. 'And he was prepared to rob you while the dog was here. The man must have been desperate. Whose house will be next?'

John understood his mother-in-law's concern. She was living alone and would feel vulnerable. For her sake he decided to treat the incident lightly. 'No, I think he's fixated on this place for some reason. And he won't be back in this neighbourhood. We scared him off for good.'

Gerry picked up on John's tack. 'John's right, Christine. Don't worry.'

She looked at both men and nodded. 'I hope you're right.'

Maureen asked. 'How good are your window fastenings? Will you think about protecting the house a bit more?'

'I don't think so. Now, let's go to the drawing room for coffee. Cook has baked some very tasty-looking cakes.'

That night as John prepared for bed he thought again about the attempted robbery. None of his locks had been forced. The door to the underside of the house had been left ajar but the padlock was undamaged. Was it the intruder who'd unlocked it, and if so how did he get the key? By the door was an empty basket and a short-handled spade. The basket suggested a woman—an accomplice? John had peered under the house and noticed multiple scratchings in the surface of the soil. Why on earth would someone come digging under Golden Hall? There were no other clues as to who this person or persons could be, in either the garden or the stables. The stables were tidy except for a bit of rope lying on the ground near the carriage, and the horses had not been harmed.

* * *

Mary Harrigan wasn't herself. It was the day after her ordeal and although she occupied herself with cleaning the house, she still felt the anxiety and fear that Barnes would attack her again. He must have some sort of job so he could gamble by day—she just had to hope it was night work and she'd be safe after dark. But Mary was worried, nonetheless. It was nearly five and she was waiting for Catherine Ryan, who had promised to visit after work. Reggie was in his room, doing his homework before tea.

Catherine came into the kitchen and was surprised by Mary's nervous greeting.

'Whatever's the matter?' Catherine asked as she sat beside her.

'Oh, Catherine I've done something stupid and awful. I went to my old house, yesterday, and looked around. I—'

'You went there! 'Did Mr Leary let you search?'

Mary blushed. 'No, the family were at Mass. I was there on my own.'

Catherine's eyes grew round. 'Oh dear. What did you do? What happened?'

'I got attacked,' Mary said, and tears came into her eyes. Of the whole disaster she'd endured, the assault by Barnes had upset her the most.

Catherine took hold of her hands. 'Oh, Mary, how terrible. 'Are you hurt?'

'No, Mr Leary came home early and the man took fright and escaped.'

'Good Lord,' Catherine said, and stood up. 'Come, let's talk outside so Reggie won't overhear us. You have to tell me everything.'

In the shade of a banksia, they sat on a bench in the little garden and Mary got herself together. 'I didn't break into the house or anything, though I do feel guilty about it. I went under it and dug in the soil, not very deep, to see if there might be something buried there.'

Catherine's eyes were wide in amazement. 'Did you find anything? What am I saying? You really shouldn't have been there at all.'

'You're right. You are. I found nothing, so I came out at the back of the house empty-handed. I was just about to shut the gate of the dog's compound when someone grabbed me. He hauled me into the stables and tied me up. I struggled but I couldn't get free of him.'

'How dreadful. Who was he, what was he doing there?'

'His name is Barnes. He used to be my husband's partner on the gold fields. He knew I was there at the house, he followed me, and he's after the same thing I am. He believes Peter must have left some treasure behind and he thinks I can lead him to it.'

'Dear Lord,' Catherine said. 'So he knows who you are and where you live?'

'Yes. It was terrible. I was ready to die of fright. But thank goodness Mr Leary came home, and that made Barnes run away. I hid until the coast was clear and got away too.' Mary pressed her hands together. 'I'm frightened Barnes will come after me and Reggie.'

Catherine thought for some time, then said, 'Shouldn't you tell the police about him?'

'How can I without admitting I trespassed at Golden Hall?' She felt her tears returning.

Catherine took her hands and squeezed. 'But you must do something to protect yourself!'

'I've thought all about it and I've decided I have no choice—I have to tell Mr Leary everything. Well, I'll tell Fawcett first and then I'll tell him. It's the least I can do to clear this mess up. And it's something I need to do so I can sleep again.'

Catherine stood up. 'It's nearly time for tea. Let me help you prepare it and we'll enjoy it with Reggie. When will you tell Mr Leary?'

'Next Sunday.'

'Why wait? What if Barnes turns up on your doorstep before then?'

'He hasn't so far. He's known about me all along but I've never caught sight of him here—he waited until I was at Point Piper.

Besides, there's a regular police patrol right along Bourke Street and I don't think Barnes likes being anywhere close to the police.'

'Do you want company when you talk to Mr Leary?'

Mary gave a smile for the first time, just a little one. 'Thank you. But this is something I have to do myself.'

* * *

Later that evening, in the Ryans' drawing room in Victoria Street, Catherine was seated with her parents and Ian McCreadie, who had been invited to dine. During the after-dinner conversation, she found it hard to concentrate on what their guest was saying. She was still horrified by what Mary Harrigan had told her. 'I'm sorry, Mr McCreadie, could you explain that to me again?'

He smiled at her with a tolerance that showed real affection. It was the third time now that he'd come here.

'The fee or the wool weight?' he said.

'Just the fee, thank you,' she said.

He started talking and she listened for a while, then her mind returned to Mary's reckless act. Mary had committed the crime of trespass but part of Catherine was excited at her daring. It was like a quest that her friend had not wanted to give up. Mary had risked a lot. Catherine herself would not like to be facing John Leary and confessing that she'd been exploring under his house. She respected him and would not care to make him look down on her or be angry with her.

Catherine looked at McCreadie, comparing him with John Leary. Both were handsome, good Catholics and older than her—and she preferred that age difference. Both were successful men in their own right, one a wool broker and the other a leading contractor. But it wasn't necessarily the position they held or their income that attracted her. It was something else. McCreadie was asking her a question about the transport of wool and she concentrated.

'You must wait for your fee to be paid,' she said. 'It's not paid until the consignment's landed. Correct?'

He beamed at her.

'Enough about business,' Mrs Ryan said. 'Let's talk about the picnic this Sunday. Ian, where do you think would be a nice place to go, somewhere close?'

Ian was only too glad, it seemed, to look forward to her company again and he started to suggest places. Soon her parents were involved and chatting away. She returned to her comparisons and realised that Ian McCreadie didn't make her feel the way John Leary did. When she was in the builder's presence, especially at something like a ball, there was a sense of excitement. More than that, a thrill. Yes, he made her feel conscious of herself, how she looked and what he might be thinking about her. It was as if he was the only man in the room. It was a strange feeling and a new one, but one she liked. Yes, she might see more of Ian McCreadie, but her heart wanted to be where John Leary was.

The front door opened and closed. Her brother Don must be home. When his tall form appeared in the room, she thought he looked tired.

'Good evening all,' Donald said. 'How are you, Ian?'

'I'm well, thank you. How's the studies going?'

'It's a struggle.' He looked at his parents. 'I might turn in.'

Her mother stood up. 'Have you had dinner? I can get cook to get you some.'

'Don't worry her,' Donald said. 'Night all.' He turned and went upstairs.

'I think I'd best leave too,' Ian said standing up. 'I'll see you all on Sunday.'

'Catherine,' her mother said, 'see Ian out, please.'

Catherine smiled at him and escorted him to the door. As she opened it, Ian looked at her. 'I enjoy your company, Miss Ryan, very much.' He paused. 'I'd like to think that you enjoy mine.'

She had to be honest with him. 'I do. And I think it's time we called each other Catherine and Ian.' He looked pleased and she took a little step back, though she smiled too. 'I'll see you on the weekend.'

He smiled back and turned to leave.

Closing the door after him, she started up the stairs and started thinking of John Leary again. It was as if he were a new toy on a string that she continually spun around her and every now and then brought closer for examination. As she made her way up, she wondered if she could share these new feelings with Donald. He was three years older but they had always confided their emotions to each other, especially when one of them was confronted with difficulties. In earlier years Catherine used to tell him about her school chums, and her jealousies and rivalries.

But this was different. She really *felt* for a man, as she never had before. How did Donald feel about women? But then she realised that Donald had never spoken about any girls he'd been attracted to, though there had to be some. He was handsome, and his cheeky smile and wavy blonde hair would attract them. He just never talked about them.

There was a strip of light under his bedroom door, so she knocked. 'Don, can I come in?'

'You're welcome, sister mine, but I'm too weary to get up and open it.'

She turned the handle and went in.

He was lying on his bed with his hands behind his head, stripped down to his trousers and singlet. She marvelled again at his physique: lean and well-muscled at the same time. He had the ideal build for fencing, which was his chosen sport. His mask and foil were propped in a corner near the bed.

He smiled at her and said, 'So Ian's sniffing around again.'

'Donald!'

His blue eyes twinkled. 'Well, he is. So, what's your opinion of our handsome wool broker?'

She sat down on the chair at his desk, which was crowded. His stacks of law books looked as though they were about to collapse at any time, his lecture notes were strewn across it and his exercise book was open, displaying random jottings. But this untidiness belied a keen legal mind. His close pal, Andrew Booth, a fellow student, had told her that Don always impressed his lecturers at Sydney University.

'Ian's a nice young man,' Catherine said.

'That sounds like the kiss of death for the blighter.'

She looked down. He was right about that. 'I want to talk to you about someone else.'

Donald rubbed his eyes. 'Can it wait, Cath? I'm really done in. I've got to be up at sparrows to swot for my torts exam. Final year and all that.'

She blurted it out: 'Have you ever been in love?'

The tiredness vanished from his face and he grinned. 'Not with a wool broker, no. Not as yet. What about you?'

She had to be careful here. 'I'm not talking about Ian … There's someone else who makes me feel really weird.'

'Dear me. In what way?'

She took his pen from the desk and got her thoughts together. 'It's hard to describe. Excitement, then self-consciousness, odd thoughts and flushes. All that. Have you ever felt that?'

He grimaced and his voice fell. 'I don't know if I've ever been in love.'

She was surprised. 'Not even once? Is there no girl who's taken your fancy?'

He looked away for a moment then back to her. 'Not a one.'

She couldn't believe that, but then what did she know about all this?

Donald got up and removed a nightshirt from his chest of drawers. 'All right, if Ian the wool broker McCreadie hasn't got your head spinning, who has?'

A fair question but one she wasn't going to answer, not yet. 'It's someone you don't know and it might just all be nothing.'

Donald pulled on his night shirt. 'Well, if this mysterious feeling you have keeps up, you must let me know. And you can tell me who's the lucky man. Now, I have to wish you good night.'

'Good night,' she said, and left. She felt dissatisfied, but at least she'd voiced her muddled thoughts.

* * *

At noon on Tuesday, Gerry Gleeson entered the Australasia Bank's site office. He wiped the perspiration from his forehead. 'Hey, Sean. Got time for a feed?'

Sean looked up from his plans and smiled. 'Your shout?'

'To be sure. The Metropolitan?'

Sean took up his hat. 'Why not?'

They made their way across George Street in the late spring heat and stepped into the coolness of the Bridge Street pub.

'Beef rolls do you?' Gerry said.

'You get them and I'll get the beers,' Sean replied.

Seated with their meals and drinks, they hoed in. After some time, Gerry said. 'John disturbed a burglar at his place on Sunday.'

Sean looked surprised. 'On the Sabbath?'

'Aye, and during the day.'

'Bold,' Sean said.

'Too true, my friend,' Gerry said. He was enjoying his food.

'Maybe it was the man John told me about: he's noticed someone watching the house.' Sean sipped his beer.

'Right. You're next to family, Sean. I think I can share this with you and John wouldn't mind. My nephew tells me that he thinks there might be something of value at Golden Hall. Something that made that robber have a go. He told me the former owner, a Mrs Harrigan, has also been hanging around.' Gerry finished the last of his roll and pushed his plate aside. 'Odd, don't you think?'

'Yes, John's told me how he feels about that,' Sean said. 'And it's funny but there's a positive side to it. Puzzling about this mystery is actually giving him a lift. It's livened him up, and I've seen the difference, believe me.'

'Another beer?' Gerry asked.

'Just the one,' Sean said. 'Then I've got to get back.'

Gerry made his way to the bar. Well, that was interesting. If this strange business was helping his nephew, then perhaps it was no bad thing.

144

* * *

In the early afternoon sunlight, Lady Dalkeith stepped back from Christine McGuire's fireplace and took another discerning look at it. 'It is indeed an excellent piece of work,' she said. 'The pattern is well dispersed. A design very much like my own.'

Christine was pleased at the compliment. 'Thank you. More tea?'

'Yes.'

Christine's maid refilled Lady Dalkeith's cup. 'Will that be all, madam?'

'Yes,' Christine said. 'You may leave.'

Christine waited until the maid left and said to her guest, 'John's uncle has been doing the renovation work for me on weekends. He took some time to find the polished marble I wanted.'

Lady Dalkeith nodded. 'A master stone mason himself, I've heard.'

'That he is.' Glad that her new fireplace had passed her friend's inspection, Christine was keen to pass on some more news. 'Last Sunday, my son in law's house was nearly burgled.'

Lady Dalkeith looked very surprised. 'How extraordinary. Any valuables missing?'

Christine sipped her tea and placed her cup down. 'No, thank goodness. John foiled the burglar by coming home unexpectedly. The man never got into the house.'

'Good,' Lady Dalkeith said.

'However, I'm still uneasy about it. It happened so close to me.'

'It's unusual to have that sort of villain lurking in this area,' Lady Dalkeith said. 'It was at number seventy-nine, yes?'

'Yes. Not the kind of place where we expect to meet the criminal element.'

Lady Dalkeith was thoughtful. 'A lovely place, ever since your late husband bought it. But weren't there some unfortunate stories about the first owner?'

'It used to belong to a successful gold prospector, Peter Smith. His Sydney business failed. The property was sold in a hurry to pay

Smith's debts after he died,' Christine said. 'Coincidentally, Mary Smith—now Mrs Harrigan—has come back here with her young son. She married again in England but now she's a widow once more. Most unfortunate. She lives in very modest circumstances.'

'Oh, what a sad fall from her previous life, my dear. Smith's death was some time ago, wasn't it? I remember the talk at the time. But you know, I've heard a much more recent rumour—it seems Peter Smith may not have parted with all his wealth before he died. Some say there's some of his gold left, if only one knew where to look.'

Christine returned her cup and saucer to the tea trolley. 'Good Lord. Do you think that's what the burglar was after at Golden Hall?'

Lady Dalkeith stood up. 'Oh no, surely not. There are so many ifs. What if Smith secreted his wealth in overseas accounts? That's not improbable. Or perhaps it's all a myth!' She smiled. 'It's time for me to leave. I'll see you in a fortnight at the Orphans' Foundation fund-raiser.'

'I'll be there.'

* * *

Thomas Barnes walked up the stairs to his William Street gambling rooms, looking forward to his Tuesday afternoon at the tables. The place was crowded, so he bought a Scotch whisky and waited his turn to play. His thoughts kept going back to the mess he'd made of trying to deal with Mary Harrigan. He reckoned he could count on her not reporting the assault to the police, but out of caution he'd steer clear of her for a while: he didn't fancy fronting up to a magistrate.

Those bloody silk curtains, he mused. Could he force Mary Harrigan to get them out of the bank? He'd first seen them in Bendigo. He'd been with Peter Smith when his partner bought some Oriental silk curtains from a man called Wo Fat. The Chinese digger was deep into gambling debt and desperate to sell them. Peter reckoned that he'd got a bargain, but he didn't know quite how valuable they were until a week later, when another Chinese gold digger, Simon Ly, saw the curtains in Smith's tent. Ly was surprised and angry. It turned out that the silk curtains formed a special screen of rare quality that belonged to Ly's family. Wo Fat had stolen them, so he could sell them on.

Ly reckoned Smith had no right to the silks but Smith was not convinced, and Barnes had backed him up, laughing at the Chinaman's cheek. Ly had made an enormous fuss, saying that the silks were very precious and had ancestral connections for him. But Smith held onto them.

A chair moved at the nearby table and a player left, creating a vacancy. Barnes prepared himself for his game, still thinking about those curtains, or screen, or whatever the bloody hell they were. Simon Ly had offered Peter Smith twice the money he'd paid for them but Smith still wouldn't part with them.

So those curtains were very valuable indeed, and Mary Harrigan had confessed that they'd stayed in Smith's possession and were now in the bank. Barnes had to get his hands on them somehow. He'd think of some way to do it, and meanwhile he'd find out about antique Oriental goods on the colonial market. Genuine pieces could be worth a fortune back in London. Peter Smith had obviously thought they were worth a lot in Sydney, too.

And what if Mary Harrigan were lying about the curtains and had them at home? One day he could go to her house and find out.

Barnes sat down at the table. He felt lucky tonight and ready to gamble high. If he got good cards in his hands he was prepared to pledge the silks as security. They weren't his yet, but they soon would be.

* * *

In the light of the setting sun, John sat on the edge of his son's bed, opened the book of fairy tales.

Richard was lying under the covers. 'What day?'

'It's Tuesday,' John replied.

Richard nodded. 'Dragons tonight.'

John smiled. 'Dragons.' He looked down at the book and started to read. 'The king had been away from his castle a long time, but no matter how far he travelled, he couldn't find the dragons. He was very tired and—'

'Why did Mummy die?'

John was startled at the question but tried to keep his answer simple. 'She was sick, and she had something that couldn't be cured.'

'Bad.'

'I know,' he said. Richard was quiet so John kept reading. 'The king lay down in the royal tent, surrounded by his courtiers. The night was cold, and the fire was not hot enough. The king said—'

'Mummy's in heaven.'

John stroked his son's forehead. 'She is.'

'Not coming back?'

'No.'

Richard forehead wrinkled. 'Sure?'

'I'm sure. Now, let's hear more about this wandering king.' Richard nodded and John went on with the story for a few minutes, then he softened his voice as his son's eyes closed. He sat there for a while and listened to the deep breathing. Richard knew his mother was gone but John felt that, at his young age, he would have few memories of her in the future. In her absence, Richard would find a place in his heart for a new mother, one who could show love and affection to him. And John realised that he needed a wife. He wanted the closeness, comfort, conversation and intimacy that a woman would bring to his life.

He turned off Richard's gas light and quietly left the bedroom. Catherine Ryan came into his head and he smiled. Yes, he could imagine getting close to her. He could.

Chapter Six

On the Wednesday after her altercation with Barnes, Mary Harrigan found herself once again outside Mrs Carter's house in Short Street, Balmain. She wanted to meet Carter personally and find out if this woman was telling the truth about her connection with Peter.

Mary walked up the path and knocked on the door.

A tall fair-haired woman with clear complexion and bold eyes greeted her. Her clothing was simple yet well-tailored.

'Good afternoon. I'm Mary Harrigan. Are you Mrs Carter?'

The woman gave a tight smile. 'I am. You're the Mrs Harrigan who's written to me?'

'I am. Do you mind if we have a chat?'

'Not at all. Won't you please come in?'

'Thank you.' Mary entered a neat, well-furnished parlour filled with an aroma of baking. Carter closed the door behind them and gestured to an armchair. 'Please sit down. Would you like some refreshments? Tea?'

'Tea would be nice, thank you.'

'The kettle's boiled and I've just made a tea cake. You came at the right moment.'

'It smells delicious,' Mary said. 'I'll come right to the point, Mrs Carter. I'm still a little vague on your relationship with my deceased husband.'

Carter raised her eyebrows but she did not look perturbed. 'We did not have what anyone would call a relationship, Mrs Harrigan. Your husband was an honourable man and an unselfish one. Let me make the tea and put you straight.'

Mary could not help feeling a little foolish at this pronouncement, but while Carter was in the kitchen she looked keenly around the room; at least she could make a guess at how well off the woman was. There was nothing here to indicate wealth.

'Here we are,' Carter said, carrying in a tray with tea pot, cups and a tea cake. The china was nondescript, and the silver was plated. 'How would you like it?'

'Black with lemon, thank you. No sugar.'

'But you'll have some cake?'

Mary nodded. 'I shall.'

'Good.' Carter said, she poured the teas and cut the cake. Her nails were neatly trimmed, and she wore a silver bracelet of a simple design, and no rings. 'Now,' she said, 'as I mentioned in my letter, your husband helped me at a difficult time in my life, and in return I was able to help him.'

'Tell me the details, please.'

'Surely. In March of 1852, my husband William was killed in a mining accident in Bendigo.'

'I'm sorry to hear that.'

'Thank you. As a widow, you'll know what that kind of loss means. Your husband's diggings were near ours. My husband was trapped when a hole collapsed one day, and your husband was one of the first to try to dig him out. It was an unselfish act and a very brave one, because the ground was unstable.'

'How terrible,' Mary said. She was genuinely shocked. 'Do you know, Peter mentioned nothing of this disaster to me?'

'I can guess why not. I lived in Bendigo on the diggings. I understand you were far away in Sydney. In the minefields there were fights, murders and terrible things going on. Why would Peter tell you about things like that? He would only worry you.'

Carter's use of Peter's first name aroused Mary's suspicions again. Then she chided herself—it might not indicate an intimate connection. 'Was your husband Peter's friend?'

'Not a friend, more a fellow digger. Men at the diggings all faced the same hardships, but they didn't always lend each other a hand. That's why I was so grateful that Peter fought to save William. It was to no avail, unfortunately. He was buried alive. It took two days to recover his body.'

'How dreadful.'

Carter's eyes glistened and she sipped her tea. 'Life goes on. Like many others, Mrs Harrigan, we just made enough money to pay our way. I was overcome by grief when my husband died but I was determined to repay yours for the risks he took.'

Mary looked at her. In Peter's letters to her from Bendigo, he had often said how lonely he was, being away from her. Had he sought the company of the widowed Carter? 'What sort of repayment are you speaking of?'

'Just before my husband died he laid claim to a quartz-bearing patch not far away from his first claim. It looked very favourable, he told me. Well, I couldn't work it myself and I had no reason to stay in Bendigo. I gifted the claim to your husband.'

'That was very generous of you.'

'No less than your husband deserved, Mrs Harrigan. After that I went back to Melbourne with barely enough to keep myself. I heard nothing from your husband for three months, and then in June of that year, I received a letter with a bank draft from your husband.'

Here comes the truth at last, Mary thought.

'Peter said that the claim I'd gifted him had yielded a very rich seam of gold and it was due to me that he'd found it. Your husband then made me a generous gift.'

'How generous?' Mary asked, then felt ashamed of her abruptness. 'I'm sorry.'

'It's quite all right, Mrs Harrigan. I think you need to see the letter that mentions the exact sum. Excuse me.'

Carter was both dignified and confident in her demeanour, but Mary was still feeling flashes of suspicion. The woman had accepted Peter's gift gratefully—but what if she'd asked for more, once she learned the true value of his strike? Would she admit to that?

Carter returned with a piece of paper and a slim book. 'Here's his letter,' she said, handing it to Mary.

Mary read it. The language was courteous and there was no hint of intimacy. Peter had sent Carter two hundred pounds, a substantial sum but not a fortune. 'Thank you,' she said, as she handed back the letter.

'And here are my bank transactions at the time,' Carter said, handing Mary the pass book, open at a page that clearly recorded the only deposit Carter had made over a period of many months.

Mary took the book, surprised and ashamed to have prompted this woman into showing something so private. But she still asked, 'This was your only deposit?'

Carter gave her a level look that made Mary even more uncomfortable, and said calmly, 'Yes indeed.'

Mary handed back the book. She felt for the first time that this woman had deserved Peter's largesse. 'We have both seen a great deal of misfortune. I'm proud that my husband was able to help you in a time of need.'

'More tea?' Carter said.

'Thank you,'

* * *

Maureen and Liam had settled in their drawing room after their Thursday night dinner. Unable to attend Mass the previous morning for All Souls Day, they recited a decade of the Rosary for their departed loved ones.

'So,' Liam said as he poured sherries for them both, 'what's on your mind?'

Maureen wanted to test her instinct about her brother. Liam was always a good and sensible sounding board. 'John.'

'What about him?'

'Have you noticed a change in him? For the better?'

Liam positioned a cushion behind his back as he seated himself. 'He hasn't said anything revealing to me. But he's pretty animated over that attempted break-in.'

'Exactly. It might have shaken him up but his spirits are restored, dear. I'm sure of it. Stella has seen it too. He's more his old self.'

'Yes, he's become more active,' Liam said. 'He's been so deep in his own world, the only person he wanted to spend time with was Richard. Now he's happy to take an interest in our Michael—he's going to build him a fort just like Richard's.'

Maureen sipped her sherry. 'My brother's showing interest in another direction, too. Romance.'

'No! With whom?'

'You men,' Maureen said and smiled. 'You don't see what's happening around you. The way he looks at Catherine Ryan tells me a lot. And it's all good news.'

'Maureen, my dear, with respect, all men look at women. It's how we're made'

She was not to be put off. 'It isn't that type of look, though she's a beauty, I admit. No, he really seems to like her for herself. I think that's great.'

'What, you think John's on the way to matrimony? Aren't you getting a bit ahead of yourself?'

'Oh I'm not saying he'll marry Catherine Ryan, Liam, although she's a good match. No, I've just noticed John is interested in women again, and in my view that's a good thing. So there's nothing wrong with my bringing the two of them together.'

Liam smiled. 'Maureen, be careful.'

She leaned forward and placed her hand on his knee. 'I shall and if it's not to be, it's not to be. John has started to show some of his old self, the loving man we know, and I'm going to do all I can to see his interest doesn't wane.'

* * *

Mary Harrigan was waiting with her son Reggie outside the Cathedral in the humid Sunday morning air. She saw Fawcett exiting the church and went up to her. 'Good morning, Stella,' Mary said with a smile. It was pleasant to be able to call Fawcett by her first name.

'And to you, Mary,' Fawcett replied. 'Hello, Reggie.'

'Hello, Miss Fawcett,' Reggie replied.

Mary kept hold of Reggie's hand. She hadn't told him that she had been attacked by Barnes the week before. She didn't want her son to be worried about living in Sydney, which was still new to him. She said to Stella, 'I realise it's short notice, but could I come back with you to Point Piper? Reggie could play with Richard.' She paused, hoping desperately for a yes. 'I'd like to confide something to you.'

Stella seemed intrigued. 'Of course, you can. Mr Leary has gone to the Georges River with his uncle for the day.'

Mary was grateful for that. The two women and the boys got into a cab. On the way they traded small talk about the weather and the antics of the children.

At Golden Hall, Stella poured them both a cup of tea and they sat on the back veranda. Once boys were happily playing in the yard, Mary's thoughts returned to the previous Sunday and her ordeal in the stables, just yards away from where she was sitting. She shivered.

'Are you cold?' Stella asked. 'In this heat?'

'No, it was just something I remembered.' She sipped her tea. Being on first-name terms made her confidences easier to share. 'Stella, whatever I say now, I hope you'll not think too ill of me. We've only been reacquainted for a few months, but I do like you and … I feel terribly guilty. I have to confess I've been deceiving you over something.'

'Dear me,' Stella said with concern. 'Have I upset you somehow, without knowing it?'

'No, no, this is all my fault. I've been snooping in this house while you've all been out.'

Stella looked shocked.

'I did it because I was desperate. But I know that's no excuse for my behaviour,' Mary said. 'I'll give you my reasons in a moment— dear me, I should have told you everything at the beginning! But I wasn't brave enough. And I've had my punishment: I was here last week and a man who was snooping around at the same time attacked me and got hold of me. I managed to escape from him, and he ran away. He was the man whom Mr Leary chased away from the stables, when he came home early from Mass. He's a character from my past, and his name is Thomas Barnes. I'm terrified of him now.'

Stella's eyes grew round. A ball landed near her feet and she picked it up and threw it back to the boys. 'How shocking, Mary. Why did he attack you? And you think he's still a threat to you?'

Mary felt overwhelmed that Stella's first thought was for her welfare, not about her trespassing at Golden Hall. She said, 'I owe you the whole story, Stella. It began when my husband, Peter, left me in Sydney to go gold prospecting. He eventually found a golden hole at Bendigo. He and his partner shared the proceeds and the value of his gold alone was close to thirteen thousand pounds.'

Stella's mouth dropped open. 'Oh, Mary. What a fortune!'

"I know. Now, with that, he built this house and started a business. But he lost it all eventually and I only inherited debts. All I could do was sell up what I still had, including Golden Hall, of course. When that was all done, I only had enough money left to fund my voyage back to England. I was too overwhelmed to think clearly about the inheritance, but I've done the calculations since, and the fact is that there should have been a lot more money left over in Peter's possession. Therefore, Peter spent it frivolously without my knowledge, or he secreted it away before he died, and didn't have a chance to tell me where it was. Stella, Peter loved me and cared about my welfare. Whenever he talked about our future he always said that this house, *this very house*, held wealth. I don't think he just meant it would have a high selling price. I think he meant that there is money here, somewhere. Peter's money.'

Stella sat back, her remaining tea untouched. Mary could not read her expression; she seemed to be thinking deeply. Stella finally said, 'And you've been looking for this treasure on the sly?'

'I have. I used my time with you to access the keys. I had kept a copy of the back-door key and I spotted where you kept the underfloor key, so I could get access in secret.'

'That's why you dug out the wine bottles!' Stella said. She did not sound angry, yet—just intensely curious.

'Yes, that gave me my first look under the floors. Last week I explored there with a basket and spade.'

'Ah. You used the padlock key to get in.' Stella frowned. 'And it was *you* who left the basket.'

'Guilty again. I'm sorry for doing this to you.'

Stella bristled. She was hurt now. 'So, when you first talked to me and I said you might be able to come here with Reggie, were you sounding me out? Were you just getting to know me so that you could use me?'

It was no use lying. 'I was desperate. I had to find out if the money was here. If Reggie's father had provided for him better than I ever could, I needed to discover the truth. Are you forgetting that I once owned this house? That my husband had it built for us?'

Stella stood up. 'I think you and your son had better leave.'

Mary took a breath and remained seated. 'Please. I came here specially today to make a clean breast. I wanted to tell you because I like you and I think we've become friends. I didn't want to keep on deceiving you.'

'I'm angry you've used me,' Stella said. 'And more than that, I'm angry you didn't tell me all this at the beginning. Not to mention Mr Leary!'

'I'm sorry.'

'And if that burglar had been caught last week,' Stella said, 'and he was under arrest and you were safe from him, would you have come and told me all this today?'

'Yes. I had to tell the truth to someone. I was molested by that horrible man, Stella, and I'm afraid of him, but that's not the only reason I'm here.'

Stella looked at the boys. Richard was laughing at Reggie, who was swinging on a branch and making faces at the boy. 'Molested?'

'He tied me up and threatened me with a knife,' Mary said and her eyes filled at the memory.

Stella softened and placed a hand on hers. 'That must have been horrible.'

'If it wasn't for Mr Leary returning home from Mass early,' Mary said, 'I don't know what would have happened to me.'

'If he comes back,' Stella said, 'Mr Leary will have him. So, you don't need to fear him. But what will Mr Leary say about you creeping into this house and under it! He'll want to know exactly what you've found, too. Tell me, what *have* you found? Anything at all?'

Mary was momentarily relieved that her friend was now more intrigued by the mystery of the treasure. 'You know the panelling above the sideboard in the dining room? I turned a lever and uncovered a little alcove in the wall. In it was a paper with Chinese writing on it.'

'Just paper? No gold, no money?'

Mary shook her head.

Stella poured them more tea and Mary welcomed it into her dry throat.

'You'd better tell me every detail of this whole business,' Stella said.

During the next five minutes, Mary told her friend the history of her long research into Peter's affairs. She enumerated the five items Peter had left with her, and how she and Catherine Ryan had investigated each one.

Stella gasped. 'Miss Ryan! Did she ever come here with you?'

'No, no,' Mary said. 'I would never have involved her in that way. I'm ashamed of what I've done. Dear Stella, can you find it in your heart to forgive me?'

Stella hesitated and Mary's concern rose. Stella had an obligation to tell her employer everything that she'd heard: including Mary getting her hands on the household keys. Even though Stella had known nothing about what Mary was doing, it would make her look careless about the safety of the house and its occupants.

Stella shook her head. 'I don't know yet. So, you had debts here and you went back to England. What happened there?'

Mary told her the rest: how she had been remarried, to a property developer who had died and left her a small income. 'Peter left me a very valuable telescope. There are very few of its kind. I sold that and paid for the fare for Reggie and me. I wanted to see whether the five things Peter left me in Sydney had any value.'

'And are they worth anything?'

'No, all except maybe the silk curtains. They used to—'

'Mummy,' Reggie said coming up to her, 'can we play in the front garden?'

'Stella?' Mary said.

Stella got up as if she couldn't sit still any longer. 'Yes, let's all go there.'

Seated under the shade of the front veranda, Mary studied Stella's closed expression. She said in a strained voice. 'Peter was a good haberdasher in some ways; at least he knew his fabrics. When he was sold some silk hangings, he snapped them up because of their quality.'

'And you still have them?'

'Yes, at home.'

Stella sat back and kept quiet for some time. 'So, perhaps they are the treasure you've been looking for. For all you know, they may be worth a huge amount.'

'Well,' Mary said, 'I certainly haven't found anything at Golden Hall, except for that bit of paper. And I've caused no damage by my actions. In fact, the only violence that's happened here is what Barnes did to me. So, what will you say to Mr Leary about me?''

Stella looked at her and said in a clear, firm voice. 'I can't keep something like this from Mr Leary, Mary. You're going to have to tell him, if you have the courage. And if you don't, I will.'

Mary closed her eyes. 'All right.'

Stella put out a hand. 'And I want your copy of the back-door key, now.'

Mary's head drooped. She pulled out the key and dropped it into Stella's palm. 'Can I come here tomorrow night and talk to him? Will he be here?'

'He'll be here,' Stella said, 'and Mary, if you tell him face to face, whatever he says, I've decided I'll still be your friend. You've done no harm yet, except to bring this on yourself.'

Mary pressed Stella's hand as relief washed over her. 'Thank you. That means a lot to me. Now, we've overstayed our visit and we must go. I'll see you tomorrow night.'

'About eight would be best,' Stella said.

'Reggie,' Mary called out. 'Come on, we're leaving.'

'Until, tomorrow, Mary,' Stella said. 'Goodbye.'

* * *

John finished dinner and read a story to Richard. He then went down the stairs into the drawing room and poured himself a Jamesons. When Stella had informed him that Mary Harrigan was coming to see him this evening, he'd pressed her for details, but all Stella had said was that it involved the break-in. John was intrigued. As the clock struck eight, he heard the front doorbell ring and Stella led Mary Harrigan in before leaving them together.

'Good evening, Mr Leary,' she said, bringing a hand to her hair. 'Thank you for seeing me on such short notice.'

'Good evening to you. That's quite all right. Would you like tea or something else?'

Harrigan stood there pressing her hands together and not looking at him. 'No thank you. I have something to say to you and following that, your view about me may well change.'

'Dear me. Won't you at least sit down?'

Harrigan looked at the lounge and back at him. 'Very well.' She sat down on its edge, ill at ease. 'Did Fawcett tell you anything?'

'I gather that this has to do with the attempted break-in.' John smiled. 'Is that right?'

'It is, Mr Leary.' Harrigan paused. 'You are aware that my husband Peter built this house from the proceeds from a rich strike at Bendigo.'

'Of course,' John said.

'His partner at the diggings was a man named Thomas Barnes and he and my husband shared the claim and the strike.'

'Yes?'

'Peter used some of his gold to start and build a business. He was a haberdasher by trade and a good one, but he wasn't a good businessman. Frankly, he was overstretched and went into debt that almost crippled us. Unfortunately, Peter never shared his business dealings with me. And I never knew how much he might still possess in assets after starting it up and building this house. He might have confided in me eventually but he died from a massive heart attack. I came home that day in the afternoon. He had collapsed in the garden near the front gate and did not recover.'

'Wouldn't your husband have put all his remaining capital in a bank account? By law it would have come to you when he died. But he left nothing?'

'Nothing but debts. I'm not talking about money in the bank, Mr Leary. I'm talking about money he might have hidden away, that he never had time to tell me about.'

'What about his partner, Barnes? Could he shed any light on your husband's assets?'

Mary shivered. 'No. His share was equal to Peter's, but he lost it all. Mr Leary, Peter told me just before he died that this house was valuable and that it held wealth. I always thought he meant there was value in the land, but now that I've researched where the gold went, I think he may have secreted some of it here.'

John was astonished but he could see she had convinced herself of this idea. And he'd had the feeling for months that his house was being watched. 'I suspect there are others in Sydney who think the same as you do. Go on, Mrs Harrigan.'

'I have something to confess, Mr Leary. I've been here when you've been absent, and I've been looking inside and under the house as well. I was here on the Sunday when you thought your house was about to be robbed. The man you chased away was Thomas Barnes.

He'd followed me here. He caught me by surprise, tied me up and threatened me. He pulled a knife on me to make me tell him where Peter's money was. Of course I don't know. I was terrified.'

John remembered the rope lying in the stables. 'Good God, you were there when I sent Mrs McGuire's groom and Parnell after him?' He added roughly, 'You weren't in this together?'

'No! I've had to do everything alone. It's been frightening and it's been lonely. But what choice do I have—Reggie is Peter's son but he'll have got nothing from his father if I don't track down the wealth that Peter hid away.'

He kept his face hard. 'Tell me everything you've done since your return to Sydney.'

Harrigan went on quietly, 'Peter left five items in storage here, at his bank. Fireside tongs, a chandelier, two hangings of Chinese silk, a grandfather clock and a miner's lamp. When I got back to Sydney, I collected them so I could look them over. I thought one of them might be a clue to the hidden assets. So far we've spent most of the time investigating the five items.'

'You say *we?* You and Reggie?'

Harrigan hesitated before answering. 'I had Catherine Ryan help me.'

'Really? That's outrageous. Did she come here to this house with you?'

'No, Mr Leary. She disapproved. She told me that it wasn't the right thing to do.'

John felt disturbed that Catherine Ryan should have anything to do with this. 'I wonder that she didn't think it was the right thing to tell *me* what you've been doing. And none of these items has proved valuable?'

'No. And I found nothing here except a piece of paper that may relate to the silk hangings. I'm sorry, Mr Leary for trespassing.'

'I ought to get the police in straight away and have them charge you and Barnes for breaking and entering.' Mary looked shocked now and John frowned at her, thinking fast. Fruin, Mrs McGuire's coachman, had lost Barnes because the man had got away so fast, and Parnell had given up the chase once he was well away from the property. Neither Fruin nor John had got a good enough look at Barnes to identify him in a police line-up. And the woman in front of him now was not a reliable witness to take to the police: she was a budding criminal herself. He watched Mary Harrigan's trembling lips.

'I won't prosecute,' John said at last, 'because you could go to gaol for your actions and I don't want Reggie to be deprived of his mother. If Barnes hadn't attacked you, would you have told me all about this?'

Harrigan hesitated. 'I think I would have,' she said.

He snorted. 'That doesn't seem like contrition.'

The woman shook her head. 'I've done wrong all along and it's all been pointless. Whatever wealth might be in this house, or under it, became yours when it was left to you by your father-in-law.'

'So, you've finally decided to stop looking,' he said dryly.

Mary Harrigan smiled sadly. 'Yes. I came here today to suggest that you look instead.'

Despite himself, John was amused. 'That's damned cheek, Mrs Harrigan.'

'If you did find anything, would you consider sharing a small portion of the proceeds with me?'

John was so astonished at her boldness that he did not reply.

'Peter used to own this house,' she continued, 'and no treasure was listed in the goods that were sold with the house and land. Possibly it could be legally proven that any unlisted goods are still mine, in which case I would be prepared to divide them with you.'

John became angry. 'I'm afraid that your proposition is not acceptable. In fact it's nonsense.'

'I'm sorry for trespassing.' She rose to leave.

'Mrs Harrigan,' John said, 'You're damned lucky I'm not taking this matter any further. In return, you'll promise me that you won't come here again unless invited.'

'You have that assurance, Mr Leary. 'Thank you for listening to me, and good night.'

Stella was waiting at the front door and accompanied Mary to the front gate. 'How did he take it?'

Mary stopped and looked down at the old Bede Hall sign, still sitting in the garden near the front gate. 'He won't have me charged with breaking and entering, provided I don't come back here. He's letting me off because of Reggie.'

Stella pressed her forearm. 'Maybe we can find a way for Richard and Reggie to keep playing together. But I'll have to ask Mr Leary first.'

* * *

It was Wednesday night, and Catherine Ryan was on her way to Glebe in a cab with her brother Don. They had just reached Broadway. Catherine was taking a chance that Mrs Forde would be at her home tonight, and she wanted to talk to John's sister about the goings-on at Golden Hall. She was only permitted to go to the Fordes tonight if her brother accompanied her.

'What did Mr Leary say to Mary Harrigan on Monday night?' Donald said.

'That whatever might be found at Number Seventy-nine, he wouldn't agree to splitting the proceeds with her.'

'He's right. As anybody knows, Cath, possession is nine-tenths of the law.'

'Explain that for me.'

'Well, when you transfer the title of a house and its land, the purchaser receives all the rights to that land and its improvements. Everything.'

'But Don, it's so unfair. If Peter Harrigan's money is still around somewhere, Mary should have it.'

He shook his head. 'That's supposition, which could be difficult to prove in a court of law. And Mrs Harrigan doesn't have the funds to bring a civil case.' He paused. 'Although ... I know of a case in common law where a priceless necklace was left in a home that was sold and the original owner made a claim ...'

'That's like Mary's situation, in a way.'

'It's very complicated, Cath, when two lawyers go head-to-head pulling the thing apart. No. This whole approach could be a waste of time and an embarrassment. Mrs Harrigan should be concentrating on ascertaining the value of those Chinese silks. Legally she does own those. Although they're known to be stolen goods. And so ...'

Catherine interrupted at once. She was sick of hearing about what the law could *not* do for Mary. 'Yes, I want those at home. I told Mary they'd be safer with me. She'll bring them to me tomorrow.'

'That's a good plan. Barnes surely wouldn't try to rob *us*.'

'You should have heard the intensity in Mary's voice, Don. She's fearful of him.'

Donald remained silent until the cab had stopped outside Maureen's house. Accompanying her to the front door, he said, 'You really want to mend her fortunes, don't you?'

'I do. She deserves some sunshine in her life.'

Donald knocked on Maureen's front door. 'You're not getting her hopes up too far, are you?'

'I'm thinking Mr Leary mightn't listen to a former owner of his house but he'll listen to his sister.'

The front door opened, and Liam greeted them. He gave them a smile of surprise. 'Good evening, Miss Ryan.'

'Good evening, Mr Forde. This is my brother Donald. We're sorry for coming unannounced but we'd like to talk with you and your dear wife, if that's convenient.'

'Of course it's all right,' Liam said. 'How do you do, Mr Ryan.'

Donald shook his hand. 'Very well, Mr Forde, and you?'

Liam closed the door after them as Maureen came into the foyer. 'I'm well also, thank you.'

'Catherine,' Maureen said smiling at them. 'What a pleasant surprise.'

Catherine came up to her. 'I'm sorry for imposing, Mrs Forde, but I needed to see you tonight. It's about Golden Hall.'

'You're in luck,' Liam said. 'We've just made some tea. Unless Mr Ryan would like something else? Something stronger?'

'Please call me Donald, Mr Forde, and no, tea's fine.'

'Good, then I won't be long.'

Maureen ushered them into the parlour and bade them to be seated. 'Now,' she smiled, 'what's so important about John's house?'

Catherine paused and got all her facts in a row, conscious that her legal-eagle brother would jump at any opinion-based or third-party information. 'Mary Harrigan is convinced that money or some other kind of wealth is secreted in your brother's house. Her deceased husband Peter didn't spend all his wealth and Mary's convinced that he hid some away, without having time before his death to tell her its location.'

'That's extraordinary,' Maureen said.

'It's a big assumption, Mrs Forde,' Donald said. 'There's no evidence pointing to anything being hidden in Golden Hall.'

'So,' Maureen said, 'why is Mrs Harrigan so convinced?' Liam came in with tray and pot. Maureen poured for them all.

Catherine waited until Maureen had finished handing out their teas. The story did sound flimsy. 'She has an instinct that there's something there to find.'

'But,' Liam said, 'I overheard some of what you've been saying, Miss Ryan, and if anything is found in John's house, it's his, I'm sorry to say.'

'Mr Forde's likely right,' Donald said.

Catherine sipped her tea and placed her cup down. 'Perhaps, but Mr Leary might split anything he found with Mary, in gratitude for getting her lead.'

'Except that he's refused to do so,' Don said.

Maureen said. 'I can understand John on that point. How long have you known Mrs Harrigan?'

Catherine told the Fordes the story of how she, her mother and Donald had got to know the widow and her son Reggie on the voyage to Sydney. Catherine was also frank in describing Mary's present financial position. 'She paid for the voyage by selling one of her husband's last possessions. Her second husband had been killed in an accident and had left her a small income. She decided to stay in Sydney for a few months while she tried to recover any wealth that Peter might have left behind. She's in a parlous position and I can't help feeling sympathy for her.'

Donald said wryly, 'She's better off—and less likely to commit more crimes—if she pursues the value of the silk hangings. Who knows what they might be worth?'

'Expensive silk,' Catherine explained to Maureen, 'that Peter Smith bought from a Chinese miner in Bendigo.'

'So,' Maureen said with irony, 'she might just solve her problems without having to half-demolish John's house.'

Catherine smiled with her. 'It might well be. Nevertheless, could you consider talking to your brother and seeing if there could be a thorough search of Golden Hall? At least it would lay the issue to rest in Mary Harrigan's mind. An obsession like that skews someone's life, and she deserves to know the truth. I like her.' She looked askance at Don. 'Despite her criminal tendencies.'

'I'll talk to John,' Maureen said.

Catherine was surprised how quickly Maureen had agreed. It seemed that Mr Forde was also surprised.

'I can't promise anything, mind you,' Maureen said, 'but it might be fun to search, and who knows what we may find. It could take some time.' Her face became serious. 'But I'm not going to ask John to share the spoils, not just yet. Let's see how the thing pans out.'

Catherine finished her tea and said hesitantly, 'I wouldn't mind being involved in the search myself.'

'I think that might be arranged,' Maureen said. 'But let's wait to see what John says about all this.'

Catherine was pleasantly surprised at her tolerance. A part of her, just a part, thought for a second that Mrs Forde suspected her interest in John Leary, and approved of it. She rose and said. 'We've taken too much of your valuable time. We must go.'

'I'm glad you talked to me about this, Catherine,' Maureen said. 'Any time you and your brother would like to visit, you'll always be welcome.'

It was nice of her to say that. Catherine smiled in appreciation. 'Thank you. Come, Don, time to go.'

Liam and Maureen saw them out. Don said. 'Good night, Mr and Mrs Forde. Thank you for your hospitality.'

Making their way up to Glebe Point Road to get a cab, Donald said, 'How do you think Mr Leary will react to your aiding and abetting Mary Harrigan in her escapades? What sort of a man is he?'

For once Catherine was not comfortable when her brother probed her feelings. 'I don't know. I've had hardly a word to say to him.'

Donald hailed a cab and they got on board. 'Potts Point, driver. Victoria Street.' He looked at her sidelong. 'With some encounters, a few words can go a long way.'

Catherine ignored him, sat back and thought about the evening. She hoped that her visit tonight would be construed by all as coming from a wish to help a friend.

* * *

The Fordes walked through the open gate of Golden Hall with their children, Michael and Irene. It was a warm and humid Saturday night, three days since the meeting with Catherine Ryan and her brother. On the way to the front door Maureen thought again about how luck was working for her. The supposed treasure wasn't that important to her; what she wanted was for John and Catherine to spend some time together, soon.

Fawcett greeted them and John joined them in the drawing room.

'Come through,' John said, smiling at them, 'dinner's just about ready.'

They sat together at the dining-room table with Irene and Michael facing their mother, and John and Liam at the table ends.

'Uncle John,' Irene said excitedly, 'we're off to find buried treasure.'

Maureen was surprised at her daughter's outburst, but it was one way to start the conversation. The children had heard them talking in the cab and were fired up in excitement.

John paused between spoonfuls of the vegetable soup. 'And what island are we going to explore?'

'Point Piper,' Michael said and grinned. 'We'll get Richard to help us.'

John seemed puzzled and Maureen stepped in. 'We'd like to look for Captain Smith's lost treasure,' Maureen said. '*The* Captain Smith, who used a telescope to look at ships from this very house.'

'Oh, that Captain Smith,' John said, understanding dawning on him. 'So his widow has been talking to you?'

Maureen, hoping for a pleasant reaction from her brother, was careful how she phrased her answer. 'Not his widow, John, but Catherine and Donald Ryan.'

John was shocked but recovered and smiled. 'Really!'

'Miss Ryan was convinced,' Liam said, 'that Mrs Harrigan was genuine, and we listened to her story. We agreed that we would ask you to think again about following up on her quest.'

John sat back and tapped the table. 'Look, I admit I'm tempted to have a look around myself. But I don't want to get everyone's hopes up. If the whole family's going to—'

'There's gold buried here, Uncle John,' Michael chirped up. 'I know there is. We'll find it!'

'Well then,' John said as the cook brought in the main course of roast chicken, 'I suppose we'll have to break out the spades and clear the decks.'

'Yippee!' Irene called out.

'Irene!' Liam said, but smiled. 'We said to Miss Ryan that we wouldn't ask you to consider sharing anything you found, because obviously it's yours anyway.'

'Indeed.' John turned to the children. 'How about you two go and tell Richard about your plans and you kids can decide where to start. Stella, can you feed my treasure hunters in the kitchen with Richard, while they nut it out?'

'Surely, Mr Leary.'

Maureen was happy that John had agreed to this. And very happy at his manner and good humour. It was all heading along nicely.

John waited until the children had left. 'I didn't want to say this in front of the little ones, but I don't think there's anything to find and therefore there'll be nothing to share. As a builder I know how things are put together and where the treasure could be held here, if there's anything at all, which I doubt. However, I've thought for the last five months that there might be something to this whole puzzle and I'm willing to get stuck in and explore because,' he smiled, 'I think it's doing me some good. You can join me in my whimsy if you like, but that's all it is. Don't expect any gold to come out of it.'

Maureen got up from the table and hugged him. 'I'm so glad,' she said. 'Mind you, Mary Harrigan would like to look as well.'

'I don't know if I can consent to that,' John said.

'And someone else would like to snoop around too,' Maureen said. 'Catherine Ryan.'

John paused with his fork in the air. 'Why, what interest could she have?'

Maureen tried to act innocent. 'I don't know. Curiosity perhaps.'

She went on with her dinner and stole a glance at her brother. John was deep in thought, and she knew that look: it was one of anticipation, and she was glad. When she looked at Liam, he had a smile on his face.

* * *

'First item, John?' Christine asked.

John bit into a chocolate biscuit and concentrated on the November board papers in front of him. 'Project status,' he said, 'all proceeding well and profitable.'

'Wattle Street wool store especially,' Sean said. 'From a slow start in September, Bob Jones has got the outside walls well up and the centre row of columns is done. I was at the Annandale factory yesterday.'

'How are the trusses going?' John said.

'Early days. Just setting up the jigs. Timber looks seasoned and their plans are detailed. We—'

'Gentlemen,' Christine said, 'you can have your technical talk any time. I want to know if we have all the risks covered on that job, or whether are there issues.'

Indeed, John thought. He sipped his tea. 'There aren't any real problems, but the trusses will need close watching, as we've never built trusses on that scale before.'

'I remember,' she said. 'Something about the wool-store owners saving money on space?'

'Yes, Mrs McGuire,' Sean replied, 'and they're special.'

'Well, I'll leave it to you both to ensure there's no problems. Now, this second item, our competitors. I've never seen this; it looks like intense research.'

'Grand idea,' Sean said. 'I like it. It shows all the jobs Shelby and Hoxtons are building and what they're tendering on.'

John explained, 'I've had a crack at what I know about jobs being built in town and the suburbs. We need to know who's building them, and what tenders are out and who's pricing them. All that adds up to what is our Sydney construction market. I want to know each month what the other builders are doing and ensure that we're not slipping behind.'

'I understand,' she said. 'We can look at this each month.'

'That's what we should do, yes,' John said.

'Now, this third item, the most important. You're proposing we consider purchasing a joinery business.' She put on her spectacles and began to read. 'Two thousand pounds goodwill ... together with the property, fixtures, stock, machinery and factory.'

'Christine,' John said, 'most of our buildings incorporate joinery.'

'Yes, of course.'

He said, 'If we manufacture our own joinery, we cut out the margin we have to pay others when we order it in. That lowers the cost of our windows, doors, architrave, skirtings. Even with these monster trusses, in time, we can reduce the cost of the total building and therefore be more competitive.'

'But at the moment, John, if I understand it,' she said, 'we get good competitive prices from many joinery businesses.'

'We do,' Sean said, 'joiners are always busy and often we're chasing delivery of the biggest things for a project—like for instance we can't do any plastering work until the windows have been fixed into position. Or we can't complete architraves until doors are in, and all that.'

'So what we can do with our own joinery business,' John said, 'is be in control. We can also save on costs by purchasing materials from the timber suppliers and the metal suppliers at wholesale rates.'

'So, this business is for sale.' Christine looked at the papers. 'Yes, here it is, Bradley & Son. The broker's report says it's a fair and reasonable price.'

'If you look at the last page of the papers,' John said, 'you'll see the profit and loss report that Dan Reynolds has done. It shows we can get our capital back in four years, including the bank loan repayments—which, incidentally, they are keen to finance.'

'Mrs McGuire,' Sean said, 'we can then be competitive in making more of these trusses, like the ones on the Wattle Street wool store and get better value in our projects. We'll cost the client less and at the same time make more profit ourselves.'

'Is this your strong recommendation?' she said, looking from one man to the other.

'It is,' John said. 'And we already have a staff member who's willing to take over the joinery business, with Mr Bradley staying on for six months for a smooth transition.'

'Rory Jenkins, a foreman of ours,' Sean said. 'He's been with us just under two years and he's proving a find. His father Rupert would also like a ten per cent share of the joinery business as an investment. I trust Rupert with his knowledge and experience.'

Christine tapped her papers with her spectacles and drank the remainder of her tea. 'Very well, I agree. Get cracking. I want to look at this again in the middle of next year to examine its profitability and, more importantly, to see if we're better off as a result.'

'Very good,' John said.

'Now, son-in-law,' Christine said. 'Has anyone laid their hands on the man who broke into your stables?'

John sat back. 'No, but I think I know who he was. Mrs Harrigan has filled me in about a man who could have a big interest in the house.'

'Mrs Harrigan,' Christine said, 'the former owner?'

'The same.' John decided that now wasn't the time to tell anyone else about Mrs Harrigan's snooping, or Catherine Ryan's interest, in Golden Hall. 'The story starts many years ago. Apparently a Thomas Barnes struck gold in Bendigo while in partnership with Peter Smith. The syndicate split the proceeds but unfortunately for Mr Barnes he went through the lot, became penniless and now chooses, I guess, to rob people's houses. Mrs Harrigan says that, unlike Barnes, her husband held onto some of his money despite his business failures. She thinks he concealed what he had left over and intended to tell her about it, but he died suddenly. So the gold or money or whatever he concealed is still around somewhere—and she's convinced herself that it's hidden in my house.'

Christine exclaimed, 'But that's absurd!'

'Well,' John said, 'she's not the only one interested in Golden Hall. I'm afraid there's some kind of mystery attached to it.'

'You've had a feeling about this for some time John, haven't you?' Sean said.

'I have. And that's what drew Barnes there—at least according to Mrs Harrigan.'

'But Barnes didn't take anything,' Sean said. 'There was no damage, there was no broken glass, nothing stolen.'

'No. But Barnes could have been looking for hidden wealth. It's not the first time he's turned up. I'm pretty sure he was the man I saw standing outside some months ago, watching my place.'

Christine said, 'This is awful. Do you think he has accomplices, John? Might he come back again?'

'I don't think so. But I'm going to keep searching. I might even allow Mrs Harrigan to help me.' He stood up and they rose too. 'Now, we have a company to run. Sean, I'll see you this afternoon at

McCreadies. Rupert Jenkins wants us there to celebrate the completion of that little job.'

'Right,' Sean said.

'I'll say goodbye to both of you,' Christine said. She smiled at John. 'And welcome back to the fold.'

He was surprised but understood. He nodded to her. 'Thank you, Christine.'

Chapter Seven

In her Glebe parlour, Maureen lifted her teapot from the low table in the middle of the room. It was Saturday afternoon and one week since she and John had talked about the treasure hunt at his house. 'More tea, Mr Ryan?' she said. This gathering had been her idea, to know Catherine's parents better.

William Ryan smiled up at her from an armchair. 'No thank you, Mrs Forde, but I'll have another slice of that delicious fruit cake.'

'Surely,' she said and took his plate to the table and cut a handsome slice. She looked at her other guests enjoying her afternoon tea and checked they were well served. Through the open French doors, Catherine was talking to Liam in the shade of the veranda. The light fabric of Catherine's dress moved in the pleasant spring breeze.

At the larger table indoors, Constance Ryan and John were talking about Ireland, their teas untouched on the cloth between them. Maureen smiled to herself as John glanced again outside to see Catherine. It was a good sign. She now had to get the pair together. On the veranda would be best, out of earshot from parents inside but still under their watchful eyes.

'Here you are,' she said, returning to William Ryan with his cake. 'Now, tell me more about Catherine growing up.'

Ryan took a bite of his treat. 'Delicious.' She waited for him to finish, eager to find out more about Catherine. Today was the first plan of a strategy. She was certain that a real connection could be made between her and John, and she was going to ensure that the connection turned to romance.

'Where was I?' he said. 'Ah yes, her studies were commendable, and she made friends easily.'

'Where did she get her interest in hats?'

He smiled. 'From her mother, as a matter of fact. Constance had more hats when I first met her than she had dresses, or so she told me.' He glanced over at his wife, who was still talking animatedly to John Leary. 'Catherine would play with the out-of-fashion hats as a child and when Constance allowed her, she would take them apart to see how they were made.'

'She had an eye for fashion so young?'

'More than that, she was intrigued by the craft required to make them.' He smiled again. 'I think she has an eye for intrigue as well. She's fascinated by the treasure hunt that's going to happen at your brother's house.' Ryan glanced outside. 'Your brother won't mind if she takes part? I'd hate to think she'd be making a nuisance of herself?'

Maureen was about to laugh. The scheme fitted perfectly with her romance strategy. 'I'm sure he'll consider her a welcome addition to the search party, whether they find anything or not. I hope *she* won't mind getting very dusty.'

'Not at all. That's excellent,' he said, and took some more of his cake.

'If you will excuse me, Mr Ryan, I'll take Catherine and Liam some more refreshment.'

'Surely.'

Maureen went to the table where the cake slices and biscuits were laid out and found Constance Ryan and John in an intense discussion about the cathedral in Cork, which Maureen's uncle Gerry had worked on years before. Constance Ryan remembered that there was a marble cross above the altar but John recalled it was in a beautiful timber that might have been oak.

As Maureen picked up a plate, Constance Ryan was saying, 'You won't convince me, I'm afraid, Mr Leary. I'm sure it was marble.'

Maureen said. 'Excuse me, but Liam was asking my uncle about the cathedral the other day, and I'm sure they talked about his work on the altar. John, why don't you take these slices and small cakes out to Catherine—her plate's empty. And ask Liam to come in and compare his recollections with Mrs Ryan's. Perhaps he can confirm that the cross is marble?'

John stood up at once and took the plate. Maureen could see he was delighted to escape outside—away from the little tussle with Constance Ryan and armed with an excuse to sit with Catherine.

Maureen watched as her manoeuvre proved successful. In a few moments John was with Catherine on the veranda and Liam had come in to oblige Mrs Ryan with his memories of Cork cathedral, which he was tactful enough to match with her own.

Outside, Catherine smiled as John held out the plate. 'I couldn't have another thing. That would be gluttony.'

'Please do. I'll sit down and help you eat them.'

'All right,' she said, and smiled. Ever since she'd entered the Fordes' house this afternoon, she had been very aware of his presence. As he sat down, in the movement of the breeze she smelt his scent, a male muskiness that affected her, in a nice way. She picked out a small cake.

'I do like my sister's cooking,' he said.

'These little cakes are delicious. Mrs Forde is a good cook.'

'Do you cook, Miss Ryan?'

'I do and I enjoy it. Mary—Mrs Harrigan—and I work in her kitchen sometimes, trying out various recipes.'

She looked down at the plate as his fingers, long and slender, took a slice and carried it to his lips. She wanted that hand to touch her and she wanted those lips on hers. She was amazed and stirred by her own thoughts.

Their eyes met. Flustered, she stood up and leaned on the veranda rail with her back to him. She tried to keep her voice neutral. 'You are a businessman-builder, are you not?'

'An interesting term,' he said. 'And yes, I am.'

She turned around to face him. There was a small distance between them but she felt as if she wanted him to fill the gap, to stand up and be even nearer to her. Her reactions both excited and concerned her. 'And you like what you do?'

'That I do. The work's not quite so physical as it used to be, of course, now that I'm more established. I spend more time planning now, working out how to juggle men and materials, and tendering …' He smiled. 'But perhaps I'm boring you?'

'Not at all,' she said.

'You're being polite.'

'I'm not, Mr Leary. I usually mean what I say.'

He smiled again at her. 'You do, do you?'

She now smiled with him. 'I do. You see, I like the ins and outs of business. There, I've said it. You probably think that a woman should not be interested in management.'

All at once his eyes were sad. She wondered how her words could have had that effect on him.

His measured reply gave her the reason. 'No, I do understand how some women may have a genuine grasp of commerce. My departed wife, Clarissa, was capable and adept in dealing with money and running a business.'

He looked vulnerable at the memory, so she did not feel he would want to talk further about his wife. She must find another subject that would interest them both. Why not the possible treasure at Golden Hall? 'The last time I saw Mary Harrigan, she mentioned that she had told you about her interest in Golden Hall. Have you forgiven her for her intrusions on your property?'

'I'm not sure. But she was the previous owner—I suppose I must forgive her curiosity about what might or mightn't be hidden in my house.'

Catherine felt herself blushing. 'I hope you know that I didn't approve of her going there without your knowledge. And I never joined in that part of her investigations.'

'So she tells me,' he said evenly. 'I must say I'd be disappointed if you had, Miss Ryan.' She blushed again at this. He noticed, and his voice grew gentler. 'However, I can understand your being curious about the legacy of the unfortunate Peter Smith.'

With relief, she took his cue. 'It's so tantalising. Mary and I went through all the five things her husband had left her, with such care and hope. But none of them led anywhere.'

'All except the silk hangings, perhaps? Has the Chinese inscription been translated yet?'

'No,' she said, remembering with embarrassment that the note in Chinese script had been found behind the panelling of his own dining room! She saw her mother coming out onto the veranda and said hastily, 'Which Mass are you going to tomorrow at St Mary's?'

He seemed surprised at the question. 'Ten o'clock, of course. Why?'

'I'll try to come then, too. I mean, if we meet afterwards you could tell me how you intend to look for the treasure.'

He looked happy at her suggestion, and she felt a rush of anticipation. He smiled at her. 'I look forward to that.'

'Catherine, come, we must be going,' Mrs Ryan said. She turned to John. 'And Mr Leary, I'm pleased to say that Mr and Mrs Forde have agreed to come for dinner at our house next Saturday night. We would be very pleased if you could dine with us too.'

Excellent, Catherine thought.

'Thank you, Mrs Ryan,' John said. 'I'd be delighted. Goodbye, ladies.'

Catherine smiled at him. 'Goodbye, Mr Leary.'

On Sunday, as the Mass was coming to an end, John was disappointed that the large St Mary's congregation did not seem to include the Ryans. The week had gone slowly for him. He'd tried to make time pass by concentrating on his projects, especially the wool store, but during gaps in his day, the young milliner had filled his thoughts. The dinner at the Ryans the night before had given him the opportunity to see her in company and at the same time relish sitting by her side. He admired her more, every time he saw her.

The priest entered the sacristy and John stood up to leave. Then he spotted William Ryan, who was at the end of the pew six down from his. Seeing that they were heading for a side door, John turned to Stella beside him. 'Please take my mother-in-law and Richard home with you in the carriage. I'll get a cab later.'

'Certainly, Mr Leary,' she said.

He genuflected towards the altar and followed the Ryans. It might be hard to talk with Catherine about the treasure hunt while they were all heading home, but whatever they spoke about, it would be enough to be by her side. Leaving the church and looking around, he spotted Catherine standing with a tall young man at the roadside. As he walked towards them, John became apprehensive that this man might be a friend of hers, perhaps a suitor even.

Catherine turned and saw him. 'Good morning, Mr Leary. This is my brother, Donald.'

John tipped his hat to Catherine. 'Good morning to you, Miss Ryan.' He put out his hand to Donald. 'How do you do, Mr Ryan.'

'I'm very well, Mr Leary,' Donald said. 'And you?'

'The same, thank you.'

'My brother and I were talking about your house, as a matter of fact. Mrs Harrigan asked me if she could write to you and discuss dates for the search, at your convenience.'

So Mary Harrigan was determined to come back to Golden Hall? He realised he didn't mind, as long as Catherine might come. 'That's quite all right, Miss Ryan. Please get her to do that.'

'I say, Mr Leary,' Donald said. 'It's frightfully hot. Can we go somewhere in the shade?'

'How about Hyde Park?'

'Good,' Donald said. 'Let's go.'

John was on her inside and Donald walked on the kerb side next to his sister. It wasn't ideal, with her brother there, and John would have to refrain asking questions about Catherine herself, just stick to the search. 'So, Mr Ryan, do you believe your sister's story about this mystical treasure?'

Catherine's eyes flashed at him, and she was about to say something when John smiled at her. She smiled back and said nothing.

'It's really Mary Harrigan who's the central character here, Mr Leary,' Donald said. 'It used to be her house.'

They crossed College Street and walked into the park. John gestured to a seat and Catherine sat down. John leaned against a tree. 'But it's my house now.'

'The search will be interesting, just the same,' Catherine said.

'You don't mind your house being invaded by prospectors?' Donald said ironically to John.

'It's of no inconvenience to me, Mr Ryan, really, provided that the times of exploration can be worked out. I'd prefer Wednesday afternoons, say after two. It's now the middle of November and summer's long days are going to be with us soon. This is the best time for digging, if we're going to be messing around in the soil below the floorboards.'

'So, Wednesdays. Can you spare us time on the weekends?' Catherine asked.

'Perhaps one or two if we get enough notice,' John replied and smiled.

Catherine fanned her face. 'Where do you think the trove might be, Mr Leary?'

Something he had asked himself many times. 'Did Mrs Harrigan tell you of the false panel above my sideboard?'

'Where she found the note in Chinese?' she said, then blushed.

He was tickled by her embarrassment. 'That's the one. I got the details from Fawcett, who was the first to hear of it from Mrs Harrigan. Well, I thought that might be the place to seek directions to the missing hoard.'

'That sounds logical,' Donald said.

'Yes. I thought it would have been unusual for Peter Smith to leave treasure behind him but no instructions on how to find it.'

'He might have thought,' Catherine said, 'that he'd never need to leave instructions. Perhaps he planned all along to access the trove during his lifetime. But he died too young, very suddenly.' She paused. 'You know, Mrs Harrigan told me that on the day of her husband's death, he was going up the front path to his house to get something, when he collapsed. What if he was actually intending to access the money, or gold, or whatever?'

John was thoughtful. Were Peter Smith's last moments important for the search? 'It's just possible. Perhaps we can find out the details of what happened that last day, from Mrs Harrigan herself. But I would hesitate to ask her such a sensitive question. The inquiry would have to come from a friend.'

Donald said. 'Well, it's a mystery that won't be solved today.' He stood up. 'Now, Mr Leary, we must go, I'm afraid.'

* * *

At four in the afternoon, and shaded by a tree, Harry Shelby waited and sweated opposite the factory in Moore Street, Annandale, a suburb or two just out of Sydney town. It was early summer, yet it felt like the middle of January. Shelby was impatient to meet the worker whom he'd sent to spy on the construction of the roof trusses in the factory. Learys were mad to try and build roof trusses of that size. Nothing like them had ever been done in the colony and they could have huge problems with them. Shelby had wanted the wool store job and he hadn't given up on the idea of winning it back for himself.

Just then his spy, Alan Coleman, walked out of Sullivan's Timber Merchants, with four other workers. Coleman was tall and slim and had the gait of a fit and hard-working man. He knew his lathes, jigs and saws like a hen knew its chicks. The timber worker spotted Shelby but kept walking on his own side of the street. Shelby set off and kept up with him. When Coleman turned the corner into Parramatta Road, Shelby caught up with him. 'Hot day, Alan. Time for a beer?'

Coleman looked at him and nodded. They set off for the pub nearby. Harry Shelby had promised to line up a new job for Coleman in a competitor's yard, with more pay and perks. Now there was a price to pay for that and Coleman would have to cough up.

The public bar started to fill with workers who were keen to quench their thirsts. Coleman paid for two beers and they found a spare space where they would not be overheard.

Coleman downed half his beer and wiped his mouth. 'I needed that.' He looked at Shelby. 'Heard anything?'

'Mr Coleman, I have it on good authority that you have the job.'

Coleman pressed his lips together then smiled. 'So, when do I start?'

Shelby smiled with him. Good. The man hadn't had any second thoughts about leaving his employer of ten years. 'You'll need to give notice?'

'Two weeks.'

Shelby nodded. Now to find out something. 'The trusses you're making for Learys.'

Coleman swore an oath. 'Bastards are big. Jigs needed remaking, cost the bosses a fortune.'

Shelby didn't wonder. 'Are they being set up?'

'The first one is. I started the jigs today. It'll take me about a week's work.'

Good timing. 'How much do you want this new job, Alan?'

'Return the shout, and I'll tell you,' the man said.

Shelby headed to the bar for the beers. The man had to be convinced, no, more than that, he had to commit to doing the task Shelby handed out. And the job had to be done so that he, Harry Ernest Shelby wasn't connected to it. He returned with the drinks.

'Right,' Coleman said. 'I'm keen to work for Maxtons. I've always thought they were a better bunch than Sullivans, with more chances of promotion. Yeah, Mr Shelby, I want this job.'

'Alan, I need something done in exchange.'

For the first time, Coleman looked apprehensive. 'What?'

Shelby smiled. 'Just arrange a simple mistake in what you're now doing.'

'What? With the jigs?'

'Exactly. See, I want those jigs set up so the first two or three trusses are made to the wrong size.'

'But ... that'll be a massive error. It'll cost the boss money and time, and guess who'll get it in the neck?'

'Nonsense, you'll find a way to set it up so the mistake's not found until you're out of there. Just make sure you engineer it so the blame lands on someone else.' Shelby was interested to see Coleman's reaction. The man was thinking about it, good.

'I don't know. I'll need some time to think of a way. But why would you want me to do it anyway?'

'Don't ask me that question again, Mr Coleman, and you won't know, will you?'

Coleman thought for a bit. 'Another beer?'

Shelby nodded and Coleman went to the bar. Would the man do it? And if he did, might he confide in someone else? Mind you, Shelby had an answer for that.

Coleman brought the beers back. 'How exactly do you want me to alter the trusses?'

Good, Shelby thought, he's taking the bait. 'Adjust the jigs to make the trusses one foot longer and higher than they're supposed to be. Surely you could manage that without being found out?'

Coleman nodded. 'The best patsy is my foreman, Forrester. He's a lazy sod and just does whatever I say, never double-checks anything. I won't go near the jigs, I'll give him the instructions verbally and he can supervise the adjustments. He won't even notice that the truss measurements don't match up with the plans. Later on I'll be gone and he'll cop the blame for it.'

'Sounds like the go. So, I'll let you work out the when and how. When it's done, let me know and I'll fix up the new job for you.' Coleman smiled. 'But don't let anyone else in on this little matter. If you do, I'll let it be known to your new employer that you *were* involved and that alone will be enough to lose you your new job.' Shelby touched his glass to Coleman's. 'Just do as I say, and you'll have a prosperous future with your new company.'

Coleman looked at him for some time. Shelby could see nervousness in his eyes, but it changed to resolve. 'I'll get it done, Mr Shelby. I will.'

Shelby finished his beer and put his hat on. 'Good man. Now, I wasn't here, but if any of your mates has spied us and asks who I am, you tell them I'm a chance acquaintance and you can't even remember my name. All right?'

'Done,' Coleman said, and Shelby left.

* * *

It was six o'clock on the Tuesday morning in late November and Simon Ly was struggling through a news article. Before his work day began in the Waterloo transport company, he used this time every day to improve his reading skills. As an immigrant of eight years, he still found the English language hard to read, but he persisted. And he had good reason to learn, because his promotion to supervisor depended on it.

He placed his newspaper down to give his eyes a rest. Sydney was different from Melbourne and its climate was milder. Today would be hot. It was now three years since he had travelled from the southern capital, carrying a reference from his employer, whose business equipped coaches and carriages with harnesses. Three years before that, he had struggled as a miner in the Bendigo goldfields. That was a time of suffering with only one brief flash of hope.

Simon had paid his own way from China to Victoria and had walked out to Bendigo with almost nothing except his clothes and the tools he'd bought for prospecting. But he had something valuable hidden in his baggage: two silk hangings from a screen that had belonged to his ancestors. His father had entrusted it to him after saving it from the ravages of the Taiping rebellion. The screen had held two panels, each three feet wide by five feet in height. Each panel had an embroidered hem in gold thread. Simon considered the silks a treasure to be kept for as long as he could protect them. But if his prospecting was not fruitful and his situation became desperate, he had considered the idea of raising funds from the silks to start a business.

Tragically, he had not been able to protect the silks: they were stolen at the Bendigo diggings. Simon had got back to his tent one night and found they had been lifted from his pack. He had despaired of ever seeing them again, but only a few days later he saw them being offered to Peter Smith, a miner who shared a claim with Thomas Barnes, not far from Simon's own claim. He was devastated to see Smith inspecting the silks and to realise that they were being offered for sale by another prospector called Wo Fat. Simon at once accused Wo Fat of stealing the silks from him, but the man denied everything and insisted that he had a right to sell them for whatever sum he chose. Simon had no hope of going to the rough and ready police at the Bendigo diggings—they refused to get involved in disputes amongst the Chinese diggers and treated them contemptuously. Shouting at Wo Fat got Simon nowhere, and Smith was too keen on the silks to turn them down. They went to Smith for a price that Simon considered grossly under their value, but it was still too high for him to buy them back himself. After Ly left the diggings, almost penniless again, he thought the silks were gone from his life for ever.

But today he had an idea where they were. Some time ago in Sydney, at a shop in the market gardens to the south of the town, Simon overheard a conversation between two of his countrymen. One was talking about a gambling night in a William Street gambling den, when an Englishman at his table had put up 'silk curtains' as a stake. The man repeated the description of the silks clearly enough for Simon to guess they were his, and said that the Englishman had got them from the gold fields in Bendigo. Simon had interjected and asked the pair about the Englishman. The man did not know his name, but could give Simon a description.

Simon had begun to haunt the William Street gambling den, and after five nights had spotted the man and followed him home. He recognised him as Thomas Barnes, the former companion of Peter Smith, when they were all in Bendigo.

Simon was desperate to get the ancestral silks back. In an alley, he had grabbed a drunken Barnes one night and threatened him. A terrified Barnes had told him that he did not possess the silks: they still belonged to Peter Smith. All Barnes would say about Peter Smith was that he had built a house at number seventy-nine, Wolseley Road, Point Piper.

The seven o'clock bell went for start of work and Simon put his newspaper away and started to prepare his orders for the day. His work was tiring but he felt energised, because he had a purpose. He would go to Mr Smith's house tonight and demand his ancestral silks back.

* * *

At dusk on that Tuesday evening, John Leary was at home, thinking of the pleasant time he'd spent with Catherine Ryan lately. He was interrupted in his thoughts as Stella stood in front of him.

'Sir,' she said, 'there's a strange man at the front door. I think he's a Chinaman. He looks clean and speaks fair English. He wanted to talk to Mr Smith but I told him he no longer lives here. He keeps going on about a silk screen, or some such thing.'

'A screen?' John said.

'Yes, sir. Should I send him away?'

John was about to tell her to do so but stopped. He was curious. 'I'll see him.' He went past Stella and out onto the front veranda. There he found a slim, tall, fine-featured and well-dressed man. 'I'm John Leary. Can I help you?'

'Good evening, Mr Leary. I'm apologise most sincerely for this unexpected visit.'

John smiled. 'That's all right.'

'I'm Simon Ly and I want to talk to a man called Peter Smith. This is his house. Where is he?'

'Mr Ly,' John replied, 'This house is mine. I acquired it not too long after Peter Smith died.'

'He is *dead?*'

'Yes. He died in September 1855.'

Ly looked disconsolate.

'It's a balmy night,' John said, 'so why don't we sit down?' John pointed to two chairs on the front veranda. Once Ly was seated, John said, 'When did you meet Mr Smith?'

'In Bendigo in May of 1852. You see, Mr Leary, Mr Smith bought two silk pieces from a man called Wo Fat. But the silks were mine and Fat stole them from me.'

'Please tell me what they look like.'

'The size was about six feet long and five feet high. Two panels. They were from my ancestors, given to me by my father in China to take to Victoria.'

'And you believe Mr Smith had them? I have to tell you there was nothing like that in the house when it came into my hands.'

'Back then, I offered to buy from Mr Smith at double what he'd paid but he wouldn't sell. He didn't believe me when I said that he had stolen property. He told me he wanted to keep the silks.'

John understood Smith's reaction. Without proof that the screen was stolen, John wouldn't have sold it or given it back to its so-called rightful owner either. 'Most of Mr Smith's possessions were lost when his business crashed. But these silk hangings, his widow might still have them.'

'Where is she?'

John wouldn't answer right away. Mrs Harrigan was already in danger from Barnes; why give her address to Ly? 'Could these silk pieces be misinterpreted as curtains?'

'Sorry, Mr Leary. Miss in what?'

'Could they be mistaken for a curtain or curtains? Like the ones you see in our houses.'

'I do know what curtains are, Mr Leary.'

'My apologies.'

'Yes, they could be,' Ly said.

John was right. The silk curtains Mrs Harrigan had described might very well be the panels that Mr Ly had owned.

'Is Mrs Smith in New South Wales?' Ly asked.

'She went back to England after her husband's death and remarried, but she has returned here. The items that her husband left her may well include these silk hangings.'

Ly's eyes became bright. 'Then I must meet her and get my rightful property back.' He paused. 'She might still have my note?'

'What note?'

'Mr Leary, I made my offer in writing to Mr Peter Smith, to buy back my silks. I could write the numbers but I could not write the words in English, so I did it in our own script. It was perhaps foolish of me but I wanted to record my offer.'

'What did you offer Mr Smith?'

'One hundred pounds.'

It was a significant sum and gave John pause. 'This is a very serious matter, Mr Ly. I believe I should get in touch with Mrs Harrigan—that is her new married name. Can you come here again tomorrow night?'

'Will Mrs Harrigan be here? With my silks?'

'I can't promise that. But I'll try to get her here and you can talk to her.'

Ly smiled. 'That's a bother to you, Mr Leary. Please be so kind as to give me Mrs Harrigan's address, and I can go there and sort all this out.'

John could do that, but he had to be wary of Mr Ly. He might be a rogue like Barnes.

He stood up. 'I think that's all we can do tonight, Mr Ly. Will you come here tomorrow night?'

Ly stood up and held out his hand. 'I will. Good evening, Mr Leary, and thank you.'

The following night was very hot. As John waited for his visitors to arrive, he was apprehensive. He was allowing Mary Harrigan to visit his house, when he'd practically thrown her out not many days before. But she had faced hardships ever since both her husbands had died and John did not think she should face Simon Ly alone. He had written her a note explaining the situation and felt grateful when she replied, agreeing to come.

A horse's whinny made him stand up and he indicated to Stella that he'd answer the door. There were two vehicles at his front gate. Simon Ly got off the first cab and to John's pleasure, Catherine Ryan alighted from a gig with Mary Harrigan. Simon Ly stopped and faced the two women. Miss Ryan was carrying a box and John suspected that inside it were the 'curtains'. Not wanting a confrontation on his front lawn, he went out to meet his visitors.

'Good evening, Miss Ryan and Mrs Harrigan. I'd like you to meet Mr Simon Ly.' He turned to the Chinese man. 'Mr Ly, this is Miss Ryan and Mrs Harrigan.'

Ly nodded to both women.

'Good evening,' the women said to them both.

'Please come inside,' John said and directed his guests into the drawing room. 'Would any of you like some refreshments?' He smiled at Catherine.

'Tea for both of us, thank you Mr Leary,' Mrs Harrigan said. Simon Ly shook his head.

John turned to Stella. 'Please arrange that, thank you.'

Mrs Harrigan seemed anxious to speak to Ly. 'When was the last time you saw my husband?'

Ly lifted his eyes from the parcel in her hands. He hadn't looked at anything else since he'd come into the room. 'In Bendigo, in 1852. Have you brought my silks?'

'Perhaps, Mr Ly,' John said, 'you could give us more information on their history.'

Stella brought the teas in and poured for them all. Ly looked at John. 'My Leary, Wo Fat stole what was rightfully mine. He—'

'Where is that man now?'

'Dead,' Ly said.

John was startled, then became wary. It would be convenient for Ly to lie about Fat and claim the silks for himself. 'When did he die, and how?'

Ly brought out a worn piece of newspaper and handed it to John. On a marked section of the *Bendigo Advertiser*, dated 1 August 1853,

John read that Wo Fat had been found dead in his tent—the cause, excess drinking. He handed the paper back to Ly. 'Thank you.'

'Wo Fat had gambling debts, Mr Leary,' Ly said. 'That's why he had to sell my silks. He needed cash fast and wanted any money he could get. He handed my silks to Peter Smith for fifty pounds.'

Mrs Harrigan put her cup down. 'And you approached my husband after Wo Fat died?'

'Yes. I told him that the screen was my ancestors'. It's my responsibility to keep it and to pass it onto my children.' His eyes misted. 'It's that precious and important to me.'

'And Wo Fat,' Mary Harrigan said, 'he stole it from you?'

'He did. I couldn't get it back from him. But I thought your husband might understand that it was really mine.'

Mrs Harrigan brought out from her purse a piece of paper.

'I can tell you what that says,' Ly said eyeing the document. 'It's my offer to Peter Smith.'

'Yes, but without a corroborative translation.' John said, 'we don't know for sure.'

For the first time, Ly looked angry. 'I don't lie, Mr Leary.' He sighed. 'But I can tell you there are two symbols on that paper you hold, Mrs Harrigan. Don't show it to me. There are two small "s's" side by side in the top right-hand corner. That's the symbol for silk, two silkworms. At the bottom right-hand corner is the mark of my family.' He brought out another piece of paper from his purse and handed this to Mrs Harrigan. 'These are the symbols of my father's name. See if they are the same as on my note.'

She took it and compared the notes. She then spoke to John. 'It's as he said, Mr Leary. He's right.'

John took the paper that for six years had been hidden in his panelling. 'All right, what else can you tell me about this?' He held it away from Ly's line of sight.

'There's a sum of one hundred pounds and the date at the top is 20 August 1852.'

Ly was right about the figures, which were in roman.

'What colour are the pieces of silk?' John asked.

'There is one panel in green, Mr Leary, with a lace-type pattern. The other panel is in red silk and both have a gold embroidered hem. Now please, please all of you. Please let me look at them.'

John was affected by the man's emotion. He looked at Mrs Harrigan, who was disconsolate, and he didn't wonder. 'Just one more test, Mr Ly. Is there anything else you could tell me about the panels?'

Ly closed his eyes, breathed in and out. He looked at John. 'In the top right corner of each panel, my father's and family's initials are stamped, same as on the note.'

'Mrs Harrigan?' John said. 'Could you check for me please? You and Miss Ryan could do so in the dining room.'

'Please let me see, Mr Leary,' Ly pleaded. 'Please.'

'Just be a bit more patient,' John said.

The ladies took the parcel away. Ten minutes later they came back into the room. The panels were draped over Mrs Harrigan's arm. She held them out to Ly. 'Here Mr Ly, please accept these back. They are indeed yours.'

Ly fell to his knees and joined his hands together. His eyes were wet when he held the gleaming pieces of fabric, as though they would fall apart in his hands. 'Thank you.'

'As these were stolen from you,' Mrs Harrigan said, 'I cannot accept any money from you for their return.'

John admired her sense of honour, and her bravery. All her chances of regaining any of her husband's wealth could now be gone.

But Simon Ly shook his head. 'You are very honourable, Mrs Harrigan but you see, Mr Smith paid Wo Fat for my screen in good faith. I offered a great deal to get it back. I cannot accept to get it now for nothing.'

Harrigan paused, torn, and finally said. 'Very well, for my son's sake, I'll accept what my husband paid for them.'

Ly nodded, brought five ten-pound notes from his wallet and gave them to Mrs Harrigan. 'Thank you again, madam.' He carefully folded the screen and placed it in the box. He bowed to John and the ladies.

"I will go now and celebrate with my family the return of this precious item.'

John saw the man out and returned to the drawing room. 'I do feel for you, Mrs Harrigan.'

'Thank you, Mr Leary,' Harrigan said. 'The money is welcomed, of course, yet it's nothing like I expected. It is disappointing and it's made me think that I should bring my expectations to earth. I feel that I should end my quest tonight. There'll be no further need to trouble you.'

John felt suddenly sorry for her. And the idea of searching further in his house was irresistible. 'Please consider this for the next few days, Mrs Harrigan. Don't be hasty.'

'I agree,' Catherine said, and John was thankful for that. 'Some of your husband's wealth could still be here.'

'Ladies,' John said, 'it's been quite a night. I'll see you out. I look forward to seeing you both on Saturday next week, so we can plan a search of this house.'

"I'm so unsure, Mr Leary,' Mrs Harrigan said. 'I still don't—'

'Come, Mary,' Catherine said. 'We'll talk on the way home. Good night, Mr Leary.'

'And good night to both of you. Until next week.'

* * *

On Friday, two days later, John set off to meet the original builder of his house, a Mr Briggs. In Kent Street, John entered the office and after being directed by a clerk, introduced himself and sat down opposite a big man like himself.

'How are you finding it?' Briggs asked.

It was always the same when two builders met. How was the market or how was the timber supply, always questions about building. 'It's not bad,' John said.

Briggs grunted. 'Might be all right for you commercial builders, Mr Leary, but our clients are getting very picky.' He waved to plans on his wall showing a three-storeyed, handsome residence. 'I'm not supplying the bricks for that. No, the client wants to save money and he'll be buying them himself. That leaves me little margin left to play with when I'm providing the rest of the materials.'

John was sympathetic. 'Yes, it's tough, even though we can get bricks cheaper than an off-the-street customer.'

'I know that, and you know that, but try telling that to Mr I-can-save-myself-a-pound-customer.' He smiled. 'Any road, you didn't come here to hear me bitching. What can I do for you?'

'You built a house for the Smiths at Seventy-nine Wolseley Road, Point Piper.'

'I did indeed.'

'I now live in it.'

Briggs smiled again. 'And you like it so much you want me to build another one.'

'Not quite,' John said. 'Now Mr Briggs, you and I know that sometimes, just sometimes,' John smiled, 'we builders cut corners. Or if the architect can't see it, we might not build exactly what's on the plans, to save cost.'

Briggs had a look of wounded pride. 'Me, never.'

John smiled again. 'Perhaps, but tell me, was there anything that Mr Smith asked you at the time that was out of the ordinary? Did he ask for, say, a hidden compartment or something like that?'

Briggs scratched his thinning hair. 'Smith? Smith? I remember him. A good client. Liked the stars, I heard. When was that?'

'Would have been in fifty-two, fifty-three,' John said.

Briggs stood up. 'Give me a moment to look at some diaries.'

Briggs returned minutes later with a thick, hardcover notebook. He sat down. 'Give me a minute Mr Leary, please.'

Briggs turned a few pages with deliberation, then with increasing frequency. John began to lose hope. Briggs did stop at one page and started reading. 'No,' he said to himself. He closed the notebook and looked up at John. 'Nothing in there, I'm afraid. What in particular were you looking for?'

'Was there anything built between the brick walls, or within the floor? A space where something might be placed, with access from the interior?'

'Like a safe, you mean?' Briggs said.

'Yeah, something like that.'

'Not that I know of.' He smiled. 'I'm sorry, Mr Leary.'

John stood up. 'Thanks for your time. If you do think of something, call on me in George Street.' He put out his hand and Briggs shook it.

'That I will. Goodbye, Mr Leary.'

* * *

Another social evening and another chance to talk to Catherine Ryan. John was in the drawing room of the Ryan house in Victoria Street, Potts Point. They had just finished dinner and Mr and Mrs Ryan and the Fordes were playing whist at a nearby table. John and Donald Ryan were talking with Catherine. John was impressed with Donald's prowess as a fencer: he'd never realised the effort, time and technique that was needed in the sport. Catherine assured John that Donald was good at it.

'You should have a try,' Donald said. 'You might like it.'

'I might, although I think my height might be a problem.'

Donald put his whisky down. 'It's not about height, Mr Leary. It's about balance and getting your body centred. It's about—'

'Mr Leary's only being polite,' Catherine said. 'Let's talk about something else. Like the treasure.'

John smiled at her. 'Or just the thought of it, perhaps.'

'Look, Mr Leary,' Donald said. 'Don't think I'm a wet blanket.'

Catherine poked her brother. 'You can be most times.'

He fended her off and barked a laugh. 'But seriously, though,' he said with his voice lowered, 'do you think it's a good thing to keep Mrs Harrigan's hopes alive? After all, even if the money or whatever is found, it's likely to be declared your property. And, if you don't find anything it'll be a double disappointment to her.'

194

John had been considering this for over a month. Perhaps he was being selfish in his quest and was just using that as an excuse to see more of Miss Ryan. What Donald said had a lawyer's clarity to it.

Catherine said. 'I've spoken to Mary about the pros and cons. She said she's given it much thought and she wants to go ahead with the search, even though it may result in nothing.'

John felt oddly grateful to Mrs Harrigan. 'Then we must get cracking. Yesterday I met with Briggs, the original builder of my house.'

Catherine's eyes lit up. 'Did he tell you something? Do you have a moveable wall or something exciting?'

'Nothing, I'm afraid,' John said.

'Did you expect something to come up, Mr Leary?' Donald asked.

'When you build a bespoke house,' John said, 'you can, in the design stage, plan for such places with ease and for very little cost, given their size compared to the whole of the house. It's more expensive to try to put these things in during building. It's really a reasoned guess that Mr Smith would have planned for such a feature, given the wealth he accumulated.'

'But, no hidden crannies in the plans?' Catherine said.

'I'm afraid not,' John replied.

Donald proffered the bottle. 'More whiskey, Mr Leary?'

John glanced at the wall clock, which showed a quarter to nine. He felt he might have overstayed his welcome, but the laughter and wit coming from the card table indicated that its occupants were enjoying themselves. 'Yes, why not. Thank you.'

Catherine was watching him, sipping her tea. 'Where do you think we should start to look?'

'The least likely place first,' John said. 'The attic, under the roof.'

Donald looked puzzled. 'Why is that the least likely?'

'Because gold,' John said, 'has weight—'

'Gold!' Catherine interrupted him. 'Sorry, Mr Leary, but why would you say gold?'

John placed his drink down. 'We have to think of every possibility. We know for a fact that not all the gold Smith found in Bendigo would have been converted into cash. Most would have been melted down into ingots and deposited at his bank. And he might have kept some ingots stored on his own premises. It's not unknown.'

'And the ingots would be heavy,' Donald said.

'Yes, requiring reinforcing timbers to support the weight. We could find them very easily if they were in the attic, though it would be tiring and dirty work.' He smiled at Catherine. 'I wouldn't think of asking you, Miss Ryan, to come scrabbling around there.'

'Nonsense. I can do that!' Catherine said with emphasis.

Donald laughed. 'You run a mile when you see a spider, Cath. You know that.'

Her lips were set in a firm line. 'I will do it. I will.'

John smiled. 'It'll take about a couple of hours to really look the area over. If you are coming, bring Mrs Harrigan. She's already acted as a peon under my floorboards.'

'She won't be able to keep away,' Catherine said.

Don said. 'I think Mrs Harrigan would be willing to join Cath under the roof.'

'I recommend you wear some old clothes, Miss Ryan.'

'Yes, Mr Leary.' She was smiling now and so was John. 'So, when would you like us?'

'Next Saturday afternoon would be a good time, say at two o'clock?'

Don said. 'I won't be able to make it, Mr Leary. I have a fencing tournament.'

'Mrs Harrigan will be with me, Donald,' Catherine said. 'She can chaperone.'

John was thankful again for Catherine's willingness to go exploring with him.

Catherine's brother looked at him keenly. 'Then I think that would be all right,'

Catherine smiled. 'The third of December. We will be there.' She put her cup down. 'So, what's the next area to search after that?'

'You mightn't have to,' Donald said, 'if you find something in the attic.'

'Your brother's right, Miss Ryan.'

Catherine spread her hands. 'Then humour me. Say we find nothing in the attic?'

'Then we look under the house. Another dirty spot but it may be easier to move around,' John said. 'We could do that the following week or at some time to suit you.'

'I certainly could do the tenth of December,' Donald said.

For some reason John and Catherine looked at each other. She looked down as John said, 'That's good. We'll do it that day, then.' John felt emboldened by her willingness to explore his house with him. Suddenly, he stood up and took a place between Catherine and Donald and the whist players. 'Could I have your attention, everybody?'

Maureen and Liam looked at him as did the Ryans, senior. 'I feel privileged that Donald and Miss Ryan have agreed to face the discomfort of treasure-hunting at Golden Hall, with little chance of a result! I would like to offer your whole family a more satisfying occasion at my country house near Bathurst. Would you all like to stay with me there over Christmas?'

John was pleased to see Catherine brighten at this invitation. But it was her parents who would make the decision.

William Ryan looked at his wife, who smiled at him. 'It's a nice thought, thank you Mr Leary,' William Ryan said and paused. 'Can you leave it with us for a few days? We'll certainly let you know as soon as possible.'

Catherine showed disappointment and John tried to hide his. But then the Ryans hadn't said no, outright. So, there might be a chance.

Maureen caught her brother's eye. 'That sounds like a lovely idea, John. Perhaps if the Ryans are busy and want to celebrate just as a family on Christmas Day, there's always the time immediately thereafter.'

Nicely done, John thought.

'Thank you, Mrs Forde,' Mrs Ryan said. 'That certainly gives us food for thought.'

Maureen stood up. 'I think we may leave, if that's all right.'

'But,' William Ryan remonstrated, 'perhaps one more game? A glass of port. Mr Forde?'

'Thank you, no,' Liam said.

Ryan senior smiled and stood as well. 'It's been a grand night. Thank you all for coming.'

As John made his farewells, he caught a smile from Catherine Ryan that raised his spirits. He was already looking forward to the following Saturday.

* * *

That night, as William Ryan was slipping on his nightshirt, he said, 'What about Christmas with the Learys and Fordes?'

'It's rather a bold invitation from a mere acquaintance, don't you think, dear? Mind you, John Leary is acceptable company and it would be novel to go to Bathurst, although it'll be hot there. I just feel that his asking us to go all that way to stay with him is a bit forward.'

Ryan sat on the edge of the bed. 'I was thinking the same. Though I'm sure his hospitality would be tip-top. So, how do we let him down without being rude?'

She didn't answer him for a while. 'There's a consideration. He might be courting Catherine. What do you think of that?'

'Really? Do you mean he has serious feelings for her?'

'Oh William, of course he has. Tonight, he couldn't keep his eyes from her.'

'Hmm.' He got into bed and propped up the pillows. 'I wonder if we should go on letting her see him. What about this treasure hunt or whatever they're calling it?'

'William, he's a pleasant, well-off, eligible man. I've got nothing against him, per se. Although I'm not sure we'd want Catherine marrying a widower with a child. And I have heard rumours that he had an affair with another woman during his marriage to Clarissa McGuire.'

'What?'

'One of Lady Dalkeith's friends let it slip one day. John Leary is known to have had an affair with a hotel worker.'

William clucked. 'That might just be idle gossip, my dear. I hear he was hit very hard when his wife died. His feelings there seemed genuine. A man's past ought not to be used against him, if his present intentions are sound.'

Constance raised her chin. 'There's no getting around the fact that he is a widower and, more complicated than that, he's got a son.'

'That he has, and a bonny boy he is.'

'Yes, he is, but that's what Catherine will inherit if we give this friendship opportunities to lead to marriage. A household that's not her own. Doesn't she deserve better?'

'I don't know about that, dear. Leary's solidly established— I'd say his person and his prospects are what any young lady in Sydney might value. Well, we can forbid her to see him if you like.' William smiled. 'But you know our daughter, dear. Forbid her to do something and she'll latch onto it with both hands.'

Constance kept quiet for a moment, then said thoughtfully. 'His family is respectable, too. I like the Fordes, I really do, and I've seldom seen you laugh and enjoy yourself as much as you did with Mr Forde tonight. So, I think it would be rude to decline Mr Leary's invitation.' She reached out and turned off the gaslight. 'And we should invite Ian McCreadie here more often. He's keen on Catherine and I want her to properly compare him with Mr Leary. Goodnight, my dear.'

William got down under the covers. 'Good night.'

* * *

On Sunday, John was hosting his regular family dinner. It was just about time to sit down and eat and he was enjoying himself. And for one of the few times in the last months he felt relaxed.

He looked around at his family in the Point Piper drawing room. Maureen and Liam were laughing at the pantomime they'd seen the previous week, telling Gerry and Moira all about it. The three children were playing on the floor with a puzzle that lay at Christine's feet. She was pointing out some hints about it to Maureen's daughter, Irene.

John got the nod from Stella. He stood up. 'Right, dinner's ready.'

The Forde children jumped up and ran to their usual places. 'Just sit still,' Maureen said, 'and wait until Grace has been said.'

The Fordes, Christine and the Gleesons took their places. Stella placed Richard in a special high chair that John had made. Stella would feed him at their table.

John said Grace then the roast was served.

'Can we join you in the treasure hunt, Uncle John?' Michael asked, his eyes eager with excitement.

John smiled. 'I think we can get you in our gang for the weekend after next. That weekend, we'll be ferreting in the ground.' John tapped his feet on the floorboards. 'Under here. If we don't find anything, you can help when we search the garden.'

'Wonderful!' Michael said. 'We'll find treasure, just like pirates.'

'What do you think is hidden?' Moira asked. 'Money or gold or something else?'

John was enjoying a juicy lamb slice. 'Who knows?' He glanced at the timber panelling above the sideboard, that reminded him of the note in Chinese. All that effort just to prove that the silks weren't Harrigan's anyway. 'So, we need a structured search. Next Saturday we'll look in the roof space first, and we need to search every nook and cranny.'

'Can we go up there?' Michael said, looking at his mother.

'It's too dangerous for children,' Maureen said. 'Not in the roof.'

'Your mother's right, Michael. Wait until you can help in the garden.'

'But,' Michael said, 'what if you find something in the roof next week and we miss out?'

'We can still have a look-see in the garden, in case there's more to find.'

Michael nodded.

'I got a letter from Kieran this week, John,' Maureen said. 'I'll leave it for you to read.'

Kieran was John's older brother. He and John's father owned a one-hundred-acre farm in county Kildare. John had lived there until he was twenty, when he'd migrated to New South Wales. 'I'll read it later,' he said. 'I hope they are all well.'

Maureen smiled. 'All well.'

'Your brother has his own parish now, Maureen,' Gerry said. 'Alf wrote to me three weeks ago,'

'Wonderful,' John said. His other brother was a devout and compassionate priest. 'I'll pray for him.'

Gerry was halfway through his meal and picked up his glass of Guinness Double Stout. 'I've had my head down these last weeks, John. Tell me, any news on those trusses?'

John knew the first three for the wool store job had been started, but the factory was having teething problems with them. He wasn't about to describe the details of such at his dinner table. 'They're being made now.'

'Any issues?' Gerry said.

'Nothing that they've said can't be fixed.' John replied.

'Gerry was telling me something about them, John,' Liam said. 'They sound monstrous, and the first for Sydney.'

'They are. And with anything that's a first,' he said, and looked at his uncle, 'there'll be issues.'

'What's a truss?' Michael said.

'It's like a giant coat hanger, one of many, that rests on top of the walls of the store and keeps the roof up.' John said.

'Does it have a hook on the top?'

'Only for a while,' John said and smiled, 'so the crane can lift it into place.'

Michael nodded.

'A real wonder,' Liam said. 'John, cut me some more lamb, will you?'

'Liam,' Maureen chastised him. 'You've had way too much already.'

Liam patted his stomach. 'It's a good cut, dear. You have some as well.'

Maureen sighed, then smiled at her brother. 'What can I do with him, John?'

'Give the man more to eat,' John replied. 'That's what you could do.'

She laughed and they started to banter about other family matters, some funny and some not so. Yes, it was a nice and loving gathering. Life was good.

Chapter Eight

Catherine couldn't believe it was finally Saturday. The time had seemed to drag by, as if by magic or guise the sixty minutes of each hour had been replaced by one hundred minutes. It was two in the afternoon, and she was with Mary Harrigan, walking up the path to John Leary's house.

'I'm excited,' Mary said, 'I really am.' She stepped up to the front door and paused. 'Ever since that business with the silk screen, I've wanted to stop this plainly ridiculous quest.' She rapped with the knocker. 'But then I felt, why not? I'm not getting any hopes up, but you never know.'

'No, you don't,' Catherine said. The door opened and Stella Fawcett greeted them. She looked at the bags they were carrying. 'Work clothes?'

'Yes,' Mary said, 'and hats.' She smiled. 'We won't win any fashion prizes at Madame La Roche's.'

Fawcett smiled with her. 'Well, as long as your clothes are light. It's hot outside and it's going to be even hotter up in that roof space. Mr Leary's already there, setting up lanterns. You can get changed in my room.'

Mary and Catherine followed Fawcett to her room, which was upstairs and right beside Richard's.

'I'll let you get organised,' Fawcett said. 'Mary, you know where the manhole is?'

'I certainly do,' Mary said.

'You'll find a ladder's been propped and braced under it so you and Miss Ryan can climb up.' She smiled at them. 'Good luck.'

Ten minutes later, Catherine and Mary were standing near the base of the ladder outside a bedroom on the landing of the first floor.

An odour of mustiness was wafting down from the dark manhole above.

'Hello there,' a voice from above startled them both. 'Come on up,' John said. 'Do you need a hand?'

'We can manage,' Catherine said, and they both put on gloves. Catherine climbed up first. When she got to the top, she felt John's hand hold her forearm and that touch affected her. It was the first time that she'd touched him and known the strength of his grip. Combined with his male scent in the heated space, it was disturbing.

John was holding a lantern in his other hand and there were another two lit at his feet. 'Just get your bearings and adjust to the darkness. Avoid looking directly at the lanterns and you'll find you can see things quite well.'

He hadn't let go of her arm and she was reluctant for him to do so. Lanterns that hung from rafters in the four quadrants of the roof space lit the cobwebs that were wafting in the draught from the manhole. Other timbers were casting their shadows onto the ceiling below. There were two dark circles under the slate, the bases of the pinnacles above.

'Now,' he said, 'look down and you'll see some floorboards fixed over the ceiling joists.'

She did so. They comprised a type of walkway two feet wide.

'Make sure you only step on them. They're nailed to joists. Keep to the boards, because if you walk on the ceiling your boot will go through.'

This was dangerous but thrilling at the same time, Catherine thought. 'I understand.'

'Now please move along the boards so Mrs Harrigan can come up and join us.'

When both women were facing him, he grinned at them. There was a smear of dust on his cheekbone. Catherine would have liked to brush that away. He explained to Mary the same instructions he'd given to her.

'Look around,' he said. 'You can see how the roof is constructed. Every six pairs of rafters are connected to each other by collar ties, for stability. Like a brace.' He walked with an acrobat's confidence and placed his hand on a beam, which was only three and a half feet above the ceiling. 'You'll have to duck under these when you come to them.' He rubbed his dusty hand on his trousers. 'The curved division in the centre is the base of the dome. As you move around it you can see the three fireplace chimneys for the main bedroom, the dining room and the drawing room. If your late husband secreted something up here, Mrs Harrigan, he might well have put it in one of those. If it was gold, then the brickwork would be strong enough to support it.'

'That's a good idea,' Mary said. 'It would have to be in a compartment, so it did not block the chimney itself.'

'Yes, I think the chimneys would be good places to start. Mrs Harrigan, why don't you examine the front bedroom chimney, and we'll look at the other two. I've placed boards down in front of each chimney for safety, but be careful, they are only tacked on, not fully nailed.' He bent down and handed her one of the two spare lanterns. 'Take this and watch where you walk. Are you sure you can keep your balance?'

'I'll be all right, thank you,' she said.

They stood and watched as Mary went forward and noticed the dexterity with which she crawled under the collar ties and made her way to the chimney that took the smoke from the main bedroom fronting Blackburn Cove.

John smiled to himself ironically. After all, she'd had plenty of practice crouching around under his house! 'Are you all right?' he called out.

'I am.'

'Good,' he said.

Catherine was alone with John at last, and excited. She tried to look calm, but her face was flushed, and she chastised herself for that, in case he noticed. However, her condition could be easily explained by the hot space in which she stood.

He was looking at her and she smiled. 'Well, let's get cracking,' she said. 'Lead the way.'

John handed Catherine a lantern and headed towards the northern side of the house. She followed him, mimicking his movements and crouching among the roof timbers, making sure to keep on the walkway. At one point her face touched a cobweb and she nearly dropped the lantern and lost balance, but instead she crouched down and got her composure. John hadn't noticed, and she was glad of that. Her gloves would become dirty and her clothes would look dishevelled but she didn't care. She was close to him. Soon they were alongside the dining room's fireplace. John hooked up his lantern to a rafter and wiped his hands.

The bricks of the chimney, because they were not on display, had no neatness of joint or bed, and there were a few gaps to be seen.

'I'm taller than you,' he said, 'so I'll look through the bricks closer to the roof. You could start around the other face. Use the lantern. Just look for any irregularity in the brickwork, any nooks and crannies.'

'Right,' she said, stepping away, careful that she kept on the boards. She rubbed her gloved hands over each surface as far as she could reach, checking for gaps or voids. They worked away in silence for a few minutes, then Catherine said, 'Tell me a little about yourself.'

His voice came from the other side of the chimney. 'Back in Ireland, I was a carpenter by trade. We had a farm in Kildare. My father thought that coming to New South Wales was better for me than staying in Ireland. I started in New South Wales as a carpenter and got my own business going not too soon after.'

'So, did you really want to emigrate?'

'I did and I didn't. But now I'm glad I did. Sydney has been good to me. I have my company and my family here and most of all, I have my son.'

Which was significant, Catherine felt. Yet, that son's mother had died. She wouldn't broach that subject. 'And your family in Ireland; you must miss them?'

'I'm lucky that Maureen is here. Wait.' She heard sounds of scratching.

'Have you found something?' she asked.

'Maybe … no, just some looseness in the bricks. I've got four brothers in Ireland: Mervin, Alf, Vincent and Kieran. They are all well. Have you found anything there?'

'Nothing, but there may be something above my height. You'll have to do that.'

'When I've finished here, I will. And what about you, Miss Ryan? Were you born here?'

'I was. A cornstalk you're looking at and because of my height, I copped that nickname at school all the time.'

'I like your height.'

'Thank you. Do you have something pointy, an awl maybe? There's some loose mortar here and I may be able to loosen a brick.'

'I have just the thing. Come and get it.'

She found her way to where he was working. He had one leg propped against the brick chimney and the other on a collar tie, and he was reaching up high on the chimney. In that posture, his trousers pulled tight against his haunches. For a moment she was distracted by his athletic strength.

'Here,' he said, leaning over towards her and handing her the tool. It was a chisel, heavier than she expected, with a bevelled edge that wasn't too sharp. 'Keep both hands on it and always strike away from you.'

'Thank you.'

Going back to her position, she continued to work carefully. 'Do all your brothers live on the farm?'

'Vincent and Kieran are on the farm. Mervin's a store manager in Newbridge and Alf's a priest.

'Did your family suffer in the great famine?' She placed the chisel down, unable to loosen the brick.

'We were lucky we didn't depend on crops. My family had cattle and a dairy herd.'

'Your parents are well?'

'My mother passed away four years ago. My Da's still alive.'

'I'm sorry.' She was getting near the bottom of her section of the work. 'There's nothing here I'm afraid.'

Suddenly he stood beside her, startling her. 'Sorry,' he said and smiled. She did too. He was looking at her eyes, then at her lips. Her heart started to beat faster, and something was taking control of her, directing her to kiss him. She hoped he felt the same. This was really making her head spin.

'There's nothing on my side, either,' he said. 'Let's move on.'

The spell was broken and a part of her was disappointed. She said dryly, 'You haven't checked above my head yet.'

Noises and light nearby got their attention. Mary was heading their way, carrying her lantern.

'Mrs Harrigan,' John said, 'don't come over here.' Catherine was excited again. Maybe he wanted them to be alone so he could kiss her. 'Would you mind using your lantern and looking into the corners of the house on your side? The roof comes down near the ceiling at those points and you'll have to crouch, but it's worth checking.'

'Very well,' came back the reply.

'If you find anything, it will be a timber structure,' John called out, 'built on top of the ceiling joists. If you see something like that, yell out and we'll come.'

'All right.'

John looked back at Catherine and smiled. 'We haven't quite finished here, have we?'

She wanted him to kiss her now. She moved closer to him. It was bold of her, but she wasn't thinking about the consequences. His look was now intense, and he seemed to be thinking as she was. Kiss me, please, she thought.

But instead, he raised his lantern and inspected the beds and courses of brickwork above them, where she had not been able to reach. So close, but not looking at her, let alone touching her. She could tell he desired her. How long did she have to wait until he admitted it?

'Let's look at the drawing-room chimney,' he said abruptly.

He picked up the chisel and turned away. She followed him across the walkways to the third chimney. She was surprised: through narrow gaps at their feet she could see daylight.

'We're over the first-floor veranda,' John said.

He repeated the lantern hanging again and they started looking. She was really disappointed. She tried to keep him talking. 'I like your sister. I admire her for the way she thinks and her attitude to women in society, especially working women.'

'But when you get married,' John said, 'you won't continue working.'

'I might,' she said and decided to be frank. 'You told me that your deceased wife worked in commerce?'

he chipping stopped and Catherine waited. Had she been too intrusive?

'She did.'

There was no irregularity in the bricks she was examining. Just like the previous chimney. She took her lantern and, watching where she trod, she had a look in between and on top of the ceiling joists, copying what Mary was doing. After another ten minutes, there appeared to be nothing unusual there. Her clothes were now stuck to her and she was getting very hot.

'Let's stop for a drink.' John said. He came over and passed a water bottle to her and she removed her gloves and slaked her thirst. It was refreshing.

'Mr Leary,' Mary said, her voice coming from the area of the manhole where they had accessed the roof. 'I don't think there's anything here. How about you over there? Anything?'

John had had his fill and recorked the water bottle. 'Nothing our end, I'm afraid.'

'What do you want to do? Keep looking?' Catherine looked at him and they both smiled. She had enjoyed the time with him and finding out a little more about him. She wanted a last chance.

He glanced around. 'Well, none of us has checked in the corner above the back bedrooms. I think we should go there.'

'All right. What's the time now?'

John pulled out his watch and read the time by the light of the lantern. 'Nearly three-thirty.' He turned his head. 'Mrs Harrigan?'

'Yes, Mr Leary.'

'I think you've done enough. Just wait there for us while we check the far corner.'

In her eagerness, Catherine led the way. Suddenly, ahead in the gloom, she could see two flat wooden boxes straddling the ceiling joists above the corner bedroom. 'Mary!' Catherine cried, her voice trembling with excitement. 'Here, come quickly.'

John and Mary scrambled up to her, Mary's eyes gleaming in the light of the lamp. 'Let me see.'

John held the end of his sleeve. 'Let me wipe the dust off these so you two can take the lids off.' He wiped both boxes. Mary removed the cover from one box and, as Catherine held up the lamp, Mary looked at the contents. Her eyes were bright with anticipation, then they dimmed. 'Ah, books. Peter's astronomy books.' Her lip trembled as she took one out. 'He was doing research into Jupiter's moons and wanted to read all about them.'

Her fingers delved deeper into the box.

'Be careful, Mrs Harrigan,' John said, 'there could be spiders.'

Mary put her gloves back on and examined the rest of the twenty or so books. There was no money. No gold.

'Can I look in the other now?' Catherine said.

Mary nodded. 'I suspect there'll be more of the same.'

Catherine lifted the lid of the second box. 'Oh, just fabric. It may have been expensive once, but now …' She removed two pieces and found they smelled of mould. Rummaging beneath them, she found more of the same.

John sighed. 'You're welcome to the books, Mrs Harrigan,' he said. 'I won't have need of them. You could sell them, or Reginald might want some. The fabrics are worthless. I'll dispose of them.'

Mary winced as she stood up. 'Thank you, Mr Leary. I will take the books. Are we finished up here? I think we are.'

He looked at both women. 'We should call it quits. I'll send a man up for the boxes. I'll escort you down the ladder.'

After the women changed and washed up, John saw them off at the front door. His man had put the boxes in Mary's gig. 'I'll see you both next week?'

'We both will be here, Mr Leary,' Mary said, 'and thank you again for letting us look. At least we're eliminating all possible hiding places. We've done the roof,' she smiled, 'bring on the underfloor.' She looked suddenly shy at this last statement, but John pretended not to notice.

'Goodbye, Mr Leary,' Catherine said.

'Have your parents decided to come to Clontarf during the Christmas period?'

'Not as yet,' she said, 'but I'll talk to them. I'd very much like to come.'

* * *

The next day, Sunday, was even hotter. Catherine was with her parents and Ian McCreadie, sitting on rugs in the shade at Parsley Bay, Vaucluse. It was very bushy and the track, which gave them access from South Head Road, was just wide enough to admit a carriage. Her father had told her the bay was named either for a plant that resembled parsley—a scurvy preventative—or more interestingly, it might have been named after a hermit who'd lived in a local cave. It was a popular picnic spot, and two adventurous men were taking a swim from its little beach. Catherine wished she could go swimming as well but that was unheard of. Just to let the cool water flow over her would be grand, especially on a day like today. Their picnic spot was only two bays from Point Piper. Her mood was still spirited from the time spent with John in the roof space the previous day.

'I don't think I could eat another thing,' Ian McCreadie said as he sat back against the trunk of a gum tree, rubbing his stomach. 'I'll just take a rest.'

Catherine suspected that her mother had invited Ian today to give her more of a choice of potential suitors. The Ryans still hadn't agreed to accept John's invitation to go to Clontarf and if they left it any later, they'd be seen as rude. She would have to ask her mother about their decision but did not want to broach this in front of Ian.

'I like to see a man who enjoys his food,' Constance Ryan said. 'It proves that he's in good fettle.'

Ian's tanned face, bright eyes and trim body were signs of a fit and healthy man. Catherine was still attracted to him but not as much as to John Leary. She waved a fly away from her face.

Ian smiled at her and handed her a fern frond. 'This might help.'

'Thank you.' Catherine gazed out onto the harbour through the trees, shimmering in the sunlight. They'd just eaten a cold chicken and salad lunch, refreshed with two bottles of homemade ginger beer. She sipped more of her drink, the ice in her glass melting and cracking.

Ian stood up and stretched. 'I might walk down to the water. Will you join me, Catherine?'

'I thought you wanted to rest?' she said and smiled.

'I could but then I wouldn't be talking to you, would I?'

Catherine looked at her mother, who smiled and nodded. William Ryan was lying down, his faced covered. The sounds coming from under his hat indicated he was fast asleep.

'All right,' she said. Catherine finished her drink. With one hand she took her parasol, and she placed the other over Ian's arm. Coming out from the shade, she put up her parasol.

'How did you spend yesterday?' he asked.

Catherine decided to surprise him. 'Mary and I were at Golden Hall, searching inside Mr Leary's roof space. Mary thinks some of her late husband's money might be hidden there.'

'Dear Lord! Why would you want to do that? With her?'

Catherine noted Ian's attitude to Mary Harrigan: he looked down on her.

Catherine sat down on a sandstone shelf. 'Mary was the original owner of Mr Leary's house. She's an interesting, educated woman who's fallen on hard times through no fault of her own.'

'And what was Mr Leary thinking? Was he with you, up in that roof?'

'Yes,' she said. 'Along with Mary Harrigan.' She smiled, reached out and pressed down the brim of his hat. 'It was all proper, Mr McCreadie. Mr Leary is a gentleman.'

'I'm glad you think so, Miss Ryan. But I've heard rather ungentlemanly things about him.'

'What?' she said, her reaction a mixture of curiosity and worry.

'I was close to Clarissa McGuire before she married John Leary.' He paused and looked down. 'In fact, I asked her to marry me.'

Catherine was surprised at this confidence. 'Ian McCreadie, I had no idea you even knew her.'

Ian looked at the water. 'Well, all she felt for me was friendship. Her love was for Leary.'

Catherine felt sad, realising she was jealous of the late, beautiful Clarissa. 'Yes, everyone said he loved her dearly in return.'

'That's what they say.'

'But you don't believe it?'

'Let's keep going,' he said.

She stood up and they walked along the start of the sandy beach. The tide was going out and some parts of the mud-bottomed harbour were showing.

'One of my closest friends,' he said, 'is in the horse breeding business. He knows Mr Henry Blackett very well, who's a leading horse breaker. Blackett is separated from his wife, who lives in Melbourne. Her name is Beth.' Ian paused and pressed Catherine's forearm. It was a touch that startled her. 'I say this to you honestly, Catherine, and it's not idle gossip. My friend, whom I trust, said that in his cups one night Henry Blackett admitted his wife had an affair with John Leary.'

Catherine's face felt hot.

Ian saw that at once. 'Oh, I'm afraid I've upset you. I'm sorry. It took a lot of courage to tell you, but I feared I must, for your sake.'

He was sweet. 'You haven't offended me. I prefer to know the truth about people.'

More worrying was that she was concerned by what she'd heard. If it was true. She took a breath. 'He was unfaithful, then? Are you sure?'

'I'm only telling you this because you are seeing a lot of him. And I'm not saying it out of jealousy, although I'd like to think that you enjoy my company.'

'So, you're not sure about this?'

He shook his head. 'No.'

'Then let's leave it at that. I'll hear no gossip of anyone.'

'But what if it's—?'

'Ian. I can't be a Catholic only on Sundays. I have strong personal principles. I'll find my own path with Mr Leary, according to my own choice.'

He looked at her for some time. 'Very well.'

They had walked the length of the beach and in that little pocket, the breeze could not be felt. 'Let's walk back,' she said. She didn't want Ian to see that she was upset. John Leary having a son was one thing. John Leary having an adulterous relationship outside marriage was appalling—if it was true, and it might well not be. Ian had stopped and again he touched her forearm.

'Please don't think ill of me about this, Catherine. I'm not the one to spread gossip and I really hope that what Blackett told my friend was false. And I'm not trying to denigrate Mr Leary.'

You might be, she mused, to see off a competitor. But Ian's face looked earnest and sincere. 'I appreciate that you only told me because of our friendship.'

He sighed. 'Thank you.'

'And let's keep this between ourselves,' she said. 'If my parents believe the gossip about Mr Leary, I'll not be able to continue the search of his house.'

He seemed to be struggling with her request but then he nodded. She was relieved.

'Now,' he said, 'will you continue to see Mr Leary at Point Piper?'

Right now, she was just trying to keep calm. 'I'm accompanying Mary Harrigan in her quest, that's all. Once we've established that there's no gold or money, I won't have reason to visit the house.' She was going to say that she wouldn't see Mr Leary at all, but she didn't. And she knew why: she was not going to examine his past failings, whatever they might have been. It was what he showed to her now and in the future that counted. Her Catholic virtues of forgiveness and non-judgment also informed her view.

'I see. Then I think that's wise. Now, on a more pleasant note, there's a musical show next Friday at the Royal Victoria. Would you like to come with me?'

Her mind was still in a turmoil over John Leary and she had to concentrate on what Ian was saying. 'If my parents approve, I'd like to come.'

He smiled and she knew that he was pleased. 'Excellent.'

'Only if my parents say it's all right,' she said.

'Let's ask them now.'

On the way back to their picnic spot, she was thinking about next Saturday and John Leary. Don said he would be available as chaperone. Perhaps it was best that he be with her. Yes, she would see Mr Leary again but from now on she would protect herself. Her mind would need to rule her heart and she would try to determine, if she could, what real stuff John Leary was made from.

* * *

The next day the family was celebrating Richard's fourth birthday at Point Piper. It was being held outside and John had left work early to spend the afternoon with his son.

'Your turn, Michael,' John said and helped his eight-year-old nephew mount a pony.

'I can use the reins, Uncle John,' Michael said. 'I'll be all right.'

John glanced at his sister, who was talking with his mother-in-law. She nodded and smiled.

'All right, you can, but just keep at a steady walk around the yard.'

'Come on, boy,' Michael said and the pony moved off. John went back to his plate and took another bite of his cake. Reginald was

215

playing with Richard and Irene was with another little friend. They were both looking at Michael on the pony. The afternoon was hot and early summer had come with a blaze.

It had been a blistering day when Richard had been born, and his entry into the world had happened at number seventy-three, at Christine's house down the road. Clarissa's face had been tired and drawn from her ordeal, but her eyes had shone at her delight. He had loved her so at that moment.

'Michael seems to like the pony,' Maureen said, standing near him. She threaded an arm though his own.

'He does.'

'You seemed a mile away just then,' she said. 'Share your thoughts?'

'About Clarissa and the day Richard came to us.'

She squeezed his arm. 'And what a wonderful day that was.' She paused. 'There'll be other days like that John in the future. There will.'

He smiled down at her. 'You think?'

'I know there will. How did you go with Catherine Ryan on Saturday?'

Michael's pony came up to them and nuzzled John's stomach. John stroked his head. 'It was Mrs Harrigan who was looking for the money, Maureen. Miss Ryan just helped out.'

His sister looked innocent. 'So, how did you fare? Any sign of the lost treasure?'

'No, just some old books and fabrics.' John helped Michael down from the horse. 'Reggie!' he called out. 'Your turn!' Reginald left his mates and came up to the pony, placed a boot in the stirrup and mounted.

'Thank you. Mr Leary. I'll be all right.'

'I'm sure you will.' John patted the pony's flank and it moved off. 'Miss Ryan learned a thing or two about me.'

'All good, I'm sure.'

'All good, Maureen. She says she likes you too.'

'And I like her. Did you speak alone together?'

'Between us scratching around like navvies, yes we did. Come on, let's organise a game for the children. What shall we play?'

'Hide and seek is best with a prize for the winner,' she said and looked over at Richard, who was trying to catch a ball thrown by Michael. 'Richard should be the winner, John. After all it's his day.'

'Good idea. Come on.'

John watched Maureen and Stella organise the game. Soon there were squeals of delight and laughter as all the children joined in. He thought again about his time with Catherine. There was a moment when he might have kissed her. He had wanted to. In fact, her eyes had been bright as well and her breathing had been uneven. Perhaps like him she had wanted to be kissed or even to kiss him. It was all new to him, after so many months, but for some reason that he couldn't define to himself, the moment had passed, and they had continued with their search.

Next Saturday they'd be under the house and he wanted to find out more about her. She liked cooking and eating but what books did she like to read? What plays made her laugh? What were her thoughts on history and how events had influenced it? All these things he felt she would have an interest in and that's what made his thoughts about her more intriguing.

They were interrupted by the applause, and a bright-eyed Richard held up his trophy, a one-foot-high timber figure of a knight that John had carved and painted. The metal armour and sword that encased the knight had been made by a metal forger friend of John's. It was another birthday present for his lad.

John walked up to Richard, picked him up and hugged him. 'Happy birthday, my boy, and many more to come.' Richard grinned, accepted his father's affection and then wriggled to be free. John set him down and he joined his friends and cousins.

Maureen smiled at him. Yes, life was good.

* * *

On the Tuesday after Richard's party, John entered his office in town. He found Sean sitting opposite his desk with a drawing and file of papers in front of him. Sean's face didn't look happy.

'The trusses,' Sean said. 'There's problems.'

John sat down opposite his partner. There had to be teething problems with anything that was this new and untested; John accepted that.

'Yesterday afternoon,' Sean said, 'I went with Ed Larkin to Sullivans. Ed got a note from them that morning to meet them. We did and there's trouble, big trouble.'

Sean wasn't known to exaggerate. 'Go on,' John said.

'The first three trusses have been made to the wrong dimensions.'

'What?' John was shocked.

'Yeah, I found that hard to take as well. The foreman, a man called Forrester, has been sacked, but that doesn't help us.' Sean paused. 'The trusses are one foot higher and one foot longer than they should have been,'

'Christ on his Cross.'

'The good news is that they'll fix them. The bad news is we'll—'

'Be delayed, I know. How long?'

'Four weeks.'

John sat back. This was very serious. The trusses were critical to the project. Without their being installed to Learys program, they could not complete the roof and then the internal finishes.

'How did Sullivans explain it?'

Sean sat back. 'The jigs were set to the wrong size. Because the trusses are seventy-five feet long, one foot longer probably wasn't picked up. But it's the height of the trusses. One foot higher, eleven feet! Surely that must have stuck out like the proverbial?'

'You'd think so.'

Sean shook his head. 'And all the internal framing that makes up each truss is now the wrong size. All got to be redone.'

'That error sounds so bad,' John said, 'you'd have to think it was deliberate.'

'Deliberate or not, we're in a bind. We've got penalties to pay if we're late.'

'I know, I know, Sean.' John was thinking about a way out of this. In the end, if they demanded the same amount of penalties from the timber merchants, Learys might not be out of pocket. 'Did we get the same penalties back-to-back with Sullivans?'

'We did,' Sean said, 'but it's our reputation that'll be hit. The trusses were a big risk and our competition will be laughing at us.'

They would be. 'It's the clients who worry me, Sean. They won't be in a hurry to sling us another job after this turn-up.'

Sean looked down. Like all true tradesmen, John and Sean prided themselves on making sure every detail was checked, twice, before any cutting or sawing was done. On one look, it was very sloppy work, on the other ...

'Do you think someone's fiddled with them?' Sean asked, as if reading John's thoughts.

'Maybe.' John exhaled. 'Get Ed to camp out at Sullivans for a week or two. I want him sweating over the new trusses like a scientist with a specimen under a microscope. Sullivans had better not complain about that, otherwise they'll have me to deal with.'

'Right,' Sean said. He stood up to leave.

'And Sean,' John said, 'tell our foreman to keep his mouth shut about this. I want Sullivans to do the same. They should, because they ought to be hanging their heads in shame, allowing this to happen. I don't want our other clients knowing too much.'

'That I'll do,' Sean said and left John's office.

Mrs Dawes brought in John's morning cup of tea and the newspapers.

'Thank you,' he said. He thought suddenly of William Ryan, who was a shareholder on the wool store. It would do no good trying to keep Ryan in the dark: the work on the wool store would be delayed because of this disaster, the architects would get to know about it at once and their clients straight thereafter.

* * *

December had advanced eight days and contractor Harry Shelby was waiting in the anteroom of wool broker William Ryan.

Shelby's good mood was heightened. Coleman had called at his home the previous night to tell him that there was now a problem with the first three Learys trusses. Good. The plan had worked, Coleman had done his magic and now Learys were delayed. All Sydney would know. The Wattle Street wool store was a prominent project and Learys would be delayed at least a fortnight if not a month. Good.

Now, he had a meeting with Mr William Ryan about the house extension he was planning. The wool broker might just be interested in a progress report on his big job and Shelby would tell him about John Leary's performance.

'Mr Ryan will see you now,' Mrs Brookes said.

Harry Shelby thanked the wool broker's secretary and entered a meeting room where Mr Ryan was seated. In front of the wool broker were a file of papers and a set of plans for an extension to Mr Ryan's house in Victoria Street Potts Point.

Ryan stood up and gestured to the chair in front of him. 'Mr Shelby, please sit down.'

'Thank you, Mr Ryan,' Shelby replied.

Ryan opened the file. 'The last time we met in May this year, you gave me an estimate of what you think this extension could cost.'

It would be a piddling job and hardly in Shelby's line. He'd spent some time on preparing his quote, probably a bit too much. But a client, or a potential one, was still a client. 'I did.'

'Then you might like to see what my architects are proposing and give me your valued opinion of whether I can afford it.'

'Gladly. Are these the latest plans?'

Ryan turned around the sketches and Shelby looked at them. The last time he'd seen something like this, Learys had not been part of Mr Ryan's life. Shelby had hoped that by working with Ryan on his house extension he might sway the broker into giving him favoured treatment on the wool-store bid. Well, that didn't happen, but Shelby might now be able to insert himself back into favour, with one of the wool store's shareholders at least. 'You've extended the plan to the east but not as far as the new stables.'

'Yes, but we've reduced the north-south direction as well, to compensate.'

'And the ceiling height's increased,' Shelby said, noting the cross-section.

'We wanted the ceiling in the new part to match the height of the existing house.'

Shelby nodded. 'And there's an additional bathroom that will definitely put your costs up.'

'We need it, Mr Shelby,' Ryan said.

Shelby spent some moments looking at the latest design. It was all very straightforward, but he wanted to give this man the impression of his own professional acumen. What he was really thinking about was how to sow seeds of doubt with Mr Ryan about John Leary, but without it sounding like gossip-peddling or sour grapes from a rival. 'Can I take these,' he said, 'and work up a new indication of cost?'

'How long would that take?'

'A couple of days at the most,' Shelby said. Ryan looked irritated and Shelby was irked in return. This moment happened all the time with clients! They would spend weeks, sometimes months, making decisions, then their architects would spend even more time preparing the drawings. And then, for reasons that he couldn't fathom, they would object when the builder needed further time to examine all these new details and adjust the original estimate! He said evenly, 'I'll be as quick as I can.'

'Very well,' Ryan said, somewhat mollified.

Shelby packed the documents away in his satchel. 'How is your new project going? The wool store.'

Ryan spread his hands. 'From my architect's latest report, fairly well.'

'I passed the site the other day and noted the brickwork to the outside walls. Mr Leary's workers have done a good job on that.'

Ryan nodded and pulled out his watch. 'I'm afraid I'll have to go shortly, Mr Shelby. Another meeting.'

'That's all right. I recall that Learys were building new trusses to span the warehouse.'

Ryan smiled. 'They are, Mr Shelby. In fact, they're so unique my architect's set up a factory inspection for me to see them.' He referred to his diary. 'It's on the twenty-second of this month.'

Shelby was disappointed—he'd hoped the inspection would be earlier. The sooner Ryan found out about the error, the better for Harry Shelby. 'I hope all is quite well there?'

Ryan gave him a quizzical look. 'You think there might be issues?'

'Like all things new, Mr Ryan, there are always things that go wrong, but Sullivans are a reputable company. I'd hate to think anything would go wrong with their work.'

'Of course. I'll see you out.'

* * *

For a change, the evening was cool and Catherine was glad as she accompanied her parents and Ian into the foyer of the Royal Victoria Theatre in Pitt Street. Over the past week she'd been thinking about John Leary. Despite her Catholic upbringing, one part of her nature was denying his past affair happened. The other was prepared to acknowledge that it might have, and perhaps forgiving him. She felt uncomfortable because her conscience hadn't formed a final opinion.

Her parents had agreed to go to Clontarf on the day after Boxing Day. Tomorrow was Saturday and she'd be in Mr Leary's company again at Golden Hall. But if it wasn't for supporting Mary in her vain quest she was tempted not to go, since she still hadn't made up her mind about John, and she wouldn't have Donald as a chaperone— there was a fencing match he had to attend.

'It should be a good night,' Ian McCreadie said as they took their seats at the theatre.

'The Backus Minstrels are from California and they're proving very popular.'

'Yes,' she said, 'so I've heard.'

The performance began, and soon the melodies and lyrics of the band were enlivening her and making her feel good. Ian was smiling too and his foot tapped out the beat. He was a nice man and she knew he liked her, a lot. Her parents favoured him also, as did Donald.

During the intermission, Ian stood with her while her parents were talking to friends.

'I'd like to take you sailing, Catherine,' Ian said. 'This Sunday.'

That would be a distraction. 'I'd love to come.'

His eyes brightened. 'I'm glad. I mentioned it to your parents when I came this evening. I hope you don't mind.'

'Of course not.'

'They agreed,' he said. 'We can sail out from Rose Bay. I'll collect you at your house. Say ten in the morning?'

'I'll go to eight o'clock mass.'

'Of course. It'll be a little wet and windy out there, so please wear something that will take a bit of punishment.'

'If I come in anything too practical I'll look a fright,' she said.

He smiled. 'You'd look acceptable clothed in a jute bag.'

She smiled also. 'I don't think so.'

'You would.'

He was looking at her in a keen way and she was glad that they'd be on an excursion together. In a boat, how thrilling!

Her father came up to them. 'The show's starting again.'

* * *

Next day, Mary Harrigan was under her former house with John Leary and Catherine Ryan. The three of them crawled through the access door and settled with their lanterns against the base of the central staircase, getting used to the dust, smell and darkness. It was a blessing that it was cooler here than in the roof space, where they'd been the week before.

'Right,' Mr Leary said. 'Where to start?'

Mary concentrated. 'Perhaps we could split up and search individually.'

'Perhaps that way,' Catherine said, looking at Mr Leary, 'we'll cover more ground more quickly.'

Mary saw a look of disappointment on Mr Leary's face. It was just for a fraction, then he seemed to force a smile.

'Of course. Mrs Harrigan, under the study for you, Miss Ryan the drawing room, and I'll tackle the rear.'

As Mary crouched and made her way in the cool darkness, she thought about Catherine's interest in Mr Leary. Up in the roof, Catherine had spent most of the afternoon in his company and they had to all appearances been more than polite to each other. So why did Catherine want to be by herself today?

Catherine scrambled over to her starting place under the drawing room. It was the right thing to do if she wanted to keep a distance from him, although she had had a moment of doubt when she'd seen his reaction. Keeping away from him here would show that her interest in him had changed somewhat. Getting out her trowel, she adjusted her gloves and started to fossick.

The material in which she worked was a combination of sandy loam and hard-packed clumps of dirt. While she was digging, she mused. She was still troubled about the hearsay concerning his infidelity, but she should at least give him the benefit of the doubt.

After thirty perspiring minutes she'd covered a fair area of ground. She was startled when, suddenly, John was behind her.

'Find anything?' he said.

She sat back on her haunches and removed her gloves. 'Nothing, I'm afraid.'

She accepted the water bottle he offered her. 'How about you?'

'Nothing. You seemed to prefer not working with me today.' He looked worried. 'Have I done anything to offend you?'

He looked genuinely concerned and she would have liked to give him an explanation. But how could she confront him about his supposed infidelity? He might have done something terribly wrong while married to Clarissa Leary, but she had no evidence of it. 'No. I just thought it would be quicker if we spread out.'

He looked relieved. 'Good. I'll duck over and see how Mrs Harrigan is doing.'

She watched him go with mixed feelings. She felt his attraction so strongly when he was near.

The following morning, Catherine stood at Rose Bay shielding her eyes from the December sun. In the heat, and with her bare feet welcoming the sand, she scanned the bay and spotted Ian McCreadie's sailing skiff. It had just turned eleven o'clock, and the north-easterly breeze was now picking up, assisting the skiff as it made its way to shore. Glancing back, she waved to her parents, who were seated on the grass in the shade. Self-consciousness about the clothes she had chosen for the outing was outweighed by her anticipation. Ian waved to her, pulled up the centre board, let go the main sheet and eased the boat onto the sand. Catherine ran to it.

He leaped out into the shallow water and held onto the transom. 'Can you climb aboard?'

Placing her bottom on the gunwale, she swung her wet feet on board and sat on the forward thwart, next to the mast.

'Well done,' he said. 'Take that rope attached to the jib—that's the front sail—and pull it tight when I tell you.' He smiled. 'Can you do that?'

She smiled as well, excitement filling her. 'I can.'

As she did that, she watched him push them afloat and climb on board. He let the centre board drop below the boat.

'Now, pull on that rope,' he said, while he did the same with the mainsail.

As she did so the boat suddenly heeled a bit, and she shifted, to keep her balance.

He pointed. 'Now, run the rope around that cleat. It will make it easier to control.'

As she did so, the jib filled with the wind, the boat heeled some more, and she held onto the mast as the skiff headed towards the Point Piper headland.

'We can't sail directly into the wind,' he said, looking at a pennant attached to the top of the mast. 'We have to go at angles to it. It's called tacking.'

She was thrilled as the craft skimmed along, at times sending up a refreshing mist of seawater. There was some water in the bottom of the boat but she didn't mind her feet getting wet. 'When you came onto the beach—'

He cupped his ear. 'Speak up!'

She raised her voice. 'When you came onto the beach, the wind was behind you.'

He nodded.

'So, you sailed in front of the wind to come in to the sand. Can't you do the reverse?'

'That's a good question, Miss Ryan. It's the physics that kills it.' He grinned. 'Do you want to go faster before we tack again?'

She did. 'Yes, please.'

'Right, when we do, you'll have to sit closer to me on the right side of the boat, the starboard side, so your weight and mine will balance the wind on the sails. Also, the boat will lift out of the water a bit. Don't worry about that.' He grinned. 'Ready?'

She nodded, excited at what was to come.

'When I say the word, take more strain on the rope on the cleat. We need to tighten the sails to make the boat go faster.'

Ian steadied the tiller with his left knee and tightened the mainsail. 'Now!' he said.

She pulled with all her strength on the rope that controlled the jib. The boat straight away leaned more and she panicked just for a moment, then she got control.

'Up on the side with you,' he said.

She held onto the rope and sat on the gunwale. Ian was doing the same but towards the stern. The boat lifted and Catherine was splashed as the skiff hit a wave. She laughed and grinned at Ian, who smiled as well. It was a wonderful absorbing feeling as the boat picked up speed and shot across the blue water.

After a little time, Ian got her attention again. 'Slacken the rope off a little, we have to go about.' She did that and the boat slowed. 'See a cleat on the other side?'

'Yes,' she said.

'When I bring the boat around, you'll need to detach that rope from the cleat and pull the sail to the other side so the wind is on our left side.'

'The port side,' she said.

'That's it. I'll be doing the same to the main. Right, here we go.'

It was exciting just to be able to do things that a man would do in her place. Yes, a man would be stronger in the physical pulling and leaning but she was doing it anyhow and she was intrigued to watch how the boat behaved in a similar way with the new direction. Her arms ached a little but she'd not tell Ian that, too excited and occupied with what she was doing.

At one moment she glanced at the shore and wondered how her parents were going and whether they were concerned about her. Then she looked at Ian's shoulders and arms, as his muscles and tendons changed shape, pulling and reefing. It was nice to see. They joked at times about how she looked—tousled by the wind—and she laughed at herself. Ian's frank admiration of her was also attractive. She liked him. The prospect of going to John Leary's Bathurst property just after New Year took on a new aspect. Were her parents intending to impress on John that she had an interest in Ian McCreadie?

Being in the country and perhaps alone with John at times, how would she be able to manage such a complicated situation?

Chapter Nine

John arrived at the meeting room early and tried to concentrate on the board papers, but he was still thinking of Catherine Ryan. For the last three days he'd been considering her changed demeanour. On the first search, up in his roof space, she'd parried and laughed with him and he felt she was very much at ease with him. Then just last Saturday, she was a different person. It had been dramatic. Even when she'd reassured him that he hadn't done anything wrong, he hadn't been convinced. Something was amiss and he wanted to get her alone again, somehow, and see what was wrong. He wanted to solve it and be in her good books again.

'Good morning, John,' Christine said coming into the room. Sean followed her and closed the door behind him.

They approved the previous minutes and read the reports, then John prepared to tell his fellow directors some good news. 'The trusses,' he said.

'Ah, yes,' Christine said. 'I was going to ask about them.'

John smiled. 'Sullivans have capitulated. They've agreed to meet the existing time frame by putting on more staff and working night shifts.'

'That's encouraging,' she said.

'At least they've agreed,' Sean said, leaning back. 'But the proof of the pudding's still to come—if they remake the trusses in a hurry, how good will they be?' He paused. 'It will set them back a quid.'

'It will,' John said, 'but they need to make serious amends to us for their error, so I gave them no choice.'

Sean nodded. 'Good. Is that all the business we have? Are we finished?'

John looked at his papers. 'We are.'

'Then how's the treasure hunt going?' Sean said.

'Yes, John,' Christine said, her face was interested too. 'Tell us.'

John looked at them in turn. 'Nothing yet, I'm afraid. Not a speck of gold in either attic or underfloor.' He shook his head. 'We're running out of places, and it looks like a waste of time.'

'Maybe,' Christine said standing up. 'Maybe. Still, it keeps you busy, John. And what about Richard and Michael? Have they been good little helpers?'

'I'm only involving the children once we get into the garden.'

She got up, nodded to Sean and waved at John as she left the room. 'Good hunting.'

Sean remained seated. 'You sure about Sullivans doing the right thing?'

'I am. Come on, we've got things to do and jobs to run.'

Sean got up. 'Right.'

As John watched him go, he thought again about the timber merchants and those trusses. Yes, of course they'd do the right thing. Why shouldn't they?

* * *

It was hot, hotter than a normal late December day for the NSW hinterland, and the southerly buster was tardy in coming. The oven-like wind blowing from the north-west was stripping leaves off the gums, flying them all over, some landing in the fast-flowing Macquarie River. In a smooth backwater, Michael and Irene were splashing and laughing.

Richard was on the bank, standing beside John. 'More dirt, Father.'

'Right,' John said. He dug his spade into the muddy loam and scooped it into the bucket. Richard took it and emptied it onto the walls of the fort he was building. The mud refused to stand upright and Richard frowned.

'Not like home,' he said. 'We have wood for fort there.'

'We do,' John replied, 'but we can make believe.' He wiped the perspiration from his brow. Richard kept on working and John glanced at the Ryans, who were sitting in the shade talking to Maureen and Liam. It was coming to the second day of the stay at Clontarf and John was concerned: Catherine was avoiding him. She made sure they were never alone together, and her manner was distant. There was no way he could find out what was wrong unless he could get her alone somehow.

'Well,' Stella said, coming up beside them and looking down at her charge. 'That's a good job you've done, Master Richard.'

Richard pulled a face. 'Do I have to go in?'

Stella looked at John, who nodded. 'It's time for your bath and you need one,' he said. John dabbed at the mud and tapped Richard's nose, leaving a mark. Richard giggled.

'Right,' Stella said talking his hand. 'Let's get you cleaned up.'

John watched them go and washed his hands in the water before walking up to his guests. As he approached them, his cheek felt the coolness of a wind change and he realised the southerly was here. It picked up speed and Maureen stood up and came down to her children in the water.

'Come in,' she said. 'Time to get dry.'

They climbed up the bank and dried themselves with towels. Maureen helped them dress and sent them back to the house. She turned to John. 'Are you going down to the traps?'

The traps were woven baskets placed underwater about one hundred yards downriver, set to catch Murray Cod and Yellowbelly.

'I am,' he said.

'Why don't you invite Catherine to go with you?' She smiled. 'I'll keep the Ryans busy.'

'Still playing Cupid?' he said ironically, though he was happy at her suggestion.

'Got a better idea, brother?'

He smiled. 'Yours is a good one. Come on.' He went and picked up a canvas bag that he'd left under a tree.

The Ryans looked ready to go back to the house and take Catherine with them, but Maureen diverted them with a question. 'Would you like to see the fish traps?'

William Ryan stood up. His face was red and he was still perspiring from the heat. 'Traps?'

'Yes,' Maureen replied and pointed downstream. 'They're tethered just down there among the reeds. It takes a bit of work to get at them but it's worthwhile.'

'Thank you, Mrs Forde,' he said, 'but no. Perhaps my wife and Catherine might like to see them.'

'I'd like to see them,' Catherine said. She turned to her mother. 'Will you come?'

Her mother laughed. 'Dear me, no. You go with Mrs Forde.'

'Right,' Maureen said. 'Then let's go.'

John wanted to be alone with Catherine, not have his sister with him. But as Maureen walked past him, she winked at him.

They set off. When they were halfway there, Maureen said, 'John, would you accompany Catherine the rest of the way? I've just remembered I have to give Michael his medicine.'

Catherine seemed to hesitate. 'Are you sure? We can do it another time.'

'No, no, don't let me deprive you. You go with John.'

Catherine looked at John. She hesitated, then said without enthusiasm, 'All right.'

The pair set off and John waited to see whether she'd say anything. He'd almost given up when she posed a question, without looking at him.

'Mr Leary, can I ask about your late wife, or is that too personal?'

Her forthrightness startled him but it was characteristic of her. He said at once, 'What would you like to know?'

She said hesitantly, 'I believe she had firm ideas, and thought that ladies should work if they wished to?'

John shooed a fly away from his cheek and smiled. 'Clarissa did. She did indeed.'

'And she worked in a company, your father's, I understand.'

'Yes,' he said, 'and she did a good job.'

She stopped. 'What do you mean by "good"?'

John spread his hands out. 'Competent, diligent, assertive. All things or attributes that a man needs in the same work. Clarissa had the accounts in order, controlled the cash flow, limited the stock and had debtors pay on time.'

Catherine nodded and set off again. 'That's very interesting. And how did the men take that?'

'Not very well at first.' He smiled and Catherine did too. 'She met a lot of resistance.'

'But she was the boss's daughter. That would have helped. They had to obey her.'

John stopped at a copse of trees that grew close to the banks. There were rushes at its base. 'Here we are.' He put down the bag and broke off a staff-length of branch from a fallen gum. 'Follow me,' he said, and stepped into the undergrowth. As she did so, he thrashed about ahead of him with the stick. 'Snakes come down here to drink. They—'

Her voice sounded a pitch higher. 'Snakes?'

He grinned. 'They're more scared of you than you think.'

He found a rope attached to a peg in the ground, put the stick down and used both hands to pull on a rope. After a short time, a woven tapered basket about a yard long emerged from the reeds. He let the water drain out, pulled it closer to Catherine and removed the toggle securing the lid. 'See?'

She looked inside at three good-sized cod thrashing about. 'Goodness!'

'Fresh for dinner tonight.' He smiled. 'I'll check the other two traps.' Both were empty and the small fish baits in them were untouched. He went to his bag and brought out a smaller cotton bag and a hessian bag. After rebaiting the single trap and transferring the fish from the trap into the hessian bag, he washed his hands and rejoined her.

'Right, let's head back.' He carried both bags and glanced up the riverbank as they walked. The wind was freshening around them but it was still pleasant to be by her side and to know the rest of their party would have reached the house. 'You have a point about the men surrounding Clarissa. But her father was an exception. He had no trouble giving her tasks that he might have given to his son, if he'd had one.' John thought about David and the ghost of guilt visited him. David McGuire, after getting to know John, had loved him as the son he'd never had. But John had let him down. 'You see, in his businesses, David wanted results. And he had an instinct that Clarissa could get them.'

'That was very unusual, for him to think that.'

'It was. He had his own logic, and he was prepared to think differently about women's customary roles if it would benefit his affairs.'

'He expected his daughter to stay single while she worked with him?'

'Oh no, of course not. He had traditional views on women as wives, nurturers and mothers. But he judged individuals by their nature and their skills, and he knew his own daughter and what she could do. He was tough: I'm sure that if Clarissa hadn't come up to par in her job, she would've been given short shrift.'

'How interesting.' She stopped and turned to him. 'And your marriage, if I may ask—was it affected by the fact that Clarissa worked outside the home?'

Her look was frank, and it was a very forward question again, but he liked that about her and decided to answer it. They were nearly back at the homestead. 'She did manage it well. She made sure Richard was well looked after at all times. Fawcett was very reliable in that respect, and she's always loved Richard. I had no hesitation in keeping her on as housekeeper after Clarissa died.' He looked away and had a flash of the good times that he and Clarissa had had together.

'I'm sorry if this upsets you,' she said. 'Please forgive my inquisitiveness.'

He nodded and smiled. 'You're forgiven.'

During the evening meal that night, Catherine was again having mixed feelings about John Leary. He had been a gracious host these last two days, charming and attentive to her. That was attractive. And he had been tolerant with her, despite her deliberate attempt to be polite and no more.

The dinner was a lively affair, and she would look at him from time to time. Fortunately, she was still able to concentrate on what others were saying, and join in the laughter of Mrs Forde's two children as they shared a joke about their father's gardening prowess.

'Delicious meal, John,' Maureen said as she placed her cutlery down. 'The fish was cooked to perfection.'

'Our cook, once again,' John said and smiled. 'Another piece for you, Miss Ryan?'

His eyes were animated and again she felt the tug of attraction. 'Dear me, Mr Leary, no. But it was tasty.'

The plates were collected and they awaited their desserts. With her baked apple pie and cream in front of her, Catherine again tried to think logically and with a cold edge. If John Leary had been unfaithful once, and to a woman he obviously loved, would he stray twice? The answer was a worrying: probably yes. But she had no proof of past peccadillos and, in a way, she did not want to find any.

Tucking into her dessert, she looked at Richard sitting at John's left and Stella Fawcett by his side. If she was going to consider marrying John Leary, her future relationship with Richard was her main challenge. Would she be able to get close to Richard? She liked him, but would the little boy ever see her as a mother?

Stella looked right at her then and there seemed in her eyes a strong look, a protective one. Stella had been a stand-in mother to Richard these past two years. Catherine smiled at her but felt nervous in her heart. Yes, the housekeeper would protect Richard as though he were her own, and might be jealous of her relationship with him.

Catherine looked down at the remainder of her sweet and another thought struck her—hard. It was only a relatively short time since Clarissa's death. John might not have fully got over her. His emotions might not be touched by Catherine as a lover—he might only want her as a substitute mother for Richard. That, she was not going to be.

She wanted a passionate partnership or none at all. How much time needed to pass before John Leary would love her for herself and not as a substitute for Clarissa?

She couldn't help thinking of Ian McCreadie, who had no previous marriage, no children, no scandalous past. So why was she so keen to keep Leary in her sights?

'I was talking to your parents before dinner,' Maureen said, 'and they have agreed to have a return match of whist at our place Sunday eighth of January. The first game of the New Year. Would you care to join us?'

Still haunted by her thoughts Catherine smiled at Maureen but said, 'Thank you, no. I have another engagement.'

Maureen looked disappointed. 'Another time perhaps?'

'Perhaps,' Catherine replied and looked at her parents, who had their eyes down. Everyone at the table seemed aware of her cool attitude towards John Leary. Perhaps that was a good thing. It might make John work harder to win her over, get him to do the hard yards.

'I hope so,' Maureen said, deflated.

* * *

On Sunday night in the first week of January, John finished reading to Richard. As his son closed his eyes, John turned off the gaslight beside the bed. He didn't move but sat thinking in the darkness. This afternoon, he'd been his polite best with the Fordes and Ryans and played a few hands at the table. But his mind and heart weren't there because Catherine wasn't there. At times Maureen would glance at him, and her concerned look told John that he wasn't himself.

He missed Catherine and he was in a quandary as to why she had changed. Going over their time spent together since that happy afternoon up in the roof, just over a month ago, hadn't brought to light anything that might have put her off him. Yet something had. The change in her demeanour had been swift. Her detachment had not disappeared at Clontarf, either.

He realised that his feelings for her were deep. Not quite so deep, yet, as the love that he had had for Clarissa, but he knew that would come. His uncle Gerry hadn't found love again until he was in his forties. But then, Gerry hadn't had children to complicate the issue. Was Richard the problem? Was Catherine slipping away because she felt she couldn't be a mother to Richard? But if so, would she tell him?

He shook his head. Catherine was a single girl who did not owe him anything and was under no obligation to him, so why should she tell him why she *wasn't* interested in him? Still, just to end the frustration, he wanted to know. Getting up from the bed, he closed the bedroom door and went downstairs.

Gerry and Moira were settled in the drawing room. His uncle was always direct with him, telling him home truths without invitation. John had to talk to another man about his worries. His sister was available, sure, but tonight John wanted a man's perspective.

Gerry looked up at him and smiled. 'The boy down?'

'In the land of nod.'

Moira smiled. 'God bless his little heart.'

John poured two Jamesons from the drinks trolley and paused. 'Can I talk to you for a moment, uncle? In the study?'

Gerry stood up and said to Moira, 'Excuse us, my dear.'

'Of course.'

Upstairs, seated in two chairs with the door closed and their drinks in front of them, John said. 'I want to talk to you about Miss Catherine Ryan.'

Gerry nodded. 'I can see that you have a liking for the young lady.'

'More than a liking, uncle. I want things to be go further but she seems to be changed for some reason.'

Gerry held his hands up, palms open. He smiled. 'If you've come to me for help in matters of the heart, I'm not your man. Still struggling to understand the better sex myself.'

John feared as much but he spoke anyway. 'There's nothing I've done wrong to her.'

'You're sure?'

'I think so, and I've asked her if I have done something and she's said no.'

Gerry waited some time before answering. 'What little I have picked up is that when women say that, there still could be something that's narked them.'

'I think there must be.'

'She might have just stopped liking you.'

'But it was so sudden. All was going well one day, then one week later when I saw her again, she was as different as pine to ironbark.'

Gerry sipped his whiskey. 'Then something else has got her rattled.' Gerry nodded. 'Maybe she's worried that you have not got over Clarissa.' He paused. 'Or there's talk about you, that she heard when she was trying to find out more about you. If that's the case, good: it means she likes you enough to dig. But …'

'But what?'

'She might have found out some things about your past, maybe in business or something like that, that she doesn't like.'

John sighed. 'How am I supposed to know what that is? But thank you, uncle.'

Gerry finished his drink and held onto his glass. 'Hope I've helped. I'll see Moira and we'll call it a night. Good night, John.'

'Good night, uncle.'

Gerry opened the study door, paused and turned to John. 'If it's something dark that the lass has found out about you—and you know your history—then it might be best to have it out in the open with her. Who knows, there may be a way to explain yourself to her.'

John paused for a moment before following Gerry downstairs to see him and Moira off. His past. Nine years in the colony, and in some of those years he'd made enemies and had done wrong. Which one of those sins had Catherine discovered?

On the following Tuesday morning, John was in his office early. He sorted letters that needed his signature, then took a sheet of paper and started to write a letter to Catherine. He wanted her to tell him what, if anything in his past, had made her change her attitude.

The treasure hunt had stalled but he could still invite Mary Harrigan and Catherine back to look for the so-called treasure horde within the grounds of Golden Hall. It might be a slightly daft idea, but he'd get ten labourers with shovels to dig up some of his yard, with the excuse that he wanted to plant more shrubs. If nothing was found, and he suspected that nothing would be, then he would plant some new bushes anyhow. But in the course of the digging, he'd have valuable time to find out what was worrying Catherine. Signing the letter, and feeling happier that he had for days, he placed it in an envelope.

He heard his secretary arrive at the office. 'Mrs Dawes?'

She stood in the open doorway. 'Good morning, Mr Leary.'

'And you. Here, please see that this letter is delivered today.'

'Surely.' She looked at the envelope, smiled and turned away.

John started on his cost-reports review and over the next two hours he was engrossed.

At eleven o'clock, Sean walked into his office, followed by Ed Larkin, who closed the door and sat down. Sean's face was as white as a washed sheet.

'I've just heard from a Sullivans joiner,' Sean said. 'They've gone broke.'

'What?' John said, shocked.

'The man came to the wool-store site first thing this morning, looking for a job. The bailiffs are in, and the place is locked up.'

John sat back, his blood racing. He couldn't believe it. He looked at the foreman. 'Ed?'

'Mr Sean's right, Mr Leary. But it's a mystery why they've gone bust.'

'You had no clue?' John said. 'Surely there were warning signs.'

'Not one. I've been there every day checking our order and not a whisper from the workers as to what's been happening lately, and that's odd. When I left yesterday the two trusses were just about completed, the third one partial but no jigs set up for the fourth. They said they'd start the fourth this week.'

'But just last fortnight,' John said, 'they promised to complete all three by today, the tenth of January.'

'Words, John,' Sean said. 'Words.'

John tried to think clearly. 'Sean, get to Annandale now with Ed. Find out yourself what's going on. Break in if you have to. I want to know what the hell is happening, and I want those two trusses to come to site. By rights we own them. I want them. Mrs Dawes,' John called out, 'get Mr Reynolds in here!'

'Yes, Mr Leary,' came back her reply.

'Right,' John said to the two men. 'On your way.'

They nodded to him and trooped out of the office.

Dan Reynolds, his accountant, came in and sat down. Dan was a trusted man and gave John straight answers. He'd been by his side in many tight scrapes where pennies were few and debts had mounted. 'Mr Leary?' Dan said.

'Have we paid anything to Sullivans for their trusses?' John waited anxiously for the answer.

'I don't think so, Mr Leary, but I'll check.'

'Do that now.'

'Right.'

As Dan left, John got himself together. If they'd paid no money out, that was something. And two trusses at least were ready for his site. Fourteen still to go.

Dan returned and stood at the doorway. 'No monies paid.'

'Right,' John said. 'Thanks, Dan.'

'Anything else.'

'Not for now,' John said. 'Thank you. Wait. Find out who Sullivans owe money to. Ask those ledger-keeper friends of yours if they can find out who are creditors to Sullivans. The timber millers would be a good start. Off you go.' This was serious. The wheels moved slowly in legal and finance matters. Sullivan's creditors would want to get their hands on the Sullivans assets, including John's precious trusses. Then they would sell them and try to get their monies back. But that all took paperwork and approvals, and the process might last weeks.

John didn't have weeks. He'd gone out on a limb with these trusses and now the job would be delayed a long time. And Mr William Ryan would find out. If they defaulted on the project's time, the owners could rescind the contract. A coldness crept through him and he shook himself. First, they had to get those two trusses any way they could, and at the same time they had to find another truss supplier.

For the rest of his Tuesday, John dropped cost reports and the woman problem and got stuck into finding a way out of the mess.

* * *

Maureen was waiting for Catherine Ryan in Mrs Wicks's tea shop in King Street. It was Wednesday at noon, in an unusually cool early January. Maureen was worried. Catherine's note said that she had to meet urgently with her about John. That was all. Now, if it was good news, especially if the friendship had blossomed into romance, then surely John would have told her face-to-face or even the pair together would have told her. No, this meeting wasn't going to be good. Maureen sensed that.

Catherine came into the shop and saw her. Her half smile told Maureen that her instincts had been right.

'Good day, Maureen,' Catherine said. 'Thank you for meeting with me. Have you ordered?'

'No, what would you like?' Maureen said. After their orders were placed. Catherine folded her arms and looked Maureen in the eye.

'I've been thinking very hard. Yesterday, I got a note from your brother inviting me and Mary Harrigan back to his house to look within the grounds.'

'So, John wants to keep searching?'

'So, it seems and Mary does too. But ...'

'What's the problem?' Maureen asked and leaned back as their teas arrived.

Catherine paused until the waiter had gone and replied, 'I think John wants to spend time with me rather than looking for gold or whatever. I know that sounds forward but that's the sense I get. And … I can't see him any more.'

Maureen left her tea alone and braced herself to hear more, trying to control her disappointment.

'Before you say anything, I must tell you that what I feel for him is more than friendship and I suspect he thinks the same about me. I'm sorry Maureen, I really am. If it wasn't for our friendship, I wouldn't have bothered telling you, but I had to.' Catherine hadn't touched her tea. 'I feel strongly that John is not over Clarissa. If I get more involved with him, I'll not be able to control things and we'll be married. I fear that in the not-too-distant future, John will realise that he's made a mistake with me. Then it will be too late. And another thing. I don't want to get Richard's life turned upside down.'

'That's a lot to think about.'

'It is, Maureen. It is. Your brother has a past and is not free of personal memories. That's my belief.'

'Not so. I'm sure that John is over Clarissa. What I mean is, of course he will never forget her, but emotionally he's ready to move on.'

'Are you absolutely sure of that?' Maureen hesitated, and that was fatal. 'You see? You are not.'

Maureen wasn't about to give up. 'Why not talk to John about this?'

'Words mean little. It's actions and time that count.'

'Do you mean his actions in the past? You don't think you could accept him because he's been married and has a son?'

'Look, I've been over and over this in my head and it's been nearly driving me mad.' Catherine's eyes were moist now and Maureen felt for her. 'It's hard for me to convince myself that he would love only me and not see me as a replacement for his dead wife. But believe me, I have tried.' She closed her eyes for a moment.

Well, there it was, Maureen thought. Brutally said. She was about to reply and defend her brother's commitment to Catherine Ryan. But in one way Maureen understood the young woman's doubts. 'Is that your final word, no compromise?'

Catherine hesitated and Maureen felt a glint of hope.

Catherine said, 'I can't say these things to your brother. But if you care for me, I wonder if you might. I think it's best that you let John know as soon as possible. If he asks you about my feelings, please feel free to tell him the truth. I see marriage as a total commitment, for life, to another person. I can only marry a man wholeheartedly, and that's how I expect to be loved in return. However your brother takes it, I still want your friendship.' She looked down for a moment then directly at Maureen. 'But you might not want to be my friend, after what I've said.' She stood up.

Maureen stood up and placed a hand on Catherine's shoulder. 'I'll still be your friend despite this setback. And unlike you, I feel that there's still hope. But that's up to John and you to work out. Meanwhile, I'm sure John wants you for yourself.'

'It's not your assurance I need, Maureen. It's John's. Goodbye.'

As Maureen watched her go, she sat back down and thought, *If John has any ambition to win this lovely young girl, then he'd better pull out all stops to get her.* Now, what could his sister do to help him?

* * *

The brilliant noon sunshine of a mid-January day warmed John's shoulders and he swore. Where he was standing now, he should be in the shade, with a partially completed roof above him, but the wool-store project had ground to a halt. It was as if a cyclone had come and clipped the roof off the building, leaving only its four massive walls.

Only sundry work was under way: cleaning the outside brick walls, completing the amenities areas and inlaid services, but the engine-room of effort, the roof structure and its covering fabric, was stalled. The two trusses were gathering dust in the now bankrupt Sullivans factory, with no sign of a breakthrough. There was no alternative truss maker that was willing to take on the completion of the fourteen trusses for the same amount as John's original budget. The only one John was talking to, Bowmans, had demanded a prohibitive price. John swore again.

'I feel for you,' Sean said standing beside him. He pointed to the letter in John's hand. 'That from the architects?'

'It bloody is,' John said. 'Come on, let's get out of this heat and into the shed.'

They walked across the vast expanse of the ten-inch-thick concrete floor that John had ordered to be poured. Ordinarily, John and Sean would have waited until the roof sheeting was on before they poured the concrete ground slab. The shade provided by the roof with its protection from the weather would have ensured that the concrete cured with less cracking. Also, with the roof sheltering the ready-to-receive compacted gravel, the concrete could be poured in any weather. As it was, the concrete floor had taken longer to lay, due to rain delays. John was worried that the slab, under the weight of the bales, would give him future grief because of the sequence in which it had been laid.

Sean opened the site-shed door and John followed him.

John slumped into a chair positioned against an open window. He flicked the letter in his hand. 'Bardells have given us notice: we're behind three weeks and won't get our contract extended.'

Sean filled up two mugs with cold water and handed one to John. 'So, what do we do?'

'Something. We have to do something, Sean.' John started to think. The structural frame for the wool store, with its massive trusses and the few columns supporting them, was radical and different from the original design that the architects wanted. It would cost months and many pounds to reconfigure the trusses and build more columns. No, better to persevere with what they had and put pressure on his only remaining truss manufacturer, Bowmans. Or ... a gleam of an idea came to mind: an alternative plan, in case Bowmans proved impossible to deal with.

'There's another thing as well,' John said. 'Mr William Ryan is on the warpath. I've heard it from a director of Superior Sheeting, who said that Ryan went out on a limb with the other shareholders of this job. They didn't want to move away from the architect's first design but Ryan did.' *I was too good a salesman there!* 'Well, he's lost face now and wants to change contractors. I'm not in his good books.'

'But,' Sean said, 'I thought you and him were friends, you know, with him being Miss Catherine's father and all that.'

On that front John knew he was on rickety ground as well. 'Different in business, Sean. Money first and always.'

Sean shook his head. 'Why not talk to the man anyway?'

'I will, but I need a plan first.'

John stood up and started to pace the shed. There could be a way; it would be a gamble, but it might work. And he could get materials from a factory in which he was a director, Superior Sheeting, formerly owned by David McGuire. 'Right, what about this? Go to the yard with Ed Larkin. Collect as many ledgers and timbers you can and set up a temporary roof here on site. You'll get second-hand sheeting from Superior. I was at their factory last week for a directors' meeting. Tell them we'll take as many sheets as we can from their seconds. The space on site has got to have enough clearance height so that we can make the trusses ourselves.'

'Here?' Sean said, his voice raised in surprise. 'On site?'

'Look, Sean, I might be able to get the costs down from what Bowmans want. If I can, then the only extra expense is on the temporary set-up. Also, we're going to work two shifts. It'll cost us some, but it'll be worth it.'

Sean didn't look convinced. 'We've never made monsters like these, John. What if we make errors, waste timber and still don't come up trumps?'

'I'm off to Bowmans now. You get Ed, and get that stuff ready. Sean, you're a carpenter and a bloody good one. So am I. These trusses are bigger than what we're used to but that's all. The principles are still the same. I agree we'll need blocks and tackle to move the bastards.'

'We've got three come-a-longs and chain blocks in the yard.'

'Should be enough. Sean, we'll save money on the transport of the trusses if we build them on site. That'll be something. I'm off.'

'Just see if you can get Bowmans down on price,' Sean said to John as he left the site shed.

John waved in acknowledgment.

On the following afternoon, John was in his office working through the logistics of building the trusses on the wool-store site. Scribbled-on papers surrounded him, filled with sketches and calculations. Meanwhile his meeting with Bowmans the day before hadn't gone well—he still didn't have their agreement on price.

Bowmans knew that they had the upper hand. Every other timber merchant had turned Learys down to make the trusses. Bowmans could call all the shots. John had no leverage. Before John had been about to leave, he'd thanked Bowmans for their time and mentioned that Learys might build the trusses on the site. Bowmans wished John luck with that and offered to supply the timber anyway, at a reduced price. When John said that they had other timber suppliers who were willing to do the same, Bowmans had shifted position on making the trusses. They said that they might be able to reduce their price a little if they made the trusses in their factory. John had thanked them again.

At least Bowmans didn't want to lose the order completely. There still might be a chance of making the trusses in time.

'Your afternoon mail, Mr Leary,' Mrs Dawes said, coming into his office.

John glanced at the correspondence. 'Thank you.'

'The business ones I've opened and sorted but there is a personal note for you.' She turned and left.

John took the envelope and opened the letter. The signature at the end gave him a jolt.

Dear Mr Leary,

Thank you for your invitation to myself and Mrs Harrigan for us to continue the investigation at your house. I've spoken to Mrs Harrigan who would be willing to accept that. She will be in correspondence with you in due course to arrange a suitably agreeable time. Regretfully, I won't be able to join her or to be further involved with the search. I understand from my father that there is a serious issue on the wool-store site that has affected its progress. I'm unsure as to the details but, suffice to say, my father's attitude to your company's performance is not good. He has forbidden me to have anything to do with you. It's disappointing that this issue has raised its head, but you can surely understand my position.

Yours sincerely,
Catherine Ryan.

John placed the letter down. The tone of it surprised him, but it shouldn't: Catherine was already acting distant with him, and the letter's language reflected that: it was commercial and formal. So, she was being forbidden to see him because of this truss fiasco. Was there a chance she might still like him, despite the father's insistence to keep away from him? He wondered if she would try to see him nonetheless. He sank back in his chair. *Who are you fooling?*

* * *

On the day before Foundation Day, Harry Shelby sat waiting in William Ryan's vestibule. He was to meet the wool broker to talk about his house additions—but Shelby wanted to leave here not with a contract for that minnow, but one for a whale. He was ten minutes early for his appointment because he was keen, keen to excise Mr John Leary from the wool-store job and install himself in his place. It had now been two weeks since Sullivans had gone under and Shelby's spy on the wool-store site had told him that Learys were buggered because of it.

Yes, Learys could spend the extra money and time going back to the original architect's design and complete the project, but if they did, they would be paying heavy penalties for being late. There was still no sign that Learys would get going again on the wool-store roof structure. Every day that Learys delayed that decision was one more day in favour of Harry Shelby. The Leary star was falling and Shelby's was on the rise.

'Mr Ryan will see you now, Mr Shelby,' a woman said. 'Please follow me.'

Ryan gestured to a seat and Shelby sat down. The wool broker opened a folder and brought out a single sheet of paper. He handed it to Shelby. 'Here's your letter to go ahead with my house additions. Send us a contract and I'll sign it.'

'Thank you, Mr Ryan.' Shelby scanned the letter. It looked straightforward, including a list of architect's drawings that Shelby would need to conform to. He folded the letter and slipped it into his jacket. 'When would you like me to start?'

'As soon as you can. Right after Foundation Day would be ideal.'

'I'll need to get materials and carpenters,' Shelby said. 'First week in February would be the soonest.'

'So be it. Is there anything else?'

'Your wool store,' Shelby said straight out.

Ryan's face went red and he slammed his open palm onto the desk. 'Bloody thing. I shouldn't have listened to Leary. Should have stuck with the architects. I won't be hoodwinked like that again.' He seemed to regret losing his temper and got himself together. 'The architects have served notice on Leary to start back on the roof frame by the sixth of February, otherwise we'll rescind the contract.'

'It's a poor show,' Shelby said in a voice that sounded sympathetic. 'It was a daft idea, building trusses that big. It was bound to be a mess. And the ground-floor slab is poured: now, that's a problem.'

'Problem?'

'Mr Ryan, for the proper layout, you'll need more columns to support the roof. Those extra columns will need footings and the construction company that takes over will have to break out the slab to pour them.'

'I see.' Ryan looked despondent.

'My company can get you out of this mess. I've got two steam-driven saws that can halve the labour time on site, build the original design and bring the job back onto program. Leary can't do that. He doesn't have the saws I do.'

'You think you could do that?' Ryan said.

'I know we could. Look,' he said, leaning forward, 'you haven't spent a quid yet on the trusses, right?'

Ryan nodded.

'Get me in there with a big band of chippies, set up the saws and you'll have the roof on in no time.'

'And the due date?'

'Learys can't finish the job to the original time. They're stuck with the big trusses, No one will build them, so they've got nowhere to move.' Shelby had another thought: he'd better find out who Learys might be getting to make their trusses and try to stop them. 'Learys will still be sitting on their duffs this time next month. Meanwhile your job will be more delayed.'

Ryan sat back and steepled his fingers. 'All right. First, put all this to me in writing, what you propose. I'll get the board to review it and if I'm still satisfied, then I'll get the board on side. I've got some fences to mend with them.'

Shelby stood up and extended his hand. Ryan shook it. 'I'll do that now,' Shelby said, 'and have my recommendation on your desk tomorrow. How are you spending Foundation Day?'

'We'll be in the Governor's Domain, with the family.'

'We might just see you there. Goodbye, Mr Ryan.'

* * *

There was a big crowd enjoying the celebration of the founding of the colony. Ten years, John thought, 1860. Ten years before, he'd come to

New South Wales as a hopeful, skilled, assisted-passage carpenter. A lot had happened in that time. From the delightful—like Richard, who was standing beside him, laughing at a dog doing tricks—to the dreadful: Clarissa's death.

'Lovely day, John,' Maureen said as she helped Liam spread out the picnic rug. 'Grab that corner, will you, and weigh it with the basket?'

'Surely.'

'Liam,' Maureen said. 'Could you watch Richard for a bit and mind that Michael doesn't play too rough with him? John and I want to walk down to the water.' Maureen turned to Christine. 'Will you be able to manage for a while?'

Christine smiled as she threw a ball to Irene, Maureen's daughter. 'You go, dear. I'm enjoying myself here.'

John was curious as to what his sister wanted to say. She put up her parasol as the late morning sun started to bite. Among the crowd there were familiar faces; the Ryans, Shelbys, Sean and his family. John spotted Catherine, who was laughing at something Ian McCreadie had said. Maureen followed his gaze and entwined her arm with his.

'Catherine came to see me, John,' she said.

John stopped. 'When?'

'Just about a fortnight ago. It was a difficult time for both of us. I'm sorry, but she told me that she doesn't want to see you any more.'

John sighed. 'Yes, I know. I got a letter from her, a week ago. It seems her father has forbidden her to see me.'

The breeze had strengthened, and they started walking again. 'Is that all she said?' Maureen asked.

He nodded. 'She's using her father as an excuse not to see me. But you think there's more? So do I. Something has got her upset about me, something I've done. I'm certain of that.' They were at the water's edge now and John sat down on a sandstone shelf. 'I'd love to know what it was, even if it's dire.' John picked up a stone and threw it with frustration into the water. 'I wish I knew, then I could do something about it.'

Maureen sat beside him. 'Catherine told me why. She also told me that it was up to me to explain her reasons to you.'

'Then please tell me. Whatever they are, I'll deal with it.'

'Are you sure?'

'Yes.'

'Before I tell you,' she said, 'I want to give you my view. I think you and Catherine deserve to be together. It's not just a sister's wish to see her brother looked after. It's more than that. You have something together that works. You're both well suited and there's attraction there.'

'Well, on my part there is,' John said.

Maureen covered his hand with her own. 'And Catherine is attracted to you. She's not quite said it to me, but as a woman I see all the signs.'

'Then what's keeping her away from me?'

'Catherine told me that, in her view, you have not got over Clarissa.'

John was disappointed but not shocked. 'Ah. But is that all?'

'She says that she can't let her affections develop, as she feels you still love Clarissa. If she just wanted you for a friend, she mightn't have cared so much.'

'But I will always love Clarissa.'

'I know.'

'Not in a physical way, Maureen, not like that, but she'll always be in my heart.'

Maureen took both his hands. 'I know that John, but Catherine thinks that you want to replace Clarissa with her, with Catherine. Not for *herself* but just because you need a wife.'

'That's not how I feel at all! What if I talk to her and explain? Was there anything else she said or maybe found out about me?'

'She didn't say, but John, you do have a history of impulsive and passionate behaviour. If you want a trusting love with someone, you must be true in every way to that person. I think Catherine would need to know for sure that all your passion is hers.'

John said in despair, 'It is! But how do I convince her of that now?'

'I did stress that you were very down after Clarissa's death, but you have moved on.'

'I was down, Maureen,' he said, 'and still am, a bit.' God, not only had his past affected his loved ones, but it could also be preventing him from starting anew. He must act. 'Maureen, I have to talk with her, now if possible.' He looked over and spotted Catherine in the crowd. 'Can you get her alone with you and then let me talk to her? I have to. I have to convince her that it's her I want in my life, not a copy of one who has gone from me.' He was pleading with his sister now, but he didn't care.

'I'll see what I can do.' She looked around then nodded. 'I'll get her to walk with me behind that copse down there. Place yourself out of sight of the others. I can't know how long you'll have together, if at all, but I'll try.' She walked off and John placed himself where Maureen had suggested.

Some minutes passed and John was getting anxious. Then he saw Maureen and Catherine walking towards him through the copse. At the same moment, Catherine saw him and stopped. She looked at Maureen and turned to go away.

'Wait!' John called. 'Please!'

Maureen nodded to Catherine and gestured for her to continue down the path in John's direction. John feared the worst as she came towards him—she looked so contained. Maureen fell back to look at some flowers in a bed nearby, able to keep her eyes on the two, but out of earshot. The Ryans' and McCreadie's picnic was within sight now, but no one seemed to be looking John's way.

John stepped over and said to Catherine, 'We've got such a short time. I wish I had more, to convince you of my sincerity.'

Catherine looked at him sadly. 'I know you still love Clarissa. I could never take her place.'

'I know.' She seemed surprised at his answer but did not speak. 'You are Catherine Ryan. Yes, you have Clarissa's qualities, value and virtues but you are not her, nor could you ever be.' She still said nothing. 'It's you that I'm attracted to, not some facsimile of my past.'

'How can I be sure of that?'

'Because you'll have my love.'

Her eyes rounded in surprise, as though she understood him for the first time. 'That's a bold thing to say.'

'I mean it. It's the truth.'

'John,' Maureen said. 'Ian McCreadie's heading this way.'

'Let him.' John touched her sleeve. 'Please, Catherine, you have to believe me. Clarissa is dead. You are my present. You are alive and you are here.'

'I need time, to be sure I'm important to you.'

'Then, give me that time. Let me help you to believe that I love you.'

'John!' Maureen said, her voice alarmed.

'I don't know,' Catherine said. She turned and joined Maureen and Ian, as John stepped back and gave up.

As he watched the three go off together, he had mixed feelings. Yes, he was satisfied that he'd talked with Catherine, but had he put his case in the right way? Seeing her walk away with Ian McCreadie, he realised he had only a few more rounds left in the fight.

Maureen left Catherine and McCreadie to join her husband and Christine, who was sitting in the shade. Christine got up and took her arm.

'Walk with me, dear. Please.' Christine waited until they were out of earshot from anyone. 'John was talking to Catherine Ryan, yes?'

Nothing much escaped this lady. 'He was.'

Christine nodded. 'I admire her but I know little of her. I suspect he has feelings for the girl. Am I right?'

John was walking back towards them. 'You are,' Maureen said, 'and he's serious about her.'

'Then I'm provisionally pleased. Is Miss Ryan of the same mind?'

'I don't know,' was all Maureen had time to say before John joined them.

* * *

In the Ryans' kitchen on the Saturday following Foundation Day, Mary Harrigan was pouring tea. 'Are you sure you won't come with me?' she said to Catherine.

Catherine shook her head. 'No. You go. Mr Leary has organised his men, so it'll be easy for you to dig wherever they've turned over the soil.' She smiled. 'You might finally get lucky.'

Mary nodded. 'I hope so.' She paused. 'You really like him, though, don't you?'

'I do, but there's an issue, a big one.'

'I see. Which is?'

Catherine sipped her tea. It was a warm morning already and the cicadas were raucous. 'I like him so much that I have to move on, or take him on a faith that I don't yet have.'

'I'm guessing that he doesn't gamble?' Mary said.

'No.'

'Violent?'

Catherine shuddered. 'No, dear no. It's all to do with his past.'

'So,' Mary said, 'men are simple souls. If it wasn't money or any of the other, then it was women. Yes?'

Catherine wanted to open her heart. 'It is. Clarissa.'

Mary said nothing for a while. 'I see. You think he's not over her.'

Catherine hung her head. 'I don't think he is. It's only been a few years since her death and I worry that he just sees me as a replacement.'

'What makes you feel that? Something he's said?'

'Oh no, he denies it. He loved Clarissa but now he says he loves me. Oh, it's nothing obvious that makes me cautious, Mary, nothing. Just my instincts and some things I've heard. Gossip about his past. It's just so frustrating.'

Mary nodded. 'This is your first brush with romance. It's all new. There are no guidebooks on this, just as there are no books on being a good parent.' Mary smiled. 'Don't be too hard on yourself. There's nothing perfect in life and that extends to the people you come into contact with. Forget gossip. It has a way of corroding your thoughts.'

'But how can I just remove my doubts about John and his past?'

'You have to replace those doubts with faith in what the man does and how he shows that to you, now and into the future.' Mary stretched out her hand and pressed Catherine's. 'In the end, you have to make that leap into a space that may seem insecure. While remembering that nothing is guaranteed, not even love.'

Catherine kept quiet for a while. 'So, I'm to replace one way of thinking for another?'

'Something like that. When Peter and I were courting, sure he didn't have Mr Leary's situation, but I had doubts about other things. Still, I gave those doubts little air to breathe and gave my faith and love for him full room to grow. It's hard, I know. But when you saw Mr Leary in the Domain—he was there, wasn't he?'

'Yes, I met him … briefly.'

'And what did he say?'

Catherine placed her empty cup down. 'He said that I was different from Clarissa. He doesn't see me as her replacement, but as myself.'

'And what did you say?'

'Nothing. I don't know that I'm willing to take on a widower with a child and a past.'

'You mean you couldn't see Richard as a son?'

'Oh, Richard's not the problem. He's a lovely boy. As long as he accepted me, I could happily care for him.'

'Then your concern is with John Leary himself?'

'Yes, Mary. How do I know he would stay faithful to me?'

'There's no certainty in marriage, Catherine. Yes, both partners can work on it to make it so, but there are no guarantees. However, from what I know of John Leary, I would say that he keeps his promises. Especially now, when he's gone through so much and has a chance at happiness with you.'

Catherine said. 'Then there's Ian McCreadie, whom I like. He's young, with no murky past, and he's fond of me.'

'But could you love him as much as Mr Leary?'

Catherine had to be honest. 'No.'

Mary took their empty cups to the sink and started to wash them. 'Well, you'll have to choose between them soon. They'll each want an answer, and you can't say yes to them both!'

'I know. Some girls would find it thrilling to have two men interested in them! It's flattering up to a point, but then it becomes difficult. What should I do?'

'I can't help you, Catherine, but whatever you do, be honest with them. They are both good men.'

* * *

On a warm Monday morning, the second-to-last day of January, John was making his way down Market Street to McCreadies, to inspect some defects that had become apparent in the addition to their office. Rupert Jenkins, who had built the addition for the wool broker many years before, was ill in bed and John had offered to take his place.

The previous Saturday, watching Mary Harrigan and the children fossicking at his home, had been a let-down for two reasons: Catherine hadn't been there and his garden had yielded no money, no gold, nothing. Mary Harrigan was now resigned to accepting that her husband Peter must have divested himself of all his wealth before he died.

When John arrived at the McCreadies wool store, he stopped in his tracks to admire the large extension that he and Sean had supervised while in Jenkins's employ. It still stood as a robust and bullish building. John was proud of it. Going up the steps to the office, John thought about Catherine, again. When he'd left her at the Domain, he'd made a declaration to her. It might as well have been a proposal of marriage. And her final words had been, *I don't know.* Over the last four days, John had clung to the ambivalence of those three words like a drunk to a half-filled bottle. She hadn't said *no*, she had said *don't know*, and that was something. Could he still get her to say yes?

He opened the front door and went to the front office.

Ian McCreadie greeted him. 'Morning, Mr Leary. Father asked me to show you the issues.'

'Morning.'

'This way.'

John followed him through the hall with its two offices attached and up the short stairs into the new mezzanine area, which comprised a new office. McCreadie went past that and into the timber-panelled meeting room, and closed the door behind him.

'We have problems with the timber,' McCreadie said. 'Here, I'll show you.'

He walked to the corner and pointed under the sill of a large window. 'Some of the boards are lifting.'

John could see straight away what the problem was. He ran his hand along them. 'Those two have reacted differently to moisture from the others. That's why they've warped.'

'But they're not supposed to warp!'

'No, they're not. However, no one can guarantee timbers won't warp with age. We'll replace them with wood that can handle moisture better, and drill extra screws to fix the new boards down.'

McCreadie nodded. 'When can that be done?'

'In about a week. The refixing is not the problem, it's getting the right timber for your purposes.'

'Will you do it, or Mr Jenkins?'

'Don't worry Jenkins, Mr McCreadie, I'll get it done. Is there anything else?'

Ian sat down on a meeting-room chair and gestured for John to do the same. 'What's your interest in Miss Catherine Ryan?'

John was taken aback with the man's frankness. McCreadie had been a suitor of Clarissa once and here he was declaring his interest in another woman, again the exact one in whom John was interested! John said shortly, 'I enjoy her company.'

'Anything more?'

'Right out there, aren't you?'

'Mr Leary, I like Miss Ryan very much and value her well-being. I liked Clarissa very much also and it pained me to see how much hurt you inflicted on her during her marriage. I don't want the same to happen to Miss Ryan.'

John bristled. 'My wife is dead, McCreadie, and I live with that and the events that led up to it, every day of my life.'

'Miss Ryan deserves to know about you and Beth Blackett.'

John was startled, then appalled. He leaned forward in his chair and pointed his finger at the wool broker. 'You've told her? How dare you.'

'I didn't go into the sordid details of your dealings with women, Leary. I wouldn't subject a delicate young lady to that type of talk. I simply indicated that you're no saint.'

John stood up, his hands clenched, and took a big breath. Hitting McCreadie would solve nothing and his reputation with Catherine would be trashed as well. 'I'm going, McCreadie. You've done what you had to do. I'll get your sill fixed.' He turned to go.

'She likes me, you know,' McCreadie said, still seated.

'Has she said so?'

'I know she does.'

John went towards the door and said without turning around, 'Then propose to her. You'll have to hope for a better answer than what Clarissa gave you.'

It was a cheap shot and John heard the chair push back and McCreadie make two steps towards him. But he opened the office door and kept walking. He was gut-wrenched with worry now. Did Catherine believe he'd been unfaithful to Clarissa? But if she did, Maureen hadn't mentioned it in the Gardens and Catherine hadn't either. Why? Had she dismissed McCreadie's remarks as gossip? He hoped so. He really did.

* * *

Ed Larkin, Learys truss foreman, looked above him at the layout of rafters, battens, beams, lifting tackle and roof sheeting that covered one half of one bay of the wool store site. 'It won't win any awards,' he said.

Sean laughed. 'It wasn't meant to. Just as long as it keeps us and this timber dry while we work.'

They both looked at the assortment laid around them: bundles of scantlings and ledgers of hardwood, irons brackets, steel rods, boxes of bolts, dollies, nails and screws and the timber saws and ropes.

'It's the first of February,' Sean said, 'and we've got under a week to see if we can make one of these big bastards. Otherwise, we say goodbye to this site and the whole deal. When are the lads coming?'

'Seven-thirty.' Larkin replied.

'Right, we've got half an hour to work out the steps we need to take.'

'Sixteen of the monsters,' Ed said. 'What about the two already at Sullivans?'

Sean had grabbed the truss plans, drawn to a scale of 1 inch to 1 foot, and was concentrating. 'What's that?'

'The first two trusses. Can we get hold of them?'

Sean shook his head. 'The accounts mob snaffled them. We hadn't paid for them, so they've used the proceeds to pay the creditors.'

'What about Bowmans? Have they brought their price down?'

'John says no dice yet.'

'So,' Larkin said, 'we've got to build sixteen trusses here, all under this roof and move them into place, crane them up and fix them.'

'Yep,' Sean said still looking at the drawings.

'I suppose once we've knocked over one, we should be able to make the rest quicker.'

'We should. All the components are the same.' Sean put down his plans and rubbed his jaw. Something of an idea was forming in his mind. What if they could make all the trusses at the same time? No. That would take more men and more space.

'What's on your mind, boss?'

'We shouldn't build just one truss at a time. We've got the space to make at least one more, concurrently. And maybe, if we throw even more men at it ...'

'What?' Larkin looked at him, mystified.

'Right, this is how we're going to do it. It's going to take three shifts working round the clock and we've got to keep this whole idea under wraps.'

Larkin looked as if Sean had lost his head and Sean smiled. Maybe he had, but it was worth trying, just the same.

* * *

On the first Saturday in February, John was on his way to Potts Point. He'd dropped a note to Mary Harrigan asking if he could meet with her and she had accepted, saying that she was staying the weekend with Catherine Ryan to keep her company. Catherine's parents had gone to the southern tablelands to a wool brokers' social gathering. The timing couldn't have been better: John really wanted to talk to Mary about Catherine, anyway. Now he would see her in person.

It was Mary Harrigan who welcomed him. 'Come, Mr Leary, into the drawing room.'

John sat down opposite her. In the eleven months since she'd been back in Sydney she had changed. There were more lines on each side of her eyes and mouth. The end of a fruitless quest had affected her. He felt sympathy. 'It was a real pity that nothing was found last Saturday.'

She smiled, which surprised him, 'Your garden looks better, that's something.'

He smiled with her. 'Indeed it does.'

'Would you like tea?' she said. 'I've made some. Or more for the weather, some cold water?'

'Cold water would be grand, thank you.'

'Just give me a minute.'

John sat back and thought about his strategy. Was Catherine actually at home? Or was she avoiding him?

Donald Ryan came down the stairs and smiled at John. 'Morning, Mr Leary. What brings you here?'

'Good morning, Don. I've come to see Mrs Harrigan about the outcome of our search.'

Donald opened the French doors to let in the sun. 'A damned pity about that. Oh, I know that if anything was found it'd be yours, but just for Mary's sake, it would've made her happy.' He paused. 'You know, there's a case last week we were studying about a diamond necklace that was left in a house that was sold. The original owner had a claim to it, as it was not listed in the contents for sale on property transfer. Her claim is being looked at and I can let you know the result eventually. Interesting.'

Mary came in with a tray and placed it on the small table in front of John, who had an idea. 'Are you in for the day, Don?'

'I've got fencing lessons from one, but until then, I'm here.'

'Good. Can you spare me some time after I talk to Mrs Harrigan?'

Donald nodded. 'Surely.'

Mary handed John his water. 'You're welcome to some tea, Don.'

'I think,' Donald said, 'that I'll get a wash up and shave. Big night last night.' He smiled again, winked at John and left them.

John's water was refreshing. 'Is Miss Catherine home?'

Mary smiled. 'Now, why did I think that you only came here to see me?'

John wanted to reassure her. 'I did come to see you, really.'

'I'm glad. Catherine is at home. I told her you were coming. At first, she didn't want to see you.' She paused. 'But I convinced her to at least talk through whatever you must.'

'Thank you for that,' he said. 'I'd really like a chance to talk to her. You see, Mrs Harrigan—'

Mary raised her palm to him. 'Whatever you have to say can wait for Catherine. It's between you two, no one else.'

'Very good.'

'Now, about Golden Hall,' Mary said and sipped her tea. 'It's clear to me that Peter's sickness or his heart condition had affected his thinking just before his death. I'm sure now that in his mind he was certain that there was more wealth, but I realise he probably gave away his money to someone, as he did to Dunstan and Marie Carter.'

'That's by no means certain.'

'Mr Leary, I have to stop this obsession at some point and now is the best time. I'll be in modest circumstances for the rest of my life and I'll have to consider Reggie's future from that standpoint. It's useless thinking about a different world of comfort and style when I don't have the money for it. Simon Ly's payment is very helpful, of course. Now I can think about a way of earning a living, perhaps as a teacher.'

John thought about his own background. If it hadn't been for David McGuire, he might still be just a journeyman carpenter. Moreover, without McGuire he'd not be in the house that Peter Smith had been so proud to build. 'Are you sure?'

'I'm sure, Mr Leary. I cannot live on phantoms of wealth and visions of gold.' She finished her tea. 'More water?'

'No, thank you. I'll finish what I have.'

'So, there'll be no more safaris there or archaeological digs,' she said, and John smiled. 'We'll draw a line on that part of my life. However, there is one favour that I'll ask, and you don't have to grant it.'

'What?' John was curious and a little on guard.

'Peter often mentioned the house by its name, Bede Hall. If I'm to move on with my life and accept how I live now, may I ask that you consider removing the sign with Bede Hall on it? Or changing it?'

John was surprised. 'Well, there's a sign saying Golden Hall near the front door. Isn't that enough?'

'I'm curious: why didn't you change both signs at the same time?'

'I didn't discover the garden sign until well after I moved in.' He paused. 'But if it will give you more peace, Mrs Harrigan, I'll take away the Bede Hall sign or replace it. It seems little enough for you to ask me.'

'Thank you. Now, are we done? I think you'd like to speak with Catherine. But perhaps Mr Ryan junior first?'

'If he's ready,' John said. 'Thank you.'

'There's just one thing I'd like to tell you and it concerns Richard.'

John smiled. 'He done nothing wrong, has he?'

'I'm good friends with Stella now, Mr Leary and she's very close to your boy, even like a mother would be.' John agreed with her. 'If another woman comes into your life, Stella will feel it deeply.'

'I'm very aware of that. I know it will be a huge adjustment for her. But she is engaged to Fruin, and one day she'll have a new life with him.'

'Nonetheless I'm worried, Mr Leary,' Mary said. 'Stella's attachment is very strong. Even, dare I say, possessive. Because of Stella's deep devotion to Clarissa, and especially the way she passed, she devoted herself to Richard, to make up for his not having a mother.'

'Yes. I'll always be grateful for the way Stella loves Richard.'

'So,' Mary said, 'when and if you marry again, and I'm sure you will, just be very mindful of Stella's feelings in all this. It will take careful and sensitive understanding. There'll be a period of transition, before she starts a new life for herself. I doubt if either she or Richard would be happy if she moved very far away from him.'

'Thank you, Mrs Harrigan. I'll take what you've said on board.'

Mary stood up. 'I'll see if Don's ready to see you. And, Mr Leary, from now on please call me Mary.' Her smile was genuine.

'Very well … Mary. And I'm John.'

A few minutes later, Donald was sitting opposite him, pulling on his shoes, his well-muscled arms reacting to the effort.

Well, here goes, John thought. 'I have strong feelings for your sister.'

Donald looked at him for some time, then smiled. 'I see.'

'And,' John said, 'I hope to talk to her and convince her that I love her very much.'

'John, I can't be of much help here. This is really between yourself and my sister. She came to see me last night and talk about things.'

'About me?' John became excited.

'We talked about things in general and about men's behaviour and motivations in particular.'

'Did she talk about me? About my circumstances, my behaviour?'

'No.'

'Well, at least she didn't speak ill of me! Can you persuade your sister to see more of me? I'd like her to know my motivation—I want her to be my wife.'

'That's up to her.'

'I know.'

'But,' Donald said, 'I hope that she does see you more often. You seem a good man, and one with whom I could be a friend.'

John grinned. 'Good stuff. Now we had better find out from the girl herself.'

'I'll see if she's ready,' Donald said and stood up and extended his hand. 'Good luck. Whatever happens, drop me a note from time to time. I've always got time for a beer.'

John shook his hand and watched Donald walk up the stairs, then walked over to the French doors and revelled in the nor-easter that had sprung up. Its coolness was refreshing. He heard footsteps behind him and turned around.

Catherine was dressed in a white-coloured bodice with a red sash and a crinoline skirt of pale blue. 'Good morning, Mr Leary,' she said in a polite voice. There was no animation in her expression.

'Good morning, Miss Ryan.'

'Won't you please sit down?'

'Thank you,' John said and sat opposite her. Catherine's back was straight, her hands were clasped, and she wasn't looking at him.

'Thank you for seeing me,' he said.

'That's quite all right,' she said, looking at the table between them.

John reached for his water and Catherine watched him take the glass.

'Why did you come here?' she said.

'To see you and to talk to you.'

She paused. 'You asked me to try and believe in you.'

'I did.'

She nodded. 'Mr Leary, this is hard for me. Frankly, I'm attracted to you. And because I'm fond of you, your character and your values are very important to me.'

'As they should be,' John said, his hopes rising at her words. 'I will answer any questions you wish to ask.'

'Very well. You loved Clarissa passionately?'

'I did.'

'And you still do?'

She seemed set in that opinion and John had to convince her otherwise. 'Yes, I remember her with love. I cannot forget Clarissa and I think it would be unreasonable for you to think that I should.'

She nodded.

'But I am attracted to you,' he said. 'You are your own person. Let me make this very clear: you are not, nor will you ever be, just a replacement for her. I see you as an individual whom I'm very much drawn to. I can't prove myself in any other way than to be straight with you. I love you.' He saw her eyes brighten and pushed on. 'You mean everything to me. You have my word on that.'

'Words, Mr Leary. Words. I'm demanding more than that. If we are to keep seeing each other, then I want actions, demonstrations of fidelity. I want to be sure I can trust you.'

Fidelity. What had McCreadie told her? He owed it to her to explain. 'In my past are faults that I'll confess to you, if you wish. You may have heard—'

'Your past is gone,' she said. 'You don't have to tell me about the sins of your past.' Catherine knew. He was certain of it now. 'I'm talking about the future, Mr Leary. I'm talking about devotion.'

Catherine was taking a big step for him, putting aside her opinion of his past failings, just believing in the two of them. It was a huge leap of faith. He felt more strongly about her now than he ever had. He would repay her belief in him with a lifetime of commitment. 'You'll have that from me. I'll prove my love to you in every way I can.'

Now she looked hard at him, as if to look behind his eyes and into him, to see if he was genuine. 'Good, because I'm going to accept that you are ready for us to move on.'

Relief filled him. 'Thank you. I really love *you*.'

'Do you?' she said her eyes were pleading with him now.

'I do.'

Catherine let out a long breath. 'Then I shall keep seeing you.'

John was filled with joy. 'Thank you. Thank you.'

'Now, tell me about your wool store. Father says you're off the job because you can't get going again and build it. Is that true?'

John was so surprised with the change in subject that he almost laughed. But then he felt relieved that she wanted to talk about anything and everything, just as they had before. 'There's a good chance that we can,' John said with a confidence he didn't have. 'My partner has a new scheme to get us back on program.'

'I do hope you can. It wasn't your fault that the timber factory went bankrupt.'

'Correct. But your father and his partners need their store built, and that's what counts.'

She smiled. 'Can I put in a good word for you?'

'Ah. As you just mentioned, Miss Ryan, actions are more powerful than words. I'll have to prove to the architects first that we can get the store back on track. Once I do that, then I think your father will realise we are the people for the job.'

'Well, I sincerely wish you good luck with that.' She stood up and so did he. He took both her hands and she didn't resist.

'Until the next time we meet,' he said.

She nodded. 'Until then, Mr Leary.' Mary came into the room and Catherine turned to her. 'Would you see Mr Leary out, dear Mary?'

Mary looked at each of them in turn and smiled. 'Surely, Catherine.'

Catherine sat back down and waited until Mary had come back into the room. She was excited. All worry about John's past was now a vapour that was swiftly vanishing. She knew that her strong feelings for him were forcing her to forget Clarissa and other matters, but she didn't care. She knew that he was telling the truth about his commitment to her. She was happy and had to tell someone.

Mary came in and stood near her. She was smiling.

Catherine grabbed both her hands and forced her to sit down beside her. 'I'm going to keep seeing him.'

Mary pressed back. 'I'm so glad. I really am.'

'He's the one I want, Mary. He is. I love him, not Ian McCreadie.'

'Mr McCreadie is very keen; I see the signs. It wouldn't surprise me if he asked for your hand.'

'Nor me. But Ian doesn't make me feel the way Mr Leary does. Do you know what I mean?'

'Peter made me feel the same. It's hard to describe. Happy, eager, wanting to yell your feelings out loud, all that.'

'Yes. That's right. I guess, I'm in love.'

'When did you realise?' Mary asked.

'After I'd spoken to Don. He said that he'd heard good stories about John and from all reports he was a man of character. Don also added that no one is a saint and that's when I remembered what you said. There are no certainties in life. But if you really love, then trust to it.'

'And what about Mr Leary? Does he know you believe in him?'

'He does indeed.' Catherine brought a hand to her face. 'Oh, my goodness, we didn't even discuss when we could meet again. We were both so dazed, we just said goodbye.'

Mary squeezed her hands again. 'I'll find a way to get us back to Mr Leary's house.'

'Thank you, Mary, thank you.' Catherine realised much later that it was the first time she'd heard Mary call her former home, *Mr Leary's house.*

Chapter Ten

John was in his George Street office early to review cost reports, especially the wool-store project. He then checked his diary. It was eight o'clock and he had to be at the wool-store site in half an hour. It was time to go. Out in the street he hailed a cab. It was Thursday the ninth of February and on Monday he'd got a letter from Bardells saying they would rescind the contract in seven days if John had not restarted on the roof framing.

What was Sean doing on the site? John had some idea that he was organising the labour. Seven days ago, Sean had sought John's approval to move twenty carpenters from the other sites to the wool store for a set period, and to employ another ten besides. What the hell did he need thirty men for? If John hadn't trusted Sean's judgment, he would've refused the request. Well, he'd find out when he'd got there.

One thing was certain, Bowmans had got wind of the architect's ultimatum. John couldn't think how, but he suspected his competitors might have whispered into their ears. Bowmans had refused to lower their price. So whatever Sean had going on site had to work, otherwise they'd be bumped off the job.

John's cab stopped at the wool-store site and one thing struck him as odd straight away. All the windows in the brick walls at ground-floor level were boarded up on the inside, preventing anyone from looking in. What was going on? John was about to mount the stairs to the gantry-supported site sheds built over the footpath, when a single door halfway down the long wall opened and Sean came up to him. He looked at John and smiled.

'You've probably being scratching your noggin for the past week, wondering what we've been doing.'

'That I have.' *Though I've mostly been thinking of Catherine.*

'Well,' Sean said, 'come in and we'll show you. I think we've got the answer.'

John stepped into the wool store. The huge area was bounded by brick walls on four sides and in the centre was a row of individually braced columns. But it wasn't the walls or columns that struck John with surprise. No, at every gridline marking a braced column, there was a gang of men sawing, nailing, bolting and lifting into position assemblies of timber. What were they? He looked at Sean.

'Instead of building one complete truss,' Sean said, 'and then lifting it up into place onto its column, we've decided to build all the trusses for one half of the site, *at the same time.*'

'You mean, those assemblies are parts of trusses?'

'Yeah, one to each bay. When we've finished one half we'll move onto the other side of the store.'

John, amazed, started to walk along to check on the teams. They were hard at work and there was an efficiency and order to their methods.

Sean said. 'We cut every timber section of each truss to size, and lay them out on each grid line. That makes it easy to lift each completed truss into place. With all the cut timber we've assembled the bolts, rods, screws and connecting plates that are needed. One team works on a certain part of one truss then moves onto the next truss to perform the same task. We've got a frame team to do the top and bottom chords, a lattice team to build the members in between, a connecting team to put the whole lot together, a measuring team for checking and a final team to touch up any unfinished work. John we're back in business. We'll be able to lift the first three trusses on Saturday.'

John looked ahead: indeed, three of the giant trusses were nearly completed.

'It's saved us heaps of time,' Sean said.

Now the reality set in. They were back in business. John slapped Sean on the back. 'You bloody beauty, Sean. You bloody beauty.' Then he pointed to the windows.

Sean grinned. 'Yeah, that's why we boarded up the site. Keep the prying eyes out.' He scowled. 'This labour will cost us a bit but we'll save on time overall.'

John was still too excited by what was happening around him to comment. It was a great idea, a grand idea. 'Let's push on big with what we have here. Get more men. What about lifting?'

Sean pointed to the row of solitary centre columns running the length of the wool store. Each column was temporarily braced until its pair of trusses could be loaded and connected on top of it. When the trusses were loaded and fixed, the temporary bracing would be taken down. 'We'll use cranes and the columns as centre load points and leverage off them. The first truss will be slow but we'll set up the crane parts, then assemble them using the same steps as the trusses.'

John was impressed. It had taken the mischief of the truss maker at Sullivans and the setback to cause another idea to germinate and be a reality. Here was the proof. 'Keep the men hard at it, Sean.'

'We're working three shifts now.'

John didn't wonder. 'Anything else you need? Where's the roof that you ordered?'

'Took it down. You asked if I needed anything. Just make sure our other jobs aren't suffering. There's a lot of men here who should be on them.'

'I'll see to that and I'll write to the architects and William Ryan,' John said, 'and get them down here on Saturday afternoon after you've got your three up. That'll show them.'

Sean grinned. 'Good, now let me be. We've got timbers to tie and brackets to bolt.'

'That I'll do.' John walked away with spirits lifted. The job was saved, and his heart had found love. Life was good.

* * *

It was Saturday morning, two days after John's uplifting visit to the wool-store site. Sitting back after he'd finished his breakfast, he was tempted to go to site this afternoon and see for himself the erection of the first three trusses. No, Sean would have it in safe hands and he should spend more time with Richard.

Mary Harrigan had asked if she could bring Reggie over to play this morning with Richard, and John had agreed. They'd be here shortly. Glancing at the timber panelling above the sideboard, he thought about the quest that had so consumed Mary Harrigan. To a degree it had helped him drag himself out of his pit of depression. If Peter Smith had buried treasure in this house or its surrounds, it would take the demolition of the house, brick by brick, and the sifting of hundreds of tons of earth, to find the elusive wealth. And that wasn't going to happen. No, the quest was over.

The nine o'clock chimes started and John stood up and left the table. The cook removed his plate and John went into the drawing room and picked up the Saturday edition of *The Sydney Morning Herald*. Through the window he saw a cab approach, and Mary and her son alight. And, to John's surprise and pleasure, so did Catherine Ryan. Why was she here? He didn't care and he dashed to the front door to join Stella, who opened the door to the three visitors.

John only looked at Catherine, who smiled at him. 'Come in, come in,' John said. 'Out of this sun.'

'Thank you, Mr Leary,' Mary said. 'Go on Reggie, go on.'

'Richard's in the back yard, Reggie,' John said still looking at Catherine, who had followed Mary into the drawing room.

'Come on, Reggie,' Mary said, 'I'll take you out and we can all play.'

Stella left them but stood at a discreet distance away. Catherine said. 'Mary asked me to come with her today. She's finally accepted that no money is here, and she wants to end this part of her life and move on. She wanted moral support.'

John didn't care why Catherine was here. She was, and that was all that mattered. 'Come in and sit down. Would you like a cool drink?'

'Yes, please.'

'Stella, a cool drink for both of us, please.'

'Yes, Mr Leary.'

John was in a daze. This was unreal but wonderful. 'Sit down, sit down.' Catherine sat on one settee and he on the opposite one.

'Father says that he's satisfied you can get his store going again.'

'I'm glad.'

'It was no outpouring of joy, Mr Leary,' she said and smiled. He did too. 'It was just that he was relieved to end his embarrassment with the other directors. I know him. He's a proud man. When he takes a chance with someone, he doesn't want that person to let him down.'

Their drinks arrived.

'I'm glad I've got back into his good books,' he said.

She smiled again. 'Well not quite onto a page but at least a mention on the back cover.'

He laughed. He had missed their banter.

'He's going to see the roof being raised this afternoon,' she said.

'Grand,' John said. He couldn't stop looking at her. 'I've missed you.'

She blushed but recovered. 'I know.'

In that simple acknowledgment, John knew that she was aware of his thoughts about her, about his wanting her.

In reaching for her glass, she nearly tipped it over and John leaned over and took her hand. She looked at him as he held onto her.

'I want to see you more often, Catherine.'

Her look told him everything. 'And I you.'

Instinct took over and he moved onto the settee next to her. She smiled at his gesture. He took both her hands in his and she didn't seem to mind. He was able to say without worry, doubt, guilt or guile, 'I meant what I said, Catherine. I love you.'

She opened her mouth a little for a moment and studied his face as if she wanted to remember it for ever. 'I love you too.'

He pressed her harder and she winced. 'Sorry,' he said letting go the grip and but still holding her. He was overcome with feelings that he'd hadn't had for years. 'Will you marry me?'

She squeezed back. 'Yes, John. Yes, I will.'

He kissed her and she responded. They hugged then broke apart to look at each other. Her eyes were wet and his were the same. This was a wonderful moment. Sounds from the kitchen heralded Mary returning from the back yard. John and Catherine separated but remained on the settee. Mary came in and pressed her face with her handkerchief.

'It's warming up out there,' she said and looked at each of them in turn. She smiled. 'Now, I think something's happened in here that's worth talking about, What do you think?' John looked at Catherine and she nodded and smiled.

'Catherine has agreed to marry me,' John said.

Mary threw her arms up and went forward to embrace Catherine and pat John on the shoulder. It was very joyful. John saw movement out of the corner of his eye and looked over to see Stella standing in the doorway. Her face looked as though she'd seen an horrific accident. She recovered and came in.

'I overheard, Mr Leary,' she said. 'I'm sorry.'

'I hope you'll be happy for us,' John said.

'Congratulations to you both,' she said, forcing a smile. Then she left them.

'And mine also, of course,' Mary said. 'Well, well. Now, you must have a lot to talk about and not much time in which to do it. Say Stella and I take the boys down to the bay for a paddle? Would an hour do you?'

'Thank you, Mary,' John said. 'That would be grand.'

'Right, I'll get things cracking.'

Now John and Catherine had the house to themselves. It was all so unreal, the solitude and just the two of them. They kissed and embraced again, knowing that the passion they gave each other was returned with interest.

It was an extraordinary sensation for John, holding her and feeling her against him.

During the next embrace, he sensed that Catherine might be experiencing all this for the first time. It wasn't arrogance on his part but from what he felt on her lips and the sounds she made when he caressed her, he suspected these responses were all new to her. He had the impression that she would let him lead her anywhere. And he was tempted to do so. So it was with regret that he eased himself away, because her eyes were excited and her breathing was rapid. 'We should talk,' he said.

She took a deep breath and smiled. 'We should.'

'What will your parents say?' he said.

She drank some more of her water. 'Mother, no problem. Father, you'll have to ask and get his permission.' She looked at him.

'Thank goodness we've started back on his job, or he wouldn't be talking to me at all!' He smiled. 'I'll come tomorrow. Is that all right?'

'The sooner the better, my darling.'

That endearment sounded a treat. 'About eleven, after Mass?'

'Perfect,' she said. 'And as I'm an optimist, I'll keep a place for you at our dinner table.'

John wanted to know the lay of the land. 'Will he accept me?'

'I'll talk to Mother and Don tonight. I'll get them to work on Father. Hopefully by the time you get your chance on stage, you'll be the star.'

He laughed and he kissed her again. 'I'll get you a ring.'

'Lovely.'

'And we'll have a party with—'

Catherine placed a finger on his lips. 'Grand, but let's wait till after lunch tomorrow.'

She was right and he welcomed her sensitivity.

'I'm not interested in a big engagement, John. Just our families and close friends will do me.'

He felt the same. 'Now, about our wedding.'

'After tomorrow.'

He grinned. 'Very well.' Then a cloud smudged his blue sky. 'I have to talk to you about something that will need careful thought and action. It's about Stella.'

'And Richard?' Catherine said.

'Exactly. Stella will feel threatened now that we're engaged. I think she fears that she won't be part of Richard's life any more. But I'd like her to be, for as long as she wants. Do you agree?

'My dear,' she said, 'I'll never replace Clarissa in that part of your heart, nor would I ever try to be a mother to Richard straight away. I've thought about this too. Stella has been both mother and governess to your son for two years now. I think she should continue in his life until she gets married, and perhaps even after, depending how they both feel. It will take time for the four of us to find our feet and make sure that her love for Richard is protected.'

Isn't she marvellous, John mused. 'Good. Very good.'

For the next half hour they talked nonstop about all sorts of things. Then the front door opened, and their crew returned. The boys were laughing and chattering.

Catherine kissed John on the cheek and Richard noticed. He then smiled. A good sign. 'I'll see you tomorrow, John,' she said. 'Good luck.'

'Till then.'

Stella put her hand on Richard's shoulder and Catherine joined Mary in the vestibule.

'Goodbye, Mr Leary,' Mary said, 'and congratulations.'

John was distracted with Catherine leaving and was only half listening to Mary. 'We will see you soon,' he said.

Catherine squeezed his hand and walked out into the sunshine.

Mary turned as she reached the front gate. 'Have you given any thoughts to changing the Bede Hall sign to Golden Hall?'

John watched Catherine go and calculated the minutes before he'd see her again. 'What, sorry?'

She smiled and looked at Catherine. 'The sign,' Mary pointed to the ground sign. 'Will you be changing this soon?'

John remembered their conversation. 'Yes, yes, of course.'

Mary smiled. 'Grand. See you tomorrow.'

'You will indeed,' John said and watched them leave. Stella closed the door and avoided John's eye. 'Come Richard,' she said. 'Time for your noon meal.'

John went to join his son for his meal and thought about the meeting he needed to have with William Ryan. He couldn't discuss the future with Stella until that meeting had occurred. He realised that Stella would be thinking the same. Would she be hoping that Ryan would refuse to let John have his daughter's hand?

The next morning, John attended the ten o'clock Mass at St Marys and was pleased to find his sister there with her family, his uncle and aunt and the Connaires. He was bursting to tell anybody he saw about his good news, but he listened to Catherine's quiet voice of reason whispering to him: *Wait till after Sunday.*

After Mass he told Gerry about his need for a new house sign and Gerry agreed to help. His uncle suggested a marble sign for the front garden, which was less protected from the weather than the one by the door. He said he would get pleasure in doing the job himself at nights, if John could pay for the materials. John agreed. Gerry said he would be there on Tuesday afternoon to measure up. John thanked him, wished his aunt a good day and greeted his sister with a hug, which surprised her. He whispered to her. 'I've got something to tell you.'

'Surely,' she said. 'Liam dear, go down to the cab stop with the children, I'll be there in a moment.'

She joined her arm with his as they walked off. 'Now, what is it?'

'Catherine has agreed to marry me.'

She stopped, pulled him to her and hugged him again. When she broke away her eyes were shining. 'How grand is that! Are you happy?'

'You bet I am! I've been given the love of a wonderful woman. One to whom I'll return that love every day.' he grinned. 'I've got to go now and beard the lion. Mr Ryan, senior. So, wish me luck. Now, no word to anybody yet. Wait until I get his approval.'

Maureen pressed his hands and kissed his cheek. 'Congratulations, my darling. You deserve it and more. She's a wonderful girl.' She waved and left him.

After leaving Richard in Stella's capable hands, John made his way to Potts Point. On his way there his joy was changing by the yard to a stomach-clenching anxiety. Dealing with William Ryan on a business basis, where John could show he was confident of what he could build and when, was one thing. Trying to convince a father that his daughter would be safe in John's hands for the rest of her life, quite another. The cab stopped and John alighted. Catherine met him at the front door. Her smile to him was polite, though her eyes sparkled.

'Father is in his study. I'll show you in.'

William Ryan stood up as John entered and Catherine walked away. 'Sit down, Mr Leary please. Care for a drink?'

'Perhaps later,' John said, 'if that's all right.'

'Straight to the point then, eh?'

John sat down and looked at his prospective father-in-law. Ryan was not tall, unlike John's six foot three, but with them both seated Ryan would not feel intimidated. As when he was in his office, he had the look of a hard-edged negotiator.

'It came as no surprise that my daughter is interested in you, Mr Leary. Nor to my wife.' He paused and moved a cigar case closer to him. 'She is a little younger than what we consider a marriageable age and we'd hoped to have her with us for longer. But then,' he smiled, 'love sets its own timetable.'

A good start, John thought. 'I love your daughter, Mr Ryan. I want to marry her.'

Ryan looked at him for a long time. 'That's what Catherine says, and she wants to marry you too.' He sighed. 'Look, Mr Leary, all parents would like their children to marry a person they consider appropriate. They also want them to be happy.' He paused. 'And Catherine's idea of being happy is to marry you.'

'Yes, she does me the honour of saying she loves me. I promise to make her a good husband.'

'I can see you're sincere, but I think there's more to discuss about your situation. You have a child and, frankly, you have a past. If we are to believe everything we hear, some of your past actions have been questionable.' He looked hard at John now. John said nothing and Ryan continued, 'Catherine has some idea of your past and begs me not to judge you on it.' He paused. 'But it's hard not to. I'm human and I have a daughter to protect.'

'I understand that, Mr Ryan, and I acknowledge what I've done. There are things I can't expunge, and they will haunt me till I die. But I have never done anything criminal, nor can my past actions touch Catherine in any way. And I live my life differently now. What I feel for Catherine is love, pure and simple. And beyond what you may have heard, I have no secrets that I need to confide to you or her. There are no skeletons in my cupboard that haven't seen Sydney's sunshine.'

'I hope so, Mr Leary. I sincerely hope so. Because we are taking a risk in believing you and we can only evaluate your behaviour on what we've seen since we've known you. Catherine believes in you, but her belief may be clouded by love. Donald thinks you're made of the right stuff.' He exhaled. 'So, we will not stand in the way of your marriage. Our blessing on you both is woven with hope and a blank cheque of trust. Let my daughter down and … no, I make no threats, John. I'm letting you know my heartfelt wishes for my daughter's happiness. You have Catherine's love, but you also have her belief in you. That's strong, yes, but it's also precious and fragile.' He stood up and came around to where John was seated. John stood up. Ryan put out his hand. 'Welcome to our family,' he said.

John was overwhelmed. 'Thank you.'

Ryan seemed moved as well. Then he gave a knowing grin. 'And you'd better make a fine job of our building project.'

'Yes, sir.'

'You'll want to see my daughter and tell her the news. Any date for the wedding?'

'Autumn, probably end of May.'

'Good,' Ryan said. 'Good. No sense in stringing it out for months. Go on, John, go on.'

John left the study and found an anxious Catherine standing in the hallway. He nodded to her and she ran to him and they embraced. 'It's all grand,' he said and kissed her. John heard footsteps behind him and they turned to her father.

'Well, get along you two,' Ryan said, 'and tell your mother. Don will be pleased as well.'

'Oh, Father, thank you, thank you,' Catherine said and hugged him.

He kissed her cheek. 'Off you go and set a place for John at the table, Catherine. He'll stay to eat.'

Catherine looked at John and smiled. 'What a good idea.'

After a midday meal complete with laughter, wine and good will, John left his fiancée and took a cab back to Point Piper. On the way, he felt the wheels were not touching the ground and he was gliding on a carpet of happiness. As he got nearer to home, however, his good feeling took a break. He had relationships to foster. Richard and Stella. The boy was of him, and the other was more than a housekeeper.

He greeted Stella at the front door. 'Come into the drawing room, for a moment. Is Richard busy?'

'He's having some biscuits in the kitchen with milk, Mr Leary. I can't keep away from him long.'

He smiled at her. 'Then we'll talk in the dining room with the door open.'

'Very well, Mr Leary.'

John was self-conscious even though he was as happy as he'd ever been in his life. 'Mr Ryan has agreed to the marriage. We'll make it official soon.'

Stella nodded. 'Congratulations. Miss Catherine will make a fine wife for you.'

'Thank you, Stella. And in time she will become a new mother to Richard.'

Stella flinched. Mary had been right: there was resistance there.

'Stella? Is there something wrong?' he said.

She looked down at the hands clasped in her lap. 'Are you not pleased with my care of Richard and your household, Mr Leary? That's why you're getting married again? I've let you down?'

John was shocked and reached and placed his hand over hers. 'Dear God, no Stella. That hasn't even entered my mind.'

Her eyes were glistening now. 'You mean that?'

'I'm surprised that you even thought that about me. You've been the captain in this rough sea for the past two years. Without you, Richard and I would have foundered.'

'I've been worried, like. With Miss Catherine being in Richard's life, I'll be left out and forgotten.'

'Richard loves you, Stella. He loves you.'

'I know he does.'

John strove for the right words. 'Catherine needs you as a companion to Richard and as housekeeper as much as I do. When I marry Catherine, if you consent to stay with us, we will be very grateful if you can stay in Richard's life for as long as it suits you. You've helped me bring him up, Stella, and your relationship with him won't end, whether you're in this house or not.' She had raised her head now, and he let her hands go and looked at her earnestly. 'Do you understand?'

She seemed relieved. 'I think I do, Mr Leary, thank you.'

'No thanks needed. It's myself who should be thanking you. Now, come on, let's join Richard.'

* * *

Gerry Gleeson was enjoying this morning's ride along South Head Road near summer's end. It was the end of February and the weather was clear and bright. Gerry was satisfied with what lay behind him in the tray of his wagon; a square marble plinth with 'Golden Hall' chiselled onto the top of it, with love. He had put his skills as a stone mason to work in this present to the new couple. He had selected, cut, honed and crafted it so it could be set in the garden in the same spot occupied by the old brass sign that said 'Bede Hall'.

'Posh houses coming up,' said Tom, who was sitting next to him.

'They are,' Gerry said, 'and there's not many like them in town.'

Gerry had wanted to bed the sign in place himself, but age was taking its toll. The low marble block weighed nearly seventy pounds, so he'd brought along an apprentice from the Bank of Australasia job that was finishing up this month. The boy, Tom, was sullen and an average worker, but Gerry didn't care. He just needed an extra pair of hands to help him.

Their wagon stopped at number seventy-nine and Tom swore. 'God, look at that. Mr Leary must be rich.'

'Just get the sign onto the trolley,' Gerry said, 'without damaging it, and get it inside the front gate. Can you do that?'

'I'm not daft. Yeah.'

Gerry sighed. 'I'll see Mr Leary and then I'll be back. Don't do anything but unload the slab. All right?'

'All right, all right.'

Irritated, Gerry grabbed a canvas bag, a seven-foot-long steel bar and two shovels, and shook his head; he'd rather have bedded the sign on his own. He dropped his gear near the brass sign and went to the front door, where Stella greeted him.

'Mr Leary and his sister and her family are in the back yard. Shall I get him, Mr Gleeson?'

'Ah. On second thoughts, don't bother him, Stella. Just tell him I have the sign and I'm installing it. I want him to see it when it's all done.'

'Very well, Mr Gleeson.'

erry smiled at her. 'Thank you.'

He returned to the front, where Tom was moving the trolley with its carpet-wrapped load towards the front fence. Gerry pulled out a pair of shears from his canvas bag and started to clear away the foliage. Tom arrived with his trolley.

'Right, let's put it on the ground and uncover it.' Gerry said.

Just as they did so, John joined them. Gerry gave a start and a grin. 'You heard us? I was going to surprise you when I had it in place.'

'Morning, uncle,' John said and nodded to Tom. 'Yes, I heard the wagon come up. You didn't think I'd want to miss this, did you? I'll give you a hand.'

When the sign was unwrapped, John whistled. 'It's beautiful, uncle. You've done a great job. Do you need a hand to set it in place?'

'Tom and I will manage, thank you. You see to your loved ones. Right, Tom, Let's get cracking.'

'I'll leave you to it,' John said reluctantly, and went inside.

'Tom,' Gerry said, 'get started with the mortar. We'll bed the slab down on something solid—this Bede Hall plate is on timber and I don't like the look of it.'

While Tom got busy, Gerry dug down deep beside the old sign. After a while he said disgustedly, 'It's a bloody hardwood base, and white ants have eaten a third of it. The brass plating is not bad, though.'

It looked to Gerry as though an expert craftsman had made the plate by heating a sheet of brass to a high temperature, then beating it down over a mould that formed the letters, BEDE HALL. It was an excellent job. The letters stood well proud of the top and the thick brass sheet fitted smoothly down the sides of the timber block as well. Once he got the whole thing out of the ground and detached the brass from the block, maybe the metal could be melted down. Underneath the dust and grime it looked surprisingly untarnished.

He grunted. 'It's set deeper than I thought.' He struggled to get purchase and lift the sign out of the earth, but it was heavier than he had expected. 'That's strange,' he said. 'Hardwood is dense but it's not as heavy as stone. Give me that bar, Tom.'

'I can do it, boss.'

'No, let me,' Gerry said. 'You attend to the Portland cement.'

After three attempts Gerry was regretting not getting Tom to do it. But by using the right combination of force and fulcrum, he managed to lever the sign out of the earth. Parnell came to inspect it.

'Go away, boy.'

Parnell was obedient and Gerry bent over to look at the underside of the timber base. To his surprise he saw two holes drilled through it.

In the past, when the timber was dry and solid, it looked as though it might have been fastened to a wall, like John's 'Golden Hall' sign near the front door. The two holes must have been drilled for the supports.

Parnell was capering around the work site, pleased to have company in the garden. As the dog raced past the front of Richard's fort, Gerry noted the two brass ferrules that the boy used as a bridge across his pretend moat. Gerry recalled Richard telling him they'd found the ferrules in the garden. On impulse, Gerry went over and picked them up. He stepped back, cleaned the dirt out of the holes in the hardwood block and tried to insert them. They fitted. He looked back at the house, wondering if this sign had once been set into the wall of the house. If so, how had it ended up in the garden?

He shrugged and pulled the ferrules out. All that effort had made him thirsty, so he went to a water tank attached to the house and drank from the tap. He splashed his face. 'How's that mix going?'

'Ten minutes,' Tom said.

Gerry spent the time squaring out the hole and removing roots and stones. Near the water tank there was a pile of leftover sand that John had bought for Richard's sand pit. Gerry got a few shovels full and used that as a base for the new sign. Tom came up with the batch of cement and Gerry supervised setting it down as a bed course. Together, they lifted the marble block and placed the base on the cement. Gerry levelled it off, packed soil and turf around its base and wiped off the excess dirt. Standing up, he stretched his back and grimaced. Parnell came up and wagged his tail, seeming to approve of the job.

'That should do us, Tom,' Gerry said. 'Let's get the other plate to the foundry and have it melted down. It should make a bit of money that we can donate it to an orphanage.'

They loaded the old Bede Hall sign onto the wagon. Tom packed up their tools and kit and Gerry washed his hands.

John came out at that moment and strode over to examine the new sign in its raw bed of earth. 'I like it,' he said. 'The marble looks more natural in amongst the greenery.'

Gerry was pleased. 'Once your flowers grow back, it'll look even better. Maybe yellow flowers, to match the name. By the way, nephew, when you put your new sign up on the wall over there, was there a space in the stone where another sign might have been inserted? Because I'm wondering whether the brass one might have been there originally.'

John looked puzzled. 'Why would you think that?'

Gerry pointed to the brass ferrules, now lying on bare earth. 'Those things fit into the base of your "Bede Hall" sign. Can't be coincidence. It looks as though it must have once been inserted in a vertical surface.'

John turned to look at the front wall of his house. 'Hang on, you're right. When I changed that sign to "Golden Hall" I found an alcove in the wall. It's still there, behind the new brass plate.'

Gerry was amazed. 'Whoa. Anything in it?'

John shook his head. 'Nothing.' He gave a short laugh. 'No gold, that's for sure.'

* * *

The Saturday was cool for the end of May, but the afternoon sun shone strong and bright onto the wedding party. Catherine exited the coach with her father, followed by her two bridesmaids and the matron of honour, Mary Harrigan. Mary adjusted the train of Catherine's wedding dress and Catherine glanced around her before she put her arm through her father's. Across College Street, Ian McCreadie was standing alone. When she caught his eye he nodded to her, his face sombre. She smiled at him and then approached the steps of the cathedral. At the top step, she could see inside the beautiful nave and her bridal march began, as she stepped down the aisle with her father.

Through the leaded windows of St Mary's Cathedral, with their glorious depictions of saints, coloured light bathed the congregation. John looked only at Catherine, taking all of her in. He thought about the last three months during which he'd experienced sunshine-filled harmony and peaceful times with her. And there were times of humour and gaiety as well. Their engagement party at her house in late March had been a simple affair, with friends and family gathered to celebrate. Since then there had been no visits from his past, no ghosts to confront, or guilt to assuage.

After hugging her father, Catherine came to John's side. Their families were behind them, his sister Maureen glowing with happiness for him and Catherine. But Uncle Gerry and his Aunt Moira were absent, which concerned John. They had said they wouldn't miss this for the world, so they must have met with some mishap.

The priest started the Mass and John was caught up in the solemnity and joy of those moments. When it came time to recite the vows, he registered that Gerry and Moira had still not arrived, but concentrated all his attention on Catherine. A few minutes later, there was movement behind them. When John glanced over, Gerry smiled at him and gave him the thumbs up. John relaxed.

After the Mass, when their union was recorded, he and Catherine left the cathedral and received congratulations from a happy crowd on the front steps. John could see his uncle was fidgeting to get near him, and finally Gerry fought his way through.

'John, John,' Gerry said. 'Sorry we were late, but I've got something exciting to tell you.'

'We're pretty excited too. You can give us your felicitations, if you like.'

Gerry blurted out, 'Of course, of course.' In his confusion he shook the hands of both.

Catherine laughed. 'And what are you so eager to tell us?'

'Golden Hall!' Gerry said, then stood there with his eyes bulging, as though he were suddenly lost for words.

John laughed too. 'Yes, indeed, that's where we're going. And if we're to reach there before our guests, we'd better be off.' He put out an arm, to hand Catherine into the waiting carriage.

Gerry gave up trying to stammer out his news. 'You're right. I'll tell you at home.'

The carriage set off and they waved to the party on the steps of St Mary's, most of whom would be joining them soon at Point Piper. John held Catherine's hand all the way home, where the reception tent and tables had been set out on the lawn.

It was a joyous afternoon filled with laughter, witty speeches and dancing. John had not been so happy for a long time.

Eventually Gerry managed to get the couple into a huddle with just himself and Moira. Bursting with what he had to tell, he nonetheless took time to fill all their glasses with champagne, raise his glass and hold it up before the amused gaze of his relatives, before downing a gulp.

'I've been lazy,' he said. 'Bloody lazy.'

Moira remonstrated with him. 'Language, Gerry!'

'Sorry,' he said, 'but I was. Remember that brass sign I dug out of the garden? Well,' he said, not waiting for either John or Catherine to answer, 'I meant to get it melted down and give the money to charity. But I didn't get around to it until this morning.'

'I was getting ready for your big day,' Moira said. 'The big man wasn't—why he had to bother himself with a bit of metal today, I don't know.'

Gerry ignored her. 'The foundry at Redfern told me they had a spare moment and I took it. It just had to be today. All I needed to do was separate the brass plating from the hardwood base and send it around to the foundry. So I set to.'

'On this day of all days. It could have waited,' Moira said.

Gerry ignored her again. 'In my shed I got the metal off the timber, no problem. It was real solid on top, and thick down the sides, too.'

He poured more champagne for them all and looked at each in turn.

'Well, Gerry,' Moira said. 'Get on with it.'

'When I cleaned it up, I could see there was no tarnishing on the surface. Looking closely, I got a fright. On the road gangs, I often ran into people who'd come to this country after one thing, and one thing only. And only a few of them had found it.'

They all looked at him, too confused for words.

'Now, you may ask what my past has to do with anything, and you'll find out. My dear ones, I didn't go to the foundry this morning. I didn't get the sign melted down. What I did was take it in the gig and go to town to an old associate of mine who knows his stuff.' Gerry put his glass down, reached into his jacket and withdrew a piece of paper. 'Read this, nephew.'

John read it, holding it so that Catherine could see the handwritten note as well. John looked up and smiled at Gerry. 'Is he sure about this?'

'As sure as there are three heads that bound our harbour,' Gerry said.

'Gold?' Catherine said.

'Gold,' Gerry replied. 'I've seen solid gold only once in my life and that was a long time ago. I'll never forget. Peter Smith more than once said to his wife that there was gold at Bede Hall. He was telling her the truth. John, all the metal that made up your sign is solid gold.'

'All of it?' John said amazed.

Gerry replied, 'I believe you'll get a certificate from the assayer on Monday.' He sipped more of his bubbly. 'It's a grand present on your wedding day, John.'

'It certainly is,' John said and smiled.

Catherine meanwhile was not looking at him—she was looking at Mary Harrigan, who was on the other side of the lawn, watching the children being given slices of the wedding cake. 'This might take some telling,' she said.

On Monday 4 June, John was playing blocks in the Point Piper drawing room with Richard and Catherine, but when Stella brought in the afternoon mail and placed it in the vestibule, he got up at once and went to sift through the letters. He and his beautiful wife had enjoyed a brief and blissful honeymoon down at the Shoalhaven. Now they were home, beginning their new life together. Both he and Catherine were intrigued to discover whether Gerry's prediction was about to come true: that Golden Hall had revealed a treasure, to coincide with their wedding.

John opened the most likely envelope. 'Dear,' he said to Catherine, 'it's here.' He read the enclosed certificate, which described the purity of the gold and its weight, and established its value at £4,500. A fortune in most people's terms.

'Well, it's proven,' he said and brought the letter over for Catherine to read it.

'Dear me,' she said, 'that's a lot of money.'

'It is indeed.'

'Are you still in the same mind as to what to do with it?' Richard tugged at Catherine's sleeve, and she rebuilt the blocks that he'd knocked over.

'I am,' he said. 'I'll write a note to Mary Harrigan and get it delivered today. I'll ask her to come here as soon as it's convenient for her. I won't give her the news; I'll simply ask her to visit.'

'How do you think she'll take the surprise?' Catherine said.

John had formed four blocks into the letters of his first name and Richard was fingering them. 'We'll see.'

At six o'clock on the following Wednesday evening, John and Catherine stood up as Stella brought Mary Harrigan into the drawing room. John smiled and gestured to his guest to sit down. Stella left them and Catherine closed the cavity-sliding doors that closed off the room to vestibule and dining room.

'Tea?' Catherine said sitting down.

'Thank you, Catherine,' she said and smiled.

After their teas were poured, John took a breath. 'Mrs Harrigan … Mary. Your husband Peter did leave wealth in this house. And we've found it.'

Mary's eyes rounded in shock, and she placed her cup and saucer down on the table with a shaking hand. 'Found what?'

'If you follow us, we'll show you,' John said.

John led them out onto the front veranda. The evening was mild for early winter. A lamp mounted near the door shone onto the Golden Hall sign on the front wall. 'This is the sign I put up when I changed the name of the house, soon after it was passed on to me by David McGuire.'

'Yes, yes,' Mary said, her voice impatient. Then she said, 'Oh, I'm sorry, Mr Leary. But please, what did you find?'

From the front steps he picked up a lantern that he had asked Stella Fawcett to place there. Stella, too, was avid to see how Mary would react to the surprise. She was probably looking through a front window as they walked down the path towards the front gate.

'Please come with me,' John said to Mary. When he stopped near the gate, the light from the lantern illuminated Gerry's fine marble handiwork. 'This is where the old sign used to sit. It said "Bede Hall", your husband's choice of name for the house. And this is where we found the gold.'

'Gold!' Mary's face for a moment looked as bright as the lamplight.

'Gold,' John said. 'Buried treasure, if you like. The gold plate and lettering on the old sign were fashioned in solid gold.'

Mary stretched out her hand and pressed Catherine's shoulder for support. She was quiet for some time. '*Gold.* Then Peter's promise to me was true.' Tears welled in her eyes and Catherine put her arm around her. 'He did leave me something,' Mary said, 'God bless him.'

'When my uncle dug out the old sign, it looked as if it had once been attached to the front wall. That would make sense, fixing a valuable sign onto the house rather than setting it in the garden.'

'That's strange,' Mary said. 'On that dreadful day, when I came home I found Peter here unconscious near the front gate, with a wagon and trolley nearby. Was he about to move the old sign? Or replace it? Dear me, four years ago—five this spring—was when he died. I'll never forget that day.'

'Come,' John said, 'let's go inside.'

Seated with a fresh cup of tea, Mary continued with her story. The others could sense that she needed them to hear it. They were also puzzled about what Peter had been doing that day. 'Reggie and I went to town in the afternoon, and when we returned, I found Peter.' She thought for a while. 'All during that week he said that he had something in the house that he could use to solve all our problems. He must have meant the sign. Possibly he intended melting the gold down for cash.'

'I've been thinking what might have happened,' John said. 'The solid-gold sign was initially installed in the wall near the front door. I say that because the cavity in which it was housed was large, to take the extra weight. Two brass ferrules were needed for strength. In fact Richard and I found those exact ferrules in the garden some time ago—without the slightest idea what they were for. I think you're right: your husband removed the gold sign from the front wall and was planning to take it to town to be melted down, on the day he passed away.'

'But then, why was it found in the garden?' Mary said. 'And wouldn't there have been a gap in the front wall after it was removed? I don't remember noticing the size of it.'

John shook his head. 'There was a plain metal plaque over that hole when the house was gifted to me by my father-in-law.'

Catherine said gently, 'You must have been in such turmoil that day, and for so long afterwards. You could see your husband had moved the sign—whether it left a gap in the front wall would hardly have been a worry to you.'

'No,' Mary said. 'I was so upset … I thought I would die too.'

'We'll never be sure what happened to your husband that day,' Catherine continued in the same gentle tones. 'But perhaps it went like this. He intended to take the gold wall sign into town to be assayed. He removed it from the wall, carried it down the path towards the gate, but suddenly he felt faint or ill. He decided he wasn't well enough to go to town, so he took out the ferrules from the timber at the back, tipped the sign into a depression so that it could have a temporary place in the garden, and planned on taking it to town another day.' She looked at them both. 'When the house went up for sale, the agents had the gap in the front wall covered over, and perhaps dug the sign in the garden further in.'

'It sounds plausible,' Mary said sadly. 'It was such a dreadful time, it all went by in a blur.'

They remained quiet for some time, then John said. 'Mary, if you hadn't suggested that I change your husband's lettering to "Golden Hall", the gold might never have been found. In a way, its discovery is due to you.'

Mary nodded bravely. 'So, what do you think the value is?'

Catherine said quietly, 'Nearly four thousand, five hundred pounds.'

'My goodness,' Mary said.

John said, 'Now, there seem to be complexities in law as to who owns that gold. I've sought legal advice and in summary, only a court could decide who owns it—the original owner, or the present owner. I'm not into engaging lawyers over this: the expense and time could run to years. And if the gold is defined as "mislaid", the finding might not benefit either of us.' He paused. 'I have decided what to do. You will have half of it.'

Mary started. 'What?'

'Half,' John said. 'That gold was won by Peter Smith, by his hand, with his effort and at risk of his life. It was not placed in my garden by me. No, the least I can do is offer you half its value.'

Mary's lip trembled and Catherine came closer to her on the settee and held her hand.

'Now you'll not have to scrimp and save,' Catherine said. 'You can invest some of this and live modestly while you build a future for Reggie.'

Mary started to cry. 'Thank you, Mr Leary. Thank you so much. It's made me happy. It's not just the new wealth, but that fact that Peter *did* look after us. And I would trade gold for him, any day.'

John looked at Catherine and smiled. Yes, he knew what Mary had said was right. 'We'll get a good price for the gold, and when the monies are paid, I'll transfer your share to you.'

Mary stood up and went to John. She leaned over and kissed his cheek. 'I've done it, Mr Leary. I've kissed you, and in front of your new wife. But I'm so grateful for your generosity.'

'John, please.' John was happy. With the extra money he could set up an endowment for Richard and for any future children. And then there was the shareholding in his company. Perhaps Christine might be amenable to selling her shares? It was worth a try. He stood up and Catherine did as well.

'I'll go straight home and tell Reggie,' Mary said. 'I will.'

'Of course, you must,' John said. 'We'll see you out.'

The Learys walked Mary to the front gate and waved goodbye as she was driven away. John put his arm around Catherine and brought her close. The salt-laden breeze from the harbour moved the moonlit branches above them. He had a son, a new wife he loved with a passion, and a future that shone bright. He was a lucky man.

Acknowledgments

Many thanks must go to my editor Cheryl Sawyer, herself a published and respected historical fiction author. The attention she gave to the relationship aspects of the novel were particularly gratefully received.

The builders of the colony deserve my thanks and admiration. Without their passion, sweat and contribution, their legacy and the world-class quality of today's built environment would not have been possible.

More Books by the Author

Unbound Justice (The Australian Sandstone Series Book 1)
Unshackled (The Australian Sandstone Series Book 2)
Succession (The Australian Sandstone Series Book 3)
Bailed Up (The Australian Sandstone Series Book 4)
The Australian Sandstone Series Boxset Books 1-3

Unbound Justice

The Australian Sandstone Series Book 1

John Leary boards ship in Ireland in 1850, a young immigrant carpenter ambitious for a new life in Australia. He sails with revenge in his heart--his beloved sister has been raped by her landlord, William Baxterhouse, who escapes on another ship with even grander plans for success in New South Wales. In Sydney, hard workers like Leary and ruthless newcomers like Baxterhouse find a city fired by the Gold Rush and dedicated to creating the finest buildings in the colony.

Leary has a double motive to make his construction company succeed: he has fallen in love with the beautiful Clarissa McGuire, whose family despise him, and Baxterhouse continues to rise in wealth and influence, seemingly untouchable. Meanwhile another woman, Beth O'Hare, is in love with John Leary, and he makes some hard choices--including a climactic showdown with Baxterhouse.

Unbound Justice is now available in ebook and paperback
from your favourite online bookstore

Unshackled

The Australian Sandstone Series Book 2

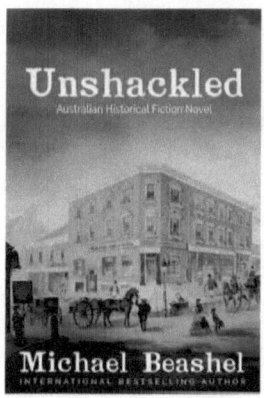

Sydney is booming in 1855 and life looks grand for John Leary: his construction dreams are coming true, his beloved wife Clarissa is expecting their first child and, with his partner Sean Connaire, he has produced some of the city's significant buildings. But success provokes jealousy, and a mysterious rival sabotages a vital Leary site.

John Leary cannot control his own company while his father-in-law holds a majority share, so he arranges a buyout on his own behalf--but this new, silent partner poses a serious risk to the harmony of his marriage. Meanwhile ex-convict Gerry Gleeson makes himself known to John as his uncle and helps him track down the saboteur.

Raw ambition, guilty secrets and undercover deals--will they bring the young builder to ruin or triumph?

Unshackled is now available in ebook and paperback
from your favourite online bookstore

Succession

The Australian Sandstone Series Book 3

Leary Contracting has to build it--the tallest hotel Sydney has ever seen. At 55, John Leary employs both his sons in his construction company, but the one he favours is his first-born, Richard. Meanwhile Richard's half-brother, Brendan, gains the respect of the Leary workers because he has 'bricks in his blood'.

John begins the massive hotel project, overcoming city red tape and the jabs of his fiercest competitor. The Imperial dwarfs all around it, with hundreds of workers busting their guts to finish the brutal program. Richard, charming but unreliable, marries well and dazzles the Sydney society of 1885, while Brendan proves himself tougher than he looks whenever real work is required.

John must choose which of his sons will lead Learys into the next century. Only after the Imperial is completed does he make his decision. Succession is the third Australian Historical Fiction novel in The Australian Sandstone Series, a magnificent view of 19c Sydney from the ground up!

Succession is now available in ebook and paperback from
your favourite online bookstore

Bailed Up

The Australian Sandstone Series Book 4

To Irishman Gerry Riordan, a pint at the Drawbridge Hotel in Cork makes the ideal end to the working week, and one winter night in 1828 he has good reason to celebrate with his friend, Lawrence Toole—Gerry is now a certified stonemason. Next day he will deliver gold tabernacle doors to St Mary's Cathedral and dare to ask the beautiful Anne Donovan to marry him.

But by the next night the gold has been stolen, Lawrence Toole lies dead and Riordan is accused of theft and murder. Anne, his boss's daughter, is the only person who believes him innocent.

Riordan escapes hanging but is transported to New South Wales. A convict in irons, with a flaming temper, he is forced to labour on the colony's toughest project, the Great North Road. As he begins working in stone again, a charming young woman, an enigmatic overseer and two convict friends seek to open his eyes to a more promising future. Meanwhile, offenders who framed him for the crimes in Ireland are also in the colony. Is there really any hope for Gerry Riordan to rebuild his shattered dreams?

Bailed Up is now available in ebook and paperback
from your favourite online bookstore

The Author

Born in Sydney, Michael Beashel is an International Bestselling Author. His Irish forebears immigrated to New South Wales in the 1860s and settled in Miller's Point. He spent his youth in Bondi, is married with adult children and lives in Sydney's inner-west.

Beashel was head of Asset Development for a global accommodation services company registered on the NYSE and has made his mark in some of Australia's iconic construction companies. In Sydney, he has restored government buildings such as the Customs House and the Town Hall and completed commercial buildings in the private sector. In SE Asia, he managed a construction division that built apartments and hotels in Bangkok and Ho Chi Minh City.

This industry—its characters, clients, tradespeople, designers and bureaucrats—provides rich material for his writing. He has an eye for the emergence of Sydney's built form, from the early days of the colony to the present, and a love of construction. He says about his writing, 'It's a passion. I revel in using the building industry as a tapestry to weave a great tale seasoned with historic facts and memorable characters. Human shelter is an essential need and I suspect people have a fascination for understanding its context and construction within their societies. Australia still is a young country in terms of large structures but there are many, many outstanding building stories.'

Beashel holds a B. App. Science (Building) from Sydney's UTS and is a member of Writing NSW. *Unbound Justice* is his first novel and Books 2 and 3 *Unshackled* and *Succession* and *Bailed Up* form the first four of The Australian Sandstone Series.

All novels can be enjoyed as standalone stories.

The stone mason Gerry Riordan appears in *Unshackled and Succession* under his chosen name of Gerry Gleeson.

If any interested reader would like to know more about me and my Australian background, please access my following sites:

My website

www.michaelbeashel.com.au

Australian History Videos on YouTube

https://www.youtube.com/channel/UCLETK6K05kne4xhKChBaVAA

Facebook

https://www.facebook.com/MichaelBeashelAuthor

Goodreads

https://www.goodreads.com/author/show/16827192.Michael_Beashel